Silver Spoons and Paper Plates

R.C. WAGNER

First Edition

PAGE PUBLISHING, INC.
Conneaut Lake, PA

First originally published by Page Publishing 2021

ISBN 978-1-6624-5934-4 (pbk)
ISBN 978-1-6624-5935-1 (digital)

Printed in the United States of America

For Sammie

Prologue

The day that Betty Sue Shaw's life changed forever started out like any other. One minute, she was contentedly walking through the old ballyard with her best friend, Sandy, talking about their respective dates for that evening long ago in a happier past, and the next, she was back in her trailer, the sun poking her in the eye and the sound of the neighbor's ancient Toyota poking her in the ear. Better than in the rear, as Sandy would say. Sandy said a lot of things, right up until her husband got sick of listening, and shut her up permanently. Sandy hasn't said anything at all for years now, and Betty Sue's life was darker for it.

"I don't wanna," she said to no one, in response to the demand that no one made. When no one answered, she sighed, sat up, and began to cough the smoker's hack that had begun her day, every day, for as long as she could remember. As she hacked, she reached over to the nightstand the fetch herself a fresh Virginia Slim. You've come a long way, baby! Her eyes adjusted to the dawn as she lit the smoke, drawing it deep into her lungs, where it could scratch the itch of her nicotine addiction. As she slowly let the smoke free from her lungs, her eyes were drawn to half-empty Bud Light next to the pack of cigarettes. Did she drink it all last night? Might there be just a little swallow left, just enough to lubricate her throat? She squinted into the neck and saw what looked like a good sip or two swirling around, and she upended the contents into her waiting mouth.

The beer hitting her stomach signaled her bladder to wake up. She shuffled down the hallway, dodging piles of dirty work uniforms on her way to the bathroom. Once inside, she collapsed onto the toilet seat, one eye closed, cigarette dangling from her slack lips, and allowed gravity to drain her of last night's Bud Light.

"What day is it?" she wondered out loud to her reflection in the mirror on the wall. She searched her memory, but the answer wouldn't come. She knew she worked the night before because she could still smell the fish that was on special in her hair. Wait. Fish meant today was Saturday because the Red Rooster Diner only served fish on Fridays. That was good. It meant she was off today. She could nurse this hangover all day if she needed to. And she needed to. She was becoming aware that this hangover was a doozy. Not garden variety. Her head throbbed with an intensity she scarcely believed possible. Every beat of her heart felt like a hammer blow to her temples. Yes, it was very good that she had today off.

She slowly rose from the toilet seat and began to rummage through the medicine cabinet, searching for anything that might quiet the cacophony in her head. Her hands shook as she knocked pill bottles over and into the sink.

"Dammit!" she shouted, then immediately regretted it. Her own voice echoed throughout her skull, threatening to break through and spill all her thoughts onto the floor. She was suddenly wracked with a coughing spasm that doubled her over. Her head beat in time with the coughs, her vision grayed with each upheaval of her diaphragm. She slowly sank to the floor and gave in to the storm. She spent the next ten minutes in a heap on the floor, trying to catch her breath and praying to whatever god would listen to stop the infernal pounding in her head. Eventually, the roar lessened, and she found she could stand up. She continued her search for chemical relief, and presently, she found the bottle of ibuprofen. She clawed it open, dumped a few into her dry mouth, and swallowed. She hoped the medicine would be strong enough to at least take the edge off, but with the way she felt, she couldn't be sure even morphine could slay the dragon between her ears.

Sliding her feet instead of stepping to avoid the shocks of impact, she made her way into the living room. She collapsed into her easy chair and closed her eyes. She tried to will the ibuprofen into her brain. After a few minutes of absolute stillness of body and mind, the pain started to abate. Betty Sue sighed with relief.

She realized with dismay that today was the day her landlord was supposed to fix the water heater. It had been running constantly for the past month, as the thermostat was broken. Betty Sue had discovered this one afternoon before work. She immediately called Ralph to report the predicament, but his level of concern did not match her own. It took dozens of increasingly impolite phone messages to convince him that intervention should be taken. It wouldn't do to forget about Ralph, not after how hard it had been to get him motivated.

As she stood up to go back into her room to change, the room spun in circles around her. She bent over and steadied herself on the edge of the recliner.

"How much did I drink last night?" she asked out loud. "Was it eight or eighteen?" She laughed unsteadily at her own joke, half-amused and half-scared. Something was off, but she didn't know what. This was far from her first hangover, but something about this particular one was different. Worse.

Worrying about it would have to wait, though. *That horny old goat Ralph would love nothing more than to catch a look at me in my bloomers,* she thought. She would have to get dressed. Once, in days long gone, Betty Sue had been extraordinarily beautiful, and she knew it. While the years had taken their toll, she still would have been a catch for old hunchback Ralph. She knew he fancied her. His gaze always strayed to her ample chest when he talked to her, and he always found excuses to talk to her longer than strictly necessary. He never did anything overtly creepy, but Betty Sue was leery of him all the same. Men always wanted something from her, the same something men have always wanted from women who looked like her. But they never cared to listen to her dreams. They weren't interested in her soul, just her crotch. Oh, sure, she was fine for a bit of sport, but Betty Sue Tucker was not someone you brought home to meet the family. At least not for people whose family Betty Sue would want to meet. That is why, at age sixteen, Betty Sue Tucker married that all-time son of a bitch, Elmer Ray Shaw. He was the first man who didn't run out the door the minute his balls were emptied. He was mean and lazy and cheap, but anything would have been better than staying home with Daddy and the boys, so Betty Sue settled, as the saying goes. One violent drunk was easier to contend with than five. Betty Sue was no math whiz, but she understood that particular arithmetic.

Back in her bedroom, Betty Sue looked for some clean clothes that were demure enough to disguise what feminine attributes she still retained. As she reached overhead to move some shoe boxes out of the way in her closet, she noticed an odd numbness creeping down her left arm. She lowered the limb and shook it, trying to banish the pins and needles that afflicted her so. As she did this, she realized that she had forgotten why she was in there. She stared at the clothes hanging in the closet without seeing them. Her mind, while conscious, was a strange blank. It was as if someone had pressed pause on her thoughts.

"Violets… Violets…" she muttered, confused as to what it was that she was talking about. Somehow, those words had an esoteric meaning known only to her, but something was blocking her memory. She felt like she had just tuned into a television show already in progress, starring her, but she didn't know the script.

"What the fuck is happening?" she asked herself as if she could answer with any real accuracy. Her thoughts were coming rapid-fire and with no discernable connection between them. Her unease was rapidly growing, and she sat down hard on the edge of the bed. She tried to purposely blank out, to deny the torrent of memories that whirled around her mind like a cyclone. She could see bright pinpoints of flashing lights obscuring her vision, and she wailed as the clock on the wall doubled, then tripled.

Adrenaline pumped through her veins, and her breath became rapid and shallow. She was aware of a sheen of cold sweat on her skin, and she felt alternating waves of fire and ice wash over her. She slumped over on her bed and squeezed her eyes shut. She tried to narrow her consciousness in a feeble attempt to make whatever was happening stop. As she lay on her bed, she became aware of a whooshing sound in her ears. It started quietly, almost imperceptibly, like waves breaking on a distant shore. It ratcheted up in intensity until it seemed to engulf the world. Betty Sue screamed, but she couldn't hear herself above the din.

Terrified now, Betty Sue bolted upright in bed. The left side of her face was tingling now too, keeping time with her shoulder and arm. She gasped as she saw her face in the mirror on top of the vanity across the room. Her left eye was now a good quarter of an inch lower than her right. The left corner of her mouth was drooping comically, and a little runner of drool hung there, mocking her. She didn't recognize herself, and she wondered who let the witch from Snow White into her room.

She stood up to run from the hag in the mirror, but her legs were no longer taking orders from management. They twisted themselves around the legs of her vanity bench, and Betty Sue was introduced to the floor. She smacked her head on the bedrail on the way down, and enormous white flowers exploded across her field of vision.

"Oooooohhhh," she moaned, and she started to curl up in the fetal position. Her world condensed down to two crimson dots in front of her eyes. She had lost her ability to form rational thoughts, and all she knew was pain and panic. Her heartbeat triple time in her chest, and her breath came in short, ragged gasps.

"Mama!" she yelped. It was the sound of an infant crying for help. She no longer knew who she was. She no longer knew anything other than something was ***very wrong***, and there was no one to help her. She was drifting down into the dark, and she didn't know her way back. Soon, all was quiet and still. She lay in limbo, aware of nothing. The doorbell rang. Ralph had arrived, but Betty Sue was leaving.

Remlee

I winced as my eardrums popped while barreling down the mountainside in our trusty old Jeep. We were heading south on I-77 in Virginia, rapidly approaching North Carolina. To my left, the eastern horizon was turning a violent pink as the sun began its daily rotation. The Piedmont of Virginia and North Carolina lay spread out like a blue and gray patchwork quilt, the low hills undulating like the form of a sleeping giant. Tiny pinpricks of light were spread unevenly across this tapestry, visible signs of human habitation.

To my right, beyond my sleeping husband, lay a sheer wall of granite, climbing so high as to obscure the fading night sky from my vision. I felt an almost imperceptible lump in my throat as I realized that if something came tumbling down off of the cliffside, I would have nowhere to go to avoid it but over the other side and into certain death. I had to consciously force myself to relax my grip and breathe slowly. I was certain that if I woke Jack up to take over for me, he'd only add that to the list of things that I couldn't cope with and tease me unmercifully. I wasn't prepared to deal with his bullshit on top of everything else that had transpired over the last twenty-four hours.

When I had woken up twenty-three hours beforehand, my life was a certain way. Wake up. Get dressed. Grab coffee. Rush to the restaurant, make sure it gets opened on time, and find replacements for any of the college girls who called off owing to hangovers. Work. Work. Work. Come home to Jack. Relax and talk, or watch TV, or whatever. Anything but talk to or even think about Mama. I'd gladly listen to Jack talk for hours about the trials and tribulations of the landscaping business his buddy Trevor owned and Jack operated, even the boring details, if it meant I didn't have to think about, to remember the woman who gave me life, if not much else. She certainly didn't seem to spare a passing thought for me during my childhood.

We had been at Jack's parents' vacation house in the Finger Lakes region of New York that evening to celebrate the old man's seventy-fifth birthday. Stuart Shephard was a partner at Bergdorf, Shephard, and Shephard, a highly respected Boston law firm. It was the kind of law firm that doesn't advertise on the side of bus stops. I don't know too much about who or what they represent, nothing too controversial, nothing that gets them on the news, or anything like that. They handle the kind of legal work that grants them extraordinary comfort in life without impinging too much on their tee times at the country club.

Jack's mom Carolyn, however, spent her working years, which only ended two years ago, on much loftier pursuits. Upon retirement, she vacated the post of director of nursing at Children's Hospital of Boston, a position which she had held for the previous twenty-four years. Retirement hasn't seemed to suit her well, and she had been devoting much of her time to various local charities in an effort to exercise her overwhelming zeal to show the unwashed masses how to better live.

Also accompanying us for the birthday feast were Jack's siblings, older brother Simon and younger sister Ingrid, Simon's shrewish, gold-digging whore of a wife, Hannah, and their disgustingly perfect children, Arianna and Judson. Simon was the other Shephard in his father's law firm and was just as stiff, smug, and altogether boring as his father. The similarities between the patriarch and his prime heir were too many to be counted. It was as if Simon were cloned, not born. From their baby-fine straw-colored hair, curiously gray eyes, and awkwardly tall physiques to their joyless, business-only, career-centered lifestyles, they were only distinguishable from one another by their age.

As much as Simon was like Stuart, Ingrid was like Carolyn. The obvious parental favorite, Ingrid, was nearly worshipped by all who knew her. Accolades followed her every step, from her first some nine years after Jack's, to her most recent, graduating from Johns Hopkins Medical School Summa Cum Laude. In two weeks, she would begin her surgical residency at Children's, keeping the Shephard name active on that roster. Although it wasn't officially acknowledged, the party that night had been as much for her as for her father.

"So, Jack," began Simon, a wry smile barely touching the corners of his thin lips, "How's things in the grass shortening racket? Any new advancements in blade technology I should know about?" His eyes gleamed with impish delight at the red shadow creeping up Jack's neck. Score: Simon, one; Jack, zip.

"Nothing new under the sun, Simon. Grass grows, I cut it. Some scumbag rapes a kid, you get him off," Jack mumbled back, not lifting his eyes from the Cornish hen he picked at on his plate.

"What's that? You wanna repeat that for me? I'm not sure I heard you," Simon said, his chest puffing up and his own red shadow rising on his neck. He started to stand, and Hannah touched his forearm, shaking her head no, but she dared not speak. She knew who paid her way, and she did not bite the hand that fed.

"You heard me," Jack said, a little louder but still quieter than Simon.

"We don't even handle criminal cases, that's not what we even do, and you'd know that if you hadn't majored in drinking back at Northeastern instead of something useful…" he started, but Carolyn had had enough and cut him off before he got rolling.

"THAT. WILL. BE. ENOUGH. OUT OF YOU TWO!" she barked, jabbing her fingers at both Simon and Jack. "You WILL NOT, I repeat, WILL NOT ruin yet another family celebration with your immature fighting. Simon, quit baiting your brother. Jack, quit falling for the bait."

I stared at the table, not wanting to see the look on Jack's face. I already knew what it looked like, and that look always broke my heart. It was the look of a child who desperately wants his mother to take his side, just for once. It's a look I'd seen on his face more times than I care to count.

"No one's baiting him, Ma. I simply asked him how things were going at work. A perfectly reasonable thing to ask of one's brother during a civil conversation. I wasn't the one casting aspersions—" Simon began, but Jack cut him off.

"CASTING ASPERSIONS? CASTING ASPERSIONS?" Jack roared, his curly brown locks quivering as he visibly shook with rage. "Is that what you call pointing out the corruption of representing scumbags in exchange for egregious sums of money?"

"ENOUGH! I WILL HEAR NO MORE!" interrupted Stuart in his famous courtroom baritone. It was like the air was suddenly sucked out of the room. All eyes were drawn to this man, this patriarch that everyone present feared a little bit more than loved.

"This is my three-quarter centennial. I will not have my reverie interrupted with the eternal penis-measuring contest you two insist on waging. You both will cease this nonsense at once," he said stoically. He returned his attention to his meal, and the silence grew uncomfortable in the wake of his reproach.

I took this opportunity to steal a glance in Jack's direction. He was seated directly across from me in the formal dining room. The low light cast shadows on his face, but those shadows couldn't obscure his feelings from me. I'd known him too long, loved him too fiercely for his famously stony countenance to fool me for a second. I could see the sensitive child, begging for acceptance, buried under the years of cheap bourbon, honest labor, and the scars earned in countless Combat Zone bar brawls. I felt a knot form in my throat like it always does when I watch Jack's family go to work on him. Their banal distaste for him hurt him more than any physical blows could ever hope to achieve.

In a characteristic attempt to move the conversation to safer territory, Ingrid asked Hannah about Arianna's chances for making the traveling equestrian team, and the mood instantly lightened. Nothing mollified Jack's family like stories of unbridled (pun most definitely intended) success. That was their legacy. That was their entire reason for existence. Excellence was expected, and excellence was rewarded with positive regard and respect. Love, for the Shephards, was earned, not given.

I sat, nibbling at my meal, hoping my face didn't betray my feelings. I will gladly acknowledge that Jack's family has done a lot for us. It was Stuart who gave me the down payment for the restaurant, Carolyn who bought the house we live in. And neither one ever hesitates to remind us of these facts at every conceivable opportunity. It's as if they helped us not out of love and care but out of shame. It wouldn't do for the folks at the country club to see a son of Stuart and Carolyn Shephard living in a trailer court, drunken blue-collar slob or not. The fact that Jack worked an honest living with his back and hands, creating beauty with earth and rock for people with more money than physical ambition, wasn't seen as worthy, as the renumeration was admittedly meager. Mere lawn maintenance was supposed to be the purview of the intellectually and culturally inferior, not a scion of the long respected and revered Shephard family.

"And then Aubrey fell right off her saddle!" squealed Arianna, reveling in the spotlight. I couldn't pay attention to her story. My mind was too worn out from the hectic day. My eyes glazed over, and I nodded and smiled in what I assumed were the appropriate pauses in the chatter. I was considering excusing myself to the bathroom, wherein I could escape the tales of elementary school excellence and maybe grab a toke or two off of the joint that was burning a hole in my pocket. As I opened my mouth to announce my intentions, I was interrupted by the insistent warbling of my cellphone emanating from my purse, which was slung over the back of the colonial-style chair I was sitting on. I gasped audibly and reached into my purse to silence the infernal racket. I looked at the caller ID, and my heart sank. Jolene. Fuck.

"Fuck!" I said, louder than I had meant to. Eight pairs of eyes instantly locked onto me. Cursing was a ***BIG NO-NO*** in the Shephard household. Judson giggled, and Hannah cuffed him.

"I'm sorry," I lied. "I've got to take this. I'll just step out into the hallway."

As I excused myself from the room, my mind spun with the possibilities inherent in this particular call. My sister Jolene was the textbook definition of a hot mess. When I finally answered the phone, it was all but assured that some ridiculous drama would immediately manifest from the earpiece of my Samsung and drag me along for at least the next ten minutes, if not longer. One of her children probably got arrested again, and Gary, her current beau, probably refused to pay the bail. Or maybe her doctor refused to proscribe any more

Xanax for her. Whatever it was, I was certain it wasn't news that she got a good job, and her kids were great, and her love life was healthy, and rainbows were spontaneously erupting from her asshole. Jolene didn't work that way.

"Hello?" I asked the phone, almost wincing in anticipation of the blow that was about to fall.

"R…R-R-R… Remlee?" Jolene's voice replied, thick and shaky with tears.

"What, Jolene? What is it now?" I demanded, impatient.

"It's Mama," Jolene started, "she's in the hospital."

Slightly alarmed but far from panicking, I replied, "What hospital? Why? Is she okay? What happened?"

"She's in St. Mark's, here in Stillwater. S-s-she h-had a s-st-stroke," Jolene answered, exploding into tears. I waited for what seemed like days until she got a hold of herself. I noticed that I wasn't surprised or even all that concerned. My lack of concern started to concern me. My mother just had a stroke, and I didn't feel a thing except for minor annoyance at having to talk to Jolene. Presently, she got herself under some semblance of control and was able to talk again.

"Are you gonna come?" she asked.

That should have been an easy question to answer, but it wasn't. Most daughters would not think twice; it wouldn't even be a question. My mother, however, was not most mothers, and I was not most daughters.

"Why should I?" was my automatic reply. Jolene started to answer but then fell silent. I waited patiently for her to pick up the thread.

"Because I need you," Jolene finally whispered, sounding small and defeated. I could picture her, in my mind's eye, her head in her one hand, a Budweiser and a Virginia Slim menthol in the other, sobbing quietly into her phone.

"I needed her growing up," I said to the mewling voice on the other end of the line. "Where was she? At Tiger's or the Legion."

"I need you, I said," Jolene said. "I ain't asking for her. I'm asking for me. There's no one else to help. Shane's out of town on a job, and Elton's back in jail. Lord knows my fuckin' kids couldn't be bothered to lift a fuckin' finger… Oh, hell!" She broke down into tears again.

"I have a life, Jo," I began, frustrated and oddly terrified. "I own a restaurant. I have employees to manage, supplies to order. I have to call that goddamn Enrique to come back and fix my fucking fryer right. I have responsibilities—"

"So do I!" Jolene interrupted. "You're not so high and mighty! I have responsibilities too." I could picture her pooching out her lower lip, just like when we were kids. I tried not to chuckle at her absurdity. I needed to stay pissed. I went on the attack.

"What responsibilities? Your kids are grown, and Gary pays for everything. You ain't got a job to go to. What possible responsibility could you be talking about? Remembering to go to the fucking methadone clinic?" I hissed into the receiver. Jolene made a sound like she had been punched in the gut.

"That's not fair," she said quietly.

"Maybe, but is it untrue?" I pressed.

"Not the point," Jolene grumbled.

"Then what is? Why should I drop everything to come rescue that hateful old bitch?" I demanded.

"Goddamn it, I told you it's to rescue me! Would you take the shit out of your ears and listen, for once? It's to rescue me! I need you to look out for me, like I did for you, when Mama wouldn't." Jolene sighed with exasperation, and I could almost smell the smoke she exhaled.

"It's like, two thousand miles," I protested weakly.

"I know," she replied.

"Jack won't be happy," I pointed out.

"Is he ever?" Jolene answered. She had a point there, albeit a small one. Jack was a Grumplestiltskin from time to time.

"Fine. I'll call you when I leave," I said wearily.

I pressed the end button on the cell and stood there, staring at the expensive artwork on the walls of the hallway in the vacation house I was standing in. I had just committed myself to spending time in an environment and amongst people diametrically opposite to my present circumstances. I felt a wave of vertigo wash over me as I contemplated my immediate future. What was Jack going to say? Would he agree to accompany me on this trip back into hell, or would I have to face this nightmare alone?

I didn't have to wonder for long because as I stood there collecting myself and preparing to brave the dining room again, Jack appeared, investigating the case of the missing wife. I must have looked shaken because he hesitated upon seeing my face.

"Hey, kiddo. You 'kayzies? Who was that?" he asked quietly, using his patent-pending soothe-o-matic tone he reserved for when I really came unglued. His tone scared me this time because it meant I looked crazed and about to erupt. That was the only time he used that particular tone. I closed my eyes, took two deep breaths, and tried to purposely slow my heart, like I read in *Cosmo* or some other rag in a waiting room somewhere. I noticed I was shaking ever so slightly, and my skin had a sheen of sweat glistening in the light from the chandelier. Jack just stood pensively, like a sinner requesting absolution, awaiting my answer. Finally, I was able to give it to him.

"It was Jolene. Mama had a stroke," said a voice that sounded like mine.

"Oh, God," began Jack, a look of horror quickly crossing his face. He started to say more, but I cut him off.

"I have to go back. I don't want to, we can't really afford for me to, but I have to, regardless." I said, and Jack tried to interrupt me, but I continued over the top of him.

"I'm not discussing this with you. I'm telling you. You can come, or you can stay and ride back to Malden with Ingrid. Lord knows she has enough room in that fucking Range Rover." As I paused to catch my breath, Jack was finally able to respond.

"Of course, I'm coming with you." He laughed, his winningest smile stretched across his face. "Do you really think I'm going to miss out on the opportunity to finally see the fabled Stillwater, Florida? Oh, hell naw, baby, I'm going with you. I'm always going with you."

The dam in my chest sprung a leak, and I felt myself collapse into his arms. I buried my face in his chest and breathed his familiar scent in. It was the scent of grass and sweat, flowers and earth. A natural smell. My home smell.

"I don't want you to see it," I whispered into his T-shirt.

"See what?" he responded somewhat lazily as if only half listening.

"It. All of it. Stillwater, my family. The way they are, the way they live…" I started, but this time Jack cut me off.

"I don't care about that. I know who you really are," he said, smiling sadly.

"But I care. It's embarrassing, man. I know it shouldn't be, but it is," I protested. He pushed me away to arm's length and held me there, staring directly into my eyes, not letting me look away. His gaze seemed to transfix me, hypnotize me.

"I. Love. You," he said, punctuating each word with a peck on my forehead. "Just as you are. For who you are, as you are. I don't care who you come from. You are not your relatives. Believe me, I know."

He didn't, though, not really. Sure, there were major issues in his family. He was also struggling with the baggage that comes with a surname of note. The difference is that the assumptions were good in his place. People thought well of him, even if he couldn't see that, and it was, in large part, due to the Shephard name. The Shephard name connotes success and respect. I was a Shaw, though, with a side helping of Tucker. My driver's license may have said Shephard due to marriage, but my genes will always say Shaw, and the connotations that go with that name are altogether different. You're expected to be ignorant, dirty, criminally oriented, and likely incestual. People clutch their belongings a little closer on the bus when they see one of us. We're the reason people in Stillwater lock their doors at night to ensure we won't gain entry and liberate their property. Most people won't even look us in the eye, either out of fear of being seen associating with one of us or out of shame for allowing the neglect and abuse to go on for generations. It's shame all over, inside and out.

I looked at him, loving him immensely, and said, "So who's driving?"

Betty Sue

It's dark here. I don't like it. Where is here? Hello? I can't feel anything at all. I'm not hot or cold, and I can't tell if I'm standing or lying down or if I'm even real at all. Am I real? I'm just a thought in the abyss. What was I just doing? I was definitely something before there was a before. How did I get here, and how can I leave? I don't like it here, not one little bit.

I'll just try to be very quiet. Maybe I'll be able to hear something. Wait, what's that? It's very faint, but I hear something thumping somewhere. It's slow and steady, keeping a bounding beat. I'm not sure if I'm really hearing this or if I'm feeling it. Maybe it's a little of both. Maybe if I focus on the beat, I can follow it out of here? Can I walk, though?

I don't like being alone here. I have to think, how did I get here? Well, I got up this morning. Yes, I remember that. The headache I had was the worst of my life. I definitely remember waking up. I'll never forget that headache as long as I live.

Hold on, as long as I live… Am I dead? Is this hell? Well, I don't see flames or smell sulfur, so probably not. It can't be heaven either. There ain't no angels or clouds or anything at all. Just infinite blackness. Maybe I'm not dead. Is there an in-between place? That must be where I am. But why? I wasn't sick or nothing. Sure, I had one mother of a hangover, but that can't ***kill*** *you, can it?*

How long have I been here? I don't remember. It seems like I've always been here, but that can't be true because I remember being alive. I remember hot, sticky summers in the cane fields. I remember my Daddy's calloused hands over the top of mine, showing me how to cut the stalk. I remember the sunshine, and I remember Daddy's moonshine too. Uncle Leo let me taste it for my eighth birthday. I remember being surprised that a liquid that wasn't hot could still burn the bejeezus out of your throat. I remember Elmer. Elmer, who took me away from one hell, only to trap me in another. I remember Shane, and Elton, and Jolene, and little Remlee. And, oh, poor, poor, sweet Jesco. Jesco, who died young. Jesco, who was stolen from me by that cursed Peterbilt. Oh, Jesco!

Please, God, I don't want to be alone in here with these ghosts! I can't bear it!

I hear something new now. It wasn't there a minute (an hour, a year, who can tell in this place?) ago. Beep. Beep. Beeping in time with the other thumping. Behind that, other noises. The incessant hum of high-wattage light bulbs. Various clicks and clacks from some invisible machinery inside the walls of this featureless tomb. I focus on the sounds with every fiber of my being. Something is nagging me, like I'm missing an obvious and important clue. I'm forgetting something vital or not recognizing something that should be as plain as the nose on my face. What am I missing here?

I struggle with these thoughts uselessly in the void. The blackness keeps stealing my thoughts. My mind goes blank for minutes (hours, years) at a time as I float here, suspended in nothingness. It's not so bad here, I guess. A person can get used to damn near anything, I suppose. It's quiet. That shitbag Norbert next door can't play his TV so loud that I can hear every moan from those disgusting pornos he watches every night, and that's a relief, let me tell you. I can't hear the young couple from the trailer on the other side fighting (or fucking). There are no telemarketers calling me a dozen times a day to try to convince me to change my electric supplier, no ex-football players trying to sell me Medicare supplements. I guess I could get used to this. This is the first peace I've ever had in my whole rotten life.

Yes, I think I'll stay awhile. There's no pain here. I can't feel the scoliosis in my back anymore. I don't ***have to*** *do anything here. No more days of taking shit from the workmen who eat their greasy lunches at the diner in hopes of eking out a tip that isn't insulting. No more being eye-fucked by every straight male I run across. No more being tossed aside as soon as their balls are drained of that nasty white stuff that seems to make them crazy. No more worrying about the water bill, or the rent, or the doctor, or anything at all. No more worries, period. That can be over here. All I have to do is let the oblivion take me away. I can hear its hungry breath in my ear, whispering seductive promises of peace. Nobody* *here to pester me, no one to know who I am and what family I belong to. No more pitying glances from the hoity-toity women in designer jeans behind me in the grocery line as I fumble with my food stamps. I don't even have to get completely trashed to forget my pain. I can just simply fade.*

Time passes, or it don't. It don't matter. I can just float here forever, safe from the world. I don't think I'll miss it. I also don't think it will miss me. Shane only calls when he needs something; Elton's the same. Jolene is as fucked up as I am, and I haven't seen Remlee in eight (or is it eighteen?) years. Wow, has it really been that long? And Jesco, ahhhh, sweet Jesco! Why did you have to die? You were the best of me, you were perfect. Everyone thought so. Mrs. Landry down at the bank once told me that you looked like the baby Jesus. But you were more than that, and now you're gone, and it's all my fault, and oh, God, I'm so, so, sorry! You deserved better than this old world.

Something is happening. I can hear voices now. I don't recognize who they belong to, but they're there, all right. I can't make out all they're saying, but they are talking about me. I've heard them say my name several times. They keep saying words I don't understand, like "elevated serum fibrinogen levels," "atherosclerosis," "posterior thalamic artery." I don't know if I should be scared or not. The voices change from time to time, and sometimes they're gone altogether, but they always come back. I decide to hide in here and hope they can't find me. I don't want to go back. I'm tired of being tired. I just want to stay here, where it's safe, and rest.

But is it safe? Is it really? There are ghosts here too. I can hear Uncle Leo, calling me with his reedy voice. He's telling me it's time for our special game. The one we can't tell anyone about, 'cuz they might get jealous. I hide from him, just like I did when I was ten. He's been dead for thirty years now, but I'm still terrified of him; his visage still haunts my dreams. I don't think he can see me here, though, because I still haven't felt his rough hands squeezing my tush or felt his sour breath on my neck as he runs his hands under the waistband of my panties. If I stay still and quiet, I'll be safe.

One person who isn't here, and can no longer hurt me, is that old snake Elmer Ray Shaw. He's still in the Florida State Prison, will be till he rots. Florida has no patience or mercy when it comes to cop killers. He may be only a few miles down the road, but even he can't contend with twelve-foot-high razor wire fences. He can't hurt me any longer, I remind myself. I tend to forget that a lot.

He wasn't always so bad. In the old days, before the factory closed, before the boozing took priority. He was so cute that day he pulled up at the pond out back in that old Thunderbird to meet up with my brother Clarence for some fishing. And when he stole a kiss that night under the willow tree, I felt released from the prison that was my home. I left with him that very night, all of fifteen years old, and was Mrs. Elmer Ray Shaw by the next month. Ten months later, Shane come along. Then Elton. Two more years, then Jesco and Jolene, the terrible twosome. Finally, Remlee. An endless cycle of diapers, spit-ups, ear infections, and fevers. And no money. Never any money. The second a nickel found its way into Elmer's hand; it was handed over to the bartender at Tiger's Saloon. How many times did the kids go hungry because that lousy son of a bitch needed to "wind down"? And why, more often than not, did "winding down" include "tuning up" on me as the main entertainment for the evening? Or the kids? When he was arrested after the robbery, I cried tears of relief. Sure, he wouldn't be around to provide for us, but, honestly, that would be much of a change. I was just glad that my children and me could live in our house like people who belonged there, instead of like hostages.

I don't want to think about him anymore. I don't have to, and I won't. I don't have to do a goddamn thing anymore. I can just **BE** *here. No judgment from the neighbors, no more shame, or fear, or loneliness. Just peace. For the first time.*

More time passes, I think. I think I slept, but am I awake now? Is this all just one long, fucked up dream?

I can hear voices again. I perk up and try to pay attention. One of the voices sounds familiar. I just can't place it, but I feel like I should know it. It's a woman's voice, as familiar as my own, so similar, like the equivalent of a mirror image for sound. I hear phrases I use that I've only ever heard my family use. Then, like a bolt of lightning, it hits me. It's Jolene! It's my daughter! Jolene is here! Can she help me?

I can't see her. It occurs to me to try to open my eyes. I hadn't thought of that yet. I give it a try, and my brain is assaulted by light so bright; it's like looking at the face of Jehovah himself. I close my eyes tight to stop the burning. I try again, but slower, only letting a little at a time. I can see the bedrails and the tubes coming from my arms. I see two nurses, one white and one black, standing at the end of my bed, talking to a figure that their bodies are obscuring. I try to move my head to see beyond them, but I'm too weak. I try to speak, to call Jolene's name.

"Mmmmuuuummmmmppphhhhaaaaaa," I say. I'm confused because this is not at all what I mean. I'm trying to call my daughter. Her name is Jolene, like Dolly's best song. Jolene. Simple. I try again, louder.

"Mmmmmmuuuuummmmmmuuuuummmmmmpppppphhh-haaaa," escapes my lips. The nurses turn around like they're on swivels and gape at me.

"Miz Shaw! Are you awake?" the black one asks me, startled by my sudden utterance. I look past her at my now revealed daughter. I can see that she's been crying. This scares me. Is she hurt? Did that piece of shit Gary beat up on her again? I try to ask her what's happening.

"Mmmuummm! Dow dow mmmuuuummm!" I hear myself say. What's wrong with me? Why won't the words come? I feel a wave of terror wash over me as the nurses, or whatever they are, come closer to where I'm lying.

"You've had a stroke, Betty Sue. You're in the hospital, and you've been here for three days. We're sure glad you decided to wake up!" says the white one in a syrupy tone I'm sure she reserves for children and morons. "How are you feeling?"

"Muuummmmuuummm," I say. I mean terrible. I think my meaning is understood, as both nurses give me the "bless her heart" look all medical professionals eventually learn to adopt.

"You need rest," says the white one. I try to read her nametag, and I'm shocked when I realize that I can't. I'm no genius, but I can read! But those symbols ain't right, I don't think. They look like letters, but I don't recognize them. I try to ask her what her name is.

"Nnnnaaaaammmm," I sputter. The nurse gives me a blank look.

"NNNNAAAAAAMMMMMM!" I yell more forcefully. I must not be making any sense to them either because any fool should be able to

answer what their name is. My eyes start to burn as they fill up with tears of frustration. I see Jolene looking at me, and I try to choke them back. Jolene's crying hard, and I just can't take it.

"Oh, Mama, what are we going to do with you?" Jolene wails. I try to answer.

"Fffuummmb...ffuummbb..." I start but then quit. I can't make the words come; it's no use. I know what I want to say, but the message is getting mixed up on the way from my brain to my mouth. I'm furious, terrified, and sadder than I have ever been, even when Jesco died. At least then I could say I was sorry! Now, I can't say anything.

This is all too much. I need to go back. Back to where I just came from. This world, the real one, is too much for me to handle right now. My head hurts so, so bad, and I'm bone tired. I just want to sleep. I... just...want...

Remlee

As the sun rose higher in the sky, our position on the map edged further south. Jack was still sleeping, and I intended to let him as long as I could. While he was usually a happy drunk, even when brawling, the morning after, before coffee, could be dicey. Jack was never violent with me, but in darker moods or unusually hungover, his tongue was sharper than any broadsword. He was always contrite after, but I've often wondered if Grumplestiltskin Jack was the real Jack, the true Jack.

Pretty soon, I'd have to pull over. I'd been awake for over twenty-four hours, at the wheel for the last ten. We were in North Carolina now, and with the new day, I could begin to feel the south. It's something in the atmosphere I can't quite describe, a thickness, not quite oppressive but undoubtedly felt. I don't know if this has to do with atmospheric pressure or just the weight of my own personal history on this side of the Mason-Dixon line. Since I left (escaped) twenty years ago, I've rarely been in a state that fought for the Confederacy and have simply not set foot in Florida at all. I've been afraid to like the state could somehow trap me there against my will. I got away once, but would I be able to again? The thought of being stuck in Stillwater made me shiver so hard, I accidentally swerved off of the road for a second. The tires growled in protest as they ran over the rumble strips, or trucker alarm clocks, as my brother Elton always called them. Jack began to stir.

"Mmgawdamn! Where? What's going on?" he asked thickly.

"Nothing. I'm just getting tired. I'm gonna pull over at the next rest stop," I replied.

"Oh, okay," he said through a yawn. "I'll take over then. My head's pounding a little, but I've slept enough. We don't want to keep

Jolene waiting." He turned over in his seat and gazed out of the window at the generic interstate scenery flowing past at seventy miles per hour. I thought he was going back to sleep when he suddenly spoke.

"Are you okay? I mean about all of this. Your mom, your sister. Going to Florida, all of it. Are you okay?" he asked, still staring out of the window.

"Am I okay?" I parroted back to him. I didn't know how to answer that question. I felt my lips quiver, and my eyes burn. A lump formed in my throat, and I couldn't speak anymore.

"Rem?" Jack asked sharply, alarmed. All the pent-up rage I had stored over the years exploded in an instant; my voice returned with a vengeance.

"NO, I AM NOT FUCKING OKAY! I have NEVER in my entire LIFE been this NOT fucking okay!" I bellowed, spraying saliva all over the windshield. I slammed on the brakes and jerked the wheel hard to the right, screeching to a stop on the shoulder. I sat still at the wheel, hyperventilating, as a cloud of road dust obscured us from view for a few seconds. A semi blatted its horn in annoyance as it barreled past. Jack gaped at me, an almost comical look of bewilderment on his face.

"I'm sorry," I sighed, laying my forehead on the steering wheel. "I'm just exhausted and scared. I haven't actually seen Mama in eighteen years or so. I'm not sure I'll even recognize her."

"I've never seen her at all, except in those couple of pictures you have in that old scrapbook. You almost never talk about her. I know it was bad, but how bad was it?" he asked cautiously. He knew he was on dangerous ground. My boobs weren't the only things I inherited from my mother. I also got her hair-trigger temper. There are few things in this world as vicious and implacable as a Shaw (or Tucker, for that matter) who has been provoked.

"Are you familiar with the author, V. C. Andrews?" I asked.

"Not intimately, but yes, I suppose. She's the one who writes all those desperation porn books, right? The ones where someone is always locked in an attic or is forced into some weird incestual relationship, and everyone is always poor and put upon?" he asked in return, looking at me as if he didn't understand why I brought some pulp fiction author into all of this.

"Yes, that's her. Well, her books are my life," I began. Jack stared at me blankly.

"I don't mean literally, you jackass!" I sputtered, nonplussed at his thickness. "I mean, my life was so fucked up as a child that you wouldn't believe me if I told you some of the things that happened. Awful things. Things I wouldn't believe if someone else told me they had happened to them."

"Is that why," he began slowly, "you always make jokes when I ask you about your life before we met?" I rolled my eyes and squealed in frustration. I buried my head in the steering wheel again.

"My God! For a genius, you sure are a fucking moron sometimes," I muttered. Jack chuckled in agreement.

We sat there in silence, each brooding on our own secret thoughts, each waiting for the other to mention the fact that we were sitting on the side of a major American highway, motorized death zipping past at breakneck speeds mere inches away from our fragile human bodies. The jeep rocked back and forth noticeably whenever a semi whooshed past. I looked to the south and saw the ominous midnight blue clouds stacked up on the horizon.

"Storm's coming," Jack said quietly.

"Yeah," I answered. "Can you drive now?"

"I thought you might ask that. Lucky for you, Captain Jack is present and accounted for. At your service, ma'am," he said, flashing that go-to-hell smile that I fell in love with the very first time he unleashed its brilliance on me.

We both exited the jeep, performing the Chinese fire drill ritual practiced the world over by harried travelers. When I reached the passenger side, I stopped to stretch out my exhausted and sore legs. My ass was numb, and I could hardly stand up straight. Ten hours of sitting had compressed my lower spine, and I needed to release the tension. I was used to being on the move, scurrying about my kitchen, certainly not sitting still. The long drive and the sedentary posture it required conspired together to make my back a despoiled battleground. I bent over at the waist, grabbed hold of both of my ankles, and slowly let the air out of my lungs, feeling the tightness melt away with the expelled breath. I returned to an upright position, breathed in deeply, and collapsed inelegantly into the passenger seat. Jack, already behind the wheel, put the car in gear and slid effortlessly into the stream of traffic, plowing ever southward. I closed my eyes and allowed myself to be comforted by the steady rhythms of the road.

"How bad was it?" Jack asked, breaking my trance. "You know, when you were growing up."

"We've talked about it," I answered testily.

"No, not really. You've told me that it was bad, but you've never really told me anything. Bad is a big word. It encompasses a lot of territory," he said, pushing back a little more than I was particularly comfortable with.

"Bad enough that I don't want to talk about it," I retorted, glaring at him and his temerity in pursuing this line of talk.

"That's too bad, Rem," he started, setting his jaw at the don't-fuck-with-me angle, "because this is real now. We are going to Stillwater. Right. Now. It's not fair to make me go into this blind. I should know what I'm about to walk into."

"Yeah, but…" I trailed off. He was right, it wasn't fair, but fair don't really come into play. I stared at him, unable to come up with anything remotely reasonable to explain why I couldn't just tell him everything. How do I explain shame that I have no logical reason to feel, yet feel it all the same, as keenly as a brush with a hot stove? My brain knows that I couldn't possibly bear any responsibility for my own origins, but my heart knows that I'm a less-than. I'm a Tucker and a Shaw. I simply can't evade that unfortunate yet undeniable fact.

"Yeah, but nothing," he continued. "I love you, as you are, because of who you are. Now it's time to tell me the why and the how. I can't navigate us through this storm if you won't let me see the map."

As the last words reverberated around the inside of the jeep, he stared stonily ahead, lighting up a filterless Camel and trying to hide the frustration I knew him to be feeling because I felt it too.

"I want to tell you, I really do. I just don't know how. It's silly, I know, but I don't want you to think less of me. I don't want to give you any weapons to use against me," I breathed in a rush, desperate to get it out before my nerve failed.

"Weapons? Wha…what do you mean?" he stammered, his eyes betraying a guilty conscience.

"You know exactly what I mean," I said in my most derisive tone. "Every time you get a bug up your ass about anything I tell you, out come the snide comments and not at all subtle insults. You always use any weakness I admit to or mistakes I have made against me to belittle me! You try to make me feel small!" I was shaking now, my words catching in my throat as I battled the onrushing tears. "You don't respect me!" I bellowed.

Suddenly, I was pitched forward in my seat, and my nose stopped short of the windshield by mere inches. Jack had spiked the brakes, and angry motorists shouted a kaleidoscope of profanities at us as they desperately maneuvered their cars away from the sudden appearance of the obstacle that was our jeep. Jack was staring intently at me, ignoring the sheet metal maelstrom outside. His shoulders heaved in time with his rapid breath and his temper twitch, a slight involuntary wink of his left eye, was working overtime.

"Jack!" I shrieked, but he raised a finger and placed it on my lips, creepily calm.

"Ssssshhhhhh," he said.

"FUCKING MOVE THE CAR!" I shouted, putting all the meager bass I could muster into my trembling voice. He turned from me, put on his right turn signal, and without looking, darted back over to the shoulder. He calmly put the transmission into park and shut off the engine. He turned back to me, looking at me with both exasperation and pity, and cupped his hands on either side of my face.

"I'm going to be as clear as possible," he began, his dark eyes never diverting from mine. "This car isn't moving another goddamn foot until you give me something here. I got nothing. I barely even know any of their names. You had what, three brothers and a sister, right? One of the brothers died. Your ma was a bitch or whatever. Nothing but vague tidbits. I just, I don't know, need more. Something more."

His chin sunk to his chest, and he seemed to collapse into himself. He turned back around and stared out of the windshield at the rapidly approaching thunderheads.

"Start the car," I said, my voice barely above a whisper. "Start the goddamn car and fucking drive."

"No," he replied simply. He folded his arms across his chest, and I kid you not, actually pushed out his lower lip, pouting like a child. White-hot sparks of fresh anger shot up and down my spine, invigorating and terrifying me.

"Will you please start the car?" I repeated, struggling to maintain a semblance of composure, my tone only rising the slightest degree.

"Not until you tell me something. A detail. A memory. Something other than a bare statement of fact," he said, still not looking at me. His temper twitch was gone, and his breathing wasn't as ragged. He no longer seemed angry, just sad, and tired. For some reason, that enraged me even further.

"You want a fucking detail?" I seethed, the venom shooting out of my mouth at his sad, tired face. "You want a memory? Oh, I got a fucking doozy of a memory for you, Jack. It's actually possibly my first memory. It's early for sure, even if it ain't the first."

I paused for breath, and as I drew it in, I noticed something in Jack's face I'd never seen before. Fear. It was really small, hiding behind his eyes, but I saw it, if only for a second. I don't know what or who the fear was directed at. I was mostly just shocked to find that emotion visible on his face at all. I stole a Camel from his pack, lit it, and continued on as he continued to refuse to look at me.

"I remember holding Mama's hand. It was so much bigger than my own, but it had the same shape. Only her hand was covered in blood, as was much of the rest of her. Only some of that blood belonged to Mama. A good bit of it belonged to her boyfriend at the time. They had a disagreement about the length of Mama's skirt and decided to settle it like mature adults. You know, with fucking steak knives."

Jack gaped at me but remained silent. Another semi roared past, sounding its obnoxious air horn far longer than was strictly necessary. I ignored both the traffic and Jack's befuddlement and continued my trip down Memory Lane.

"I remember the nurse called me sweetie pie and kept trying to keep me from looking at the blood. But I couldn't take my eyes off of it. I wanted to see Mama, and Mama had blood everywhere. She looked like someone had spilled paint or Kool-Aid all over her. And the smell! It was like someone put pennies over my nostrils." I continued my outburst while Jack silently regarded me with mounting horror.

"This is just one of many lovely stories I could tell you. It's not even close to the worst. I don't tell you because I don't want to think about that part of my life. I want the past to remain in the past. I ran away for a reason, and it took me years to put it all behind me. I don't need you to bring it all up! Just because you insist on having emotional diarrhea, it doesn't mean everybody else is going to! Can you please just fucking drop it?" I pleaded, hot tears running in rivulets down my cheeks.

"Okay," Jack said quietly, his hands extended like he was trying to calm a cornered badger. "I'm sorry. I didn't mean to push. It's just that everything before twenty years ago is a black hole with you. I'm just trying to understand—"

"Well, you don't, and you can't," I interrupted. "I know you think your life was tragic, but it just don't compare. Your momma just didn't kiss your ass enough to satisfy your giant ego. Mine forgot to buy groceries and pay the light bill and spent her paycheck at the bar."

Jack recoiled as if I had struck him. I noticed his knuckles go white as he gripped the steering wheel. It was a low below, and I knew it.

"Geez, Rem," he said. "I'm sorry. Okay? I'll drop it. We'll just get back on the road."

I nodded gravely, and Jack started the engine. Within seconds, he had nosed out into the southerly flow and joined the stream of travelers and delivery men heading down one of America's many arteries. I stared out the window at the bland Interstate scenery, trying to hypnotize myself into sleep. I knew I owed more to Jack than I had given, but I just wasn't ready. Not now. Not when I didn't really even know myself what we were heading into. Jolene is the only family member I had talked to at all, and I tried to keep that to once a year, maximum. The familial politics we were about to be immersed in would be as unfamiliar to me as they were to Jack. They may have been blood, but it's been so long, they may as well have been strangers.

"It's not your fault, Remlee," Jack said quietly, breaking into my pre-slumber fog. "You can't choose your parents, your family. You just have to, I don't know…" he trailed off, not sure of what to say next. "I'm just saying I don't care about them. I know who you are, you have nothing to prove."

I rolled my eyes, exasperated, and said, "I'm not trying to prove anything."

Determined to end this conversation, I turned over in my seat and faced the window, resting my head on the glass. I closed my eyes and started to drift off again. I was almost asleep when Jack hit a bump in the road, startling me to full consciousness once again. I noticed that it had started raining.

"Perfect," I said, mostly to myself, and went back to sleep as Jack drove ever southward, taking me to my appointment with the past.

Betty Sue

It's dark again. That's okay. The lights back in the world were brighter than I remember them being. I'll just float here in the warm place and collect myself. The nurses said I had a stroke. I ain't educated, but I've seen episodes of Dr. Oz about strokes. Strokes is bad juju, honey. I wonder how bad it was. I can't seem to talk right; my traitor mouth won't do what my brain tells it to do.

I'm worrying about what happens next when I notice that I'm lying on something. Just a minute ago, I was floating. Something is happening. Somehow, I left the warm place. I'm somewhere instead of my cozy nowhere. I can hear sounds now: insects are buzzing, I hear a cow lowing somewhere nearby. I can smell a familiar smell all around, the heavy yet not altogether unpleasant tang of manure. I can smell honeysuckle underneath that. It must be summer here. I can see light now, shining on the other side of my eyelids.

Opening my eyes, I shake my head in disbelief. I'm back at the farm! This can't be possible, but I can't deny it. I'm in Daddy's barn. There's the old Farmall over there in the corner, only it isn't old anymore. It looks like that he just bought it yesterday. Okay, I know where I am, but when am I? Did I time travel?

Wait, I must be dreaming. That's it, I'm just sleeping. But if I'm sleeping, this is the realest dream I've ever had. I can feel everything here. The air has substance. If I'm dreaming, why can I smell cow shit? I've never smelled anything in a dream before. This can't be a dream, but what the hell is it?

I look down at myself and gasp at what I see. I've shrunk! No, that's wrong. I haven't grown yet. I remember this dress! It's my favorite yellow play dress. It's so soft and loose and comfortable. The powerful Florida sun can't touch me when I wear it. If I'm wearing this dress, then I must be, what, eight? Nine? Somewhere in there. Before Bobby Lee died…

Bobby Lee! He still alive! I've got to go find him! He should be around here somewhere. I miss him so much. He's the only brother who is ever nice to me at all, even if it isn't always. Those awful zipper heads haven't killed him yet!

I run out into the barnyard, looking back and forth frantically for any sign of Bobby Lee. As the scene sinks in, I'm stopped in my tracks. There's so much I forgotten! Of course, I remember the house and the barn, but look! There's the tire swing daddy put up last year. I remember now. He used one of those giant tractor tires when it got replaced. All of us kids used to get on that thing at the same time, and Daddy, my giant Daddy, the strongest man in the whole world, would push All of us so high, I thought we would fly off and over the barn. I laughed so hard!

I scan the property to my left and see the see of our lifeblood here on the farm, sugarcane. The giant green stocks are dancing to the music of the wind, rustling secret poetry for only the ears who would listen. I don't understand business or economics, but I do understand that we eat better for a while after we cut down and sell it all. All but what Daddy keeps to make the shine, that is.

I turn to the right and see the house. I'm flooded with warm feelings, mostly, with only a little ugly underneath. I'm still young yet; things haven't gone completely wrong yet. Beyond the house, I see the path that leads down to the creek. My brothers are probably down there now, fishing or trying to explode frogs with the M-80s they stole from Mr. Nelson, two properties down the road. Daddy says he uses them to destroy the dams the beavers tried to build upstream. I feel bad for the beavers. They just want a home too.

I feel lightheaded, like I stood up too fast on a hot day, which I suppose is just what I did. I sit down hard in the dust in front of the barn, scattering the few chickens that had come over to see if I was bearing food. They squawk at me, irritated that I'm empty-handed. I notice a small headache coming on, crouching, mostly hidden behind my left eye. I try to ignore it and focus on when it is that I have come to relive, if reliving is even what you could call what I am experiencing.

Is this a memory? That seems more right. Time travel is just some Twilight Zone bull-pucky. If so, this ain't like any other memory I've ever had before. Is just so real! But I remember things that happen after right now. Oh, my head hurts! I think maybe I've gone crazy. That's it. I'm over the rainbow, just like Granny. Dr. Oz says that dementia runs in the family, and that's what killed Granny. Oh, Lord, don't let this be that!

I close my eyes and sit very still. I try not to think about anything, to just flow back into the warm place. All these sights, these sounds, these smells from the past are too much to bear. I don't understand what is happening to me, and I'm scared. I can't put a face or a name on that fear. It's just a stone in the pit of my stomach that I can ignore. I open my eyes again, just to see if it's all still there. As my eyes focus, I see a figure come from out behind the house, ambling in my general direction. I squint hard to see who it is; the form seems ghostly, ethereal. My breath stops as I recognize Bobby Lee.

As my mind convinces itself that it is Bobby Lee I see, he becomes real. It's like a fog that somehow freezes solid. He sees me and grins, like he has a joke to tell me. He wags his pointer at me, calling me over to him. He looks so young, so alive! Nothing like the pale imitation in his coffin five years from now, after Uncle Sam chews him up and spits him out. I feel myself drawn to him, like clothes on a pulley-fed clothesline. I look and see I'm floating, not walking. I don't feel scared, but maybe I should.

It dawns on me that I haven't tried to speak since coming here. (Home? Hell? Memory? Limbo?) I don't know what the rules are here, but since I'm moving without actually moving, I suppose anything at all could be possible. I decide to try.

"Bobby Lee!" I shout jubilantly. I can speak! Reality floods into me like a waterfall. I feel my feet on the ground again for a split second before Bobby Lee picks me up in a giant bear hug and swings me around and around till I'm so dizzy I might faint. He finally sets me down and grins.

"Mama?" he asks in someone else's voice. "Mama? Wake up, Mama."

"Why do you sound like that?" I ask him, fear and confusion swirling madly in my brain. "You sound like my daughter, Jolene, but she ain't been born yet. This ain't right." I back away from Bobby Lee as he stands there looking puzzled.

"Mama? Please wake up, Mama!" Bobby Lee pleads in that stolen voice.

"Stop talking like that!" I roar, and suddenly my eyes open, but for real this time. I am no longer in my memory, I'm back in the hospital, and I'm looking at my daughter, Jolene. The house, the barn, and Bobby Lee have all disappeared, almost like they just melted away.

"Mama! You're awake!" Jolene squeals. "Are you feeling okay? Do you need anything?" She reaches down for the call button and mashes it repeatedly. I try to speak, worried that I won't be able to, now that it counts.

"Yu yu yu mmump," I say, but that's not right. Jolene's eyes grow wide, and her hand involuntarily covers her mouth.

"What? I don't understand you, Mama," Jolene says as she takes my hand into hers. I concentrate as hard as I can on her name.

"Jjjuuuhhhlllnnn," I say, almost spitting the word out like a sunflower seed.

"Yes! Jolene!" she says excitedly, pointing to herself like she is talking to a child.

I'll look around the room to see if anyone else had come with her. Where are Shane and Elton? Wait, Elton is in jail again. I remember that. I wonder if Remlee is here. I haven't talked to her in years, but maybe she came. Oh, I hope she did. I miss her so much. I wish she didn't leave. Oh, please, let her have come!

"Rrrmmmlllll?" I ask, but Jolene just looks at me blankly.

We are interrupted by the nurses brought by Jolene's panic button mashing. I don't know if it's the same nurses as before. I can barely remember before. I'm just so confused and scared. The nurse on the right must see this in my face, and she comes real close to the bed and takes my other hand, the one not being held by Jolene, into hers, and looks straight into my eyes

"Miz Shaw," she begins, honey in her voice. "You are okay. You're just in the hospital. You've had a stroke. It was pretty bad, but we're gonna take real good care of you."

Jolene bursts into a fresh round of tears at this, and I turn my head to look at her. She looks so tired and sad. Them circles under her eyes tell me she's been using again. Can't put that needle away. I try to tell her she looks awful.

"Yu yu yu," I stutter. Jolene stops crying for a moment, and the talkative nurse takes the opportunity to talk to me again.

"Miz Shaw, we want to find out how bad the damage was, so the doctor has ordered an MRI. Do you know what that is?" she asks.

"NNNNOOOO! YU YU YU! MMUMFAH! YU YU!" I yell in defiance. I do know exactly what one is, and there ain't no way anyone's getting me in that contraption.

"Take it easy, Miz Shaw," the other nurse says, edging closer to the bed. "Nobody's gonna hurt you."

Jolene breaks in, cutting off the second nurse. "It's okay, Mama. I'll be here with you," she says in her toddler-calming voice. That tone just pisses me off even more. I try to tell her I'm not a damned baby, but only more gibberish comes out. I begin to cry in frustration.

"OOMBAH NOHMAH! YUUUU YUUUU!" I wail, waving my arms and pointing to the door. I hope they understand that I want them to leave. The first nurse, the smarter one, pats me on the head, trying to soothe me. I slap her hand away.

"YUUU! GIMBA GUNNZOH DDOOOM!" I roar, pointing to the door. The nurse looks stunned and a little bit scared. Good. This little bitch don't know who she is fucking with. I may not be able to talk, but I can still claw your fucking eyes out.

"Okay, okay! Calm down, Miz Shaw. Nobody is gonna hurt you. I can see you're upset right now, so we will come back later. You just rest," coos the nurse.

"I'm so sorry, ma'am," Jolene begins, clearly horrified. "My mom hates hospitals. She never—"

I interrupt. "YUU! MUMMRA!" Don't be telling these strangers about my business!

The nurse ignores me and answers Jolene like I'm not even in the room. She tells her that they'll come back to try again in an hour. I tell her not to bother, but she ignores my noises and continues to talk about me to Jolene. I quit trying to follow them. It is too tiring. I think I'll just close my eyes for a minute. Just…for…a minute…

Remlee

It was dark when I woke, but from the weather more than from the hour. Rain lashed the Jeep unceasingly, the wipers unable to clear the torrent away from the windshield. We were crawling along as fast as Jack dared, which, in this weather, wasn't very fast at all. Jack may be seemingly fearless, but he drives like a timid little grandma. I tease him all the time about this, but I decided that it probably wasn't the best time for that right then. His blue eyes were beyond bloodshot, and I could see that he was struggling to keep them open.

"Where are we?" I asked him after clearing my throat. My voice cracked from dehydration, and I reached for the bottle of water in the console. I drank greedily, the lukewarm liquid flooding my dry throat with relief.

"Just south of Savannah. Will be in Jacksonville in an hour or so," he replied, his eyes never leaving the road. "How did you sleep?"

"I'm not sure it's accurate to call it sleep," I answered honestly, "but I guess I'm vaguely more rested than I was. What I really need is a shower and a bed. What about you? Wanna stop for the night?"

Jack looked perplexed. "But we're so close," he stammered, looking at me as if I had just grown a third leg. "We are, like, three hours away. I can push through."

"I don't want to have to face this looking and feeling like I do. I want real sleep and clean gutchies before I have to deal with this," I said. Jack opened his mouth to say something, then thought better of it and closed it again. After a minute of mulling it over in his head, he finally spoke. "I have to admit," he began, "I am a bit on the tired side myself. And a mite thirsty, if you know what I mean," he winked at me.

"Yeah, I figured," I sighed and turned my gaze back out the window. There wasn't much to see in the gloom, but I wanted to keep my eye out for exit signs. I had to make sure I paid attention, or else Jack would just pull into any old fleabag motel. I'm no snob, but I'm not sleeping in a place that charges by the hour.

My mind, however, started to drift. Being this close to Florida was triggering wave after wave of memory to crash over me. Little details took on almost mythical significance as the Jeep drove us not only south but back. I had forgotten how sad and stately the trees looked, draped in Spanish moss. I had forgotten how loud the cicadas were, how their mingled emanations seemed to fill the whole world, but mostly, I remembered the day I left.

All throughout my childhood, whenever things got too bad at home, I would go stay with my Granny Lettie. I loved being on the farm with her and Peepaw. Almost all of my good memories of childhood are from there. Granny was Mama's stepmom, and their relationship was less than cordial, but Granny loved me all the same. It was Granny who taught me how to cook, not Mama. Granny was the one who taught me almost everything of value that I know. The remainder was taught to me by Peepaw. He delighted in hoisting me up on his shoulder and taking me out to the fields with him. I felt like a giant up there, my head above the sugarcane stalks. God, I missed them both so much.

It's not like Mama didn't love us. She did. She was just too damaged, two wild, to ever be a proper mother. Children are just so needy, and Mama just didn't have much to give. When I was really young, I remember weeks going by with no sign of her. Shane was already gone, and Elton was too much like Daddy to be in charge, so Jolene would do her best to be "Mom." Of course, by the time she was fourteen, she was a mom herself. And then again eleven months later. By the time I was eight, Jolene had moved out with her newest baby daddy, and I went to live with Granny and Peepaw basically full time.

The next five years or so were the most stable and peaceful of my life up to that point. I got into the routines of the farm, went to school regularly, had friends. I spent my days in the fields, or in the pond, or in a tree with my nose in a book. I never missed a meal, and the electric was always on. I no longer had to dodge the landlord. I was happy and thriving. The only time there was any real strife during this period was the sporadic visits Mama would make. She would blow in from this biker rally or that long-haul semi drivers rig and demand to take me home. She and Peepaw would fight like demons about it, Mama threatening violence or legal action, Peepaw stoically weathering her storm. Eventually, Mama would peter herself out against the granite will of Peepaw and leave in a huff, not to be heard from again for another few months. I don't think I ever missed her when she was gone.

Things went on this way for some time. The years bled into one another, and everything was pretty much the same from one day to the next. Until it wasn't. I've never been naive or sheltered, and at thirteen, I knew full well about Peepaw's illegal income stream. I had witnessed enough in my years to understand that not all that cane became sugar. A good third of it became white lightning, which Peepaw and Uncle Clarence distilled, bottled, and sold. Granny always said that the shine would be the death of him, but I'm pretty sure she didn't think it would happen the way that it did.

Peepaw died in my thirteenth year, his seventy-fourth. It was two weeks before my birthday, and he was making a special batch of shine to serve our sprawling family at my birthday party. I was in my favorite tree, reading a book, when I heard the explosion back in the barn. My tree was easily two hundred yards from the barn, but I felt my face, arms, and legs pelted with shrapnel and heat. I fell out of the tree, and everything went black for a minute. When I came to, I looked up to see an inferno where Peepaw's barn had been.

When the smoke finally cleared and the police concluded their investigation, the verdict was death by misadventure. Apparently, Uncle Clarence had been remiss in his duties and had not been maintaining the still properly. One of the exhaust ports had gotten clogged, and the pressure buildup caused the whole works to go up while Peepaw just happened to be in there. They found pieces of him three hundred yards from where he had been standing when the explosion hit.

I stayed on with Granny. Things managed to plug along well enough for a few months. Granny was sad, heartbroken even, but she was not defeated. She marshaled my three uncles into service on the farm, and she was determined to keep it running. I helped as much as I could, but Granny wouldn't let me quit school to stay home and work. She said I was meant for better, and I think she really believed it. It wasn't long, however, that the family began to notice Granny slipping. She'd forget recipes that she knew by heart, ones that she'd used for forty years. She was always a Nazi about turning the lights out when we left the room, but now she was leaving every light in the house on. Occasionally she would seem to forget who I was or even think I was my mother or my Aunt Lola. At first it seemed benign enough. She was still paying the bills, keeping up the house and such. She just said she was getting forgetful, that's all.

After a few months, however, it was becoming impossible to ignore that granny was declining rapidly. I would often find her in the bathroom, crying inconsolably like an infant, her eyes rolling wildly in their sockets, not seeing me, looking through me at something invisible to me, yet utterly terrifying to her. I would have to hold her tight in my arms to keep her from injuring herself as she clawed at her phantom tormentors, often injuring me in the process. I did my best to hide this from the world at large, to keep up the facade that everything was normal. I had friends in Florida's Child Protective Services' care, and none had anything good to say about the experience. I did everything I could to fly under their radar.

I maintained this charade for six months or more before it finally caught up with me. My middle school guidance counselor happened to notice that I was absent more and more frequently. She then took it upon herself to drop by one afternoon after a three-day absence. Her timing couldn't have been worse. She let herself into our house just as I was trying to catch Granny and bathe her. She had taken a dislike to hygiene as of late, and she fought me like a wildcat whenever I appeared with the sponge. Mrs. Shontz had the dubious honor of meeting Granny just as she had been born, naked and screaming. It took her all of six seconds to get CPS on the phone.

When they arrived twenty minutes later, the ambulance pulled in right behind them, sent by the nursing home to collect Granny. The last time I saw Granny was from the back seat of the government issue Crown Victoria, as my new minders, the State of Florida, drove me away from all I had ever known. I refused to cry in front of the sincere-as-saccharine social worker in whose care I had been temporarily placed. It was explained to me, very matter-of-factly, that nobody in my family had been willing or able to take me in, so I was being placed in the custody of a very nice Christian family, three counties over, outside of Tallahassee. I was promised that they would treat me real fair and nice, just as long as I didn't give them no "guff." What exactly "guff" was wasn't ever actually explained to me.

When I arrived at the home of Mr. and Mrs. Rodger Heimbaugh, I was already planning my escape. That I would be well fed and cared for didn't compare to the tempting siren call of freedom, almost in my grasp. I might only have been fourteen but was an experienced, worldly fourteen, or so I thought. If I couldn't be with family, I may as well go out on my own. The Heimbaughs were nice enough, but their lifestyle seemed corny and boring to my already jaded eyes. I dreaded the idea of spending the next four years having the highlight of my week being family game night with Monopoly and RC Cola. I knew that there would be no mud-bogging, no moonshine-filled bonfire parties in the back forty here. I had recently taken the Shaw family rite of passage, my first Marlboro, and that certainly wouldn't fly here. By the time they finally bid me good night, roughly four hours after I had arrived, I had already decided to leave. I just didn't know where to go.

I knew I didn't want to stay in Florida. The shadow my family cast over North Central Florida was legendary. Everybody knew about the inbred moonshiners out on Platt Junction Road. It was like walking around with Hester Prynne's letter, only it was the letter "W" for white trash, and it was in my DNA, not just all my dress. I know people generally try to be fair-minded, but too many mentions in the police blotter of *The Daily Times* tend to color people's perceptions, conscious or not. The fact that most of the rumors, even the most outrageous ones, had at least some link to reality didn't help.

I was tired of the staring children, the looks of pity on my teachers' faces, the whispering behind (and shouting in front of) my back. What really set me on my course, though, was that after all those years of being told I was trash, both obliquely and overtly, I was starting to believe it.

I was actually afraid that by staying, I'd somehow taint this lovely family who had taken me in. You can't keep clean if you roll in the dirt, you know? I doubt I was consciously thinking this at the time, but just looking at their three perfect, beaming, friendly, helpful, intelligent, cookie-cutter children, I knew I was an impostor. Clean sheets every night? Someone who not only cared if your homework was done but would actually help you if you needed it? Not for the likes of me. I was just Remlee, youngest daughter of the infamous bank robber and cop killer, Elmer Ray Shaw, and the less association you could have with me, the better. I knew I'd only let them down; it would be best not to get attached. There was no question in my mind that within a month. This lovely couple would be frantically calling CPS, begging them to take me back. Better to leave now and avoid all that inevitable unpleasantness.

I waited, fully dressed under the handmade quilt, for the Heimbaughs to all be fully asleep, and quietly walked out of their house and into an unknown future. My mind raced with mingled fear and excitement as I crept silently down the driveway. I scarcely breathed, irrationally fearing that Rodger Heimbaugh had superhuman hearing and would catch me before I could get away. I paused at the end of the driveway, looking back at the house. I distinctly remember thinking that maybe I could give this place a shot. I wasn't crazy about the rules here, and church just left me cold, but I'd be safe. After a short but intense internal war, freedom went out over safety. As it always does, for me anyways.

I felt bad about leaving without saying anything (and about stealing a hundred dollars from Mrs. Himebaugh's purse), but I knew they'd never just let me go, so it had to be this way. I struck out into the night, just myself, my brother Elton's hunting knife, and a backpack full of clothes. I had no real destination in mind. I just knew it had to be north, as there wasn't much further south I could go. I was alone but not that scared. I was a Shaw. We're made of sterner stuff.

My train of thought was halted when Jack's voice cut through the cloud of memory. "There is a Red Roof at the next exit. That sound all right to you, Rem?" he asked.

"Yeah, yeah, sure," I replied, still not quite in the moment. "They're usually clean and cheap enough. I don't need the Four Seasons. Just no cockroaches or bloodstains. I'm sure we'll have our share of that if we go to Jolene's," I cracked, only half joking.

"Eeeewwwwww!" Jack squealed playfully. He guided our Jeep onto the off-ramp and signaled to the right. In the distance, I could see one of the neon *Oases* that tend to cluster around the exits of interstates all across America. I could see signs for Denny's, Wendy's, and various other one-name joints that litter the realm, suffocating us all with their bland sameness. Presently, the familiar Red Roof logo appeared, two traffic lights ahead. I sighed loudly with relief as Jack turned us into the parking lot and then let our poor beast of burden finally rest.

"Home sweet home," he cackled with a cheesy grin. I smiled in spite of myself at his goofiness. I think that's why I fell in love with him. No matter the tragedy, no matter the stress, Jack simply refuses to take anything too seriously and tries his damnedest not to let me, either.

"I'll go get us checked in, just wait here," Jack said as he bounded away, likely driven as much by the need for a drink as his need to see to my comfort. The slight shaking of his hands on the steering wheel over the last few miles hadn't escaped my attention. Neither had the Miller Lite sign in the window of the adjoining establishment. I knew where I would find Jack once I got done showering if I had the energy and motivation to bother to look. I doubt it I would.

After a few moments, Jack reappeared, brandishing a key like it was some magical talisman. We were lucky in that our room just happened to be two doors to the left of where we parked, so we just grabbed our knapsacks and walked over to our room for the night.

"Shall I carry you over the threshold?" Jack asked with a wink.

"Well, I'm pretty sure you know I'm no virgin." I laughed. "But you never did give me a real honeymoon."

"I know," he said, his eyes full of mock contrition, "Somehow this doesn't seem festive enough for a honeymoon. Visiting your estranged mother after a massive stroke. Not very romantic—"

I cut him off. "We aren't romantic people," I said.

Betty Sue

I'm back in the trailer. This must be before Remlee was born because I can see the Pacer in the driveway, and Elmer sold that off right before she was born to pay off the light bill he run up without telling me. He was taking our bill money down to Tiger's or the Honey Pot and blowing it on broads and booze. It must be a school day because I can't hear the constant racket that constantly pours out of that pack of godawful gremlins known as my children. I go to the cupboard and pour myself three fingers of Beam. I swallow it whole, not tasting it, just feeling its warm fingers working their way through my guts.

I walk to the screen door and peer out across the dooryard at the busy highway beyond. Cars and trucks and semis and buses galore go whizzing past at speeds far higher than Johnny Law says is kosher. The noise from the road is a part of the atmosphere here, as commonplace as the cicadas. I hardly notice it anymore.

I'm not sure why, but something feels off. I know this is just a dream, I'm used to this now, but that ain't what's wrong. I feel this brick of dread in my guts, but I don't know why. The sun is shining, a cool breeze is blowing, everything is shipshape. Why does it feel like it's all a lie, and the horrible truth is just waiting to jump out of a closet at me?

I walk outside on the rickety porch and shield my eyes from the sun. I begin to notice the sound, ever so quiet, coming from behind the shed next to the Pacer. It almost sounds like a baby crying, but strangely muffled, and barely even noticeable. I take a few steps toward the shed, my ear cocked like a coonhound, listening hard. Something about the sound is both terrifying and familiar. My heart skips a few beats in my chest as the crying gets louder, more frantic. I find myself drawn toward the shed, and I can't seem to stop myself from walking toward it. I tell my legs, out loud, to quit moving, but they ignore me, pulling me ever closer to the wailing.

As I approach the shed, I notice the smell, a sharp stink filling the air. I stop and retch, my guts threatening to empty. It's the smell of rotting flesh. I know it well. One year, a possum crawled up into the ductwork and died there. It took Elmer two days of fiddle fucking around to find it once I noticed the smell. The smell is like that, only stronger. It feels solid almost, like you ran into a wall. It's coming from where the sound is, and this makes me even more scared. I don't want to know what is behind there, but I can't stop myself from looking.

The crying is so loud now. I wonder how the world can hold it. It seems to come from everywhere now, like the whole sky is bawling. The sun has disappeared, and dark clouds circle furiously overhead. I feel my hair dancing wildly on my head, and it seems like the air is full of electricity you can feel, just like before a godawful thunderstorm. Lightning flashes nearby, and I cringe as I await the coming boom. I don't wait long. The roar is so loud I worry that my eardrums will split.

Suddenly, I realized what, no, who, is crying on the other side of the shed, and my blood freezes in my veins. The crying is coming from the spot behind the shed where the kids would stand and wait for the bus. The place where Jesco breathed his last because I was too hungover to wait with him. I don't want to go any further. I can't see him like that again.

My traitor feet resume their march, bringing me closer to the sound and the smell. In seconds, I'll see him lying there, half his face gone, smeared all over the bumper of the Peterbilt he ran in front of. I can't bear it! I try to close my eyes, but I can't even do that. I feel like a puppet, or like someone in those silly voodoo movies Bobby Lee always used to sneak us into when we was kids.

"No! Please, God, no! I don't wanna see it again!" I shriek into the wind. I try to plant my feet and grab the corner of the shed, but that invisible force just keeps pushing, and I fall on my face into the mud behind the shed. I can hear that the source of the crying is just inches from me. I lie still, face buried in the mud like an ostrich, and refuse to move. All other sounds have stopped now. The wind has died. It's only me and the crying thing that used to be my son. I refused to look at him/it.

"Mama," it croaks, and I scream into the mud as chunks of wet earth fall into my open mouth. I gag again. I wonder if I can die in a dream, like in those Freddy movies Shane and Elton loved so much.

"Mama, why weren't you here?" it asks, stabbing through my heart with its words. "It huuuuuuurrrrrrrtttttttsssss! It hurts so bad, Mama!"

"I'm sorry!" I wail into the mud. I can't raise my head to look at him. I'm too scared.

Seemingly reading my thoughts, the thing that was Jesco screams, "Look at me, Mama! Look at what you did!"

I feel bony fingers tangle themselves in my hair and jerk my head up until I'm face to face with the leering ruin that was my beautiful Jesco's face. His right eye and ear are missing, along with most everything else on that side of his newly misshapen head. Black blood has dried all along his neck and mouth, and his remaining eye rolls in its socket like a spooked mare. The stench of the grave pours out of the gaping maw that was once his mouth, suffocating me. I feel the world spin, and my stomach does another flip. I look on in horror as a giant maggot, bigger than any I've ever seen, crawls out of the empty eye socket, an obscene parody of a tear. I scream a wordless protest at all I am seeing, willing it to not be real. The hand holding my head lets go, and my face slams back into the muck. The thing is still there, but its cries have died down to whimpering and sniffling. Its breath hitches up every now and again, and a sob bursts through, but all in all, it seems to be calming. Dying. I ain't sure which.

"I never meant for this to happen to you," I bawl, still afraid to look it in the face. "I just had a hangover and couldn't get out of bed. You and Jolene had gotten on that damn bus near a hundred times before, no problem. I never thought…" I burst out crying again, unable to say the rest.

I feel the thing's cold hand touch my shoulder, tenderly stroking it. I shiver away from it, repelled by the unholy force that is keeping it alive. I shut my eyes tight and plug my ears, and try to will myself awake. I don't want to be here anymore. I don't like the hospital, but at least the dead people there don't talk to me. They have the common courtesy to act like a corpse ought to, quiet and unmoving.

Slowly, the feeling of the mud surrounding me begins to fade. I realize I'm in a bed, not on the ground behind the shed at the old trailer.

The thing that was Jesco is gone too, as is the sound of traffic. All is still, except for the rhythmic beeping of the machines that are attached to me. I open my eyes and see that I'm indeed in the hospital bed, but it's evening now. I can see the pink strip in the sky where the sun has just been. I look around the room to see if Jolene is still here, but I see that I'm alone. Even the bed next to me is empty. I can hear the low murmur of conversations just outside the room in the hallway, but I can't make out anything they're saying.

As I wake up more, I begin to think about my predicament. I'm trapped inside my own body, and I don't know how to tell anybody. I start to wonder if this stroke affected anything else besides my ability to talk. After a few panicky seconds where I'm not sure I'm in control, I managed to sit upright. I start to feel a little dizzy, but I bear down and swing my legs over the side of the bed. I sit like this for what seems like a long time, waiting for the room to stop spinning. When it does, I carefully put one foot down on the floor, then the other. So far, so good.

I start to notice that I have to pee. That only makes sense. I don't know how long I've been here. Time is messed up. I realize I don't know what day it is. I'm not even sure what year it is. How long have I been here? I start to walk to the bathroom, when my left arm is suddenly jerked backward. I just catch myself from falling over. I look down at my arm to see who done grabbed it and see the tubes running out of my arm and into two large plastic bags of some kind of clear liquid hanging from a post on the bed. I realize I'm basically handcuffed in place. I start to holler.

"WUBBLUM DEE! YUYU YU YU DEE! WUBBLUM!" I yell at the top of my lungs. I hear movement in the hallway coming in this direction.

"WUBBLUM DEE!" I yell again, not quite realizing that I'm not actually saying words. In my head, I'm saying, hey, I gotta piss! Somebody, help me piss! The noises I'm making aren't lining up with what I mean. I start to get angry. Finally, a nurse pokes her face in the room.

"Miz Betty Sue! You're awake! What do you need, honey?" she asks in her made for kindergarten voice.

I try to tell her that my back teeth are floating, and I really could use to pee, but I'm stuck to this goddamn contraption, so could you please hurry your narrow little ass over here and unhook me?

"MMMNNNAAAMMMMANNN! DINGU YU YU YU! SUMBA YU YU YU YUUUUUU!" is what I actually say. I moan in frustration and try to point at the door to the bathroom. The nurse looks blankly at me. Is she really this fucking dumb?

"MMMNNNAAAAH! YU YU DINGA YU YUU!" I say again, pointing at my arm, then the bathroom door, jabbing my finger in a rage.

"Honey, I'm sorry, but I just don't understand what you're trying to say to me," the nurse coos, and in that instant, I hate her more than the devil himself. Feeling trapped and ashamed, my bladder lets go, soaking the front of my gown, and puddling on the floor. I feel like a runt puppy who can't get the hang of house breaking. I hang my head in shame.

"Yuu maa mumm," I say to the floor.

"Oh, Miz Betty Sue, you've tinkled all over yourself!" the nurse gasps, rushing over to me but trying to avoid the mess on the floor. I just stand there, defeated and quietly crying in a puddle of my own piss. I feel lower than the family dog. I allow her to lead me back to the bed, careful to avoid the piss, where she sits me down and pulls off my gown in one quick motion.

"I'll go get you a new gown, honey. You just lie down and relax. The doctor is making her rounds right now. She will be in to see you soon. She'll be better able to tell you what's going on," the nurse says soothingly over her shoulder as she glides out the door. She reminds me of Tinkerbell in Peter Pan, all cute, sweet, and happy. I hate her.

I wrap myself up in the blanket and try to calm down. I ain't never been no good at that, but things are different now. I got to think about all of this, but I ain't never been no good at that, neither. Everything is foggy now, though. Thinking is like swimming through Jell-O. I wish that fucking nurse would get back with some clothes! Oh Lord!

After a spell, she finally comes bopping back in with a fresh gown. I can see it's another one of those stupid backless getups, the kind that shows your ass to God and everyone. I really don't want one of those kinds. Don't they have something decent for a person to wear? I ain't no damned animal. I tried to tell this to Nurse Tinkerbell.

"Yu yu yu mmpah! Yumpa yu yu," I babble. Damn it!

"That's right, Miz Betty, it's a fresh one! That's so much nicer, isn't it?" she sings at me. I shake my head back and forth violently and try again, slower.

"Yu…no…d…duh… YU YU YU MMMPAH!" I spit at her, pointing at the gown in her hand and shaking my head "no," trying to keep eye contact.

"Well, we have to get you dressed," she huffs, completely missing my message. "It won't do to have you parading around in your birthday suit!" She giggles, amused at her own joke.

I ain't amused. I'll never understand why some nurses and other hospital people act like all their patients are children. Quit talking down to me. I know I ain't educated, but I'm a grown-up, and I demand you treat me like one.

Nurse Tinkerbell comes at me with the gown, but I'm a spry old lady, so I manage to dodge her first lunge. I can see she starting to lose her temper with me. Good. No reason I should be the only one who's mad. I try again to tell her I just want my ass covered. I'm not asking for Bon-Ton or JCPenney.

"Yu yu…mmmmmmm…yu," I begin, my tone quieter, more relaxed. "Bbbbuuuummmbaah doe yu yu yu?" I implore. Tink ignores me and manages to get the gown over my head. I let her, too tired to fight it anymore. I just won't get my ass off this bed till they bring me some goddamn pants.

I sit back on the bed and glare at nurse Tinkerbell. She continues to ignore me and flits about the room, looking at the machines I'm hooked to and writing things on her little clipboard. She's humming some silly pop song under her breath, and it's starting to set my teeth on edge. I'm just about to tear back into her when another woman, this one much older and sterner, walks into the room and up to the edge of my bed. She's just as small as Tinkerbell, but wiry, not soft. Where Tink is all sunshine and rainbows, this new woman is all about business. She stares at my chart for a few minutes, then finally speaks.

"Ms. Shaw," she begins, not looking up from the clipboard, "My name is Doctor Nguyen. As I'm sure you've been told by now, you've had a stroke. A particularly nasty one at that. It appears to have affected the part of your brain that controls speech. You are experiencing a condition

known as aphasia, which means that you have lost the ability to talk. Do you understand what I'm telling you?"

I stare at her for a moment, then I nod yes. She nods back, looks at the chart some more, then continues.

"We still don't know the extent of the damage, and I'm going to order an MRI, so we can get a better look at what's going on up there," she says, pointing at my forehead. "I can't say yet if you'll get your ability to speak back. You're most likely get back some, but after a year, your progress will likely plateau."

I start to get real nervous when I hear her say MRI. I feel my heart start to beat faster, and my breathing gets faster. I don't want no MRI. Not today. Not ever. You ain't getting me in that big old tube. I'm scared of tight spots, no use in denying it. I'd rather go to bed with a nest of rattlers, then get into some tight closed in spot. I must look scared, 'cause the doc reaches over and holds my hand.

"It'll be okay, Ms. Shaw. Will give you some medicine so you can relax. It's really important that we see what's going on, and the MRI is the best tool we have. You'll be completely safe the whole time, and there's a panic button for you if you need it," she says calmly, if not exactly kindly.

"Yu yu yu… AAAAHHHHHHFFFF," I say, breaking into tears. I'm too scared and confused to fight anymore. I lie back down and turned my back to the doctor. You win, for now, I think, and I try to ignore her as she goes on and on about the procedure. Finally, she tells me that they'll come in a few minutes to give me something to relax me, and she walks out of the room. I stay on my side, refusing to budge. I just hope the dope they give me is strong enough. There's no telling what I'm liable to do if they can't knock me out.

A few minutes later, Nurse Tinkerbell comes back into the room. She's carrying a little Dixie Cup and two pills. She thrusts them at me and tells me to take them.

"Yu yu yumma," I say, meaning only because I have to. I swallow the pills and the water, then turn my back on the nurse and lay down again. I pull the thin, almost useless hospital blanket up to my neck and close my eyes. I wait patiently for the sleep I know as soon on its way. When I wake…up… I'll show…

Remlee

The highway leading into Stillwater is the main thoroughfare running down the center of Florida. Daddy always used to joke that it was the vein in America's dick, but I wasn't feeling particularly humorous when we crossed the border from Georgia to Florida, just North of Jacksonville. The sense of impending doom I felt was at odds with the crystal blue skies and warm sunshine presented to my eyes. The previous day's storm had blown over, and everything was postcard perfect. It was this weather that seduced so many into living here, staying here, even though everything here, from the insects and other wildlife to the hurricanes and gangbangers, was actively trying to kill you. Say what you will about snow, but I'll take a blizzard or a deer over a hurricane or an alligator any day. I can always put on a sweater.

Don't get me wrong; Florida has its upsides. Miles upon miles of beaches and low taxes are great, but for me anyways, my history with the place overrides the temporary pleasure of a dunk in the sea. As we drew ever closer to our destination, my sense of unease grew. Jack was driving, listening to the local morning show, and seemingly lost in his own thoughts. We hadn't spoken much that morning, I think mainly because Jack was nervous. He knew how uncomfortable I was, and he knew of my propensity to fly off the handle when stressed. I think he was just girding himself for the upcoming spectacle.

Before long, I started to recognize landmarks. Things had obviously changed over the years, but not everything. We passed the gas station where granny would take us to get boiled peanuts, and like Pavlov's dog, I felt myself getting hungry. I rolled down the window, and the familiar smell filled the car. I thought about having Jack stop so we could get some, but instead decided it better to just push on through and get on with this coming unpleasantness. Hungry as I was, my nerves had me nauseated, and I decided hunger would just have to wait.

When we passed the gargantuan Ford dealership across from the tasty freeze, I knew I was home. The next red light would be the start of Stillwater proper, and St. Mark's was now less than five minutes away. My heart started racing, and I began to breathe in short gasps. I felt a panic attack coming on, and I bore down hard, trying to stop it in his tracks. I began trying to breathe slowly and deeply, fully filling and emptying my lungs with each breath. I sat on my hands to try to keep from fidgeting. Jack noticed my distress, and he pulled into the parking lot of a Walgreens.

"It's okay, Rem. I'm here, everything is okay," he said quietly as he put the car into park and killed the engine.

"I know," I said between breaths. "It's just real now. I didn't think seeing an ice cream joint would affect me so much, but seeing all this," I said, pausing, using my hands to gesture all around us, "it's just more than I thought. I realized that I have a memory attached to every place you see. My aunt used to work at that tasty freeze, and she'd always sneak fries out the back door to us kids. My brother Elton first got arrested trying to steal a Mustang from that Ford dealership across the street. He was fourteen, and it was my birthday. He knew Mama didn't have anything for me, so he decided to give me a ride in a hot rod. When they finally pulled him over, he just laughed and said that he was only borrowing it." I stopped and looked up at Jack. He was looking at me with both pride and pity. I didn't really know how to feel about that.

"That's all in the past now, Rem," Jack said.

"Maybe so, but being here, after so long, it's like the past never ended. Like, right now, I'm just waiting to see Shane's work truck come pulling out around the corner any minute now. I know it's silly, but everything is just, I don't know...weird," I replied, knowing that he didn't really understand what I meant because I didn't either.

I lit up a smoke and breathed in its calming but ultimately deadly fumes, trying to get a handle on myself. Jack grabbed one from my pack and lit up too. He pushed his seat back, put his feet up on the dash, and started to blow smoke rings. One of the many great things about him is that he never rushes me. I've never met a man more unconcerned with time. He would gladly have waited all day in that parking lot with me if he thought I needed it. As nice as that was, I decided not to take advantage of his largess that day. I needed to get this over with.

"I'll be fine," I said to him, not really believing it. "Let's just get going. The turn is just up ahead."

"Yes, ma'am," he said with jovial gravitas, "Your wish is my command." With a jaunty grin, he set the car back in motion and guided us back out into traffic.

St. Mark's Hospital looked much the same as it had the last time I had seen it: cold, imposing, sterile. The parking lot was near full, and it took several minutes for Jack to find a place to park. As it was, we ended up parking what seemed like fifteen miles from the entrance. In a cunning move born of procrastination, I lit up another smoke, knowing that would trigger Jack to do so as well. I figured that might buy a few more minutes to prepare myself.

It had occurred to me that had been a long time since I'd seen Mama, and I wasn't sure I'd even recognize her. She was in her early forties the last time I saw her, and the years between forty and sixty tend to be full of physical changes, especially for women who live as hard as momma did. She'd been smoking since she was ten, drinking since not much older. She's been in more than her fair share of brawls with both women and men. I wasn't sure if I would even be able to pick her out of a lineup. I was trying to guess what she might look like when I heard a familiar voice coming from behind and to the right of me.

"Remlee, is that you?" Jolene shouted from a few rows over.

I turned around and put on my winningest smile and said, "Yes. Hi, Jolene."

Jolene came running, winding her way between the parked cars. I braced myself as she nearly tackled me in a giant bear hug.

"Oh, Remley, sweet baby," she said into my ear.

"I missed you too, big sis," I said, laughing with both honest joy and slight embarrassment. Jack stood off to the side, looking on with an amused smirk on his face. I flipped him off behind Jolene's back, and he laughed out loud.

"So is this the famous Jack?" Jolene asked, finally releasing me and turning your attention on Jack. "Ain't he just a handsome one," she said coquettishly.

"Aaawwwwww, shucks," Jack said in his best (lousy) Southern drawl and shook Jolene's hand. Jolene took this gesture and used her big sis judo to pull Jack into her arms.

"Whoa, there fella, we're family. Handshakes are for strangers," she said, finally releasing him. Jack looked amused and embarrassed. I caught myself laughing again. I obviously hadn't prepared him enough for what was to come. The cold, distant manner in which his family expressed themselves was the polar opposite to the typical Shaw bravado and bonhomie.

"How is she?" I asked, eager to get on with it.

"Oh, God, Rem," Jolene began, her voice quavering, "It's just awful. She can't talk at all. I mean, she makes noises that almost sound like words, but none of it makes no sense."

"Does she know what happened? Does she know where, or who even, she is? I asked.

"Nobody seems to know for sure yet. She seems to mostly understand what she is told, but she can't say nothing. The doctors have some fancy name for it…oh, what is it? Affaxis, or efegis or something," she said, pausing to think back again. "Wait, no, it was aphasia! That's the word." Jolene beamed her bleary smile at me, proud that she remembered. Jolene was touchy about her lack of education.

"How is she doing physically?" Jack asked, trying hard to remain in the conversation.

"She seems basically fine," Jolene replied, "She can't be feeling too bad. The staff had to save a nurse from her yesterday. Mama was showing out over not wanting to take an MRI test, and she had that poor little nurse hiding in the nurses' station. She can't talk, but she'll still cuss you out."

"Jesus," I said, "those poor staffers have no idea what they're in for, do they?"

Jolene laughed and returned, "Oh, I think they're getting the idea. Come on, let's go in. She'll be so happy to see you."

"She probably won't even know who I am," I said.

We walked into the entrance, and I let Jolene take the lead. We followed her through the maze of corridors and elevators until we came to room 328. There was a little sticker under the room number that had "Shaw" scribbled on it in Sharpie. I stopped short as I felt a wave of ice wash over me. I stood rooted to the spot, unable to move.

"In here, Remlee," Jolene called from inside the room.

"I… I'm not… Not ready," I said in a whisper. It had been so long since I'd seen her, and the thought that she was less than fifteen feet away was terrifying.

"It's okay, Rem, I'm here," murmured Jack from right behind me. "Maybe she'll be sleeping."

I forced myself to begin walking, and slowly, gripping Jack's hand for dear life, we entered the room. It looked like every other hospital room I'd ever been in. Lying on the bed was a woman I had never seen. The mama I had known was the three Bs: blonde, buxom, and beautiful. This person, this impostor in the bed, had limp, greasy gray hair, and it was slightly matted from a lack of attention. Mom's once fierce brown eyes looked nothing like the dull yet slightly scared eyes looking at me from the bed with mom's name on it. The left side of her face drooped comically, looking like a wax statue that had been partially melted. Even her pride and joy, her legendary bosom, seemed deflated. I couldn't believe the revenant in front of me was what remained of the Valkyrie that was Mama.

"Oh God, Mama," I gasped quietly. Jack squeezed my hand, then let go. I slowly walked to the edge of the bed and sat down. The shell of Mama regarded me warily as I took her hand in mine, and she winced when I reached out to smooth her brow. After a few minutes, I was able to fight back the stone on my throat, and I spoke to her in person for the first time in decades.

"Mama," I said, my voice shaking and husky, "It's me, Mama. It's Remlee."

A single tear escaped mom's eye and began a slow journey down her face. She began to slowly shake her head back and forth as she gaped at me. I did my best to smile at her, even though smiling was the last thing my face felt like doing. A low keening began to issue from mom's throat as mortiers joined the first, and the flooding began in earnest.

"No!" Mama yelled, shaking her head furiously. "Yu yugama yu yu gumm!"

I almost fell off the bed in my haste to get away. Mama was crying like a baby now, uncontrollably an inconsolably. I felt a quick wave of nausea wash over me and then leave as I watched my mother howl and cry.

"Yumba guma yu yu," continued Mama, obviously trying to say something very specific but frustratingly unable.

"It's okay, Mama," interrupted Jolene, quickly sliding in next to Mama and putting an arm around her.

"Maybe I should leave," I said, but Mama put her hand up in the universal stop gesture and shook her head furiously back and forth.

"No. Yu yu... No... Remlee stay," Mama said, spitting each syllable out with concentrated will. Jolene's mouth dropped to her chest.

"Those are the first real words she said since all this shit started," Jolene said in awe.

"Mama," I said, edging back over to the bed and sitting down, "It's okay, Mama. I'm staying. I'm not going anywhere."

Mama scooted over close to me, and I hugged my mother for the first time since I was little. After all these years, she still smelled the same. I close my eyes against the tears I felt welling up.

"Yu yu gunta gimba downah," Mama babbled between sobs.

"It's okay, Mama," I kept repeating. I hoped I wasn't lying.

Betty Sue

I can hear the rain pounding on the barn roof as I pull smoke deep into my lungs. I hold it in for a second, savoring the earthy tang, the scratching of the itch in my chest. I open my eyes as I exhale, and my best friend Sandy is sitting on a bale of hay across from me. An ugly purple bruise paints the left side of her face, and I can see she has been crying. I've been here before. I realized this is the night that her boyfriend, soon-to-be husband, tuned up on her for the first time. She's here to ask advice, seeing how Elmer has been clobbering me for the past three years now. She figures my experience makes me wise. She is dead wrong.

She shows up here bleeding and crying, and luckily, Elmer's out. Probably with one of his whores from down Gainesville way. I am very glad because Elmer don't approve of me having too many friends. He says my mind needs to stay on my family, not on a bunch of bullshit shoveled in by the whole town. Elmer ain't the most community-minded.

"What am I going to do?" she wails at me, "I got his baby in my belly now. Mama and daddy kicked me out, said I got to marry him. I ain't got nowhere else to go."

"Well, damn sure Elmer won't let you stay with us. He'd never agreed to get in between you and Hollis," I say gravely. Hollis Chalmers is Elmer's oldest friend and usual partner in illegal activities. Elmer would kick me to the street before taking sides against him.

I want to tell her that it will get better, but I don't, because that's a damned lie. It's just the way of the world. Men are mean by nature, and if they're dumb, and most of them are, more comfortable talking about their feelings with their fists than with their words. All my life, I have had men run my life through force and intimidation. It will be a few years before I finally start to fight back, so as I sit here with Sandy, I'm still biddable. At least a little.

"All I can tell you is to just try to do what he tells you," I say, knowing that it's hollow advice. Hollis Chalmers ain't burdened by reason or mercy.

Sandy lets out a pitiful little laugh and says, "Doing what he told me is what got me here. I mean, he didn't exactly rape me, but I didn't exactly consent neither. Sure, I thought he was handsome, and I can't say I wasn't flattered, but he's a grown man, and I'm only sixteen. I don't know."

But I know. I ain't got the heart, know the guts, to tell her that her own daddy sold her to Hollis over some shady deal they had. Their meeting wasn't no accident. She thinks she had a choice, but I know better, and it kills me. I want so badly to tell her, to warn her, but if Elmer or Hollis ever found out it was me who told her, my life wouldn't be worth the hair on a skunk's ass.

I stand up and walk over to the open door of the hayloft and look out of the sky. The deep blue clouds swirl around, dancing to a song that only they hear. I fight the urge to turn to Sandy and tell her everything and damn myself internally for my betrayal. Behind me, Sandy starts to quietly cry again, each sob tearing at me, breaking my will. God, I need a drink.

As if she can read my thoughts, Sandy pulls a flask out of her hip pocket and puts it to her lips. She smiles and says, "Meet my new best friend. His name is Captain (sip) Morgan (sip). He helps me through a lot."

"Oh, we've met. Been pals for years, as it stands," I say, trying not to giggle. I'm not sure if she's joking or just going a little crazy. We all do, from time to time.

Sandy hands me the flask, and I greedily pull deep from it. Liquor doesn't burn me like it did when I first drank shine ten years back, so I nearly drain it before Sandy pulls it away from me.

"Hey, Mama, I'm the one who got beat here," she says, mock-scolding me.

"Don't worry. I got more," I tell her and scurry myself down the ladder and out the door into the rain.

"Come out here, Sandy," I call to the open door in the hayloft. "We'll let Mother Nature wash our sins away."

I begin to dance around crazily in the dooryard, and I see Sandy has come to the main doors. She hesitates just inside, not sure if she wants to get wet. I skip over, splashing mud and water all over her, and she squeals in both joy and anger.

"You're gonna get it," she roars and bears down on me like a razorback. I'm laughing too hard to dodge her, and we end up in a pile of muddy limbs about halfway between the barn in the house.

"You're a cunt," Sandy says from her perch on my chest.

"If you only knew," I reply, twisting out from under her and making a mad dash for the house. I hear her scrambling up behind me, laughing and cursing as she struggles and slips through the ever-increasing muck. I pause at the back porch and walk under the eave, so as to wash off any mud that is still on me before I go inside. Granny's a stickler about footwear in the house—"Just 'cause we're poor, don't mean we got to be filthy"—so coming in covered in mud, looking like a swamp creature, is a sure way to get her set off. And you don't want granny to get set off. Unhappy times are what's in store for those who set off my father's mother. And anyone else who is in a twelve-mile radius.

By the time I find Daddy's stash of white lightning, Sandy is beside me, dripping but clean. She knows about Granny. That's good. I pour us both respectable size shots (Mason jars) and toast Sandy to her glorious future. We both gulp the booze in irresponsible amounts for a few minutes in silence. Finally, I asked the question that I'm not sure I actually wanted answered.

"Do you love him?"

She sits there quietly, not looking at me or saying anything at all, really. I start to wonder if she's going to answer when she does.

"Does it matter?" She asks, her eyes downcast and defeated.

"A little, a lot, some, I don't know. Who cares if it matters? Fine. Sure. It matters to me, okay? It matters to me, so please answer the fucking question. Do you love him?" I ask, gripping her shoulders and almost shaking her. She looks startled and gasps. I let go before I get carried away.

"I don't know," Sandy whispers, and I know it's the truth. I nod but stay quiet. If she has more to say, she will. I watch an internal war play out across her face while she wrestles with my question. I can see the

emotions flicker in rapid succession on her features like at the drive-in Bobby Lee always snuck us into.

"Parts of him, I guess," she begins with a sigh. "He's strong. He provides. Sure, it's mostly illegally, but I ain't hungry. I got a roof. This baby will have a home."

I nod knowingly. I've said this very speech to my sister Lola, word for word.

"I know he'll protect me. Ain't nobody gonna fuck with Hollis Chalmers's wife and get away with it, and everybody knows it. On top of all that," she continues, blushing and giggling, "He ain't exactly hard to look at. And, Lord, the things he does at night when the lights go off… Well, I'll be a lady and leave the details to your dirty little imagination, but it's safe to say I have no complaints in that department."

She takes another gulp of her drink, then lights up a cigarette. This reminds me that I want a cigarette. Weird how that works.

"On the other hand," Sandy says dramatically, the shine starting to work its magic, stretching out her drawl into a slur. "He also scares the ever-living shit out of me. When he goes off, well, God help whoever is on the receiving end. It's like he becomes, I don't know, an animal or something. One time, last week, old Kenny Frazier accidentally backed into the side of Hollis's truck on account of his dog jumping on his lap. Halls dragged that poor man out of his car and whooped his ass so bad, I thought he killed him. And it didn't hardly leave no scratch on Hollis's truck, by the way. He damn near killed that poor man over a scratch you wouldn't see unless you was really looking for it. What kind of a man does that?"

She stops to take a long drag off her smoke and waits for an answer I don't have to give. When she sees I got nothing, she continues on, the plug finally pulled, and her feelings pouring out all over the kitchen.

"I'm not stupid. I know he ain't faithful. I just ain't sure I care. If he's out whoring, he ain't at home clobbering me or whatever. Let them nasty sluts down Gainesville take some of his shit for me. Why should I take it all?" she asks me.

"You shouldn't," I say, "You should keep quiet about all that. Elmer fucks six different sluts a month, and I'm glad of it. That means he's leaving me alone. It's better that way, you're right about that."

We walk back out to the porch, drinks in hand, to watch the storm. Storms always call me, ever since I was a youngin'. It's like all that chaos in the air cancels out the chaos of my life, makes it seem smaller, insignificant. The fury of nature somehow validates the fury of my world. I laugh at this thought and turn to tell Sandy, but Sandy is gone. I blink a few times and realized that somehow, I've stepped out of the farmhouse and into the cemetery down the road apiece. I'm looking down at Sandy's grave, and I realize it's later now. Sandy's dead, and it's somewhat my fault. I could have, should have warned her. Sent her away. Rescued her. She could be alive now, if I wasn't so selfish and scared. I didn't want to be alone, I needed her, so I stayed quiet. Now, Sandy is quiet forever. I start to cry silently, my breath seemingly knocked out of me. I close my eyes and lie down on the sparse grass that covers what's left of Sandy, other than memory. I lie there, listening to my own sobs blotting out everything else. I am still for a long while.

Time passes here in the void. I'm starting to be comfortable here. I seem to have some control here. In those weird dreams like I just left, it's like watching a movie of my own life, but out of order and scrambled. The good and the bad both come through. When I'm awake, well, no one can control anything in the real world. But here, in the warm dark, I can forget. I only see what I want. I just don't know how to stay here. I can't purposely leave the dreams, and I can't be sure I'll come straight here when I go to sleep. There's nothing to grab onto here, nothing to anchor to.

I hear voices again, and hospital equipment, and I know I am awake again. Something exciting happened last time I was awake; I can feel it. I can't quite remember yet; things are still foggy. I open my eyes and scan the room, looking for clues or people, anything that will remind me what I'm forgetting. I know whatever it is, it's huge. Earth-shattering. It made me so happy. Oh, Lord! Why can't I remember?

I sit up in bed and rack my brain, wondering what news I could have gotten that would leave the unfamiliar residue of joy coating the fringes of recent (not quite, but almost) memory. What in my miserable failure of a life, now made worse by a stroke, could possibly account for this bizarre and seemingly inappropriate optimism?

Nurse Tinkerbell is on duty again, and she flits into the room, humming cheerily to herself. In my present hopeful mood, I only hate her a little bit.

"Well, hello there, Miz Shaw," she says in her child's voice. "How are we doing today? How was your visit with your daughters yesterday?"

"Mumblow tow. Yu yu..." I start to say, then stop. I know that isn't right. I bear down, almost like I'm in labor, and concentrate as hard as I can, and try again.

"D...DAW... No... Oh Lord... D...Daughter?" I asked, nearly exhausted from the effort but delighted at the success. I said a word. A word I intended to say. I look at Tinkerbell eagerly, searching her face for recognition.

"Yes! Yes! That's right, Miz Shaw! Daughters!" the nurse says, clapping and hopping up and down like a child at a parade. I'm elated that my word was recognized but also confused by the implication. Daughters. As in more than one period, how could that be? I only have two daughters, Jolene and Remlee, and I haven't seen Remlee since...

Oh my God! Remlee! That's what I can't remember. Remlee was here, just last night. Remlee came back. Dear sweet Jesus, my Remlee came back.

"Doo...Doo... Yu Yu Yu... Unfu memby," I begin rushing again. I want to know if they have been back. Are they coming back? Is Remlee staying? Oh Lord, I have so many questions to ask, damn it. What I wouldn't give to be able to talk again. I never realized how much I would miss having a voice. It honestly never occurred to me that loss of communication was really possible before now. I'm overcome with panic for a moment when I think of just how big my problem really is. How am I going to do anything? Pay bills? Order food? By a fucking six-pack? Pointing and grunting? Even I'm too proud for that.

Nurse Tinkerbell understands none of this. "How are you feeling today?" she asks, concerned only with her own agenda. "Did you eat anything? Have you used the bathroom?" she asks these questions rapid-fire, hardly pausing for me to respond. I guess she figures I can't anyway, so why bother? I try, just to spite her.

"Gumba." (Horrible.)

"Yu yu bam." (A little oatmeal and some orange juice.)

"Nam ooh minke." (I pissed a few times.)

She continues to write stuff on her little clipboard as I answer her, and I wonder for a second if she understands what I'm saying and she's recording my responses. I tried to peek at her clipboard, but she never really stops moving, and I can't quite catch a glance. I'm not sure it would matter if I could because so far, my ability to read is still gone.

"Here in a few minutes, Miz Shaw, Miss Tracy is gonna come see you. She's our occupational therapist. She's real nice," Nurse Tinkerbell tells me in her child's voice, the voice that I've grown to dislike something fierce. "She just wants to talk with you and see how you are doing. See if maybe she can help you. Would you like that?"

"Yu yu yu moown pen," I muttered. Like I have a choice. If Miss Tracy wants to come in and see me, what the hell could I do about it? They won't even let me wear pants, for Chrissakes! It's not like I can really go anywhere right now. Even if I could, I'm not sure I could remember my way home. It seems like months since I've been there. I can barely even picture it in my mind. This scares me a little, but I push it aside. Another problem for another day.

Nurse Tinkerbell prattles on about the benefits of the therapy, but I'm not listening. I'm thinking about Remlee. I can't believe she's here. I figured I'd never see her again. I know I wasn't the best mother, but all my other kids forgive me. At least a little bit. Not Remlee. She don't believe it, but she's just like me. Stubborn. I knew it from the day she was born, she was mine, not Elmer's. Oh, I let him give her that name, his name in reverse, but it don't mean nothing. She's mine through and through. Jolene was too wrapped up in Jesco, and vice versa, to ever be like either her daddy or me. Elton basically dropped straight out of Elmer's ass, and Shane was only slightly more civilized. Probably because he's the oldest, had big brother responsibility in all. Remlee, though, she's mine. My baby.

When Mama Lettie died, I figured Remlee would come live with me. I was trying to get me my own place right about then, I almost had my shit together. When I went to the funeral, Remlee had already run away. I was more hurt by that than my stepmother's dying. Mama Lettie was old, and she had the dementia. Her dying was a mercy, I guess. What was worse was that Remlee was in the wind, and no one else seemed to care. That bitch sister of mine, Lola Mae, had the nerve to say she thought Remlee was better off on the street than with me. I was asked to leave after Lola Mae had to pick up her teeth off the floor.

How do I tell Remlee I'm sorry now? I've been praying for this opportunity for years, and now it's here, and I can't fucking talk. I often wonder what I did to make God hate me so much. I know I ain't perfect, but I ain't never done nothing to Him. I pray to Him. I believe in Him. Why can't he let just one thing go my way? I wonder if I can even pray anymore. I guess He can hear my thoughts, or He translate my gibberish. I laugh a little, real quick like, then I burst into tears.

"Oh, Miz Shaw! It's okay, Hun. The therapy won't hurt," Tinkerbell says, misreading situation.

I had forgotten she was even there. I realized that she has turned into Charlie Brown's teacher, an annoying drone in the background to be disregarded, full of information to be ignored. This makes me laugh again, hard this time. I double over, on the edge of complete hysteria. Nurse Tinkerbell's eyes go as wide as two harvest moons, and she finally stops yapping. She just stands there staring at me, her mouth slightly opened, as if caught in the act of being naughty. I bark out two more hard bursts of laughter, then I managed to contain myself.

"Are you sure you're all right?" she asks, less alarmed now that I'm not laughing maniacally, but still cautious.

"Mumboo yuh," I tell her, nodding. I mean "Of course not, you twit, I just had a fucking stroke," but I doubt she understands. For educated people, it sure seems like a lot of these medical people ain't got the sense God gave an opossum. Too many books, not enough living, I guess. 'Course, I done a lot of living and look where it got me. I look at that Nurse Tinkerbell and try to smile.

"Oh, bless your sweet little heart," she says.

Remlee

After we left the hospital, Jack and I followed Jolene into town. The plan was to get something to eat (and drink) at the unofficial family watering hole, Tiger's Saloon. As we wound our way across town, I felt a sense of unreality coloring my perception. Everything had changed, yet nothing had. The library right would often hide from my family, and my problems was still there, but the building seemed smaller now. In my memories, it was a stately old manor, full of bound wonderment. Now, it seemed decrepit and seedy, with its flaking paint and roof with missing shingles. The diner that Mama worked at when we were kids was still there, but now it was called Rhonda's Skillet instead of Leland's BBQ. The park that seemed like a mythical forest to my eight-year-old self was now full of litter and devoid of children. The site of the ice plant, now burnt to the ground, leaving a scar where the giant building used to be, caused me to audibly gasp.

"What's that?" Jack asked, mistaking my shock for an attempt to communicate.

"Nothing… Just seeing how everything has changed," I replied, not wanting to elaborate. Jack grunted, seeming to understand that I had said all I intended to on the subject. We remained companionably silent as we follow Jolene into Tiger's parking lot and made use of it.

"It's not fancy, but it's cheap and delicious," Jolene called to us as she crossed the parking lot toward us and the entrance. "I think our cousin Becky is working tonight. Do you remember her? She's uncle Earl Three's oldest daughter."

"Oh yeah, she's the one who told Granny that I stole her cigarettes when she got caught with them," I said grimly.

"But you did, Remlee," Jolene pointed out.

"Not the point, Jolene," I said, watching Jack try not to laugh over her shoulder.

"Whatever," she said, rolling her eyes. "Try to be nice, that was forever ago."

"Whatever nothing, Peepaw hid me something fierce over that. She got caught, not me. She should have taken hers like a man," I said, not ready to give up.

Jolene raised her eyebrows at me, just like when she would scold me as a kid. I lowered my head and meekly walked through the door to the bar, chastened. It struck me how easily I reverted to the role of an obedient little sister.

The bar hadn't changed a bit from the days when we would have to come down and drag Mama out so she could go buy us groceries. The lights were so low, you almost couldn't see, the air was full of smoke, and the dulcet tones of David Allen Coe poured out of the juke. It was the song that seemed to fill my every memory of this place: "You Never Even Called Me by My Name." I chuckled quietly to myself, amused that the song I associate most with the joint was playing as I walked in. I wondered, in a paranoid flash, if somehow Jolene had planned that, but I almost immediately dismissed the possibility. Jolene was not a planner.

"As I live and breathe, if it ain't Remlee Shaw," came a voice from behind the bar, big as a mountain. "I heard you was coming back to town. It is so good to see you."

I turned to look and see who the voice belonged to, even though I already knew. Standing behind the bar, beaming, was my cousin Becky. While she still had the blond curls, I remembered from so long ago, little else about Becky was as I remembered. It seemed that in the intervening years, Becky had managed to lose most of her teeth. The chubby girl I used to go swimming with was no more, replaced with the gaunt zombie before me. Her sunken eyes regarded me from deep within their darkened sockets. Had I seen her on the streets back home in Boston, I would likely have crossed to the other side.

"Becky," I said with the cheerfulness I didn't feel. "How have you been?"

I noticed as I approached her that she had a liquid ton of concealer on, but it wasn't hiding the sores on her face. In fact, the cheap cosmetic applied by her in expert hand actually seemed to draw attention to them rather than hiding them.

"Oh, I can't complain," she said with a bitter laugh, exposing a lonely pair of black stubs that used to be teeth. "Nobody would give a shit anyways. I was sorry to hear about Aunt Betty Sue. How is she?"

I sighed as I sat down at the bar. I noticed Jolene and Jack taking positions on either side of me. Somehow, this comforted me, and I began to relax.

"Physically, she's basically fine," I began, "but her brains are scrambled. She can't talk."

"Can't talk?" Becky gassed. "Oh God! That's gotta be damn near impossible for her. She was always such a loudmouth."

"Yeah, no shit" said Jolene, laughing. "She still cusses them nurses out no. They just can't tell what she's saying."

"I'll bet," said Becky. "So can I get y'all something to drink?"

"Yes, please," said Jack instantly. Becky paused to gape at him for a moment, then directed her attention back to me.

"And who is this fine gentleman?" she asked, rancid honey dripping from her lips.

"This fine gentleman," I said, possessively clutching his arm, "is my husband Jack Shepherd. Jack, this is my cousin Becky Tucker… Wait… Is it still Tucker?"

"Yes, yes, still Tucker," she said, absentmindedly waving the question away as she placed her hand on Jack's arm. "Well, Jack Shepherd, let me be the first to welcome you to still water, home of the infamous Tuckers and Shaws. What all you have, sweetie?"

Jack shifted nervously in his seat and said, "Bud Light, if you have it."

"I sure do," she said, grabbing a pint glass, "and you, cousin? And other cousin?"

"Same," Jolene and I said together. Becky bustled off to pour our beers, and Jack lit a cigarette.

"Friendly lass," Jack said under his breath. I stifled a guffaw.

While Becky was busying herself with our drinks, I got up to stretch out my legs. I looked around the mostly deserted bar and felt a strange feeling of jealousy. This was the place that Mama loved more than us. Mama would rather look at posters of girls in bikinis selling Miller Lite than her own kids.

"So I get off in two hours," Becky said as she set our beers in front of us. "Y'all want to come out to the farm tonight? Daddy and Uncle Jed will be there, so will Earl Four, Nathan, and Uncle Rawlie. Jed just finished a new batch last week, and it's been crazy at the farm ever since."

"Uncle Jed's still making shine?" I asked, shocked at my own surprise.

"Oh, no, honey, not shine. Crystal," Becky said, almost patronizingly. "You really have been gone for a long time."

"Crystal meth?" I asked, horrified. "When did that start?"

"Shit, your brother Elton started that mess ten years back or more," Becky said, looking confused. "Didn't you tell her, Jo?"

"No, she seems to have forgotten to mention that tidbit," I said, glaring at Jolene, who was ducking my gaze. "Is that why he's locked up this time?"

"No," Becky said, her eyes giddy with the opportunity to gossip, "Not really directly anyways. He done kicked the shit out of Hank McDaniel's boy over some stolen wheeler parts, and ol' Hank sicced the law on him. Hank's boy says that Elton owed him them parts in one of his cockamamie drug deals. Either way, it don't matter, 'cause he's locked up now, and Hank's boy come and took the whole wheeler. He better not be around when Elton gets out, that's all I know."

I looked over at Jack and watched him taking it all in. He looked like an anthropologist coming across a tribe he's only read about for the very first time. While Jack was far from sheltered, his experience rarely, if ever, occurred on this side of the proverbial tracks. Sure, he hung out with more working-class types than aristocrats, but it was still a middle-class working man that he was familiar with. He didn't pal around with his old prep school buddies, but his friends had jobs, families they actually carried about, you know, lives. There were plenty of alcoholics in his world, himself included, even a few weekend cokeheads, unrepentant stoners, and gambling addicts, but those are more "acceptable" vices. There isn't the same stigma attached to his class's foibles. Alcoholics are funny uncles who sometimes say ridiculous things. Cliff Klaven, Peter Griffin, Homer Simpson. Silly, fun, and mostly harmless. Junkies and speed freaks, however, elicit the opposite feelings, and the examples people tend to think of are not in any way positive. Thieves. Whores. Disease. Charlie Sheen.

Taking my silence for indecision, Becky said, "Oh, don't worry. Y'all don't have to do no crank if you don't want to. Just come out to the farm. You've got to see everyone."

"Yeah, Rem, we should go. I want to see the fabled farm you've told me so much about," Jack said, winking at me.

"There's plenty of room out there," continued Becky, determined to impose her will. "Y'all don't need to be spending no money at one of these dumps around here that call themselves motels."

"Well, okay," I said, resigned to my fate, "but can we at least get something to eat before we go?"

"Of course," Becky cooed. "I still got a few hours before Arletta comes in. Hang out here, and I'll get y'all some menus." she turned and bustled away. I rounded on Jolene.

"Fucking meth? Like shine wasn't bad enough. At least the law turned a blind eye to alcohol. Cops hate meth. What the actual fuck, Jolene?" I hissed at her, trying not to drag the admittedly small number of patrons into our touching family moment.

"What do you want me to do, Rem?" Jolene asked, a lonely, defeated tone in her voice. "Elton's an adult. He's older than me, tougher than me, and meaner than me. And Earl Four is tougher than him. And so on. Do you really think any of those Neanderthals are gonna listen to a fucking thing I have to say? Oh, bless your sweet little heart," she said with a small, sarcastic laugh.

"Look," she continued, "I'm no Angel, all right? We both know that. And between all my kids' bullshit on top? I don't have time to fool around with Elton and them too. Colton got himself hooked on Xanax, and his girlfriend is always trying to take his kids from him. So now I'm practically raising his kids, my grandbabies, just so they don't have to be around him nodding out or them fighting. And Lizzie's boy, Jamari, he's on a whole another thing."

Jolene stopped abruptly and seemed at a loss. She opened her mouth a couple of times, trying to go on, but then she gave up. She took another gulp and looked at me through watery eyes. I felt a twinge of guilt, and so I softened my tone.

"Hey, I'm not blaming you, sis," I said, putting my hand on her shoulder. "Just… Why didn't you ever say anything? I know we don't talk a lot, but…"

"What good would it do?" Jolene interrupted. "You live clear up in Massachusetts. I can't do shit from three miles away. What the fuck are you gonna do from all the way up there?" She had a point.

Becky came bounding back over, menus in hand. She gave us all one to look at and preceded to roll herself a cigarette on the bar while we decided.

"Look," she said as she let her jailhouse smoke. "Y'all ain't gotta worry about nothing, all right? It's pretty crazy on the farm right now, sure, but nothing outrageous. There have just been lots of people in and out. Y'all don't have to worry about drama. Uncle Earl Three runs a tight ship."

"No, it's okay, we'll come out. I want to see the place again. I can't lie," I said. "I ain't been gone long enough that a little petty drug crime scares me away."

Jack laughed at that, spraying beer down the front of his shirt and onto the bar. He scrambled around, looking for napkins, mumbling nonsensical curses under his breath. Becky handed him a rag, and she walked to the end of the bar to tend to the only other patrons.

Grinning like a gremlin, Jack made a show of cleaning up his spilled beer. He waved the rag around in an ungainly flourish, clowning as usual. I rolled my eyes and diverted my attention to the menu in front of me.

"Hey, Rem, they still have that alligator gumbo here that Mama would always bring home," said Jolene.

"Alligator… Gumbo?" Jack asked, aghast. "That's a thing?"

"Hell yeah!" I exclaimed. "It's the best thing ever in the history of ever." Jolene nodded in agreement.

"What's it like?" Jack asked, his curiosity obviously piqued.

"It's kinda like chicken, but kinda, I don't know, chewier," Jolene said. "That's the best way I can describe it. You gotta try some."

"That's what I'm getting," I said, doing my best to goad him.

"Well, when in Rome," Jack said and polished off his beer with a hearty belch. He raised his bottle at Becky, beckoning her over to take our order. When she returned, we ordered our food and another round of beers. I made a mental note of how many drinks Jack had drunk and immediately felt a stab of guilt. I hated clocking his alcohol intake almost as much as he resented it. It has always felt uncomfortably maternal, and I made an effort to avoid doing it, but not always successfully. My mind rarely does what I tell it.

I sat quietly, sipping my beer and listening to the jukebox. David Allen Coe had been replaced by John Fogerty, singing about being stuck in some dead-end town, and I wondered for a minute if he had ever been to still water. I began to watch Jack and Jolene chitchat, and I felt myself relax a little bit. He seemed to be getting along with her just fine, and some of my worries left me. My family can be a bit much, and I had been worried that Jack's more reserved nature would not mesh well, but he and Jolene seemed like fast friends already. It hit me that my own prejudices toward my family were trying to poison the well for Jack, and a wave of shame washed over me. What did it say about my attitude toward Jack, that I thought he judged my family? Maybe the only one judging anyone here was me.

Becky came bustling over with our food, placing a steaming bowl in front of each of us. I laughed quietly to myself as I watched Jack try to pretend that he wasn't grossed out by the idea of eating gator.

"To new experiences," he said, tipping a piece of gator meat on his fork at me and Jolene in an off-kilter toast. He plopped the morsel into his mouth and chewed with theatrical aplomb. A giant smile spread across his face as he swallowed.

"Yep," he said, "Just like chicken. But chewier."

With that, he tore into his gumbo with gusto. Stifling a laugh, I joined him in eating the warm stew, its flavors transporting me back thirty years. Finally, I knew I was home.

Betty Sue

I'm beginning to panic a little. Not being able to talk is harder than I thought it would be when they first broke the news to me. It's so strange, I'm here in a hospital, surrounded by hundreds of people, yet I feel utterly alone. I can nod "yes" and shake my head "no," but that's about it. Every once in a while, I manage to squeeze out a sound that somewhat resembles the word I mean, but most of the time, it's like I'm speaking a language that doesn't exist. I don't even understand myself.

How am I going to take care of myself now? How will I pay my bills? How will I do damn near anything? Sure, I can cook, clean, and wipe my own ass, but I can't even read anymore. How will I even be able to pay when I can't tell the bills apart? My cousin Billy is a long-haul trucker, and he gave me some Canadian money he got in Toronto one time. They got the right idea up there, then Canucks. Their money is all different colors, so it's easy to tell the bills apart. Why don't we do that here? Shit. What am I going to do, write my congressman to complain? Ha!

I don't want to have to move in with any of my kids. I'm too proud for that, and who am I kidding. None of them would have me anyway. Shane is polite, but he don't care enough about me to walk across the street to piss on me if I was on fire. Elton's locked up again, but even if he wasn't, I'd be afraid to stay there. That boy is a maniac, God love him. Jolene would probably let me, but it's Gary's trailer, not hers, and they ain't got no damn room anyways, what with all them grandbabies she has crawling all over the place. That just leaves Remlee, and I ain't too sure where I stand with her. Two weeks ago, I'd have told you she felt like Shane, but now I ain't sure. She actually came to see if I was okay. If anything good came out of all this mess, it's that I finally got to see her again, if only that one time. I hope she comes back, but I'm not holding my breath. I don't think she's fully forgiven me, if at all. I'm not sure if I deserve her forgiveness anyways. I tried my best to be her Mama, all their Mama, but I just ain't no good at it.

What scares me the most, though, is the County Home. I ain't got the money for one of them fancy places like you see on the commercials. If I can't live on my own, and my family won't take me, there's nowhere else for me to go. I'd have to go to the County Home; that's all there is. I don't know fuck-all about politics, but even I know that if the government runs something, it's bound to be shit. Don't believe me? Just go to the DMV. Those people that run those places don't give a flying fuck about nobody. They just want to put in their time till they can retire at forty-five and drink mimosas for the rest of their golden years. They ain't got to worry about ever getting stuck in one of those places. They got benefits and such.

The doctor says if I work hard, and if I have a little luck, I might get some of my speech back. That sounded hopeful, but then she told me that whatever I don't get back in a year will most likely stay gone forever. The thought of being imprisoned in my own head terrifies me more than anything else I've encountered so far in this scary old world. Hell, I'd go back to daily whoopins from Elmer if I could just bitch about it afterward. Black eyes heal, but this enforced silence might kill me just as dead as a bullet to the head.

I turned the TV on, hoping that Dr. Phil or Dr. Oz can distract me from my current problems. I keep going over it all in my head, and it's starting to make me crazy. Okay, fine. Crazier. I try to follow what's going on, but reality keeps butting into my thoughts. Leave me alone, you bitch! Eventually, I'm able to shut down the voices in my head, and I absorbed myself in the story of Jane, the bulimic housewife. I feel my eyes grow heavy as Dr. Phil lectures the poor woman about her dangerous habits. I'll just close them for a minute, give them a little rest.

When I open them again, the hospital has disappeared. I'm back in the trailer again. It's later than the last time I was here. I know this because I'm holding baby Remlee, and she's bawling her head off. Startled, I stand up fast, almost dropping the screeching bundle in my arms. I look around the room, desperate to gain my bearings, searching for clues as to what moment I am currently reliving. I steel myself for what lies ahead because I haven't forgotten how fun these little trips down Memory Lane can be. I walk over to the playpen in the middle of the room and put

Remlee down in it. I walk away from her, but I don't worry. I know she lives past whenever this is.

I walked back into the hallway, ignoring Remlee's distress, much like I did throughout her life, and searched to see if anyone else was home. The rest of the kids (except poor, dead Jesco), should be in school, except Shane, who would have dropped out last year to take that job on the oil rigs. Should be, unless they was playing hooky again. That seemed to be Elton and Jolene's favorite game. Lord knows they were good at it.

I get to the bedroom in the back and see that other than Remlee and the cat, I'm home alone. I breathe a sigh of relief when I realize Elmer isn't home. I laugh at this because I know this has already happened, so he can't really hurt me here. At least not any more than he already did, and I survived till now. My head reels from trying to get it all straight. I lie down on the bed, overwhelmed and gun-shy, waiting for whatever horror from my past to spring out like a demented Jack in the Box and torture me some more. I wonder if I'm not really in Hell after all, and the hospital is the real illusion. This thought makes me nauseous, and I dashed to the bathroom, opening the toilet seat just in time to empty my roiling guts into the old, discolored bowl. Partway through my sudden emptying of my insides, it occurs to me that I still don't really understand the rules here, wherever, or whenever this is. Some things seem flexible, mainly my own actions, but everything else seems to be on some kind of track or something, unable to do anything other than what really happened. I decide that I'm too dumb to understand it all anyways, so I just roll with it, baby, just like Steve Winwood.

After what seems like years, my belly is finally empty, and my body has given up on trying to eject anything else. I collapse in a heap on the bathroom floor, gasping and trying to work the awful acid taste of bile out of my mouth. I can hear Remlee, still whimpering in the living room but winding down. I struggled to get up, but I'm just too tired to do so. I lie there, wondering how it's possible to be tired in a dream when a new sound invades my ears. It's very faint, very far away, but there's no mistaking what it is. Sirens. Police sirens. Growing louder by the second, meaning closer by the second. I force myself to my feet and stagger out onto the front stoop, scanning the horizon for any sign of the oncoming ruckus. The sirens grow louder and louder, seeming to fill the world, and

I hold my hands to my ears in a pathetic attempt to block the sound. Suddenly, I see Elmer's Dodge come whipping around the bend, staggering dust behind him like a smokescreen, hiding everything behind him in a cloud. It hits me all of a sudden when it is that I am. Today is the day Elmer goes to jail for good. Today's the day I earn the scar on my left shoulder. Great, 'cause that was so much fun the first time I lived it. Why can't one of these living memories be of something. Why can't one of these living memories be of something fun? Or at least something not awful?

Elmer's truck turns wildly in the driveway, barely missing the drainage ditch is on either side. He careens to a stop just feet away from the trailer and jumps out, the sun glinting off the chromed steel of the .38 he holds in his large, bloody hand. He barrels up the steps of the stoop, all but tackling me back into the trailer. Kicking my tangled legs out of the way, he slams the door shut and peers out the window next to it.

"FUCK! THAT MOTHERFUCKER!" he rants, pacing back and forth, his eyes bulging as he pulls curiously at his hair with the hand not holding the gun. "There wasn't supposed to be anyone there today. When I get my hands on that little pussy, I'm going to gouge his motherfucking eyes out!"

I look up at him from the floor, my hair in my eyes and the taste of sweat and fear in my mouth. He's beside himself with anger and panic, his hands shaking as he tries to reload his revolver. He spills shells everywhere, and he roars at the ceiling, his rage taking him beyond words. The sirens are on top of us now. I can see the oddly reassuring red and blue lights reflecting through the window onto the TV screen and beyond. Elmer is bathed in the dueling colors, and for a second, he looks positively demonic. A moan escapes my lips because I know what happens next.

"Get up, you dumb cunt," he growls at me, grabbing me by the hair and dragging me to my feet. "It's time you be useful for something other than warming my cock."

I can see out of the window next to the door, and out in the dooryard are what seems like every cop car in the state of Florida, parked all over the place. Every surface is bathed in the alternating shades of red and blue, and every cop has drawn their gun, and they're all pointing them at the door I'm standing behind. I tried to move away, to say something different, to do anything that might change the outcome I know is coming, but I'm no longer in control of myself. The feeling of watching my life as a movie is back, the feeling of a loss of control. I tried to scream no over and over, but since this is a living memory, I follow the script as it happened.

"What did you do, Elmer Ray Shaw?" I wail, terrified.

"It don't matter what I did or didn't do," he says quietly, dangerously close to my face. I can smell the whiskey on his breath, the fear in his sweat. I realize he's as scared as me.

"What matters," he continues, his voice rising an octave, "is that the God damned army is outside, and they are looking to kill me, all right? They ain't just taking me to jail this time. I got one of 'em, Okay? Is that what you want to hear? Well, I popped one of them motherfuckers, and now they want revenge. You hear me, woman? Revenge."

I gape at him in shock, unable to respond. Elmer pushes me to the side again, takes haphazard aim out of the window, and squeezes off three shots into the crowd of police in our dooryard.

"The baby!" I scream at him, my voice cracking with the strain. "The baby is in the goddamn playpen! Stop shooting at them, you fucking moron!"

He doesn't hear me, though, because at that moment, the police return fire. I tear myself out of his grasp and dive over the love seat, determined to get to Remlee. As I'm flying over the furniture, I feel a hot, wet explosion in my shoulder. I hit the floor on the other side and inelegantly roll onto my side in front of the playpen. I tried to use my body to shield Remlee, who is now howling at the top of her lungs directly into my ear. The shoulder not on the ground feels like someone jammed a hot coal into it, and I glance at it to see what is wrong. Where my shoulder used to be, now sits what looks like two pounds of ground beef. My once blue shirt is turning a strange brownish maroon color as the blood leaks out of the ruin that is my shoulder. My vision greys for a second, and I feel the room spinning.

"Elmer Ray Shaw, come out with your hands up. You are surrounded. There is nowhere for you to go," says an amplified voice, booming through the broken window.

"Fuck you!" Elmer screams in return, firing three more potshots into the crowd. Instantly, the air in the trailer is once again alive with flying

lead as the police return fire. I close my eyes and clutch Remlee through the playpen screen as close to me as possible. Hours seem to pass while I hold Remlee close under the storm of death raging not six inches above where we lay.

The pain in my shoulder has taken on a life of its own. It's a huge beast, raging and rampaging, yet somehow, I'm only dimly aware of it. I suddenly feel very tired. I find myself directing most of my energy to just staying awake. I'm vaguely aware of Elmer screaming a litany of profanities, and I realize he's hit too. I smile a little to myself, knowing that cocksucker is hurting bad now too.

"He's down," I hear a stranger's voice say, as the trailer begins to shake from several pairs of heavy boots stomping their way inside. "Don't move, motherfucker, or I will shoot you. Don't give me a fucking excuse!"

"Hey, there's a lady and a baby over here!" a closer voice calls out. I feel hands, gentle hands, reach underneath me and roll me over. I look up into a pair of hazy blue eyes, full of concern.

"Are you all right, ma'am?" the owner of the hands asks me.

"Remlee, my baby," I stammer, barely able to speak.

"We have her, ma'am, don't worry. We're taking care of her. Are you hurt anywhere else besides your shoulder?" the officer asks, trying to call me. I try to answer, but my voice has finally given out. I shake my head no weakly and close my eyes again. I feel myself drifting back to the warm, dark place, and I breathe a sigh of relief. The warm, dark place is safe. Oblivion is a comfort.

Remlee

After dinner and several more drinks, Becky shift ended. It was decided, after much quibbling, that Jack and I would follow Jolene and Becky out to the farm. Apparently, Uncle Clarence had gotten even more paranoid as the years passed, and any unfamiliar vehicle pulling into the driveway was likely to be shot at.

"He don't believe in warning shots," Becky told us with a nervous laugh.

As we drove through town, making our way back north, I pictured the farm as I remembered it. Granny Lettie had always kept a garden in the front, so the first things you would see were her enormous lilac bushes on either side of the driveway. The house sat on the left of the driveway, and the barn was at the end of the driveway. Beyond that, a sea of green, the cane that provided for everything the family had, little as that may have been. I could still picture the old Farmall tractor sitting in the dooryard, waiting for Peepaw come back to work after his lunch break. I wondered if the ruthless pack of chickens still held sway in the dooryard.

When Jack turned onto Platt Junction Road behind Jolene's rusty old Cavalier, I felt my heart skip a beat. The old lean-to that was put up as a school bus stop was still there. That lean-to was where I first kissed a boy, Tyler Briggs, while all the neighbor kids looked on and laughed. I never been the nostalgic type, but I felt a knot form in my throat.

I must have made a noise of some kind because Jack looked over at me, concerned, and asked, "Rem, hon, are you okay?"

"I'm fine," I said, harsher than I meant. I could see the hurt and irritation flash across Jack's face, but he stayed quiet, not wanting to give me a reason to start a fight. I continued to stare out of the window, watching my past come to life. Every few feet we traveled brought more memories. It was becoming overwhelming, and I began to fish through my purse, looking for my stash box. Jack had his ways of self-medication, and I had mine. I pulled a half-smoked joint out of the Altoid tin and let it, savoring the sweet smoke as it set off the receptors in my brain. I felt myself calming down, and I began to breathe easy again.

I had myself prepared by the time Jolene pulled into the familiar driveway. I noticed that Peepaw's handmade duck mailbox was still in attendance. I smiled to myself, pleased that not everything had changed. As we parted further down the driveway, however, I began noticing how many things had. The garden was a memory, flowers replaced by half a dozen rusted-out cars in various stages of disassembly. The house, while never a mansion, seemed smaller, and Peepaw's diligent hand was obviously sorely missed, as the house was just this side of decrepit. The roof sagged like a swaybacked mare, and a couple of the windows had plywood panes instead of glass. Kudzu, that voracious interloper, had found its way onto the left side of the house, and it seemed to be in the process of devouring it whole.

Jolene pulled into an empty spot, next to a handful of vehicles that looked like they were actually functional, if not entirely glamorous. Jack pulled in next to her and then killed the engine. He looked over at me and grinned as he lit up a fresh Camel.

"So this is it, huh?" he asked, his head on a swivel, as he took it all in. "This is the farm where they grew you."

"Yup," I agreed, trying to stall. I felt slightly panicky as I watched Jolene and Becky get out of the car and head toward the barn, beckoning to us as they went. I could hear music and raised, boisterous voices coming from within.

"Rem, seriously, are you okay?" Jack asked, sensing my hesitation.

"Dude! Will you quit asking me that?" I answered testily. "I'm not made of porcelain. I'll be fine."

"Geez," Jack said quietly, "I was just..."

I cut him off. "Honey, listen. I'm fine. I'm not going to wig out. It's just weird being back here, that's all. I never thought I would see this place again."

Seemingly satisfied, Jack opened his door and stepped out into the steamy Florida evening. I took one more toke, stashed the roach back in the Altoid tin, and joined him. Suddenly, the bushes behind Jack seemed to come to life, appearing to move on their own. Jack turned to face this arboreal menace as a giant German shepherd came bounding out. It reared up, snarling, teeth bared, and knocked Jack over onto his back. I stood frozen on the spot, unable to reconcile what I was seeing, as Jack curled into a fetal position under the drooling monster's jaws. I was reminded of the old Stephen King novel *Cujo*, what with us being harassed by a giant dog in front of a barn. A rough voice cut through the air like a knife, seeming to silence everything.

"That's enough, Rocky! Back off 'im," it thundered. I turned to look at the owner of the voice and was immensely relieved when I recognized my Uncle Clarence.

"Is that Remlee?" he asked from across the dooryard, a broad smile cracking his Stony face. "I heard you was in town. How long has it been anyways?"

I turned back to Jack and was relieved to see that the hellhound had relaxed, sitting back on his haunches, regarding Jack with mild curiosity. Jack stood up, wiping the dust off his pants, and laughed nervously at the drooling cur in front of him.

"Good doggy," he said, a strange hitch in his voice.

"Don't worry, fella, he won't hurt you now. He's a good pup, ain't you, Rocky?" Clarence said as he ambled down the steps toward us. The years hadn't changed my favorite uncle all that much. He still wore big rubber chore boots, Big Yank brand overalls, no shirt, and a Dale Earnhardt baseball hat. His curly mullet was grayer and thinner than I remembered it, but otherwise, he was the same.

He grabbed ahold of me in his giant arms and hugged me close, and I could feel that the years hadn't weakened him any. It felt like two steel bands had enclosed me, and escape was unthinkable. I had forgotten just how strong Uncle Clarence was.

"And who's this fella here, who came so close to being dog food?" Clarence asked with a laugh, releasing me and turning to look at Jack.

"This is my husband, Jack Shepherd. Jack, this is my Uncle Clarence. He's my mom's second oldest brother," I said, watching Jack closely. Though not nearly as rambunctious as he used to be, Jack was still known to be a bit mouthy when drunk. And he was close to drunk now, if not quite there. I silently prayed to whatever God would listen to keep Jack's mouth in check. Jack was no chump, but Clarence was twice his size and three times as crazy. He was also on his home field, surrounded by family members of equal vigor and brutality. I hope Jack recognizes.

"Good to meet you, sir," Jack said stoically, grasping Clarence's paw firmly.

"Sir?" Clarence laughed, "Naw, son, I work for a living. Call me Clarence." He clapped Jack on the back, rocking him on his base a little. I sighed in relief when I saw that Jack was taking it all in stride. I began to relax a little more.

"Y'all come on back to the barn," Clarence said, putting his arm around my shoulders and guiding me along. "Everybody's back there fooling around. Get yourselves a drink of the family stock, see how everyone is."

As he let us down the driveway, I looked around some more at the property. The sun was starting to set, and the shadows across the dooryard were growing longer. I saw that the old tire swing was still hanging from the willow out back. I remembered the countless hours I spent in that thing, trying my damnedest to touch the clouds. One summer, I tried too hard, pushing myself out of the swing at the highest point of its arc. For a few sweet but fleeting seconds, I was flying, but then gravity and reality reasserted themselves, and I found myself crashing shoulder first into the gnarled tree roots below. I spent the rest of the summer in a sling, and I didn't get to go swimming at all.

"How is Betty Sue doing, anyways?" Clarence asked abruptly. "She holding up okay? The nurses want to throw her out yet?"

I chuckled a little before I replied, "Well, she can't really talk, so I don't think they know that she's cussing them out."

"No shit," Clarence agreed. "That woman ain't never been one to do as she was told. I'm kinda surprised she ain't try to bust out of there yet."

"Give her time. It's only been a couple of days," I pointed out.

As we approached the entrance to the barn, the door crashed open as Jolene came bounding through, several Mason jars full of moonshine balanced precariously in her hands.

"Get your asses in here!" she shouted gleefully. "Y'all are far too sober!"

"I couldn't agree more," Jack said, grabbing a glass from her in gulping the liquor greedily.

We followed Jolene inside, and I was struck by a feeling of deja vu. I looked around the barn and saw half a dozen faces that I hadn't expected to ever see again. Everyone began greeting us all at once, their voices tripping over each other and blending into allowed amorphous din.

The next few minutes were a whirlwind of reconnections and introductions as Jack and I were passed around the room like a beach ball at a Jimmy Buffett concert. After everyone was satisfied with the formalities, I went to go sit at the picnic table next to the tool bench with my cousin Sarah. We had been inseparable when we were little kids until CPS took her and the rest of Uncle Rawlie and Aunt Lola Mae's kids away to foster care. She came back a few years later, after Aunt Lola Mae convinced CPS (shockingly) that she was responsible enough to have her kids again, but we had grown apart during that time, and didn't see much of each other after that.

"So how did you meet Jack?" she asked as she lit a new Camel off the embers of her last.

"It's a boring story, really," I said, stopping to light a smoke on my own. "His boss's sister worked with me at the restaurant, and she introduced us." While this was indeed true, it wasn't the whole story.

I first met Jack about a year after I had arrived in Boston. I was still couch-surfing with friends and working under the table, cleaning office buildings at night. The pay was low, but I didn't need an

ID to get the job. Most of my coworkers didn't even speak English. It's amazing how easy it is to get by outside of the system, if you're willing to clean toilets for less than minimum wage and live semi-nomadically. I wasn't about to buy a Porsche, but I wasn't hungry or cold. And I was free.

On the night in question, I had been dropped off at a building that the company I worked for had only recently acquired the contract for. The supervisor I was with that evening, Mrs. Mendez, was beyond ready for retirement. At the ripe old age of seventy-six, Mrs. Mendez's eyesight was less than optimal. As we walked into the foyer, she gripped my arm like I was her seeing-eye dog. She had me lead her to the elevator and summon a car to head down into the bowels of the building where our supplies were kept. While we waited for the car to arrive, Mrs. Mendez rambled on and on about her troublesome nephew and all the ways he tried her patience. I pretended to pay attention, too lost in my own thoughts to concern myself with hers. I was so lost, in fact, that I didn't hear the bell ding to announce the arrival of the summoned car.

Apparently, Mrs. Mendez's ears were as bad as her eyes, or maybe she was as lost in her monologue as I was lost in my trance. Either way, neither of us was looking when the elevator doors open. Unfortunately, the occupant over the car was also distracted, though not with conversation or woolgathering. The man in the elevator was carrying three large file boxes in his arms, and they blocked his view almost completely. As he stepped out of the elevator, I turned around and was promptly crashed into by the man and his precariously balanced load. I fell over backward onto my ass, as did the man with whom I had just collided. Mrs. Mendez stood, perplexed, in a snowfall of papers, unsure of what had just occurred.

"Oh my God, I'm so sorry," he said from the floor, embarrassment plain in his voice. I looked up toward the sound of his voice and encountered the most startlingly blue eyes I had ever seen.

"No… It's my fault… I wasn't looking…" I said. I felt the color rush to my cheeks as I stumbled to my feet. "Let me help you pick all this up."

"It's okay, ma'am, I wasn't looking either," he said. Then he smiled. The smile. The smile that stops my heart every time.

"No… No… I'll help… I'm… No… It's okay… I'll…" I stammered, dazzled by the intensity of the warmth his smile emitted. Unable to complete the thought, I busied myself chasing down the escaped paperwork. I couldn't look at him, but I sensed him nearby, equally pursuing our prey.

Within a few minutes, we had managed to capture all the errant papers and had them hastily stowed away in the boxes again.

"The old man's gonna have a coronary when he sees these files. They are all mixed up," the man said with a laugh.

"I hope I didn't get you into any trouble," I said, sincerely meaning it.

"Oh, don't worry, my dad already thinks I'm a fuck-up. He doesn't expect much out of me. He'll just be happy I got his files home without setting them on fire," he said in a tone that was somewhere between humor and tragedy. "But you're okay, right?"

"Of course. It's nothing. Just a bump on the ass," I replied, laughing nervously.

We hastily said goodbye and went our separate ways. I didn't see him again, but I caught myself looking for him whenever I was assigned to that building. Over the next few years, I found myself fantasizing about him often. I would build intricate scenarios in my mind where we were reunited in some cheesy romantic comedy-styled manner. I only looked upon him for a few moments, but his face was imprinted firmly in my head, down to the smallest detail. I felt haunted by him. I dated sporadically but never anything serious. I think I was always waiting for my mystery man to reappear. Then one day, he did.

As I was finishing up my edited version of this story, Jack ambled over and sat down, listening in with obvious delight. I continued artel for a few minutes before he broke in with his assessment.

"She's rambling again," he said with a wink. "I'm ashamed to admit it, but I don't remember it happening like that. That can't count is how you met me. I was drunk and didn't even remember you."

"Okay, fine, I'll get to the point," I said, reclaiming control of the narrative. I began to recount to Sarah, and now Jack, how we ended up together.

When I was nineteen, I started working at the restaurant I would eventually own. It was located near Northeastern University, and it specialized in big, greasy breakfasts and artery-clogging burgers. I was tired of scrubbing toilets for chump change, and the tips I could earn in one weekend at McCurdy's Grill would be more than what I could make in an entire week as a custodian. I breathed a sigh of relief when Mel, the owner, hired me because the job meant real financial security for the first time since I ran away. I may not have been able to buy a Cadillac, but a used Honda was no longer out of reach. No more being crammed in like a sardine with a bunch of strangers, none of whom seem to bathe, riding the bus all over town.

After a few months, I became friends with a coworker, Ronnie. We were roughly the same age and had several shared interests (books and hiking), and both were looking to improve our living situations. We found a cheap but reasonably close apartment in Southie and swore the secret oaths of cohabitation. We were inseparable during this time, working, living, and partying together. Life was good. I felt like the earth was solid under my feet. Now was the time for someone to swoop in and sweep me off my feet, only in real life, things never go so smoothly.

One busy Saturday, a few weeks shy of my twenty-fourth birthday, Ronnie and I were both working. Ronnie's brother Trevor and a few of his buddies came in, and the hostess seated them in Ronnie's section. I was on a coffee run, checking all the sections, when I stopped at Trevor's table to top them off. I had met Trevor a handful of times, and he was a nice enough guy, but much to Ronnie's dismay, I just wasn't interested in him. He grinned up at me as I poured him more coffee, his round face lit up by the glare coming off of the windows.

"Can I get some too?" an oddly familiar voice asked, and I turned to look at the person who was speaking to me. His intense blue eyes sparkled as they locked onto mine. My breath caught in my throat as I instantly recognized the phantom fantasy man I had been thinking about for nearly a decade. "Yeah...s...s...sure," I stuttered, feeling my cheeks flame up in embarrassment. I focused my will on pouring the coffee, staring intently at his mug, determined not to spell a drop despite my obviously shaking hands. I held the pot with two hands and managed to fill his mug without completely humiliating myself. Ignoring the caffeine needs of the rest of the customers, I scurried back to the waitress section and collapsed onto the top bag of a pallet of potatoes. What was wrong with me? He was just a man. Sure, a particularly attractive man, but not really different from the countless others I had encountered on a daily basis. Why was I reacting so strongly to this particular one? I didn't know his name, we'd hardly even spoken, yet for reasons I still don't understand, I just knew I was meant to be with him.

"Hey, Rem, what's up?" Ronnie asked as she came into the station and began entering her tickets into the system. "You all right? You look like you've seen a ghost."

"I kind of have," I said with a chuckle. "Remember my mystery man? From the office building?"

"Yeah, I guess so," she replied, unsure where I was going with this.

"That's him. At that table with your brother. The one with the dark hair and the Bruins T-shirt," I blurted out in a rush. I felt giddy, like I felt my first dance in the middle school cafeteria three months before I ran away into my premature adulthood.

Ronnie gaped at me in astonishment. "Jack?" she asked after a moment's hesitation.

I don't think she meant for me to notice her reluctance, but I did. My heart sank as I realized that Ronnie had her heart set for him. She managed to keep the smile on her face, but it dimmed a little, the spark in her eye gone.

"I guess so," I said, trying to seem nonchalant but certain I was failing.

"His name is Jack Shepherd," she began, a thin smile on her face. "He's been working for my brother for a few months now. Trevor says his family's loaded, but you'd never know it to talk to him. I don't know much else about him."

Damn. I was hoping she'd mention his relationship status without me having to ask. Ronnie was too smart, too good at the game to make that kind of rookie mistake.

I walked away and went about the rest of my duties. I didn't mention Jack to Ronnie again, and she didn't mention him either. Jack became the invisible cloud that hovered over every conversation. Both Ronnie and I wanted him, but neither of us wanted to hurt the other. This would have been fine if it had been any other man, but Jack had a power over me that I can't explain. He's had it since the day he knocked me on my ass in front of the elevator. Seeing him again only intensified my obsession. The tension grew for the next few weeks as Ronnie and I jockeyed for position. Jack had taken to coming in nearly every day, and Ronnie and I made fools of ourselves, trying to outdo each other in an effort to win his affection. For his part, I'm still not sure if Jack even noticed.

This ridiculous drama continued for about six weeks. Jack would come in for lunch, Ronnie and I would throw ourselves at him, and he barely seemed to notice. I finally tired of this silly high school game, and one Tuesday, when Ronnie was off, I decided to make my move. No more innuendo, no more beating around the bush. I was just going to ask him out, direct and upfront. I gathered up all my courage and marched up to his table. He put the newspaper down slowly and started talking before I could speak.

"Wanna go out with me sometime?" he asked.

Sarah and Jack both started howling at this, and shortly I joined in with them

"That sounds like something off the fucking Hallmark Network or something," Sarah said through guffaws. Hard as I tried, I couldn't disagree.

Betty Sue

It amazes me how tired I get sitting here doing nothing. I've never been ambitious, but I always worked, or played, or something. Now, I just sit and watch TV, eat, do stupid therapy that don't work, piss, shit, and sleep. I find myself wanting to sleep more because at least in my weird time travel dreams, and in the warm, dark place, I can speak. I mean, sure, I can babble in the real world, and if I concentrate real hard, I can even say the word I mean every once in a while, but that's a far cry from being able to have a conversation. I've never really been a people person but being effectively cut off from everyone else is far more terrifying than I ever could have imagined.

My real Mama died birthing me, but Daddy remarried within the year. People tell me that it raised quite the stink in the Bradford and Alachua counties, him marrying so soon, but most everything our family did was looked down upon anyways, so he didn't pay it no mind. Both Daddy and Mama Lettie always told me I didn't talk until I was almost four years old. I would just stand as much out of the way as I could and play quietly with myself. I was the only girl, so far anyways, so nobody thought it was all that weird that I was basically silent. Then, all of a sudden, it was like a dam burst, or so I'm told. Almost overnight, I became a chatterbox. Certainly, nobody that knows me today would ever believe I was capable of shutting up. They should come see me now.

I'm watching my stories when the time comes for my next therapy session. They call it "occupational therapy," but I don't understand why. I'm a waitress, and I don't see how any of this has to do with serving truckers greasy eggs and coffee. The therapist is a wispy young fellow, no more than thirty. He fidgets a lot, and his Coke-bottle glasses are distracting. I find myself staring at his comically magnified eyes, unable to follow his monotonous drone. That isn't really all that surprising, though. I'm having trouble following a lot of things lately.

"Can you point to the one that is your phone number?" he asks me while showing me a piece of paper he is written on. I realize that I recognize the symbols, that they signify numbers. I try to remember what a phone number is and if I even have one.

"It's okay, Ms. Shaw, take your time," he says, in an attempt at soothing me. It makes me think of a robot with a pet human. I shut her for a second and try to look harder at the numbers. They seem to dance about the page, never seeming to stand still long enough for me to wrap my mind around them.

"SUMBLA NOOM OH," I grumble. Tell them to stop moving around.

"Yes. That's right," The Robot says in his emotionless voice. "Which one of these is yours?"

I stare intently at the paper, trying to will the symbols to stop their rioting on the page. I take a deep breath, hold it in, and close my eyes. I try to forget about all the worries swirling around in my brain. When everything is gone quiet, I open my eyes and look at the paper. The numbers are behaving. They remain as still as the inanimate objects they are should act. I study them for what seems like weeks, trying to find the sequence that should be familiar. I blink quickly a few times and look again at the list.

(904) 466 2139
(724) 441 0037
(904) 824 4409
(814) 827 7574

I notice that two of them start with the same three numbers: 904. That seems familiar. Yes, it's one of those two. I point rapidly to both of the numbers while trying to explain that I know it's one of these two.

"Numb summ," I say. "Numbo sum, numbo summ."

"Yes. That's right. It's one of those two," The Robot says, patting me on the arm with an uncomfortable (for me) detachment. "Can you point to which one is yours? You almost have it."

I stare at the paper again. The numbers are still cooperating, sitting still on the page. I repeat each sequence over and over in my mind, trying to find any other digit that strikes a chord. I begin to feel the telltale quickening of pulse and breath that comes before I start to lose my temper. I look pleadingly at the therapist, begging him with my eyes to let me quit, to leave me be. This is harder than any day in the field, pulling weeds in the sun.

"You can do it," he says firmly as if there could be no question. I wonder where he gets the faith to say that. I'm not convinced.

"Yu yu yu shwinger tempo neu," I blabber, meaning that's easy for you to say.

"Just try one more time. Which one is your number?" he says, ignoring my pleas.

I look again, and suddenly it hits me. I break into an enormous smile and jab my finger at the paper: (904) 824 4409. That's my phone number. That one is mine! I recognize it!

"Very good, Ms. Shaw," the therapist says, a trace of happiness creeping into his usual drab voice. "That's right. Very good."

He continues to prattle on, but I stop listening. I'm excited because maybe I can get better. For the first time since this started, I feel like there is a path back to where I was. Okay, maybe not all the way back, but closer. Close enough that I might not have to go to the County Home. Close enough that I'll be able to manage my own affairs and stay in the trailer. I can't stand the thought of not being in charge of my own life. I promised myself when Earl got locked up for good, nobody but me is gonna run my life ever again. I may be a fuck-up, but my mistakes are my own.

After a while, the robot man stops lecturing me and leaves me alone in the room again. I'm not unhappy with this. I've been lucky so far, and as much as the hospital has been relatively slow, so I have yet to deal with a roommate. I have enough problems without having to listen to some stranger's ordeals. I ain't trying to be uncaring. It's just tiring enough dealing with my own nightmare, thank you very much.

I can't remember everything about my reunion with Remlee, but I remember she said she's staying for a little while anyway. I hope she stays long enough for me to get better enough to tell her I'm sorry. I doubt she'll be here long enough for me to be able to try to explain myself. That will take too many words. I just wanna be able to say two words clearly to her: I'm sorry. I want her to hear those words from my lips. No, I need her too.

She may not forgive me. I probably don't deserve it. I just want the chance to ask her too. I just want the chance to let her know that I know I fucked everything up royally, and that if I could take it back, I would go back and do it again, right this time. I would do that in a heartbeat, no questions asked. I want her to know that it wasn't never anything to do with her. I was just weak and ignorant. I always loved her; I just couldn't show her is all.

I lie back on the lumpy mattress and close my eyes. Visions of Remlee as a baby flash across my eyelids like an old home movie. I see her taking her first step. I see her riding her tricycle up and down the driveway, blowing raspberries at the top of her lungs. I see her chasing the ducks from the pond around with a stick, trying to get them to form a line and march in an impromptu parade across the dooryard. I see her crooked smile, the one she uses when she's telling fibs to get out of trouble. I see it all at once, and it's too much. I start to cry, and I fade out into the warm dark period.

I float for a while in the nothingness, basking in the peace of oblivion. My fears, my worries, my problems, they all melt away, leaving only peace. Nothing can happen here. Nothing has happened here. Nothing will happen here. All is well, all except a quiet gnawing somewhere in the background, out there in the infinite dark. A tiny spark of worry flits about, pestering me like his mosquito. What if I get stuck here, in the warm place? I like it here, but am I ready to give up on life yet? I don't think this place is death, but it's also not life. Am I ready to be done? Like, for real, done, dead and gone, pushing up daisies? I can almost feel something beyond, like I could go on to the after, whatever that is, anytime I want. It would be just like jumping off the tire swing, letting go completely of any control, and following free. No, not yet. I have to somehow make it up to Remlee to really apologize. I could go, if only if I could manage that.

Slowly, the darkness fades as I feel the creepy dream state take hold once more. These ghosts of Christmas past are getting to be routine. I feel like laughing at the craziness of my new life. I wonder with dread what awful bit of my unfortunate life I get to relive this time. I open my dream eyes and begin to gather in the scene, looking for details that might help me guess which demon will be appearing tonight. Not that it would likely help, but it would be nice to try to prepare. For an uncomfortable moment, I can't truly decide if any staying alive is really worth all this relived horror, but the moment passes, and I turn my attention to the movie/memory/dream currently playing in my brain.

I'm young again, probably around ten. My two front teeth have fallen out and regrown larger, but not all of the baby teeth are gone, and there are a few fresh gaps soon to be refilled. I'm getting taller, but awkwardly, not in proportion. My legs are long, but my torso is still small, and my elbows are all hinky. I feel like the flamingos I saw when Uncle Leroy took us to that animal park down near Ocala that one time. Everybody thinks flamingos are beautiful, but I don't. Their gawky, funny-looking things that don't look like they should even be able to walk on those ridiculous legs. That's how I feel, klutzy and just in my own way.

I look around and take in my surroundings, looking for clues to when I am at, I recognize my old bedroom, the one I share with my younger sister, Lola Mae. We still basically like each other at this point. Hormones and boys and worse haven't driven a wedge between us yet. I feel a strange pang of deja vu as I recognize the wallpaper. It's old and cracked in places, but the violets in a row pattern is unmistakable. A chill works its way down my spine, and I wonder, vaguely, while this particular detail bothers me so.

Lola is sleeping soundly in the bed on the other side of the room. The blanket she is snuggled under rises and falls slowly and steadily to the rhythm of her quiet snoring. Outside the window, I can hear the hum of dozens of mingled conversations hovering through the air. I tiptoe over to the window and peer outside to see what I'm missing up here in my age in forced exile. A large bonfire is burning out behind the barn, and I can see the forms of my family members dancing and hooting and hollering in friendly clumps around the ring of the fire's light. A vicious jolt of jealousy hits me, and I decide to brave the wrath of my elders and sneak out to spy.

As I'm slithering my way carefully over to the door, I hear footsteps climbing the stairs outside in the hallway. I freeze, afraid to even breathe, as the footsteps come closer to my door, then stop right outside. I slowly began to work my way back to my bed, desperate to not be caught out of bounds. Youngins have to be in bed by sunset on weekdays here at the farm, no questions asked. It's just how things are done.

I reach my bed and carefully climb back in, silent as a gator sneaking up on his prey. My heart stops when I see the knob slowly turn, making that awful squeaking noise that puts my teeth on edge. I close my eyes and pretend I'm sleeping. I force myself to lie still, to really sell it. Quiet, shuffling footsteps come close to my bed, pause, then move over to Lola Mae's side. They pause again for a few seconds, then move back to the door. They stop there, and an eternity passes while I wait for something to happen.

I lie still, straining my ears for any sign of movement. I can hear the footsteps' owner breathing heavily in the doorway. He reminds me of Rufus, are Bluetick/Saint Bernard mix, after a particularly rambunctious game of fetch. I can picture drool falling from the open mouth of the otherwise faceless figure in the doorway. I push this lot away, determined to remain calm. I'm just a little kid sleeping in her own house, and monsters only exist in movies. Bobby Lee told me so.

Lola Mae murmurs something about rabbits in her sleep, and I hear her rollover inside. The breathing in the doorway stops suddenly, and I hear furtive movements rustling from in that direction. I roll over too, hoping whoever is there will leave, not wanting to wake us. The footsteps recede into the hallway, and I begin to relax. I hear them move on down the hallway, and I breathe easier, feeling I've escaped some horrible unknown fate. I begin to drift off to sleep, my curiosity forgotten.

I'm almost asleep when I hear the bedroom door close. The clicking latch drags me back to the surface. The footsteps are back, creeping over to the edge of my bed. A thick, acrid smell assaults my nostrils. It's a heady mix of alcohol, smokes of various origins, motor oil, and an underlayment of well-cultivated body odor. Her rough hand gently touches my shoulder, and my skin crawls with gooseflesh. I hold still, hardly breathing, terrified of what I now fully remember is about to happen next.

"Betty Sue," a rough voice croaks in my ear, its foul breath consuming my face. "Hey, Miss Betty Sue. It's okay, just be quiet. I'm just here to play."

I keep my eyes shut tight, refusing to admit I'm awake. If I just keep pretending, maybe he'll go away. His hand moves slowly down my back, and it feels like it leaves a trail of filth, almost like a snail. I can't bear it any longer, and I involuntarily jerk away from his uninvited caress.

"Oh, it's okay, Little Betty. It's your old Uncle Leo. We always play games together, right? Well, now it's time to learn a new game. A secret game, okay? Can't tell nobody, though," he breathes into my ear. I try to breathe in through my mouth to avoid the fetid swamp issuing from his rotten mouth. A whimper escapes me, and I feel the hand recoil for a second.

"Hey, relax, honey child, I ain't gonna hurt you. You got the wrong idea. I wanna make you feel good," he says huskily.

I wonder what he means because I feel anything but good right now. I don't know exactly why, but this feels wrong in ways I don't have the words or experience to describe. I remain silent, unable to protest, unable to even move. I feel a cold sweat break out all over, and I begin to shiver. The hand reappears at the small of my back, slowly creeping toward my butt. I squirm a little, and the figures dig deep into the muscle of my butt, hurting me as well as scaring me. I go limp and begin to breathe shallowly and rapidly.

"This will be our little game," my Uncle Leo says, his fingers creeping around my waist, flickering at the waistband of my pink panties. "We gotta keep it between us, though. We don't want to make the other kids jealous. They wouldn't understand. They are not special, like you."

I hear him fussing around behind me, and I feel him slide into the bed with me. My skin crawls as I realize that he isn't wearing any pants. Something warm and strangely firm presses insistently on my backside, and I try to squirm away, but he has me held too close. Every wiggle just seems to draw me closer into his crushing arms.

"No, no, no," I whisper, unsure of what is happening, yet feeling both fear and unimaginable shame. I don't know why, but I can sense that this will taint me somehow, mark me. Set me apart. A tear escapes my eye, and my uncle stops for a second to tenderly wipe it away. I realize that in his own twisted way, he loves me. Deep down, he loves me, even if it damns him to the deepest hell. And he intends on expressing that

unholy love in the most intimate and physical manner available to men and women. But I'm not a woman, I won't be for years.

"I'm sorry," he cries as he plunges his finger deep inside me, tearing me. My eyes open wide, and all I can see are the violets on the wallpaper. They are so pretty, even after all these years. I focus on the flowers as my uncle has his way with me. I lie completely still and limp, my mind only on the faded flowers on the wall. I'm vaguely aware that my uncle's breathing is going faster, like he's running from the devil. I feel something warm and wet splash across my back as a low moan rolls out of his fetid mouth and into my unwilling ears.

Suddenly, he is gone, and I hear him padding away toward the door. He stops as he opens the door, and I turn to look at him. He looks haggard and confused, like he just woke up after a month-long nap. His clothes are disheveled, as a put on in a hurry. He sees me looking at him, and he raises his point your finger to his purse lips. Sssssssssssshhhhhhhhhhh!

"Remember, our secret, right?" he whispers, then he turns and quietly closes the door from the outside. Silence fills the room, and I begin to breathe again. I feel exhausted and humiliated. My nether regions are on fire, and I worry that he may have broken something. A few quiet sobs escape my lips.

Lola Mae shifts around some more, and I wonder if she's awake too, a witness to my defiling. I look over at her for a long time until I'm sure she isn't faking. I pull the pillow over my head and cry. I cry for a long time until exhaustion finally wins out over panic, and I slowly drift back to the warm, dark place.

Maybe I will stay here in this nowhere after all.

Remlee

The party lasted most of the night. For an event on the Old Tucker Farm, it was relatively subdued. Nobody fought anybody, and nothing important got broken. I was worried at first, but Jack and my family got along like they've known each other from birth. I felt a stabbing of pride, seeing my family more or less accept Jack. My clan wasn't typically all that friendly to outsiders, so seeing Jack and Uncle Rawlie trading filthy jokes set me at ease.

I spent the night bouncing around the barn like a pinball, reacquainting myself with the family I tried so hard to forget. The more I talked to them, the more guilty I began to feel for abandoning them. Sure, none of them were saints, not by a long shot. I still wouldn't trust most of them with the keys to my house, but my complete radio blackout seemed like overkill in hindsight. For the first few years, I stayed incommunicado because I was a runaway, and I had no intentions of going back. I certainly wasn't going to help the Florida authorities track me down. By the time I reached eighteen, it had been so long. I simply didn't care anymore. I had my new life and my new friends, and I didn't want to complicate that with the inevitable bullshit that goes along with any interaction with my family.

Jack seemed even more at home than me. He drank alongside my kin in with gusto, easily matching their endless thirst for alcohol. He was among his "spiritual brethren" here, as he called it, pun fully intended. Jack was unique in that he simply refused to recognize class. Period. It most likely started as a rebellion against his hyper-judgmental family, but unlike other ideals and attitudes he affected to horrify his parents, this particular quirk stuck. Jack would be as comfortable under a bridge with a pack of hobos as he would be in the Country Club bar with his father's associates. As long as liquor was available to lubricate his mind, Jack could hang with anyone, anywhere.

I kept my eye on him throughout the night, and I began to envy how easy Jack could open up to anyone. When he talked to a person, he could always tell immediately what that person was all about. I marveled how he could completely disagree with someone yet somehow seemed to be on their side anyway. He probably should have been a politician, except he was far too honest for that. I wondered how he could be so easygoing. If someone cuts me off in the grocery store parking lot, I'm ready to kill them and their entire family, going back three generations. Given the same situation, Jack would end up with the parking space and a new friend. Most of the time anyways.

About an hour before everything died down and everyone went their separate ways for the night, the only tense moment happened when my cousin Lindie showed up, looking to score a bit of Uncle Jed's newest batch of speed. A noticeable hushing took place as she walked into the barn and cornered Jed. They argued quietly in the corner for a few minutes, but try as I might, I could only make one word in ten. I notice about a third of the people in the barn were watching his intently as I was, although it was likely they had more context to draw from. I decided to gather some of that context for myself and made my way over to Uncle Clarence.

"What's that all about?" I asked, nodding in the direction where Lindie and Jed were still in a mildly heated discussion.

"Can't trust that one," Clarence said, lazily pointing in Lindie's direction. "She can't manage her vices. She done stole from half the people in this room. She owes money she borrowed to the other half. She's probably trying to pull some type of con on my dipshit brother right now, and he'll eat it right up. He does every time. You watch, that minx won't be leaving here empty-handed." He spat as he said this, almost as a curse. He readjusted his ancient Earnhardt hat and continued.

"Your brother just can't seem to keep a leash on her. He tries, but she always finds—" he started to say, but I quickly interrupted him.

"Why would my brother have to keep a leash on Lindie? What the hell are you talking about? How is she his problem at all?" I asked sharply. Clarence gaped at me for a few seconds, obviously as confused as I was.

"What do you mean "what do you mean"?" he asked slowly as if talking to a small child. Not a particularly bright small child at that.

"I mean, what do you mean about my brother leashing my cousin?" I asked, truly baffled as to what my uncle was saying.

"Half-cousin," he corrected.

"Whatever," I replied, exasperated. "Seriously, what in the fuck are you talking about?"

Slowly, a look of recognition spread across my Uncle Clarence's face, and it was quickly replaced by a rapid succession of other emotions fighting for control until he settled on semipaternal concern. He gently touched my elbow and let out a low sigh.

"Nobody's told you." It was a statement, not a question.

"Told me what?" I asked, my temperature rising. I could feel the panic monster clawing at the doors of the cage I stuff him into, deep in the bowels of my mind. I swallowed hard and tried to ignore the rising dismay and focus on what Clarence had to say.

"About your brother," he started, suddenly unable to look me in the eye.

"Which brother? I fucking have two, you know," I seethe at him, barely containing my temper.

"Shane," he said. "I'm talking about Shane. Remlee, there's no easy way to say this, so I'll just say it straight: Shane and Lindie, they're together. Like, biblically. Got themselves two kids now, Ashley and Shane Junior." He stopped to look at me, to gauge my reaction.

"Huh," I said and felt myself plop down on the cooler that was behind me. Once again, my family had found a way to surprise me. Why can't these surprises ever be something good?

"I thought you talked to Jolene every now and then," he said quickly, trying to absolve himself. "She never said nothing?"

"Must have slipped her mind," I said dryly, glaring over in her direction.

"Yeah, well..." he said, fading off awkwardly. He began to scan the room, looking for a way to escape the suddenly uncomfortable conversation. I made it easy for him and made a beeline over to where Jolene and Jack were sitting. I must have looked angry because I saw Jack batten down his hatches to weather the storm he saw coming his way. I sat down hard on the bench next to Jolene and turned to face her.

"So," I said, my eyebrows arched to the ceiling, "Lindie and Shane?"

"Remlee," she began, but I raised my hand, stopping her. Jack perked up, his attention on us fully now.

"What. The. Fucking. Fuck? How does that even happen? How long?" I asked her, blaming her as if she could have done anything to stop Shane from doing what Shane wanted to do.

"Honestly," she began, her voice lowering as if conspiring with Jack and me, "I think for most of their lives, on and off. You was so young when he moved out, you wouldn't remember how they was. They was always close. Maybe too close. I remember Mama was a little suspicious all along. I think she might have caught them playing doctor or something and just kept it to herself. I know you don't remember Daddy, but he'd likely have killed the both of them if he would have found out anything like that."

"But isn't... Isn't that illegal?" I stammered, still thunderstruck.

"Well, kind of, I guess," she said, "but they ain't married, just shacked up. Plus, they ain't full cousins. Mama came from Granny Viola, but Jedidiah was Granny Lettie's oldest. They are only half-cousins."

"Oh, well, that makes all the difference in the world," I said with a sarcastic laugh. Jack giggled from beside me, and I elbowed him. He quickly put on his pensive face and held his tongue.

"It's weird, I know," Jolene said with a defeated sigh. "It caused a whole pile of trouble at first. Most of the family was actively against it when they first came out of the closet, that is. Damn sure nobody thought it was a good idea. But it's been five years or so now, so most of us have just accepted it. They're family, above all. No one else is going to look out for no Tuckers or Shaws, so we gotta look out for each other."

We sat in silence for a few minutes, the three of us, each mulling over their own secret thoughts. I looked at Jack and saw that sleep would soon steal him away for the night. His left eye was already shut, and he was weaving back and forth on the bench, ever so slightly. Watching him struggle to remain awake reminded me that I could use some shuteye myself. I was about to say something to Jolene when I notice that she was engaged in a battle of her own. Her eyes, so much like my own, were red and puffy now. I can see tears on the verge of spilling, and I washed his Jolene fought valiantly to keep them prisoner.

"What is it, Jo?" I asked softly.

"N-n-n… N-n-n… Nothing. It's nothing, really," she said in a rush, refusing to meet my eye. I didn't push, but just put my arm over her shoulder and laid my head on her chest, just like when I was little. I felt her hands automatically assume the familiar positions, one hand around my waist, the other stroking my hair. I closed my eyes and listened to the thumping in her chest, and I was momentarily at peace.

"It's just… I don't know," Jolene said quietly into my hair, "as it is, I've never had what Shane and Lindie have. He'd straight up die for her. Maybe what they have is wrong in most people's eyes, but it's real, what they have. I sometimes wish somebody loved me like Shane loves Lindie."

I sat up and looked at my sister with wet eyes. Unsure of what to say, I lit a cigarette and said nothing. I looked over at Jack to see if he was still listening, but he had slumped over on the picnic table and was snoring quietly.

Pointing at Jack, Jolene said solemnly, "Like he loves you."

"But what about Gary?" I asked.

"Fuck Gary," she answered through clenched teeth. "He only wants me to be his maid. Or his whore."

"Then why do you stay with him?" I asked, my voice cracking as it rose an octave. "Every time we talk, every motherfucking time, it's the same thing. Gary this, Gary that. Blah, blah, blah. Why don't you just fucking leave him?"

"And go where?" she retorted, her tone rising to match my own. "I've got nothing. Forty-six years old and nothing to my name. That piece-of-shit car out there? It's not in my name. That goddamn nasty fucking bug-infested trailer? His too. What am I gonna do, Rem? Go strip again? Who am I kidding? That train left the station long ago. No one's gonna pay to see this naked."

"That's not true," I said weakly, but she kept talking over me.

"I'm a middle school dropout with four kids to three daddies. Two of them have babies of their own. Ain't a one of them that ain't got a whole mess of their own problems. Nobody who is worth a damn is gonna wanna touch me with a ten-foot pole. Gary sucks, all right. I know. He sucks fucking hard. But what other choice do I got?" she asked, her shoulders and head dropping in defeat. A single tear broke free from its shackles and began tracing a slow descent down her cheek.

"You always have a choice," I said lamely, but I knew better.

"I am addicted, all right?" she said, almost too quiet to hear. "We both know it, no need to try to hide it from you. I know you ain't a moron. If I didn't have that methadone clinic, I'd just come unglued. That's what I do. If I could just get clean, I could leave him. I would leave him." She stopped for a second, and I wondered who she was trying to convince, me or herself. Maybe both.

We sat a while longer, neither one of us wanting to break the silence, both unsure where to go next. As I always do when faced with awkward social situations, I reached into my pocket and pulled out my stash. I lit a fresh joint, pulled deep into my lungs, and handed it to Jolene. She took it gladly, and we casually passed it back and forth until it burned our fingertips. I looked around and noted that other than Jack and the hellhound, we were the only ones left in the barn. I glanced out the window and saw the first pink streaks appearing in the eastern sky.

"We should probably get some sleep," I said, standing up and walking around behind Jack. I started the process of trying to get him around, mildly prodding him with my knuckle in the ribs. He moaned and slapped my hand, but his eyes remained shut.

"Leave him," Jolene said. "He'll be fine. Rocky'll look out for him."

I decided she was right but still managed to get him to lie down on top of the picnic table before following Jolene back up to the house. Halfway up the lane, I turned back and saw Rocky pull himself up beside Jack on the table, circle around him clumsily a couple of times, then lie down with a huff, snuggled close to Jack's back.

"Look at him," I said, trying not to laugh too loud.

"He's a Tucker now," Jolene replied. I couldn't argue.

Betty Sue

I am starting to understand why my stepmom always called the TV the idiot box. It has always been a part of my life, at least since Daddy brought our first one home in '56 or '57. I always watched it some, but until now, I always had something else to do, what with work and kids and all. I ain't had nothing to do for damn near a week now, maybe more. Times kinda fucky right now, so I ain't certain how long, really. I just know that sixteen hours of that nonsense every day for days on end tends to make a person a bit squirrelly.

The nurses have taken to let me putter through the hallways. They say the exercise will do me a world of good, and I got to admit, I feel a sight better than I did just a few days ago when I was still glued to the bed. I finally got the nurses to understand I wanted a better gown, or some PJ pants, or something, and a comfy pair of sweats appeared on the chair the other morning when I got up. Nurse Tinkerbell told me Jolene brought it, but I don't know if I believe her. It would be nice to think Jolene would think about me like that, but that's just the kind of lie them do-gooders like to tell, so I don't know. I'm just glad my ass ain't hanging in the wind no more.

I just walk and walk the hall, round and round the nurses' station, mumbling to myself. I know I must look crazy, but I don't care. I just want to be able to talk again. I figure if I keep trying, it's eventually gotta work. It's not like I got much else to do. Every once in a while, I manage to string two or three intelligible words together, but when I rush over to the closest staff member to show off, I never seem to be able to repeat it. Oh, they smile and pat me on the head, but I know when I'm being patronized.

I feel a grumbling in my belly, and it tells me it must be about lunchtime. I shuffle my way back to my room and sit down on the bed, ready for the next boring part of my boring day. Here comes some boring aide bringing me some boring mashed potatoes and boring Jell-O of a flavor I can't exactly identify. I eat it anyway, partly out of hunger, partly because I don't know what else to do. I wonder if the blandness of the food is a result of shitty cooks and substandard ingredients, or if it's just another wonderful gift that I can add to the pile of garbage this stroke has given me. I haven't had any outside food since coming here, so I have nothing to compare it to. Remlee asked the nurses if she could bring me some Long John Silvers, my favorite, but they said no. Something about me needing to go on a special diet on account of I can't swallow very good anymore. Sometimes, I can barely even drink without spilling a little. My left side, especially in my mouth, is still a little numb. It's a weird feeling, like pins and needles, but not exactly. The fun never ends on this trip, I tell ya.

I finish eating, pushing what's leftover back onto the side table. I'm about to get up and go to the bathroom when I hear two voices right outside the door. They're talking low, so I can't really hear what they're saying. I try to decide if I should rush over and use the commode now before whatever therapist or orderly or nurse has the chance to poke and prod at me. I decide my need isn't that strong yet, so I'll just get through whatever annoyance they have in store this time.

I get ready to start hollering, not out of any real alarm, just to mess with whoever is unlucky enough to have drawn this duty. There isn't much to do to entertain myself here, so torturing the staff has become my go-to move. They get paid better than I ever did at any of my crappy jobs, and it's always air-conditioned in here. A little bit of getting cussed at ain't gonna hurt nobody.

"Mama, are you decent?" I hear Remlee say, and instantly, all my ornery ickiness washes away. She comes into the room, leading that slick-looking fellow that was with her last time, what was that, yesterday? Day before? Oh, who cares?

"Rrrrrrrrrrreeeeeemmmmmmmllllll," I manage to say, giving what I hope is a reasonable approximation of a smile. I've noticed my face don't react the way it used to.

"Hey, Mama," she says and gives me an awkward hug. I hold on as long as she will let me, but it isn't enough.

She sits down next to me on the bed and motions for the guy she is with to come over and sit in the chair across from us. I take him in as he saunters over. He's tall, probably six feet, maybe more. He has messy dark hair and huge blue eyes, like Rutger Hauer. He smiles boldly at me as he drops bonelessly into the chair.

"Mama, this is my husband, Jack Shephard," she says, a proud gleam in her eye.

"Yu yu yu? Mamode tee? Mamode tee?" I ask, hoping she understands. She doesn't.

"What?" she simply asks.

I try again to ask her when this happened, how this happened, why she didn't tell nobody, but only more gibberish comes out.

"Oh Lord!" I say.

She starts to tell me the story of how they met, but I only half listen. I can't stop just looking at her. She's a woman now, not the gawky teenager I remember. As she goes on about her life, I feel a deep sadness growing in my guts. I don't recognize the people she's talking about, the places, any of it. This woman is a stranger to me. She's even lost her accent now. I'd never have known she was Southern had I not birthed her here myself, in this very hospital.

What strikes me the most, what I can't get over, is how much she looks like me. It's kind of like looking into a window into the past. When I look at her, I see my thick blond hair, my round hazel eyes, my crooked, almost too-small nose, my full lips parted over my pointy teeth. Even things that ain't about how she looks are from me. Her brisk, take-no-prisoners walk, for example. Or the way she pulls on her hair when she's trying to remember something she forgot. Everything so familiar, yet different.

I can see her father too. She's long and lean like he is. That's new. She must have had quite a spurt later on, 'cause last time I saw her, she was a little shorter than me. Now she towers over me like a giant sunflower. She also has that damned dimple on her chin, just like her Daddy. I used to kid Elmer that he was Kirk Douglas's stunt double, but eventually, that started to rub him the wrong way, and he let me know the way he always did. I stopped after that.

"You know, Mama," she says after a particularly awkward silence, "I never really blamed you." She goes quiet, and her man looks at the floor, obviously wishing he was just about anywhere else.

"No, that's not true. I did. I do. I don't know, Mama," she says, her eyes glistening. She looks at me all over, and I can see her trying to hold back her feelings. I can see in her eyes that she loves me, but underneath, I can also see that she hates me too. I don't think I blame her.

"I know you had your demons or whatever. I know some of the things that happened to you. I'm trying to give you leeway, but..." she trails off, and her hands fidget restlessly in her lap. When she speaks again, I can see the hatred in her eyes fully. The naked fury almost takes my breath away.

"But I don't care," she spits at me. Her whole body is trembling, and her breath comes in hitches. Her eyes are wild, and for the first time in her life, I'm scared of my daughter.

She continues on, unaware or simply unconcerned with my distress, her voice low and raspy, saying, "I don't care, because you didn't care. You left. I know things got bad sometimes, but that's no excuse. Families stay. No matter what. How was I supposed to not think you hated me? You couldn't stand to be around me! Sure, you'd come around, acting all sorry, saying things would be different. Better. And they would be, for a week, or a month, maybe even six months, but that's pushing it. And every time, every fucking time, I would fall for it. Because I wanted it to be true. Because no matter what, no matter how much you hurt me, no matter how many times you hurt me, I loved you. God help me, I still do. I love you, Mama!" She bursts out crying, and I reach out to hug her.

"No!" she says sharply, like I poked her with a needle. "I don't want your fucking hugs now. I needed them when I skinned my knee learning to ride a bike or when I didn't make the junior cheerleading squad. Or when a boy broke my heart for the first time. You weren't there. You had the choice to be there, and you didn't choose me."

I glance over at the husband, but he is busy making a show of pretending to be interested in whatever Joy Behar is saying on the TV. I don't know why I'm looking at him to rescue me from this cussing out, he don't know me from Adam, and his wife is the one doing the cussing. I give up on that front and try to defend myself.

"Ghinga do modique! Oh, Lord! Do modique!" I say. This isn't fair, I can't talk! Oh Lord! I can't talk!

She ignores me and plunges on, taking full advantage of my weakness. That's another instinct she got from her father.

"It's not only the bad you missed, though. You missed the good too," she points out, her voice softening a smidge. "I didn't get to share my life with you. You robbed me of that. I had to go to the mother-daughter dance with my sister. My sister! There are so many times I wanted you to be there with me, to see me grow, to laugh with me. But I wasn't fun enough, I guess. Or maybe I was too much work. Or maybe you're just broken. I don't know. But I can't just…forget it all. I guess I forgive you, but how do I forget?"

I try to hold her gaze, hoping I can convey something with my eyes. I want her to know that it wasn't her fault, it never was. There wasn't never anything wrong with her. The problem was with me. I'm just not cut out to be a Mama. I loved y'all kids, I really did. It's just that life is so damn heavy. Just carrying myself through this world is hard enough, I wasn't strong enough to carry anyone else too. Too many beatings, too many scars. I want her to understand that she was better off without me, but how do I tell her that? How the hell do I tell her anything?

"Oh, Mama," she sighs, and I can see the anger is gone, or at least on the way out of the door. "I'm sorry, I don't mean to yell at you. It's not fair. And none of that matters now anyways. We can't change what happened now, right?"

I try to take her hand, and this time she lets me. I try to visualize my feelings and thoughts and will them to her through our touch. It feels silly, like something Elmer would have called hippy-dippy bullshit, but I can't think of anything else I can do. I imagine all my love and all my sorrow, all my hopes for her as a warm red light. I imagine myself pushing that light down my arm and into hers, spreading warmth throughout her wrist and beyond. I have no idea if it's actually working, but I am feeling a little better, at least.

We sit there quietly, hand in hand, for a long time. The hubby minds his own business, never once intruding. I think I like him. So far, anyways, but I reserve the right to change my mind.

"Rrreeeemmmmmllleeeeeeee," I say, just to say it. As wonky as it sounds coming out of my mouth, I'm still happy I can say it. Every word

counts. She smiles thinly at me, and I know it's fake. She hasn't forgiven me, no matter what she says. I'm not sure she should.

"Look," she says after a while, "Jack and I are going to go now. I think Jolene said she was gonna come here after lunch, but you know how she is. Either way, we're going to go explore a bit. I haven't been home in forever, you know. I'll be back to see you soon. We're not going back home for a little while. Just behave yourself and try to get better."

She stands up, and her hubby follows suit. Remlee gives me a stiff hug, and I can tell she is relieved when I finally release her. The hubby steps in close and grasps my hand in his. They're rough and strong working man's hands.

"It was so nice to meet you, Ms. Shaw," he says in his velvet voice. "You've got an amazing daughter here." What a charmer, this one! Or a snake. I decide to keep an eye on him.

She turns to leave, and I feel a hitch in my throat. She promised to come back, but will she? As she just pointed out, I promised her the same thing when she was little, and I rarely kept my word. It would serve me right if she didn't, I suppose, but I sure hope she does.

Hope. That's a strange concept now. Things have changed so much that I wonder if the word will ever mean what it used to. What do I really have to look forward to? How can I ever have a meaningful relationship with anyone now, romantic or otherwise? I can no longer relate to anyone in any real way. Sure, people can talk ***AT*** *me, but no one is able to talk* ***TO*** *me. I'm doomed to be alone in a crowd for the rest of my life. I've never felt so lonely in my life. Lonely and tired.*

I lie down in my lumpy bed and pull the threadbare blanket up to my chin. Why do they keep it so damn cold in here, anyways? With the money they make, you'd think they could keep the joint comfortable. All these thoughts and more swirl around in my brain, and I can't seem to grab one idea and stick with it. I wonder how long I'll be here and where I'll go when I leave. The answers are too scary, so I try to stop thinking about it. I'm too worn out now. I can't deal with this now.

I feel myself drifting back into the warm, dark place, and I'm relieved. This place, whatever it is, has become my refuge. I think I'll stay here for now, just relax and float in this sublime nothingness, where nothing can touch me. Right here, where I belong.

Remlee

The next morning (okay, afternoon), Jack and I went back to visit Mama. Jack was a little surly after waking up next to the hellhound instead of me, but after some coffee and a little hair of the dog, he was more or less amiable. He spent the whole drive to the hospital, mock whimpering and complaining about his sore back, and I think he was just trying to distract me. I came close to breaking down the last time we had been at the hospital, and I'm sure he was keen to avoid more the same, or worse.

The visit went less smoothly without Jolene there to temper me a little. I lost my shit and probably said things I shouldn't have. It was just having her there, unable to twist what I'm saying, unable to straight-up lie to my face and deny what we both know happened, that made me snap. I only meant to say one little thing, but it felt like the floodgates opened, and I just couldn't stop. I have no idea if I hurt her or not. She always was a tough old bitch, but I really didn't mean to if I did. It was just that once I started, I couldn't find a way to stop until it all came out.

I'm not even sure she understood what I was saying anyways. The doctor told us that she's basically the same in there, that she hasn't lost her mind, just her words. Talking to her, I got the feeling that she was there, at least most of the time. She did have moments, however, where it seemed like she was almost in a trance. A couple of times when we were in there, I was talking to her, but I could tell she wasn't really hearing me. I'm not sure if she was even seeing me. Then she'd snap out of it and be present again.

After my little tantrum, we just sat, holding hands, until I couldn't stand to be in the room any longer. It felt like the room was closing in on me, but slowly, sneakily. It was like, out of the corner of my eye, I could see the walls were slowly inching in, stopping dead once I shifted my gaze onto them fully. I made some lame excuse, grabbed a still slightly drunk Jack, and all but ran out into the parking lot. I found my way to the Jeep and sat down, my ass resting on the curb in front of it. I felt the contents of my stomach began to rise, and I wondered hazily what could even still be in there other than beer and shine. This thought pushed me over the edge, and my curiosity was soon satisfied as I spilled the entire mess out of my mouth and all over the pavement in front of me. I spat and coughed maniacally for a few minutes, fighting hard to catch my breath. Jack had finally caught up to me, and he was instantly on his knees beside me, careful to avoid the stomach muck puddle that was spreading rapidly toward our car.

"Whoa, babe!" he said, startled. "What's… Oh, shit… Babe, are you okay? Do I need to take you back inside?"

"No, no," I said between gasps. "I'm fine now. I just need to breathe."

He sat down next to me and lit a cigarette, perfectly content to sit on the curb and smoke while I got myself together. After a few minutes, I stole his smoke and stood up. I waited for a second to make sure the vertigo and nausea had passed, then indicated I was ready. We got into the Jeep, him driving, me still holding his cigarette ransom. He tried to steal back, but I held it just out of his reach, outside the window.

"Come on, man, smoke your own," he complained halfheartedly.

"Nope," I said teasingly, "I stole it fair and square."

"You do realize that statement is inherently contradictory, right?" he asked, carrying the banter along.

"It's my prerogative as a woman," I replied with a coy laugh.

It was moments like these, where he injected whimsy into an otherwise stressful situation to short-circuit my fight or flight mechanism, that I truly appreciated the person that Jack was. He may have his flaws, but everything he does for me, even the subtle things—no, especially the subtle things—more than make up for trivial offenses like drinking a little too much, a little too often.

"So where are you taking me?" he asked, genuinely excited.

"I don't really know," I admitted. "I don't really have a plan. Everything so different now. I mean, I still recognize the place, but it's just, I don't know, different. Like an alternate universe Stillwater. I don't really know where to start."

He chewed on that for a moment, then his eyes lit up with delight as he said, "I've got it! Most everything on this chip has been kind of a bummer, right? But you've got to have at least a few good memories of this place. Is there somewhere around here it only has good memories attached to it?"

"Well," I said after a few minutes of reflection, "there is Ichetucknee Springs—"

"Ajax you what?" Jack interrupted, his voice taking on a cartoonish cast.

"Ichetucknee Springs," I repeated, ignoring his antics. "It's just down the road aways. It's definitely the most beautiful place in Florida, for my money."

"What is it?" Jack asked, his curiosity piqued.

"It's a natural spring. They also called the Ichetucknee River, but it's nothing like the Charles River back home. It's crystal clear, like swimming in a bathtub. Uncle Rawlie used to take us there at least three or four times a year. You could rent inner tubes at one end of the river and float down to the other where they'd have a bus to pick you up and bring you back," I said.

"Don't you have to worry about gators?" he asked warily. Jack wasn't particularly fond of animals that could eat him.

"No, actually," I said, proud of my scientific knowledge. "The water is too warm. They stay away, in cooler waters. It's probably the safest place to swim in all of Florida outside of a pool."

"It sounds wicked awesome," Jack said, his excitement growing. "We should go there."

"Yeah, we should," I agreed. "Turn left two lights up."

"What about our clothes and towels and stuff?" he asked, already knowing my answer.

"We'll pick something up along the way," I said, confirming his unspoken prediction. "We're bound to pass a Walmart or Dollar General along the way."

"No shit," he replied with a laugh. "I swear Dollar General is building a new store every eight hundred feet."

We drove along, him following my direction, and the idea of our impromptu day trip grew more and more important to my psyche. As the minutes and miles passed, it felt good to forget about the stress for a while. We talked of trivialities as we traveled, light subjects like the local architecture or flora and fauna that was unfamiliar to Jack. It struck me that Jack was seeing this for the first time. He had no emotional ties to the scenery; he could simply bask in the subtropical paradise that surrounded him. I felt a twinge of jealousy, then bit it back.

"I learned a lot last night," he said with a mischievous laugh. "Your cousin Mookie? The one with the cleft palate?"

"Yeah, that's Mookie. His real name is Nathan, but he's been Mookie since he was a toddler. Why? What did he teach you?" I asked, playing along.

"Did you know that there are three different methods for making crystal meth and a two-liter bottle?" he asked in mock seriousness. His bushy eyebrows arched high into his forehead, almost disappearing into his thick, wavy locks.

"No, I did not," I said with equally sarcastic enthusiasm.

"Oh yeah," Jack continued, enjoying himself fully now as he continued his report. "It seems young Mookie prefers the shake and bake method. Apparently, not only is the method faster, but the end product is far superior to boot."

"My family is full of such useful information," I said with a sigh.

"What did you learn?" he asked, trying to keep the game alive.

"You mean besides the fact that my brother is banging our cousin? Sorry, half-cousin?" I asked with more vitriol than I had intended.

"Well, yeah, besides that," Jack replied sheepishly, and I could tell he wished he could take his question back. I quickly tried to turn the conversation back to lighter (relatively) topics.

"Well," I began, sugaring my tone, "Uncle Jed and Uncle Clarence ain't seeing eye to eye right now. There appears to be a civil war brewing in the family right now."

"About what?" Jack asked.

"Uncle Clarence doesn't like the meth business. He'd rather stick to making moonshine. Uncle Jed thinks they should quit bothering with the shine altogether and focus solely on crystal. Clarence says crystal is too risky. The cops don't care so much about hooch, so as long as you don't make a nuisance of yourself. Meth's a whole different story. They don't look the other way for that shit," I said, summarizing what Clarence had told me the previous evening.

"Makes sense," Jack said. "Booze has always been more socially acceptable than other drugs."

"Yeah, I know, but you gotta understand Uncle Jed," I said, further explaining the situation at hand. "He's the youngest boy out of his siblings and also the smallest. He's always had a chip on his shoulder, even bigger than the chips his brothers had. He's also probably the craziest. Clarence will fuck you up, no doubt about it, but if he does, there's a logical reason behind it. He may opt for violence long before most people would, but his violence always, I don't know, makes sense, you know? Like, yeah, maybe he does go overboard, but you at least understand why he did whatever he did. It ain't like that with Jed. He'll be fine one minute, just sitting drinking in the bar with a buddy, and all of a sudden, for reasons nobody knows, probably not even Jed himself, he'll be beating his buddy within an inch of his life with a broken beer bottle over some innocuous comment."

"Geez," Jack breathed, awed by the visions I had created in his mind. He was quiet for a second as if deciding which questions to ask and in what order.

"So, erm…which side is…winning?" he asked, unsure how to word his inquiry.

"Nobody, really," I said. "About half agree with Clarence and half with Jed. There's more money in meth, more by a long shot, but also way more risk. I remember when I was a kid, the Sheriff would stop by and buy a pint or two of the shine. I can't see that happening with meth."

"Nothing surprises me anymore," Jack said sardonically.

"The old heads mostly agree with Clarence," I continued. "Uncle Earl Three is so against it, he threatened to turn them all into the law. It almost came to gunfire over that. Clarence got him to back off, but he's far from happy."

"What about your brothers and Jolene? Where do they stand?" he asked, enthralled by the sordid details.

"Shane's against it, but he doesn't have much to do with the family anyway. He's a roofer, so he's out of town most of the time. His, um, wife, Lindie's hooked on the shit, and they fight about it all the time. Elton's all for it, but Elton's a criminal, through and through. He and Daddy are just alike. Jolene…well, Jolene's complicated," I said with a sigh, suddenly tired.

"She's mostly against it, but I think that's mostly because she's not crazy about the buzz," I explained, noticing the puzzled look on Jack's face. "It's useful, you see? Even if she doesn't like it for herself, she can trade it for shit she does. My sister doesn't like to go fast, she's on a downer trip. Alcohol, opioids, benzos. Speed is a life drug and energy drug. It, I don't know, makes life somehow bigger, more."

"Yeah, like coke," Jack interjected dreamily.

"Exactly," I agreed. "Jolene doesn't want to feel life. She wants the opposite. She wants to forget. I don't blame her. I do too. And she's older, remembers more. She never got to escape to Granny and Peepaw's like I did. She never got to leave at all. I can't stand to see what she has become, so much like Mama, and I shudder to think that that could have been me, too, if I hadn't left."

Jack remained quiet, wisely giving me some space. I tried to push the thoughts away, to focus on the beauty of the countryside as we trundled along on our way to Fort White, the town that held the aquatic wonder we sought. I smiled as I let warm nostalgia work its way in, pushing out the cold truth of my family circumstances. I'd forgotten how lush my homeland was. I'd spent too long away in the cold urban wastes of the north, scores of miles from any substantial tracks of unspoiled nature. The forests of the north were different in other ways, as well. The number of animals that pose serious risks to humans in Massachusetts can be counted on one hand. That statistic for Florida would require both hands and feet of several people to accurately tally. An inexperienced buffoon could wander off into the wilderness in New England, and given that it wasn't winter, most likely wander out generally unharmed and within a day or two. That same buffoon would not be so lucky here in the sunshine state.

Before long, we began noticing signs indicating we had reached our destination. We parked hastily in the parking lot, careful to park in the shade of some lofty cypress. We hopped in the back and hastily changed into the water gear we had purchased at the Dollar General a few miles back. We quickly locked up the Jeep and ran, giggling like schoolchildren, to the rental kiosk where the inner tubes were stacked. I noticed, with almost matronly pride, that Jack was grinning goofily, his eyes dancing as they took in all the splendor that surrounded us. At Jack haggled with the intendant over pickup times at the end of the river, I closed my eyes and listened to the music of the seemingly thousands of birds that filled the air. The humid air was thick with the smell of flowers, and for a second, I understood how Eve must have felt upon awakening in Eden.

Having secured our conveyances for the afternoons lazy trip down the river, we made our way down the worn, gray boardwalk that led to the docks. Live oak and cypress lined the way, creating a canopy of green that seemed almost ethereal. We spotted several small deer flitting about in the scrub, and we saw raccoon tracks in the sandy soil running parallel with the boardwalk. It was almost impossible to believe, at least while you were here, that anything as vulgar as a city could exist in a world that contained beauty such as this.

"Oh. My. God," Jack said in amazement as we turned a corner and the Ichetucknee River came into view.

"Yes, indeed," I agreed in an awed voice.

We stood spellbound at the sight that lay in front of us. The river snaked by us at a turtle's pace, its water as clear as the air. We made our way to the docks and slipped into the gentle current, mesmerized by the living aquarium that passed slowly beneath us. Jack was a child again, excitedly pointing out each new fish we saw. Early in the journey, we came to a kind of fork, with a sign pointing the way to a place called Blue Hole. We took the slight detour and found ourselves in a deep pool, forty feet or more. I told Jack about how my cousins and brothers would have contests to see which one could dive the deepest. This idea excited Jack to no end, and before I could say anything, he disappeared over the side of his inner tube. In the clear water, I was able to monitor his progress easily. I laughed out loud when, about halfway to the bottom, he turned up to face me, and he gave me the "V" for victory salute that everyone now associates with Nixon. He kicked his way back to the surface, sputtering for breath as he pulled himself back into the safety of the inner tube.

"Man!" he said excitedly, "It doesn't look that far up from here, but from down there? You looked like you were miles above me. I almost panicked when I saw how far away you looked. I wasn't sure I'd make it back before I ran out of breath."

"I think you smoke too much to be deep-sea diving," I said teasingly.

"Yeah, no shit," he replied affably.

We paddled our way back to the river proper, but casually, in no hurry. Once we were back on course, we stopped talking and started listening to the sounds around us, feasting our eyes on the riot of color on the banks. I let my mind float as my body floated, unconcerned with anything other than soaking up as much of this paradise as I could store.

Too soon, the current had brought us to the end of our journey, and refreshed but sorry to leave, we trudged up the gangway and loaded our inner tubes onto the side of the waiting transport bus. We smiled and made small talk with the other people returning to their lives after their own magical interlude down the river. When we got back to the parking lot, we climbed back into the rear of the Jeep and put our dry clothes back on. We got back out, and I insisted on getting pictures at the sign near the entrance. Jack set the timer of the camera, but in his haste to get to me in time to mug for the camera, he tripped. The picture that resulted was mainly of Jack's ass as he tried to stand back up. I can be seen in the background, doubled over with laughter. I still use this shot as my screensaver to this day.

The ride back to Stillwater was a quiet one. I drove while Jack nursed a six-pack of Bud Light and took in all the scenery. He had always been a city boy, so are infrequent jaunts into the wild fascinated him. I was content to just drive with the windows down, the thick, humid air blowing my hair around my head like a cyclone. I had a somber edge creeping into my mood. Everything seemed bittersweet in the waning sunlight. Soon, we would be back at Jolene's, and the stress and dysfunction would begin anew. I fantasized for a good five minutes about turning around and heading back to the springs. It was just so beautiful, so peaceful. I wondered if I could convince Jack to camp there but decided he would probably not want to. He spent his last night sleeping on a picnic table, cuddled up with a hundred-pound ball of drool and fleas. He would want a bed tonight, or at least a couch. As much as I wanted to avoid it, our little sojourn would have to come to an end.

As we reached the outskirts of Stillwater, I called Jolene to get directions to the trailer she lived in with Gary. Within minutes, we were parked behind her old Cavalier, and I killed the engine. Jack popped out of his seat instantly, eager to stretch his legs and empty his bladder. He trotted up to the door and rapped a staccato rhythm on it, hopping awkwardly, side to side, in the universal pee-pee dance. I giggled to myself as I watched him, feeling lazy and unmotivated to exit the vehicle. Jolene came to the door, and I couldn't make out exactly what was said, but Jack disappeared inside in a flash.

"C'mon, girl," Jolene yelled, her hands on her hips as if scolding me. "Come have a drink with your big sister."

I made my way inside, and she stopped me at the door. She gathered me in a hug and made a noise that was either a sob or a chuckle. I couldn't tell which. I hugged her back stiffly, just wanting to sit down. The day's excursion had worn me out.

"I'm so glad you're home," she whispered into my hair.

I wasn't sure if I was, so I remained silent.

Betty Sue

I open my eyes, and I'm blinded by brilliant light. Overhead, the sky is crystal blue, and the clouds are giant pillows thrown haphazardly about. I can feel motion, and the limbs of trees blur past the edges of my vision. Whatever I'm lying on is hard and lumpy wherever I am was not designed with comfort in mind. I turn my head and see short metal walls surrounding me. I sit up in the bed of Daddy's truck and take in the view surrounding me. We're on the highway, heading to the fair. I remember now.

The fair is a yearly tradition in our family, an event I look forward to all year long. I love the sounds of the midway, the smell of sausage and onion sandwiches mingling with that of funnel cakes, the strange electricity in the air. This year, I'm showing the other occupant of the truck's bed, my giant pink pig, Horace. This is the last year I'll be showing. Daddy says we won't have the money to spare for a useless hog no more. He plans on selling him at the fair to the slaughterhouse, and I'm devastated. Horace is my friend, not a giant piece of bacon.

I put this all out of my mind when I see the top of the Ferris wheel come into view. The traffic is heavy, and I can hear Daddy cussing through the rear window. Mama Lettie's trying to calm him down, but as usual, she ain't having a whole lot of luck. I can hardly stay put as we inch closer to the parking lot. I hear the sound of a brass band playing while a barker announces times for the tractor pulls. There are people everywhere, more than I've ever seen in any one place at one time. Everybody is smiling and happy just to be alive.

After we park and get Horace registered and squared away, Mama Lettie gives me ten dollars and tells me to have a good time. I take off like hell was on my tail, bursting with excitement but unsure where to direct it. Should I ride first? Or eat? I decided to ride in case I get motion sick.

You can't puke what's not in your belly, or so goes my reasoning. Soon, I am whirling around in a sheet metal death box, screaming my lungs out in pure joy. I ride the Scrambler ten times in a row before the fun wears off a little, and I decide to move on.

I spend the next hour risking my neck on every hastily constructed contraption currently on offer. I feel a giddiness, a freeness from worry as I'm whipped around like a rag doll in Mama Lettie's new dryer, drunk on thrills, laughter, music, deep-fried sugar, and dare I say it, the stirrings of teenage hormones.

I most keenly notice the latter's effects while standing in line for the Tilt-a-Whirl with Janie McKinney from up the road apiece. We just sort of find each other in the line for caramel apples, and since neither of us knows anyone else, we team up as riding partners. We ain't exactly close friends, but we ain't enemies neither, and in a huge crowd like this, having a familiar face for a companion just feels safe. We giggle and gossip as the line inches forward, poking fun at blue-haired old ladies and clumsy toddlers. As we round the corner in the line, I see him.

I don't normally like boys all that much, on account of most of my experiences with them, having been bad. My brothers have always taken pride in how miserable they can make me. Except Bobby Lee, most of the time, anyways. He's over in the 'Nam now, and we ain't heard hide nor hair from him in a few weeks. This boy in front of me, however, something about him catches my eye today. He's handsome, but not remarkably so, not like a movie star or nothing. He's kind of tall, but not so much that he sticks out. It's his eyes and his smile I'm drawn to. He's talking to his buddy; it must be about something funny because they're both laughing. When he smiles, his eyes crinkle up so tight, they're barely open at all, and he just looks so kind. It's not that smoldering heartthrob smile, the one that hides a mean heart. His smile is full, touching every part of his face, no, his entire body. I can almost see the goodwill enjoy flowing off of him in waves.

"And then Kathy told me she was the one who kissed… Hey, Betty, are you listening to me?" Janie asks, flustered, and I realize I've been staring at this boy and not even hearing her. I try to cover.

"Yeah… Kathy kissed Terry Jackson," I sputter, my eyes still locked on the Earth Angel ahead of us in line.

"Nooooooo," Janie says, drawing it out to show her annoyance, "not Terry Jackson, Larry Jackson! Honestly, it's like you ain't listening to me at all. What are you staring at anyways?" She hops up and down, trying to see past the ogre in front of her, hoping to spot what could be more interesting than her incredible news about Larry Jackson.

"Oh, hey," she says, brightening. "It's my cousin Scooter up there. Hey! Scooter! Hey!"

She hops up and down, calling the Scooter character's name, and everyone's heads turn to see what the commotion is. I look ahead and see my angel is looking right at us, a grin of recognition spreading across his radiant face. He waves at us, and my heart does jumping jacks in my chest. I turn to face Janie, feeling the red rising to my cheeks.

"That's your cousin?" I ask, my voice sounding like it's coming from the other side of the county.

Oblivious to my flustered state, Janie replies simply, "Yes."

All throughout our wait, I'm unable to rip my gaze from Scooter. Janie continues to yap about this and that, but I'm hardly paying her any mind. She don't seem to notice, probably because she talks so much. I wouldn't have had a chance to say much anyways. I start dreaming up scenarios where this boy and I walk off into our Golden Sunset. For a moment, I feel silly, like a character in one of those trashy novels Mama Lettie reads while Daddy watches the Braves, but I'm still young enough to believe all that "true love" bullshit, so the moment passes.

Our turn finally arrives, and we strap into the clamshell-looking cars. I scan the crowd, searching for the dreamboat that is Janie's cousin. As the ride starts, I have a moment of panic, worried I won't be able to find him after this human spin cycle spits us back out onto solid ground. I don't even enjoy the ride, and when the attendant unlocks our safety bar, I all but sprint down the gangway, leaving a blustering Janie in my wake.

"Hey, wait!" I hear her yell, but I ignore her, pushing my way out of the ride enclosure and rushing out to the midway, almost frantically searching for Scooter. I stand amid the pulsating throng, my head swiveling like an owl as Janie comes pounding up to me.

"What's with you?" she asks, standing more worried than angry.

"Nothing... I...I...was just looking..." I stammer, unable to come up with a believable lie on the spot.

"Well, whatever," she says, rolling her eyes. "Look, there Scooter over there, by the Skee-Ball. Let's go see what he's up to."

My heart races as she grabs my arm and half drags me across the midway to the row of carnival games. I'm almost panicking, I just wanted to watch him, not talk to him. I don't even know what to say to a boy. My mind quickly plays movies in my head of embarrassing myself in front of him in a thousand different ways. As we arrive at the Skee-Ball he is currently lobbing balls at, I notice my skin is clammy from a cold sweat. I cursed myself for being such a ninny.

"Hey, cuz," the angel named Scooter says, slapping her five in an elaborate ritual that must have taken days to choreograph. I stand there awkwardly, not sure where to look or put my hands. I decide on flat to my sides, stiff like one of them guards they got in England.

"Who's your friend?" he asked, turning his gaze to me. It's like having the sun shine directly on you, and only you. I feel my blush grow deeper.

"Oh, this is Betty Sue Tucker, from down the road apiece. Remember that old tractor daddy sold last fall? Her folks is the ones who bought it," she says nonchalantly.

Taking my hand and smiling, he says, "Well, Betty Sue Tucker, it is a pleasure to meet you. My name is—"

"Scooter," I interrupt, and I gasp in embarrassment.

"Well, yes, it is, as a matter of fact," he says with a cheerful laugh. His eyes never leave mine, and his hand gently grips my hand in his. I feel a heartbeat in my palm, I and I wonder if it's his or mine.

"And this," he says, motioning to his buddy, "is my partner in crime, Mr. Lance Underwood. How would you two like to join us on the Ferris wheel? It's awful big, and we sure could use someone to protect us." He laughs again and winks at me. My knees turn to jelly for a second, and I hear my voice speak up.

"Yes, we absolutely would," it says, and I wonder who used my voice to say that. Betty Sue Tucker would never be so bold, would she? Janie catches my eye and gives me a mischievous grin, clearly as smitten with Mr. Lance Underwood as I am with her cousin. We fall into step,

casually weaving our way through the gathered masses. Scooter is all talk, regaling me with tales of fishing expeditions and hot rods, nearly steamrolling me with his overwhelming energy. I just watch him talk, only half hearing the words, just basking in the rollicking rhythms in gentle tones. This boy is so unlike my brothers, seemingly uninterested in the casual sadism that is the hallmark of so many of their hobbies. It strikes me that scooter probably ain't ever seen the inside of a police car or even had the thought to occur to him to do anything that could land him in one. I'm not sure what to make of him.

We wait in line for the Ferris wheel, him talking, me sort of listening. I'm almost overwhelmed, my senses working overtime. Time seems to have slowed, and all the little details stand out. The sun is brighter, the air fresher. The Pepsi we share while we wait is a little bit crisper. His elbow brushes mine, and goosebumps march out in lines from the point of contact. Every nerve is on high alert. I am fully alive, fully present, here with this boy I have just met, and I have no problems. My family don't matter. Being poor don't matter. Here, in this moment, nothing else but the two of us matter.

When it's our turn, he gets in first, and I squeeze in next to join him. The gondola is so small that we're jammed in close together, but I don't mind, and he doesn't seem to either. Janie flashes me a "V" for victory sign as the ride takes us up into the sky. I hear her giggling from below, her voice rising above the general din. Scooter laughs gently and shakes his head.

"That cousin of mine has the biggest voice in three counties," he says with obvious pride. "You could hear her from a mile away during a hurricane."

I nod in agreement, inwardly cursing my sudden inability to say more than three words at a time. What AM I so scared of?

"You don't talk much," he points out as our car stops at the top of the wheel, the whole of northern Florida spread out in front of us.

"That's not what my stepmom would tell you," I say quietly, almost to myself. He looks at me, all solemn for a moment, then he burst out laughing.

"I don't believe it!" he says. "You ain't said but ten words this whole time."

"That's 'cause you ain't shut your yap since we met," I say, more sharply than I mean to. He looked stunned for a minute, like he can't reconcile my words with the facade delivering them. He starts laughing again, his cheeks getting redder by the second.

"Okay, okay, you got me," he says, clutching his heart like he had been shot by invisible arrows. He play-acts an elaborate death scene as the wheel brings us back to earth.

"I do talk a lot, I know," he admits as we step off the ride.

"That's okay," I say with a shy smile. "I like to listen to you."

He favors me with his heavenly smile, and my heart beats faster as I feel him take my hand is in his. It's longer than mine, but not the rough, calloused hands of the men I'm used to. His long, slender fingers are graceful, fine instruments, not the crude bludgeons my brothers and father are equipped with. While not baby soft, these hands haven't seen that many hours of hard work. These hands belong to a boy who has it much easier in life than I do. I feel a twinge of jealousy, but it quickly passes.

We spend the next hour or so strolling hand in hand through the animal exhibits. He makes up funny stories about the cows and the goats, and, at times, my sides hurt from laughing. I've never met a boy so free from worry, and I try to picture his house. I bet it's beautiful.

As evening closes in, I have him wait by the dunking booth while I go to the bingo tent to check in with my folks. When I find them, Daddy is hammered, and Mama Lettie is knee-deep in bingo cards, her eyes scanning them feverishly as the caller calls out the numbers.

"Yes, go on, git," she says, her eyes never leaving the table in front of her. "Just make sure you're at the truck by ten." My freedom secured for the rest of the evening, I scurry back to Scooter, who, happily, is still waiting for me, a giant stuffed bunny in his hands.

"I won this for you while you was gone," he says with uncharacteristic shyness and presents it to me like an offering.

"Oh, I love him!" I say breathlessly. Nobody has ever given me something before. At least nobody who ain't kin, and never just for the hell of it.

"Where do you going at call him?" he asks, taking my arm and leading me toward the back side of the fairgrounds.

"I don't know," I say. "How about Bingo?"

"Bingo Bunny? That works for me," he says, and at that moment I know, I just know I'm going to kiss him. Electric sparks shoot up and down my spine in anticipation. I can see he knows it too, and we make our way to the parking lot in silence, each nervous but not wanting the other to see. The lights start to get dimmer, the voices of the crowd quieter as we get to the field that is used as a makeshift parking lot. There are far less people around. Most everyone is either heading to or already at the grandstand, waiting for the evening's band to start their show. He seems to be looking for something specific, his head swivels around looking down the rows.

"There it is," he says excitedly and breaks into a run.

"There what is?" I ask his fleeing form, then realize he's not stopping. I take off after him, determined not to let him get away. He stops short at a newer model Ford, eyeing it lovingly.

"This is my Old Man's," he says with obvious pride as he clambers up into the bed. He reaches down and helps me in with him, and we sit down next to each other, resting our backs against the rear window.

"I like you," I say suddenly, surprising myself as much as the boy I'm saying it too. His eyes go wide, and he stammers, trying in vain to respond. I lean in and kiss him before he can say anything, and everything stops. The band is silent, the birds stop singing, and the earth stops spinning. His eyes are wide open, and he stiffens for a moment, caught off guard by my sudden move. I can see forever in them, and I bliss out, my senses completely overtaken with him.

"Well," he breathes as I pull away, my eyes downcast. I can't bear to look at him right now. I'll melt if I do. He reaches over and gently cups my chin, and I'm forced to look at him. I start to swoon as his lips lock firmly back on to mine, and I lose myself in his arms.

We neck for what seems like an eternity, our hands exploring each other hungrily. I feel a strange heat take hold of me, an urgent need I don't know exactly how to fill. I clutch at him, pulling him as close as I can. I want to merge with him. My skin is on fire. My heart races as I feel his hand over top of it, under my shirt. I gasp for breath as his lips move greedily to my neck, seemingly consuming me. I close my eyes and lay my head back, and a bright light glares suddenly into my face. My eyes open on their own accord, but I can't see anything. The light is drowning everything out.

"What the hell is going on here?" a voice behind the light thunders, and Scooter's hands vanish from my chest and behind.

"Mom!" Scooter shrieks, his voice suddenly two octaves higher. "We wasn't doing noth—"

"I know what you was doing," the voice interrupts. The light lowers from my face, and I can see Scooter's mom now. She don't look too happy to see me.

"And just who are you, young lady?" she asks with naked contempt. "What are you doing with your hands all over my boy?"

I can't say anything. I just stare at her. I feel like a deer in headlights, frozen in her furious gaze.

"This is Betty Sue, Mama," Scooter says sheepishly. "She's Janie's neighbor."

Scooter's mom looks closely at me, studying me like I'm some kind of strange bug. A signal goes off in her eyes, and the fire in her eyes burns brighter.

"I know who you are," she spits at me, her son forgotten for the moment. "You're one of those Tucker brats. You keep your filthy mitts off my boy. You ain't dragging my boy down into the muck with you. I know all about you and your kin. You're all lowlife trash and probably inbred to boot."

She whirls on scooter, her voice full of icy venom.

"I'll not have you soil yourself with trash like this," she says to Scooter, but he doesn't look at her. He just stares at his feet, looking like a beat dog. She reaches in and grabs his ear, pulling it to its limit. He crawls up behind her and stands there, not looking at either of us.

"I don't ever want to see you near my boy again, you hear?" she says, thrusting her bony finger at me. "Now, get out of here before I sic the law on you."

I climb out of the truck as fast as I can and run back inside the fair, not daring to look back. I'm crying so hard; I can hardly see where I'm going. I bump into several people as I rush back to the other parking lot where our truck is. I climb inside and lock the door. My whole body shakes with sobs as I wail to myself.

What did I ever do to that woman? What's so wrong with me that I'm not good enough for her son? She ain't no better than me. Is this what my life is always going to be like? Will I be good enough for anyone?

These thoughts turn over and over in my mind as I slowly wind my crying down to light whimpering. I feel so tired all of a sudden, like I cried all my energy out along with my tears. I lie down and close my eyes, trying to shut this horrible night out of my head. When I grow up, I'm going to leave here. I'm going to go where nobody has ever even heard of a Tucker. I'm...gonna...be somebody.

Remlee

"Y'all want a Budweiser?" Jolene asked as I sat down on the over-stuffed couch, mindful to avoid the cat who was nested comfortably in the middle. It eyed me warily, as if it was unsure if I was going to encroach on its territory in the sunbeam. After an intense moment of scrutiny, I apparently passed its test because it promptly laid its head down and fell back into its afternoon coma.

"Not really," I answered. "Do you have any sweet tea?"

"So sweet, the straw stands up by itself," Jolene said with a grin. She set about pouring me a glass, then brought it over to me and sat down beside me. I drank deeply. The day's events had really worn me out.

"Oh, thank God," I gasped, the glass all but drained. "Jack is such a Yankee. He won't let me put the sugar in when it's still boiling. He hates sugar in his iced tea, he says I can always add it, but he can't take it out once it's in there."

"But it don't mix right if you don't put it in while it's hot," Jolene said, an incredulous tone coloring her voice.

"I know, I know," I said, echoing her bewilderment. "I've told him that over and over, but he doesn't care. I told him to make his own separate, so I can have mine done right. Sometimes he does, but usually, he doesn't." I sipped the last remnants of the glass, savoring its nectar.

"It's been too long since I've had a proper glass of sweet tea," I said, mostly to myself. I got up to pour another glass, and Jack sauntered in from the bathroom. He followed me into the kitchen, his radar locked onto the refrigerator and the fermented barley and hops that were ensconced inside. I handed him a bottle, and he wandered to the door.

"I think I'm going to take a walk up the road a bit, stretch my legs a bit," he said.

"Just watch out for snakes and don't take any rides from strangers, you hear?" Jolene replied with a wink in my direction. I can tell she was as relieved as I was that he was removing himself from the room. She obviously had something she wanted to say, in private, and Jack, to his credit, caught the vibe immediately.

"Scout's honor!" he said, snapping us a sloppy salute before gliding out the door and into the thick evening air. I watched him walk away, beer in one hand, smoke in the other, and I smiled, knowing he'd return an hour or so later, practically bouncing up and down with excitement about something or another that he had discovered. That was one of the things that drew me to him, his childlike exuberance. Everything was an adventure to him, from mountain climbing to walking to the 7-Eleven for some smokes. He always found something he thought interesting, and he had a knack for transferring that energy directly to me. His runaway id, while admittedly a source of occasional trouble, was the consistent sunny spot in an otherwise often dismal world.

"It's awfully quiet around here," I said after a while. "Where is everybody?"

"Gary's over next door at his mom's trailer, fussing with some fool thing or another," she answered, her tone full of distaste. "He's over there every night after work, basically waiting on her hand and foot." She lit a cigarette and seemed to think deeply for a minute, her eyes far away, looking at answers visible only to her.

"I mean, it's good to care for your Mama and all," she finally said, her story now straight in her mind, "but goddamn, there comes a point where it's just ridiculous. That man ain't touched me in over a year. A year." She stamped her foot weakly to emphasize her point.

"I ain't in this relationship to be alone," she said, and I could see the honest pain in her eyes. I reached out and patted her hand awkwardly, not sure how to comfort her. It had always been her job to comfort me. She was the big sister. She looked up at me, her eyes bleary with tears, and smiled weakly. I returned it, hoping the discomfort I felt wasn't reflected in my eyes.

"I just don't know what I'm going to do," she said, "Mama can't take care of herself. You saw that."

"Move here in the here then," I replied as if it could possibly ever be that easy.

"Gary won't have it. I already asked after that first night when I saw her in the hospital," she said.

Incredulous, my voice cracked as I asked, "What you mean he won't have it?"

"He just flat out said no," she answered, a shadow crossing her face. "He said, 'We just don't have no time,' and blew me off. I asked him how come it was okay to look after his Mama but not mine, but he just said, 'That's different,' and wouldn't talk no more about it. I tried to raise a fuss, but he just went over next door to his mom's like the little fuckin' baby he is."

"Well," I said, trying to reason this out, "why don't you move in with her?"

"Oh God no!" she answered, horrified. "I could never… No… That would not ever work—"

"Why not?" I interrupted. "What's the difference between this trailer and her trailer?"

"That HER trailer, that's what," Jolene said, a solemn look on her face, like a child caught being naughty. "HER rules. HER name on the lease. I ain't givin' that woman home field advantage. She'd be difficult enough here, where she ain't got no say."

"But she can't talk… How much trouble can she really give you?" I asked, knowing full well what the answer would be.

"Have you met Mama?" she asked back, snorting with derisive laughter. "Plenty, that's how much, and you damn well know it."

We sat in awkward silence for a few minutes. I had a dawning suspicion that I knew where this conversation was headed, and I felt butterflies of panic fluttering in my guts. She was going to ask me to stay, there was no doubt about it, and I could think of nothing to forestall this inevitable calamity.

"So," she began coyly, "how are you and Jack liking it down here? Did y'all have fun at the springs?" Clever.

"Oh yeah," I said, playing along, "it was great."

"Y'all ain't got nothing that pretty in Massachusetts, I bet," she said, pressing further.

"Well, no, not so much," I admitted. "At least not the same kind of pretty, anyways."

I refused to go on, hoping my terseness would shake her, cause her to quit now. I was trying, I guess, to give her an escape from the upcoming disappointment she was bound to feel. If I could just prevent her from asking the question, then I wouldn't have to tell her no. Unfortunately, before I could come up with a new destination to steer this conversation toward, Jolene destroyed my hastily laid plan.

"You two should move down here," she said abruptly.

"No," I replied with equal sharpness.

"Aren't you even going to consider it?" she asked. "Just no?"

"I can't, Jolene," I said. "I've got responsibilities—"

"Yeah, I know all about your responsibilities," she seethed.

"No, I don't think you really do, or you wouldn't even ask. How could you?" I asked, my voice raw with the bile of rage.

"How could I what?" she asked, her voice rising along with her body as she stood up. Her eyes were wide, and I noticed her nostrils flaring as she huffed and puffed. I stifled a laugh when I thought that this woman had once intimidated me back when I was young. The years of self-abuse had whittled her down to a manageable size. The Valkyrie from my youth had desiccated into this gaunt, pale waif in front of me. My courage soared as I realized our relative power levels had switched, making me the more formidable entity.

"How could you understand responsibility?" I shot back, my disgust revealed in every nuance of my tone and expression. "When have you ever been the least bit responsible?"

"When I was making sure your ungrateful ass didn't starve," she said icily. "Who do you think made sure you had dinner? Or got the bills paid? Shane? Elton? Yeah, fuckin' right. It was me. If it wasn't for me, you'd have starved. You ought to show me some fucking appreciation." She began stalking around the room as she said this, gesticulating wildly to emphasize her points. I remained rooted my seat, afraid that if I moved, I might just attack her. All those years of resentment of my less than idyllic life threatened to boil over at that moment.

"It's not as simple as you make it seem," I said through clenched teeth. "I own a restaurant. I can't just "call off." I'm lucky I got the time away that I did. I got good people, don't get me wrong. Kelly and Tommy had been handling my shit for me well enough so far, but I have to go back. It's the same for Jack. He can get some time because he's tight with his boss, but he can't be gone indefinitely."

"Then let him go," Jolene said stubbornly. "Run your little restaurant from your phone. This is the future now. You don't need to be up there to take care of stuff now. That's what the internet is for."

Growling with frustration, I shouted, "It's not that easy!"

"Sure, it is," Jolene said with absurd confidence. "You don't cook no more anyways, right?"

"Well, not that much," I stammered.

"You don't wait tables, neither, right?" she pressed.

"Well, sometimes, if someone calls off," I answered meekly, my resolve wavering momentarily.

"I'm not asking you to stay forever," she said, her eyes pleading as they held mine, "just until we get Mama settled somewhere, get her out of the hospital and squared away, you now?"

"But what about Jack?" I asked, playing my trump card, my unimpeachable excuse.

"What about him? He's a grown man. Are you telling me he can't fend for himself for a couple of weeks while you care for your mother?" she asked incredulously, clearly not buying my ruse. "Or maybe you can't make it without him."

Ouch. That was close. I thought for a second before I answered. Did I rely too much on Jack? It's true; since we first began to date, I had spent very little time away from him. It never felt clingy, though, just that with him was where I was supposed to be. Just like salt goes with pepper, Simon with Garfunkel, Clintons with corruption.

"That's not the point," I started but was unable to finish.

"You're right," Jolene said. "The point is that your mother and sister need your help. No need to make it more complicated than that."

"But it is more complicated than that, and you fucking know it," I snapped. "She was never there for—"

"She wasn't there for any of us," Jolene cut in, her emaciated body shaking with emotion.

"It wasn't just you, you know. When Jesco died, years before you were even born, that was bad. You act like it was so bad for you, and maybe it was, but you didn't have to pick her up off the ground like I did. At six fucking years old, my twin brother smashed across the highway, and I gotta pick her up off the ground. Nobody ever picked me up. You had me, at least. I might have fucked up a lot, but you had me, and I tried. I had nobody. Just two older brothers who were damn near feral anyways." She sat down on the chair opposite me with a defeated sigh and stared at the floor while her words bounced around the inside of my head.

"Jack would never agree to it," I said desperately.

"I thought you were a modern woman. You don't let no man tell you what to do," she said with a sneer.

"I just don't think I can," I said. She wasn't buying what I was selling.

"You can," she said, her eyes boring deep into mine, "but you won't. There's a difference. You're just going to run away again and leave us all behind."

"Run away? Is that what you think happened?" I asked, my voice rising once again. "I ran from CPS, not you guys. I was only in CPS' hands because none of you had your shit together enough to take me. Quit acting the martyr, you were no saint. You were strung out then, and you are strung out now."

Jolene's eyes narrowed in fury. "That has nothing to do with this," she hissed.

"Oh no?" I asked mockingly. "So it's not the drugs' fault that you can't care for one single old lady? There's some other reason why you can't handle a senior citizen?"

"Fuck you, that's not what I said," Jolene said in response.

"Then why? Tell me, Jolene, why can't you do this? Why do I have to put my life on hold to help you? You wanted me to come down, and I came. I saw the old bitch, I saw everyone else, and I just want to go home—"

"This is your home, Remlee," Jolene interrupted. "Can't you see that? Your blood is here."

"My blood? What does that even mean? I'm supposed to feel some kind of loyalty to this place, these people, simply due to an accident of birth? I didn't choose this family. I endured it," I said. I felt myself shiver a little as this previously unspoken sentiment crossed my lips.

"Nobody chooses their family. Do you think I would have chosen these fucking dipshits if I had the choice? But I stayed. I could have left too, but I toughed it out. Because I'm a Shaw. And a Tucker. Double damned and I ain't sorry. I stayed, Remlee, to be with my family, like people are supposed to," Jolene said, her face a mask of steely determination.

"You stayed because you had to," I said, my cruel streak breaking loose. "All those kids of yours worked like an anchor. Don't get all sanctimonious. You stayed because you had no way to leave, not with all those kids."

"My kids are the best part of my life," she countered. "You wouldn't understand, you don't have any."

"Goddamn right, I don't!" I roared. "I'd never bring another person into this rotten world, this shitty family. I'm not so selfish as to bring that on another person just because I was too lazy to get some fucking birth control."

"No," Jolene replied sadly, "you don't have kids because you're too scared."

"Scared? Of what?" I scoffed.

"Scared you'll be like Mama," she said, her eyes locked intently on my face.

"That's... That's... No... That isn't why," I sputtered. Her statement had rocked me because deep down, I knew that she was at least partially right.

"I couldn't stay forever," I said, lowering my gaze to the floor.

"No shit. I ain't asking you to," Jolene said.

"I'll have to work it out with Jack and my staff and so on," I continued, not listening to her. "Where would I even stay?"

"You can crash here some nights, Gary won't mind too much, and you can always stay at the farm," she said, a grin of hopefulness spreading across her wan face.

"Yeah, I'll pass on the farm," I said with a chuckle. "I don't need to get swept up in that drama too."

"You don't have to stay there," Jolene said quickly, keen to say whatever she felt was necessary to placate me. "We can figure it all out. There is a shit-ton of us, I'm sure there will always be an open bed somewhere."

We sat quietly for a few minutes, me considering, her silently praying. I knew Jack would be against the proposition, would fight in cajole me to leave, but I also know that ultimately, it would be up to me. Jack wouldn't forbid me. That wasn't how our relationship worked. He'd be upset, furious even, but he wouldn't try to stop me from doing whatever it was I had decided to do.

"I'll talk to Jack," I finally said, my voice barely above a whisper.

Jolene rushed over to me and entangled me in an awkward bear hug. I could feel her trembling, her body wracked by sobs of relief. The role reversal, me comforting and taking care of Jolene, me being the one in charge, made my head spin for a moment as the absurdity of it all struck home.

"Thank you, Rem," she said quietly as her weeping abated. "You're saving my life."

I just held her, unsure of what to say. Conflicting emotions battled for supremacy as I considered my situation. I was not happy. It was the last thing I ever wanted to do. I fought off waves of panic as I came to the realization that Stillwater was already working its black magic on me, conspiring to trap me in its bosom forever. I had escaped at once, and it didn't mean to let that happen again.

Betty Sue

The warm dark goes on forever and ever. I lie here, floating, hearing nothing, seeing nothing. Just being. No past, no future. Just this indeterminant now where time as a concept does not exist. It's not existence. I have no thoughts to speak of, no memories to ruminate on. This is peace.

Thoughts occasionally sneak their way in, but I can ignore them. The worries of the world are like gnats, always flitting about the edges of consciousness but easily swatted away. There's no pain, physical or mental, as long as I let my mind remain still, so as to hide from the invading thoughts.

Sometimes, I feel a tugging, like I'm being drawn either up into the world or down into the dreamscape. I fight these tugs, trying to entrench myself into this pocket of nothing between dreams and life. But is there a difference between dreams and life? Can you dream if you aren't alive? Is this pocket I'm in just like Death's vestibule, where you shed your clothes (body) before entering the house proper? The thought makes me shiver.

Fuck. That shiver has dislodged me, and I'm falling down, down, down into the dreamscape again. This is worse than waking life, at least so far. These dreams (memories) are never pleasant, but then again, neither is my life, for the most part. I won't lie and say that there weren't some moments of indescribable joy, but not many. It was mostly a series of indignities of various magnitudes, over and over, with no break in between. I ain't so dishonest as they claim that the majority of my misery was other people's doing, I know that I'm a fuck-up, but goddammit, it just seems like whenever an issue concerning luck arises, I always come out on the losing end.

I feel a seat appear underneath me, and I can suddenly hear the rumbling of a motor. I opened my eyes to find myself in my old duster. I recognize the dream catcher hanging from the rearview as my own, and

I'm able to guess roughly when I am. I'm sitting in the driveway at the farm, and I see my Daddy, striding tall out of the fields, walking toward me with a sad but resolved look on his face. He stops to wipe the sweat out of his eyes, and he stretches. He so big, he seems to block out the sun. I feel myself getting out of the car, that movie-like feeling back, and I seem to float up to him.

"You can't have her," my father, the infamous Earl Tucker Junior, says to me, skipping any pretense of civility and getting right to the meat of the matter.

"You can't keep her for me," I say, planting my feet and jamming my fists into my sides, like I am bracing for a particularly violent gust of wind.

"I can, and I will," he says, unimpressed by my protestations.

"She's my daughter, she belongs with me," I say, appealing to his sense of familial hierarchy. He doesn't buy that either.

"It's true, she may be your daughter," he replies, his stern voice never rising in tone or volume, "but she don't belong with you. You're no good for her. Period. Where are you gonna stay, in some trucker's sleeper cab?"

"I got me a place now," I say, aware of the desperate keening in my voice. "It's a trailer, two-bedroom. It's real nice, and Rem could have her own room, and—"

"She has her own room here," my father interrupts, but I continue talking over him.

"I really got it together this time, Dad," I say, knowing he's heard this exact speech nearly a dozen times now. "I'm done with Roscoe, he's gone, he's out of the picture. For good. It'll just be me and her."

"She don't wanna go with you, Betty Sue. That's the plain truth," he says, his eyes showing sympathy for the first time.

"I don't believe you," I say, but I do. I just refuse to admit it.

"Believe me or not," he says with a shrug, "makes no matter to me. But it's true. She's happy here. She's got her routine, now, and friends. A girl needs that. You know this, Betty Sue, you ain't stupid."

"But this time is different," I say, clutching at straws.

"So was the last. And the one before that. And the one before that. We've all heard this before. Fool me once," he says, letting the rest of his pet saying unsaid.

I begin to feel panicky; I can tell he means it. He truly means to keep Remlee from me, and I don't know if I can stop him.

"I'll call the law," I say, throwing my Hail Mary pass.

"You could do that. Yep," he says, a glint of humor in his eyes. "I wouldn't if I were you, though. I plum forgot to tell you, see, but your probation officer came round here looking for you, oh, last week sometime, I reckon." He rocks back on his heels, his thumbs hooked into the loops of his overalls, clearly enjoying himself.

"Seems you're behind on your fines, and you ain't staying where you told him you were," he continued, his voice serious now. "I don't think you want the law here any more than I do. If the law comes, you won't be leaving with Remlee, you'll be leaving in cuffs. So no, I don't think you will be calling the law at all."

All the air is sucked out of me as I realized the trap I'm in. He's got me. He's won. My lip trembles, but I refuse to cry. I won't give him the satisfaction. He won this battle, sure, but I ain't quitting this fight.

"Can I at least see her?" I ask, my voice small and weak, signaling to daddy that he has won, that I won't fight him no more, at least not today. His gaze softens, and he touches me gently on my shoulder.

"I suppose a few minutes won't hurt nothing," he says gently. He turns to lead me out back to wherever my daughter is currently playing but then stops. He hesitates for a full minute, not making a sound. He turns back to me, and I can see his eyes are moist.

"I still love you, little Betty," he says, his usually stony countenance softened by a tentative smile. "I know you done your best, but—"

"Don't, Daddy," I say, unable to hear his mea culpa. "Just don't. Just take me to my girl so I can see her again for a bit." He nods and strides away quickly. I stumble after him, hardly able to keep up. He leaves me behind the house, then points at the picnic table under the tree, grunting.

"Wait here," he says, then disappears into the cane. I wonder where he's going and I'm able to mark his progress by the bending stocks. Minutes later, the green sea parts, spitting out my Remlee an annoyed scowl on her precious little face.

"Hi, Mama," she says, pretending to be fascinated by her shoe.

My father emerges from the cane as well and gives me a sharp look. Don't rile her up or give her false hope, it says. I decide to heed its warning.

"Hi, my baby doll!" I say, trying to keep my voice and the mood light. "What are you doing today?"

"Nothing," she replies, still refusing to look me in the face. She's squirming a little, like she has to pee.

"Mama just wanted to stop and see her baby," I say tentatively. I have no idea what to say to this child, I realize. The awkwardness grows in the silence that follows until I can't take it any longer. "I miss you, you know," I say, taking her hand in mind. She finally looks up at me, and the hatred in her eyes takes my breath away.

"No, you don't," she says matter-of-factly. She raises her chin in defiance at me, this little miniature me, and I stifle a gasp. Her sudden fury catches me off guard, and I stutter a rejoinder but am unable to string together a coherent rebuttal.

Like a predator sensing wounded prey, she closes in for the kill. Her little body quivers as she draws herself up to her full four-foot seven-inch glory, wagging her finger in my face.

"Don't lie, Mama!" she says. "Don't you fucking lie! You do not miss me. If you did, you'd be here."

"It's not that simple," I implore, unconsciously backing away from her.

"Yes, it is, Mama," she says, holding her ground. "You could be with me if you wanted to. You just don't want to, you never did."

"You don't know what you're talking about," I say, my guilt and fear turning slowly to indignation. "You was just a kid, you just don't understand."

Fresh sparks of rage fly from her eyes as she interrupts me, "I understand that you weren't there then, and you ain't here now."

"But I am here," I say, looking to my father for help. He looks away, unwilling to step in to rescue me from my deserved tongue lashing.

"Yeah, and you're leaving again, right?" she asked, her hands on her hips in an uncomfortably accurate parody of me scolding my kids. I look again to Daddy, and again he leaves me to my fate.

"Well, yes," I admit sheepishly, "but I got me a place in town now. I can come see you every day if you want."

"Don't bother," she says, and the chill in her voice draws gooseflesh down my arms. I stare after her, dumbfounded, as she stalks back off into

the cane, never looking back. A single sob escapes my lips, and I see a tear slip from my Daddy's eye too.

"Just let her be," he says gently. "She'll come around someday. She can't hate you forever."

"She most certainly can," I say with a rueful laugh. "And I reckon she will. Lord knows I've given her ample reason to."

Daddy starts to say something, but then he shakes his head and stops. He looks at me hard, studying my face. He shakes his head again and starts to walk away.

"What?" I asked. "What is it?"

"Oh, nothing," he says, a faraway look in his eye. "It's just she looks so goddamned much like you."

He turns and wanders off, leaving me shell-shocked and alone, sitting at the picnic table. I sit there for a long time, watching the cane sway in the afternoon breeze. I began to get drowsy, so I lay my head down on the table and close my eyes.

Instantly, the dark takes me, and the only sensation I feel is relief. I'm back to my comfortable oblivion, and the heartbreak has faded to dim memory, soon to be forgotten once more. Time goes on, or it doesn't. I don't care. That's what's so freeing about all of this. I don't care. It feels good to say that and truly be able to mean it. Back in the world, everything and everyone is real. It may not seem like it by my actions, but back in the world, I cared. I cared about my kids, my friends, my family. The catch is that caring isn't enough. There are other characteristics, other skills besides caring that someone needs to be able to be of use to anyone, and I don't have many of those. Something, I don't know what, seems to have been left out when they built me. If I knew what that something was, I might be able to learn it or get it somehow, but I don't. Back in the world, I'm a broken thing, but here I'm nothing. I'm not sure which is better, but I do know that this void sure is easier.

That just figures, though. Daddy always said I take the easy way out, every time. Looking back on it all, I know he was right. I make excuses, put the blame anywhere I think I can make it stick, but deep down, I know that I am my own worst enemy. It seems no matter the situation, no matter what sage advice I'm given, I always choose the option that requires the least amount of effort on my part. I'm not proud of this, quite the opposite, but there's no use in denying it. Even though I know I will suffer as a direct result of my inaction, I just can't motivate myself to do what I need to do. It's almost like there's a secret side to me, one that not even I know about that's intent on destroying me. Over and over, the pattern appears. Betty Sue avoids something unpleasant, reaps the reward of something worse. Why can't I seem to learn from my mistakes? Am I doomed to keep fucking up again and again till I die?

Look at Remlee. I didn't see her for two decades because I couldn't get my shit together enough to care for her. I'm so ashamed. Mothering is supposed to be the most natural thing in the world, but I can't do it. Everywhere you look, you see families, smiling and happy. The children are clean and fed, and you can see in their faces that they know someone cares for them. My kids never looked that way. They were always in threadbare clothes, handed down so many times, the original purchaser long forgotten. They had a gone, haunted look to them, like refugees from some war-torn nation. I suppose, in a way, that's exactly what they were. They were refugees from the war between myself and the world, and it shames me to no end to know that their misery was mostly, if not entirely, my fault.

But was it? It's not like I came from the land of milk and honey. I knew the strap from nearly the beginning. My first whipping burned into my memory as deeply as my father's face. We was always poor, always wanting, and not just for material things. A person only has so much to give, and when you got to split it between a half dozen needy children, the share each one gets is meager. All I know, until Elmer took me away, was toil, teasing bordering on torture, and the distinct feeling that I just wasn't enough to really bother paying attention to. I guess that's how my uncle got his slimy mitts on me. Nobody was really paying all that much attention. What bothers me most, though, is the possibility that my problems didn't go unnoticed; it's just that no one cared enough to stop it.

I wonder how God decides who is born into which family. Does he just assign souls randomly, or does he have some kind of system? Did I maybe do something up in heaven, before I was born, that pissed him off, so he stuck me with a shitty family? Maybe it's a test, some trial to prove my strength. If so, I bet I'm failing miserably.

I remember Mama Lettie taking us to church, and the preacher told us the story about a guy named Job. This guy is the best, most faithful human on the whole of the earth. The devil tells God that Job's only so good and faithful 'cause his life is good; he's a rich man, owns lots of land and livestock, has a large family, and so on. So God lets Satan fuck with Job, killing his whole family, ruining his farm, giving him goddamn boils and pustules, the whole shebang. But Job never quits praising and worshipping God. I know the point of the story is that you just have to accept the suffering and worship God anyway, but I can't lie; that's really fucking hard sometimes. Oh, I believe in God, all right, but he's got some questions to answer.

Something keeps me tethered here. There must be some reason I'm here. I start to think there may be some hope, however faint. Remlee is here again. I saw her with my own eyes today (yesterday, tomorrow, last year, who knows). I don't know why, but if there's anything I've learned in this life, it's not to look a gift horse in the mouth. No need to think about it too hard. Don't want to jinx it. She's back, for now anyways, so there's a chance. I don't know how I can do it, but maybe I can tell her I'm sorry. I just want her to know there wasn't never anything wrong with her; she just got unlucky. Or maybe God's testing her too. He seems to like to do that.

As this spark of hope grows, the warm dark fades to a hazy pink. The sounds of my hospital room reassert themselves, and I feel my safe break out in gooseflesh. Why is it always so goddamn cold in this place? I open my eyes, and momentarily, everything comes into focus. The TV is on, but the sound is off, and I spend a few moments watching two ladies brawl it out on Springer. I don't need the volume to know what they're saying. It's always the same: you slept with my man, you stole my girl, bang, crash, pow. I wonder how it's possible for Mr. Springer to keep finding these people after all these years. I understand family drama, sure, but how can so many people be willing to show out on national TV? I can't talk, though, 'cause here I am watching it.

I locate the clicker, and just as I'm about to turn on the sound, Mr. Roboto, the therapist extraordinaire, comes in, walking his stiff walk. I groan at his sudden appearance, and the smallest hint of a smile touches the corner of his mouth.

"I'm happy to see you, too," he says in his emotionless voice.

"Gombloh danuta?" I stay back. Who said I'm happy?

"Well, either way, we've got work to do. Let's turn that TV off and get to it, huh?" he says, pretending to give me an option. I give him my fakest smile, dripping with all the sarcasm I can muster, and turn off the idiot box. He's right, and I know it. If I ever want to, some kind of peace with Remlee, I'm going to have to get my voice back. There's just no two ways about it.

"Oh Lord!" I say. "Oh Lord!"

Remlee

As predicted, Jack had indeed made an exciting discovery on his little excursion and was nearly bursting to show me when he got back. He was carrying the remaining four beers of a six-pack, and I hoped that the bar he bought it at wasn't what he was excited about. I didn't mind his drinking so much, although I tended to abstain, but I really did not enjoy the atmosphere most bars had on offer, and I usually resisted his attempts to get me to accompany him on his frequent trips. That was his thing, and I didn't begrudge him it. I just didn't really want to participate too. The noise, the smoke, the oppressive press of bodies, all of it left me cold.

He pulled me outside after paying lip service to Jolene, promising to bring me back unharmed momentarily. I played along, eager to avoid the conversation I knew was imminent.

"You've got to see this," he said breathlessly, his eyes aglow with rapturous delight. "It's the most beautiful thing I've ever seen."

"What?" I asked, getting caught up in his infectious excitement.

"You'll see, it's a surprise," he said, making a game of it as usual. He practically skipped along, tugging me after him. I took note of the air around us as he led me along, the stifling air like soup, filling the background of my every childhood memory. Northern air, even in the summer, just doesn't have the physical weight as the air in Florida. The sweat hangs on your skin because the air can't hold another drop of moisture, and you wonder if maybe you shouldn't try to develop gills to breathe easier.

"It's just over here," Jack said, leading me into the local playground. I felt a twinge of memories stirring as we made our way past the slide where I spent countless hours as a child. He suddenly came to a stop in front of an enormous magnolia tree, its lofty branches draped with Spanish moss. The waxing crescent moon was framed by its branches, and it swayed gently in the breeze.

"This magnificent tree you see before you makes every inch we've driven over the last four days utterly worth it," he said, staring in awe at the massive trunk.

"You're drunk," I said, laughing at his earnestness.

"Yes, I am. Not the point," he said. "That tree is as perfect of a thing as there ever was on this earth. Look at it."

I took his advice and looked at the tree. It was impressive, its majestic limbs reaching out in all directions, its massive roots gripping the earth. I thought about those roots and how deep they must go. I wondered how many animals this ancient tree had provided a home for over the centuries. This tree had been there since before my granddaddy's granddaddy was taking his first steps. Barring any human intervention or other natural disaster, it will be here long after everyone alive today is gone.

Jack had walked over and sat down on one of the many gnarled roots and cracked open a fresh beer. He sat back, resting his back on the trunk, and smiled at me, delighted that I was enjoying the tree as much as he. I went and sat next to him, laying my head on his shoulder. He absentmindedly stroked my hair a couple of times, then he began to quietly speak.

"They just can't see it," he muttered to himself.

"See what? Who?" I asked, suddenly lost, like I started reading a book halfway through.

"My family," he said, his voice suddenly thick. "They just think I'm lazy. Or maybe…unmotivated, I don't know. They can't understand how I can be satisfied only making twelve bucks an hour. Everything is about money with them. It would never occur to them that I might do what I do for reasons other than the money. They can't see the value in being outside, in the sun, in the rain, just breathing in air that hasn't been recirculated. I really don't think they understand how good it feels to sweat, to be physical. They would rather spend hundreds of dollars a month to run in place in front of a TV screen, then go outside and get dirty." He paused to sip his beer, and I could see the years of resentment etched into his face.

"My old man, especially," he continued, his voice raw with barely suppressed rage. "How can that man judge me? He spends his days looking for loopholes and technicalities in order to use the law to enable his clients to pick the pockets of others. It's so, I don't know, just fucking dishonest. He uses words to twist the law into weapons to be wielded against others, not to help them. I spend my days creating. I plant gardens, dig ponds. I beautify landscapes. I shape nature to create symphonies for the eye to feast upon. It's the epitome of honest."

"Why do you care what they think?" I asked. He sat silently for a minute, considering my question.

"I don't really know," he said, a bemused half grim ceiling across his face. "I guess everybody wants their parents' approval."

"Yeah, but you don't approve of them, so why do you care if they approve of you?" I pressed.

"Well, I guess," he started to say, but I interrupted him.

"I mean, if you disagree with them so much about what's important in life, then shouldn't you be glad they don't approve? If they did approve of what you were doing, wouldn't that make you question yourself?" I asked, hoping he would see my logic.

"I suppose," he said with a shrug. A group of children rode past on bicycles, chattering away about whatever big plans they had in store for their evening. Jack smiled as he watched them pass.

"I envy you, you know," he said, still watching the kids as they continued on into the night. "You got to grow up here, out in the hinterlands. There's so much room to run here. Look at those kids. They couldn't be out like that, at night with no parents, back in Boston. Not at that age, what are they, nine, ten? Can you imagine those kids in Southie? You'd have to be nuts to let your kids roam free in that 'hood."

"Yeah, well, small towns ain't always what you seem to think," I said. "Especially if you're poor and your family's always in trouble with the law. I promise you, you can begin to really crave the anonymity of the city. I bet, right now, even though I've been gone twenty-six years, if you watch closely, people round here keep their distance. I look enough like my kin that they don't need to know my name. It's written in my curly blond hair and hazel eyes. It's written in the way I walk, the way I carry myself. I might as well have a name tag that says, 'Hello: My Name is Shaw.' It's almost like being famous, I guess, only more like infamous, really."

Jack sat quietly, taking all this in. I leaned back and close my eyes, frustrated because I didn't think he really understood what I meant. Then he spoke and proceeded to prove me wrong.

"We are exactly alike, you know," he said gently.

"What do you mean by that?" I asked, sincerely puzzled.

"We can't escape our families. Like it or not, our last names have dictated our lives," he said. "It's like, there are expectations, you see? Neither you nor I had any say in what those expectations are, but they're there, nonetheless. Shephard means one thing. Shaw another. And the world won't let you choose. You're just supposed to be what a Shephard is or what a Shaw is. The minute you do anything different, anything not in line with the parameters that have been set, then that's when they go to work on you. The world goes to work on you, but so does your family. The pressure comes from within as well as from without. It's just…some kind of fucking trap." He emptied his beer and cracked open another. He started to say more but then fell silent. I reached out and touched his hand, but he continued to look away into the night.

"People look at me, too, you know," he said quietly. "I see their faces when they see me cutting their grass. 'Hey, look, there's Stuart Shephard son, sweating in the sun like a common workman. How sad.' I can see the pity in their eyes when they hand me their check to pay for my services, and my whole day's work amounts to about five minutes of my father's billing rate. I want to scream in their faces, 'Fuck you, you arrogant prick! What useful thing did you do to contribute to the world today?' but I don't, I can't. That's the rub. While I rarely respect them, these idle rich whom I cater to, I need to please them. They have the money, so they are the boss. And that makes them better than me, in their eyes. I know it shouldn't matter, but it does." He grew more animated as he talked, and by the end, he was on his feet, shouting and gesturing maniacally.

"Sssssssshhhhhh!" I whispered, "You'll wake the dead."

"Are there many dead around here to wake?" he retorted cheekily.

He calmed down; our banter always worked like that. We seem to be able to tease ourselves back to serenity. Humor is weird like that, I guess. That's why Jack was so important to me, and I to him. For my part anyways, and I'm sure he'd say the same, we acted like a kind of Valium for each other. Somehow, and I couldn't begin to explain the alchemy, our decidedly different dispositions managed to mesh in just the right places, and we each instinctively knew what buttons to push, and what buttons not to push, what words to say (or not say) to be exactly what the other needed. Sometimes it almost seemed fake, like we were just characters in someone else's idealized romantic fantasy. I'm not a believer, never really have been, but my relationship with Jack sometimes seemed too perfect to not have been preordained by some benevolent deity. I honestly don't know if I could have survived had I not met him. He was the one brilliant spot in my otherwise dingy life.

I began to feel nervous, knowing I still had to inform him of my change of plans. So far, he was content to lead the conversation, and I was relieved he hadn't yet asked about my talk with my sister. I considered revving him up again, just to stall some more, but thought better of it. Although he was easy enough to manipulate when he had a buzz on, I always felt sleazy for doing it afterward, so I reserved that particularly nasty tactic for emergencies only. As much as I wished differently, I simply couldn't convince myself that this counted as one. I mustered up my courage and plowed straight in.

"I'm gonna stay," I said abruptly, surprising even myself. He looked at me blankly, not catching my meaning.

"What, here? In the park?" he asked incredulously. "What the hell happened while I was gone?"

"No, not in the park. I mean, I'm going to stay here, in Stillwater," I said, the words falling out on their own accord.

"Wait… What?" he asked, his eyes widening as he began to realize what I was saying.

"I'm gonna stay here and help Jolene with Mama for a while. Just until we can get her settled," I continued, scared to meet his gaze.

"But... But what about the grill? Who's gonna run that?" he asked, his mind spinning tire, trying to gain traction.

"Kelly and Tommy can handle it for a little while longer," I explained, trying to convince myself as much as him. "I mean, they do have the internet down here, we're not that backward. It will be fine—"

"*Fine*?" he cut in, his voice dripping with sarcasm. "*Fine*? Oh, okay, she says it will be *fine*. Don't worry about half of our livelihood, it will be *fine*."

"Oh, come off of it," I said, my voice full of exasperation. "That restaurant has all but run itself for years, that's why your dad agreed to give me the down payment. It was a safe investment. They can get by without me for a little while longer."

"Yeah? How much longer?" he asked, theatrically crossing his arms across his chest like a toddler throwing a tantrum. I had to stifle the urge to laugh so as not to provoke him further. An enraged Jack was an unpredictable thing. An enraged, drunken Jack would be completely unmanageable.

"I don't know, Jack," I said, exasperated. "Two weeks, a month, it depends."

"On what?" he pursued, his lips seemingly frozen in a pout.

"Jesus, Jack, on any number of things! How long they keep her in the hospital, how much and how quickly she covers, who knows? It won't be forever, but how the fuck am I supposed to know how long it's gonna take? It's not like I've ever had to do this before. I'm flying blind here," I said, my words starting to catch in my throat as I fought back tears of anger, fear, and profound sadness.

"Why do you even have to do it at all?" he asked. "How is this even your responsibility?"

"Because she's my mom," I answered simply.

"On paper," he said, his voice coated with disdain. "Why can't Jolene do it?"

I rolled my eyes as I answered, "Really? Do you really need me to answer that?"

"Well, what about your brother? The one who isn't in jail," he asked, desperate to find an out.

"He doesn't have anything to do with her," I explained.

"Neither did you, up until a few days ago," he pointed out.

"I know, but…" I stammered, but he talked over me, refusing to back down.

"But nothing, Remlee," he said, his eyes pleading. "I don't understand. Why are you doing this? Why, all of a sudden, do you give a flying fuck about that woman? What has changed?"

"Nothing's changed," I said. "It's just…like…maybe this is my only chance to…to make it right with her somehow."

Jack burst out laughing. "How the fuck are you gonna do that? She can't even talk!"

"Exactly," I said, chuckling a little myself. "She can't fuck it up by saying anything."

This got us both laughing, our hysterics feeding off each other. It felt good to laugh, and the tension eased considerably. I stood up once I had gotten ahold of myself and grasped Jack's hand. He kept his face turned for me, but he didn't let go of my hand. I could feel the strength in his rough grasp, and I tried to draw energy from that well.

"I've got to do this," I said, trying to catch his eyes.

"I know you think you do," he replied with a sad smile. Our laughing session seemed to take the fight out of him, and he seemed to almost shrink just the tiniest bit as he resigned himself to defeat.

"You can stay too," I said hopefully, flashing him my winningest smile.

His sad smile remained as he said, "You know I can't. I was lucky that Trevor gave me a week and a half. He may be my friend, but he still got a business to run… You know, like you."

"That's not fair!" I shouted, slapping him hard in the chest. He ignored me and continued.

"Yeah, probably not," he admitted, "but none of this is fair, is it?" He stopped and ran his hands through his hair and loudly sighed.

"I'm not gonna fight you on this, Rem," he said wearily. "I trust you. You know that. If you feel you have to do this, then you have to do this. I don't want you to resent me. I just wish you had talked to me."

"This is me talking to you," I pointed out, and he flipped me off and kept on talking.

"You know what I mean," he said. "Like maybe talk to me before you have made your decision."

"Yeah, sure, fine, whatever," I said impatiently, not desiring to be lectured on responsibility and communication by my husband. Something about pots meeting kettles came to mind.

"Well," he said, taking me by the arm and leading me back toward Jolene's. "What are you going to do with yourself down here, anyways? It's not like you'll be at the hospital the entire time."

"I don't know, really," I admitted. "I guess I'll just rattle around town, get reacquainted with my family."

"Don't be getting too close, if you know what I mean," he said with a wink. "You should avoid the temptation to join the family business. My father isn't admitted to the bar in Florida, you know."

"I wouldn't want no Yankee lawyer, anyways," I said with a laugh. "My family would string me up before I even got to trial."

We both fell into gales of laughter at this. After a few minutes of gasping for air, we were able to continue back to Jolene's trailer. We walked in amicable silence, each lost in our own private worlds. I knew Jack would be fine back home, but his little jab about my family's criminal activities hit close to home. I couldn't admit it to Jack, but I was a bit worried myself that I might get dragged into their sordid little affairs, whether I liked it or not. It was just a risk I was going to have to take. Something in my mother had awakened something in me, a longing I couldn't quite put a name on but somehow couldn't deny. I thought that I was above it all and that I had successfully killed off that part of me years ago, but the truth was becoming too obvious to ignore.

I missed my Mama.

Betty Sue

Apparently, I'm an impatient patient, or so Nurse Tinkerbell tells me after my latest speech therapy session. I don't think I am, though. It's just really frustrating, I don't seem to be making hardly any progress at all. It seems like the harder I try to say something, anything, the worst the blockage becomes. Every once in a while, things get through, though. It seems like if I'm startled or surprised, a thought can somehow escape my mind without being corrupted somehow. Earlier, the Needle Lady came by to take yet another sample. (What in the hell do they do with all that blood, anyways? Geez, I'm surprised I have any left). She stuck me without warning. I was watching TV, paying her no mind at all, and I think she thought she could pull a fast one. Or maybe I just didn't hear her. Either way, she stuck me unawares, and I yelled out as clear as day.

"What the fuck, bitch?" I shouted, each word crisp and completely intelligible. I was so shocked that I said the words I meant to say, I forgot why I was even angry.

Tinkerbell flits around the room in her Technicolor Disney scrubs, Mickey's cheery face plastered all over her clothing like a walking billboard. I figure that's why she's in this racket to begin with. Where else can a grown woman wear cartoon characters on her clothes to work every day and still be taken seriously? I doubt this wisp of a girl has ever truly known suffering, how else could she be so goddamn perky all the time? I want so badly to be able to talk, to be able to tell her that she's only so optimistic because she young and obviously cared for. I can tell, just by looking at her, that she never missed a meal growing up. Not that she's fat, oh no. She's got the firm body that only comes from organic foods and exercise. My guess is softball. She's got the build. Her momma and daddy cherished her, made sure she got to the doctor, made sure she did her homework. This one's parents cared who she hung out with, probably intervened more than once to protect her from bad influences. I hate her because I envy her. I admit it. I sometimes wonder what I could have been if someone had just given a damn about me.

I'm jealous because she's young, healthy, beautiful, successful, and smart. She's everything I'm not, everything I can't ever be. I'm in my sixties, I can't talk, I live alone, and half my family hates me. I don't know if I deserve the hatred. I probably do to some extent, I guess. This nurse is a walking reminder of how nice life could be, if only I was someone else.

She's babbling on and on about how great I'm doing, how I just need to be patient and do the work. I only half listen to her; her cutesy little voice grates on my nerves. I don't know how she figures I'm doing good; I still can't say two words on command. Sure, I was able to say yes by the end of this last session, but that's only one word, a word I don't need anyways. I could always nod. I wish I could figure out how to say words I don't already have a way of communicating. If I'm only going to get a certain number of words back, I don't want to waste any.

Finally, she finishes talking and leaves me be. I'm beyond relieved. There's only so much good humor I can take. People like her, people who are happy all the time, I just don't trust them. They only see the good side of life, that's what I think, and that makes you half-blind. I don't know a lot, but I know that things don't always work out, that Prince Charming ain't coming, that fair is only a word in books. If you don't know this to be true, like I'm sure Nurse Tinkerbell don't know, how can you be trusted to know about anything at all?

Tinkerbell tells me, over and over, that if I just try, things will get better. But she don't know me; she don't know the first thing. I never was good at learning. When I run off with Elmer, that was the last school I ever saw, not that I really saw all that much, to begin with. My hands were always needed on the farm, and things were different back then, for better or worse. Schools didn't chase kids down, like they do nowadays, at least not in Stillwater, Florida. If you didn't go, well, it was no skin off their nuts. Every once in a while, some do-gooder would try to intervene, but Daddy always shut them down. Book learning wasn't important to Daddy, so it wasn't important to no one in the family. History class and algebra wouldn't get the fields sown and harvested, only hands, backs, and sweat would do.

I never liked going to school anyways. All that sitting still and being quiet was like torture to me. I would sit in class, wishing I was outside on my daddy's land, the sun on my face, the breeze blowing my hair about, singing Hank Williams songs with Daddy and my brother Earl Three at the top of my lungs. Nobody corrected my grammar in the fields; nobody cared if I said "ain't." There wasn't no freedom in that schoolhouse; every minute was scheduled in advance. But home on the farm, things happened when they did, and not a minute before. School felt artificial, unnatural. The people at school wanted, needed to mold me into something I wasn't, but home was where I could be exactly who I was and was always meant to be.

I turned the TV on, hoping to distract myself from these memories. I'm tired. Tired of remembering, so I think I'll check out for a while, live someone else's life for a while. My stories are on, I discover to my delight, and I cozy myself down to watch the problems of other people for the time being. Sure, the stories are ridiculous and far-fetched, but that's what makes them fun. That's the horrible secret at the heart of life. Most of it, even the bad parts, is boring. Dull, repetitive, same old, same old, day in, day out. The thought that keeps me up at night isn't the thought of what might happen to me. It's the thought that nothing might happen to me that really scares me.

That is probably why I was (am) such a shitty mother. It ain't that I don't care; it's just that the monotony of child-rearing is more than I can take. It's not that I don't love my kids; it's just that boredom scares me more. I know it's a lousy excuse, and I don't expect any one of my kids would ever accept it, but it's all I got. I can't explain it any other way. No matter how hard I try, sooner or later, the routine begins to wear on me, and I find myself searching for some kind of escape. Usually, that ends up being a man, but not always. These last few years have been peaceful, I admit, I guess even I'm getting old, but I'd be lying if I told you I wouldn't ride off into the sunset with the next biker or trucker that paid me any mind. Well, if I could talk, that is… Damn.

It's just something in my blood, something wild carried over from primitive ancestors that makes me this way. If there ever was a fully civilized Tucker, I ain't never met him. Or even heard of him. We ain't all complete outlaws and scoundrels, but ain't a one of us anywhere near saintly. I ain't judging; it's just the truth. We just ain't like most folks, I guess. I don't mean to say better, and I don't mean worse. Just different. We live hard lives, harder than most, and we learn to make do without all that fancy stuff the uppity folks can't seem to live without. We may not be as comfortable as those folks, but if the shit ever really hit the fan, we'd be able to survive. We ain't soft. Deprivation makes strength, or so Daddy always said.

I try to pay attention to my show, but I can't seem to follow it today. I keep falling back into my mind, the show reduced to flickering images in front of my eyes that are hardly even registered. One of the many downsides of not being able to talk is that your mind never quits. Those thoughts never get to escape. That's what I think anyways. A person can only hold so many thoughts at one time, and if she can't get them out, things start to go haywire. Talking, even if it is about nothing, even if no one can hear it, is like some kind of relief valve, and mine is blocked. I worry I might explode, like Mr. Creosote in that old Monty Python sketch. What a mess that would be, my thoughts and memories splattered in Technicolor across the once sterile white walls. Where would you even start to clean that up?

I begin to feel drowsy, but I don't want to sleep. I like the warm dark place, prefer it even, but I can't really control where (or when) I go once my eyes are closed. Like is not, I'll end back in my time travel nightmare, forced to relive some horrible past event, to reopen the scars and bleed once more. I fight hard to remain here, awake and present (or so I assume, anyways). It occurs to me that maybe this hospital is the real illusion, and I'm just really stuck out of time, living my life out of order. The thought makes me dizzy, so I try to put it out of my mind. I tried desperately to keep my eyes open, but it feels like there are weights attached to them, pulling them close. Goddammit, I don't want…to…sleep…

I open my eyes to the sound of birds calling. Their song fills the air as I shake my head and try to adjust to my surroundings. I'm still not used to these weird dreams; I can't quite seem to understand the rules. Maybe that's where I'm going wrong, assuming that there are rules, to begin with. That thought chills me to the bone, and I feel myself shiver despite the oppressive summer heat. The idea that there truly are no rules, that the earth can open and swallow me whole at any time without any rhyme or reason, for no logical reason at all, well, I'm not sure how long I can live in such conditions. The knowledge that I can slip into these time travel dreams seemingly at the drop of a hat, with no warning and no recourse, fills me with an all-consuming dread.

I'm sitting under the Willow, the sun making mandalas on my skin where it shines through the leaves. I'm basically grown now. I have the body, if not yet the mind, of a woman. It's the body I will come to abuse so grievously that I end up in this state, but still new, not yet rode hard and put away wet by this mean old world. Everything is tight, smooth, and where it was originally located. I can feel the energy of youth surging through me again, coursing through me so hard I nearly burst from trying to contain it all. I feel ten-foot tall and bulletproof. Sure, my brothers are mean to me, but it's made me hard, unconquerable. I'm no prancing fancy. I'm a wildcat, daring anyone to try to leash me.

I stand up, and it's all I can do to suppress the urge to run. Not out of fear, mind you, or even to catch something. Just run to feel the wind on my face, to see the cane become a green blur as I rocket past. I twirl around like a ballerina, drunk on my youth and vitality. I've forgotten how it feels to not have years of hard living weighing you down. I reach my hands to the sky, stretching myself as much as I can, luxuriating in the feeling of limber muscles and flexible joints. I step out of the shade, raising my face to the sun, and I let its warm rays caress my skin, turning it a glowing, golden brown. I feel alive again, fully, and I forget all about my problems for a minute.

I let myself go and give in to the urge, and I begin to run, slowly at first, trotting, really, just feeling the strength I possess warming up. I pick up the pace, everybody part working together in perfect harmony. I am a machine built for just this very purpose. My lungs fill and empty, fill and empty, two efficient power plants fueling my motor. I'm at full throttle now, legs pumping in time with my arms, all to the beat of my steady heart. My eyes begin to tear up, not from sadness or even joy but from the wind whipping my face, the molecules furiously trying to hold me back. They can't, though; I'm too fast, too strong, too wild. Not even nature can contain me.

If I can just run fast enough, maybe I can outrun all this darkness I feel on the edges of my reality. It's still mostly kept at bay, but sometimes something evil can get through and catch me. Like Uncle Leo. So I keep running. Shadows like Uncle Leo are still mostly too slow to catch me, long as I pay attention, so I keep running.

Finally, I come to the pond at the back of our property. Whatever evil was chasing me is far behind me now. I have escaped for now. I stop, my chest heaving, and drink in the air in greedy gulps. I bend at the waist, my hands on my knees, and recapture the wind that I have run out of me. I slowly sink to my knees, my breath slowing. I lie flat on my back and watch the clouds put on their show for me, my mind at peace and my excess energy temporarily spent. I watch for hours, or minutes, or days, unconcerned with anything, barely even thinking. It's a peace I've rarely felt, and I revel in it, everything else forgotten.

Sometime later, I have no idea how much, a low rumbling catches my attention. It grows louder as it approaches, eventually revealing itself to my ears as the growl of a poorly maintained vehicle. I can hear its broken exhaust blatting, and I can smell the acrid smell of its foul breath besmirching the air. I sit up to see who is intruding on my private paradise, and that's when I see Elmer Ray Shaw for the very first time.

He's driving through the brush with my brother Clarence in a Ford Thunderbird convertible, several fishing poles hanging out of the back seat. The radio was blaring, almost loud enough to cover the noise coming from the obviously neglected Ford. John Fogerty is singing about not being fortunate, and both my brother and this golden stranger are singing along at the top of their lungs. The car clunks to a stop a few feet from me, and they hop out, still unaware I'm even there.

I saunter over to where they sit, baiting their hooks and bantering, and they don't notice my approach. Realizing my presence has still failed to register, I am overcome with an irresistible urge to try to scare my brother. Lord knows he's gotten me enough times, and it's about time he got his for once. I squat low in the brush, my short stature for once an advantage. I stifle my giggles as I creep up behind Clarence. My steps are slow and measured. My blood pounds in my ears and time with my racing heart, and I wonder if this is how the cougar feels right before she pounces. I'm so close now. I can smell his aftershave, its rich, musky scent barely disguising the stale sweat soaked into his shirt after a long day at the gypsum plant he was currently close to being fired from. Neither he nor his new friend knows I'm here, and this thrills me so much I almost squeal. I can barely contain myself as I crouch deeper, winding up to spring. Every fiber twitches as I prepare to strike, every hair stands up straight, like the air is full of static electricity, and I'm drawing it all into me, consuming its power, getting ready to unleash…

"What are you doing, Betty Sue?" Clarence asks casually, not even turning his head. "Are you all right?"

I can't answer; it's like the wind has been knocked out of me. How did he know? I was so quiet, so careful.

"I saw you as soon as we pulled in off the road," he says, reading my mind. "It was over before you even knew it started." His voice is kindly, but I know better. He wants me to know he's still in charge, still bigger, stronger, faster, smarter, and just all-around better than me. I am just his kid sister, and no matter what, I'll never, repeat never, get over on him. It's better I just accept that now, his voice says without saying, and life will be easier for all involved. Arrogant prick.

"I wasn't hiding," I say, too quickly, trying to be nonchalant. "You'd never see me comin' if I was."

He chuckles at this and finally turns to look at me. He smiles his shark's smile at me, all teeth, but cold eyes. I don't think he hates me, but his eyes tell me he doesn't love me, either. I'm just scenery, background, not a cherished family member. I don't take it too personal; he's like that with everybody. I ain't exactly sure he's really a person on the inside sometimes.

"What's your name, girlie?" his friend asks, and I look at him closely for the first time. He's older than me, older than Clarence even, by a few years, but still youngish. Probably under thirty, anyways. His mousy brown hair is slicked back, greaser style, and a toothpick dangles precariously from his lips. I find myself fascinated by it, unable to figure out how he manages to keep it in his mouth as he simultaneously chomps his gum rapid-fire, like a goat with a particularly tasty clump of grass. An image of those talented lips planted squarely on mine flashes through my mind, and I feel momentarily disoriented, like I simply forgot what planet I am on.

"That's my little sister Betty Sue," Clarence says when I'm unable to answer. The stranger glides over to me, takes my hand in his, and gently kisses it.

"My name is Elmer Ray Shaw, Betty Sue," he says, his voice dripping honey into my ears. I can only gape at this man through eyes that feel like they are popping out of their sockets. I sputter and stammer, unable to speak, hypnotized by him, intimidated by him, nearly scared of him, but incapable of looking away.

"Hey, Clarence, you never told me you had such a cute sister," he says to my brother. I look around for someone else, convinced he couldn't be talking about me. This man is grown, full, and strong. He's bigger than Clarence, and until now, Clarence was the most frightening-looking man I'd ever seen. What could he want with me? I'm barely more than a kid.

"You never asked," Clarence replied dully, uninterested in me or his friend's interest in me. "Are we gonna fish or what?"

"You go ahead, I'll catch up," Elmer says, his attention solely on me.

"Whatever," Clarence grunts, then stomps off through the brush in search of a honey hole. His departure leaves me feeling nervous, and I consider making an excuse to disappear. Instead, I sit down on a stump at the edge of the pond, hugging my knees close to my chest. I try to calculate how far from the house I am, trying to decide if I can run from this man if it becomes necessary.

"So what do you do for fun around here anyways?" he asks, leering at me like I'm a particularly tasty cut of beef. I can feel his gaze on my skin, just like he's actually touching me. I'm surprised that I don't feel revulsion. Something about the way he's looking at me excites me in a way I don't fully understand. I understand what sex is, of course. I'm no ninny, but it's only academic at this point. I refuse to count my uncle's abuse as a legitimate sexual experience. I've only ever kissed one boy, and that ended badly. So badly, I've avoided boys like the plague ever since.

"I don't know," I say shyly in answer to his question. In truth, there isn't much fun to be had around here. I look up, and he's right there, towering over me. I feel so small as I stare up at him, and he smiles back. It's the smile that hypnotizes me. His smile is warm and inviting, but underneath, just below the surface, you can see the danger lurking there. I find myself transfixed, unable to look away. I'm reminded of that Harry Hamlin movie with Medusa, and I wonder for a second if maybe I've turned to stone.

He regales me with more small talk, and I try to listen, but my mind is too busy processing everything to really follow him. This doesn't matter anyway. He talks so much, I scarcely have a chance to get a word in anyways. He's pulling out all the stops, trying hard to impress me. It's working. I find myself admiring his physique, imagining his enormous arms encircling me, protecting me from harm. I begin to feel warm, the blood flowing faster in my veins.

As he talks, he slowly edges his way closer, his progress barely noted by me until he sits right next to me. He leans in close, and I can feel his warm breath on my neck. A shiver of unfamiliar pleasure ripples down my spine, and I gasp out loud.

"I could take you away, you know," he whispers in my ear. These are the words I've been praying to hear for years now, and I blink rapidly, unsure if I heard what I think I did. I look up, and everything is blurry. I realized this is because I'm tearing up, and I push it all down. It won't do to cry now.

"From here, from all of this. I could take you away, if you wanted," he says, pleading his case further. "We can go anywhere you want. I got a car, my own trailer, we would be set up real nice." He reaches over and cups my face with one of his enormous paws. It's so big. My head fits right in the palm. He leans in and kisses me, and my breath catches in my chest. My heart stops, and so does the entire world around us. Suddenly, everything's to spin out of control, everything blurred together as a fuel myself spinning around and around and around. I feel Elmer's rough hand leave my face, and he lets go of me. I'm tossed into the hurricane, spinning wildly, my vision unable to focus, leaving everything a dizzying kaleidoscope. I close my eyes to stave off this vertigo, and I feel solid ground under my feet. I open my eyes and nearly scream at what I see. I've jumped forward in time, nearly a month. I'm wearing the white dress we found at the Goodwill, and Elmer has on the hideous plaid suit that we got at the same time. We are in the local courthouse, and it's our wedding day. I am nervous and alone. There's no one here to bear witness other than the justice of the peace and his stenographer. The judge's droning on and on, reading from a well-worn book he holds in his polished fingers. I can't look away from his hands. I've never seen a hand so smooth on a man before. I glance at my own, and I chuckle a little when I see

even mine are more accustomed to work than this so-called pillar of the community.

I want to scream at myself to run, run away, but I can't. This is more dream than time travel, I remind myself. I can't seem to change anything here; I'm just doomed to relive it all. Still, a small part hopes for a loophole, some tiny oversight that will allow me to squirm free and save myself from this monster. I know now that the protection I thought he would provide would not come; in fact, it is exactly Elmer that I'm going to need protecting from.

"I now pronounce you man and wife," the judge says, his voice full of boredom and mild disdain. "You may kiss the bride."

Elmer grabs ahold of me, lowering his face to mine, ready to seal the deal, and I stiffen in his arms. His mouth opens slightly as he leans in for his kiss, and I smell the grave pouring out of it. I try to scream, but he clamps his lips onto mine before I can. My eyes roll back into my head, and I find myself falling back into oblivion, back to the warm, dark place.

I've never been more relieved.

Remlee

I barely slept that night. Even though Jack and I had agreed, I knew he wasn't happy. He wouldn't fight me any longer, it was true, but I had a sinking feeling that I just had given him enough ammo to use against me for years to come. I lay on Jolene's couch, eyes stubbornly refusing to close, and remained captive to my mind run amok. Nightmare scenarios unfolded with hellish detail, one after the other, and ran riot through my imagination. Every possible permutation of misfortune played out in high definition on the low-light reel looping before my eyes.

I tried to play it nonchalant with Jack but being away from the restaurant weighed heavily on my mind, much more so than I let on. I trusted my staff well enough, but that trust wasn't enough to ease my concern. I knew I was being irrational. Modern technology made communication over large distances instantaneous, but that fact did little to comfort me. My real problem was deeper than worries about the day-to-day operations.

Much as I would have liked to claim my stress was merely due to the practical concerns of running a business, deep down, I knew better. I was in control at McCurdy's Grill. What I said went. No matter the chaos outside, I could control what happened on the inside. Sure, there was responsibility, but I welcomed it. The restaurant gave me something to think about, to focus on. It gave me a reason to keep going, an excuse to not think about the past. Things move too fast in the kitchen to ruminate on old news. Working was much cheaper than therapy.

In Stillwater, however, the past was all around me. Everywhere I looked held memories and ghosts. Without a job to go to, I wondered how I would pass my time. I could only spend so much time at the hospital. I knew Jolene would likely drive me crazy quickly if I was forced to be in her company too much, and I barely knew anyone else in the family anymore. I wasn't sure I wanted to, either. I'd like to think that I'm not a snob, but I couldn't deny that I felt better than, somehow, superior to these people. That feeling created feelings of guilt and confusion, and a chain reaction was set off in my skull, my emotions waging an apocalyptic war of attrition that I couldn't declare asylum from.

I must have dropped off at some point because the next thing I knew, I was startled awake by the sound of Gary's diesel outside in the driveway. My mouth began watering almost immediately. The heavenly scent of freshly brewed coffee hung thick in the air. I sat up slowly, my back muscles seemingly on strike in protest of Jolene's lumpy couch, and scanned the room. Jack was sitting at the table with his back to me, a steaming cup to his right, an ashtray holding a lit Camel to his left. He was cradling his head in his hands, working his fingers gingerly at his temples. I winced, knowing immediately that he was hungover and, therefore, as friendly as a rabid raccoon with its foot caught in a trap. I considered lying back down and feigning sleep until he had some time (like two hours) to self-medicate himself back to a civilized (well, almost) human form but chose instead to brave the beast. This was likely my last day with him for a while, and I decided to waste none of it. I knew I'd miss him immensely over the coming days or weeks, and I was determined to squeeze as much in today as I could, regardless of the arrows that might fly from his mouth. I was used to his verbal barbs, had suffered far worse. I knew (hoped) he didn't mean the shitty things he said when he flew off the handle. It's just that his mouth works six times faster than his brain.

"Morning," he said thickly, sipping his brew. "Joining us in the land of the living, I presume?"

"Not sure yet," I said dryly. "Jolene up?"

"Not yet," he answered. "Gary just left. Friendly chap. Said all of three words to me."

"That's probably for the best," I said, probing his mood.

"Yeah, I guess that's probably true," he agreed, chuckling ruefully. My spirits rose a few notches, his laugh identifying his mood wasn't completely black. I continued to tread lightly, though.

"How did you sleep?" I asked, hoping to keep things light.

"Some," he grunted and took a long drag from his smoke. I walked into the kitchen and poured myself a cup of liquid morning before sitting in the chair opposite him. I took a long sip, luxuriating in the warm explosion spreading from my belly outward. My head began to clear as the caffeine worked its chemical magic.

We sat in silence, neither of us willing to address the elephant in the room. Jack pretended to peruse the sports section from the previous day, but we both knew it was just an excuse to avoid having a conversation. Sensing turbulent waters, I decided to excuse myself to the porch, hoping to drink in the summer morning along with my coffee. Although I had been converted to a city mouse years ago, my inner country mouse never really died, and she was starved of unspoiled nature. Suburban Boston is too crowded, too developed to ever feel like a summer morning in the rural South. There's too much noise, too much concrete. While I thrived on that chaos, depended on it for motivation, the sterile, soulless din of the city never really nourished me like the calm, more sedate rhythms of pastoral life. It's like the city was one of those trendy energy drinks, full of empty calories and poison, and the farm was cool, clean spring water, full of nothing but hydration. The former was more exciting, more hip and fun, but the latter was far better for my health, physical and mental.

I breathe deep, filling my lungs with the sweet air, the honeysuckle in bloom next to the trailer. A tranquility washed over me, and I sat down on the steps to watch the goings-on in the early morning sun. Part of me was exciting to be staying, though I have never admitted it because moments of real peace like this were few and far between at home. It's not that Jack and I fought a lot; we didn't. It's just a feeling, a vibe that you get in places where loads of people are all stacked on top of each other. This strange tension grows, filling the city like an unseen fog, affecting everyone. No one is immune from the insistent pressure that city living exerts on all who take part, but I don't think most people are actually aware of it, at least not on a conscious level. It's too insidious for the general public to easily recognize.

It was already sweltering, although the sun had barely topped the horizon. I could feel the cotton of my tank top sticking to me, the sweat had already begun. I laughed out loud at the irony of it all; the very thing that most people come to Florida for, namely the weather, is also the thing that makes your life the most miserable. There's something about humid heat, especially when it drags on and on, that wears on a person. It's like being forced to wear a trash bag wherever you go. The sweat just won't evaporate and serve its purpose. Everything seems just a little harder, like having weights attached to various parts of your body.

The door opened behind me, and I heard Jack come out onto the porch. He stood quietly behind me for a few minutes, taking the morning in. I stole a glance at him, and all the signs pointed to his hangover being mild. I silently thanked the gods of alcohol for sparing him the worst of their wrath. He sat down next to me on the step and laid his head down on my shoulder.

"Pretty here, huh?" he asked amiably.

"Yeah, it is, mostly," I replied agreeably. He stared off into the distance, appearing to be searching for some unknown query. I could tell he wanted to say something but couldn't decide on what course of action to pursue. I kept quiet, not wanting a confrontation, hoping that wasn't what he was working up to. Finally, he looked at me, his eyes sober and solemn, and began to talk.

"I don't like this," he began quietly, his eyes never leaving mine. "I'm not trying to talk you out of staying or anything, but I won't deny that I'm unhappy."

"I know, babe, I..." I said, but he continued to talk over me.

"No, listen," he said, his tone brooking no argument. "I just worry about you, is all. Not that I think you can't handle yourself." He began to blush, something he does when he knows he's pissed me off but still thinks he's in the right.

"I know you can, Rem," he continued, the blush deepening and spreading across his face and neck. "I really just worry you're gonna want to stay. Like, forever."

"Would that be so bad?" I asked, mostly out of spite. I had no intentions of moving back to Florida permanently, but suddenly, his honest and reasonable worry struck me as patronizing.

"Well, yes," he said, flabbergasted. "Our whole life is in Mass. You own a business, I got a job, we got family…"

"You got family," I said, harsher than I meant. "I don't have family there, you do."

"We are married, Remlee, c'mon," he said, trying and failing to hide his exasperation. "They're your family now too."

"And this is your family here," I pointed out. "Why can't we move here to be with them?"

"You've got to be kidding me," he said with a derisive laugh. "You haven't spoken to most of these people in decades! You don't even like them!"

"And you don't like yours, either," I said, a satisfied smile emblazoned across my face.

"Yeah, well…" he sputtered, unable to manage our respectable comeback. He stared suddenly down the lane, pretending to be interested in the activities of a stray tabby cat who was strolling toward us.

"It won't be for that long," I said soothingly, gently touching his shoulder.

"I know," he said, his tone conciliatory. "I know there's no reason for me to worry. It just feels wrong, being apart, you know?"

I did. Since our first date, we'd rarely been apart for longer than a shift at work. It had been me and him against the world for quite a while, and the thought of going through a whole day apart from him was like trying to go through my day with only one leg. Our lives were so intertwined that I wasn't even sure I knew how to function as an individual anymore. I counted on him for so much, it was sometimes hard to tell where I ended, and he began. Under normal circumstances, this synchronicity would probably be enviable, but these circumstances weren't normal by a country mile. I was nervous that neither of us would be able to hack it without the other, and though he'd never admit it, I could see Jack was worried about the same thing.

Jack and I weren't exactly hermits, but we were anything but social butterflies. We both had a handful of friends, but given that we were a childless couple in our mid-thirties, there was a dearth of suitable candidates to pick from when considering widening our social circle. Neither Jack nor I was what you would call people persons anyway, so it wasn't like there was much of a void to fill. It had never really occurred to us that being apart was even a possibility, so finding and maintaining lots of friendships took low priority. We always had each other, and that was honestly all either of us really wanted. Ours was a world of two.

Jack stood up, stretching and yawning, and smiled brightly at me. He hopped up and down a few times, then cracked his knuckles, all part of a familiar ritual performed by Jack daily. He called it high-speed yoga, but in reality, it was just a quick stretching routine he cobbled together to get his blood flowing. He swore it was the ultimate hangover cure, something about getting oxygen into all the deep nooks and crannies. After thirty seconds of his spastic-looking dance, he came to rest, standing at ease in front of me.

"That's better," he said cheerfully, and I felt my spirit brighten. I stood up next to him and grasped his hand.

"I'll get over it," he said reassuringly. "It's really not a big deal. I'm just being a pussy. I am almost forty, for Chrissakes, I think I can handle being on my own for a while. I'm just so used to you, you know?"

I chuckled at that. "Oh, how romantic! He's 'used to' me," I said coquettishly, pouting for the invisible camera. We both laughed at that, the tension between us fading to manageable levels.

"You know, it's not like you have to leave immediately," I said pointedly. "I know you really can't stay much longer, but you don't have to leave right now, huh?"

"I wasn't leaving right yet," he said. "Geez, I haven't even finished my coffee. Relax."

"I'm just saying," I continued. "We still have today, right? Trevor's not expecting you tomorrow or anything."

"What do you have in mind?" he asked, his eyebrows raised comically.

"Oh, nothing in particular," I admitted. "I'm just not quite ready to face all this alone."

"Can't blame you there," he said with genuine sympathy. "I have a feeling I'm getting the better end of the deal here." He paused and nodded toward the trailer. “I’ve seen what you’re up against,” he said gravely.

We started to walk down the lane casually. We remained mostly quiet, each lost in thought. For my part, I was trying to be balanced my sorrow at the impending separation from Jack and my budding optimism at the admittedly remote possibility of reconciliation with my mother. I had spent so many years missing here, then hating her, and finally basically forgetting her. The thought of being in her life again was dizzying. I had written her off years prior. I didn’t think I needed her. But then, just a few days earlier, she was right in front of me, in the flesh, ravaged by time, barely recognizable, but there. I couldn’t deny her anymore. The stroke had somehow broken her out of the deep dungeon I had thrown her in and exposed her to the light of day. What surprised me most, however, was my reaction. I was happy.

Jack noticed me smiling to myself, and he asked, “What are you grinning like that for? You look like the cat that swallowed the canary.”

Unsure of how to answer, I shrugged and continued walking. Jack held back for a minute, confused, his head cocked a bit to the side like a dog. He sprinted a few quick steps and caught back up with me, easily falling in stride with me. As we approach the end of the lane where the trailer court met the main road, I paused, grabbing him by the wrist.

“You have a few hours before you need to get going. Let’s have an adventure,” I said breathlessly.

“Our whole life is an adventure,” he replied with a hearty laugh. I couldn’t disagree, and it couldn’t be happier for it.

Betty Sue

I wake with a start as the train rumbles by on the track behind the house. I open my eyes and see that I must have dozed off in my rocker. I'm on the porch of the Orchard Street house, so this has to be after Elmer got locked up for good. I watch with disinterest the flurry of activity across the street at the ice plant, the same one that will burn down some years later. I hear the raised voices calling back and forth across the planet, the collective din of commerce. I chuckle to myself for a minute when I'm struck by the irony of sweating through my clothes while less than one hundred yards away from tons upon tons of ice.

I stand up and begin peeling my sodden clothes away from my skin. It becomes obvious that I'm wasting my time. The clothes are simply drenched. I head inside to change into something fresh, and I wonder if I should even bother. It's going to be hot like this for months. There's simply no escape. Sometimes, when it gets to be too much, I walk the kids down to the Piggly Wiggly to pick up a few groceries. We take our sweet old time in the store, soaking up every last second of sweet conditioned air that we can. One time, it took us an hour and a half to buy a half gallon of milk and a loaf of bread. We probably would have stayed longer, but the store was closing for the evening.

Things are tighter than ever, money-wise. Elmer wasn't good for damn near anything, but he did provide. Sort of. Yeah, he was irresponsible and blew a lot of our money on booze and whores, but we had a roof over our heads (mostly), food in our bellies (if not quite enough), and clothes (rags) on our backs. Now, all that is on me. It ain't easy housing, feeding, and clothing kids on a waitress's salary, let me tell you. But nobody who will pay me anything decent will hire me. This town's too small, everybody knows who I am. It don't matter that I ain't never done nobody no wrong, because my kin sure did. It don't help that my husband is the one that killed old Deputy Wiggins in that robbery. No, that didn't earn me no points at all.

I guess I'm lucky in a way because Shane's already grown and moved out. He got himself hired on with some roofing outfit, and he's on the road all the time. I miss having him around, but I'd be lying if I said I wasn't glad he's gone. He was getting himself into trouble more and more, just petty shit mainly, but he seems to have turned that all around. I hope so anyways.

I still have Elton, on paper anyways, but that's not really true. Sure, his address is listed as being here, but that boy just runs wild. He's only fifteen, but there ain't too many grown men he can't whoop. I can't control him, haven't been able to for years, and I quit trying. All I can do is love him and make sure he always has a place to stay, if he wants it. He don't come around too much, mainly just to eat or try to hustle some money from me. I ain't had much to give lately, so I ain't seen him in weeks. He's probably hiding out one of his little delinquent buddies' houses, drinking, smoking, and plotting all kinds of mayhem.

I guess Jolene counts as one and a half kids because she done got herself knocked up. I was mad as a hornet at first, but I wasn't a year or two older than her when I done had Shane, so I guess ain't got no room to talk. I just wanted better for her, that's all. I kept telling her not to mess with them boys, but she wouldn't listen. What could I do? I can't be home all the time. I got to work. These damn bills won't pay themselves. Honestly, I don't know what I would do without Jolene. She watches little Remlee for me all the time. I ain't proud of it, but she often has to play hooky just so I can go into work. I tried to take Remlee to work with me, just kept her in a playpen in the back, but Raymond, the owner, about had a conniption one day when he found her back there. He started yelling about the health inspector and so on, so that was the end of that.

Don't get me wrong; I'm glad Elmer's gone. I thank God every day that they locked that no-good son of a bitch away for life. I don't want him back, but I wasn't prepared to do all this alone. It's just so exhausting. It's just work, work, work, kids, kids, kids, sleep. Repeat. Over and over, day in, day out, no changes, no vacations, no rest for the wicked. The world is just this dull, gray place of drudgery where there's never quite enough time and never quite enough money.

I admit, most nights, all I got from Elmer was the back of his hand, but not every night. We did have five children together, after all. There were times, although they were few, where I truly loved that man, and I felt that he loved me. That's a fine feeling, the kind of feeling that can sustain a person through a world of shit. I never get that feeling anymore. Maybe that's why this is so hard.

I have been looking for that feeling, though. I see the proof of that lying fast asleep on my bed as I enter my room to change. His name is Darryl, and I met him three weeks ago at Tiger's. He ain't good for much, I suppose, but he keeps the bed warm at night, and I hate drinking alone. He ain't what you'd call a role model for the kids, but he ain't mean to them, so I don't complain. He's here for me, anyways, not them. They got their toys. Why shouldn't I have mine?

I'm tired of living for everybody else. When Elmer and me was together, I never got nothing for myself. There just wasn't any spare money or time. I'm done living that way. Elmer getting locked up is what set me free, and now that I got a taste, I ain't never going back.

I open my closet and look for something else to wear. It's so goddamn hot, I don't really want to wear anything, but I can't get away with that. I pick out a tank top and a little skirt, short but not too slutty. I quickly change into them, and I'm about to leave the room when Darryl stirs in bed, rolling over onto his back and murmuring.

"Whachuwanadoaday," he mumbles, wiping the hair and sleep from his eyes. He flashes the dopey grin that caught my attention in the first place, and I feel the beginnings of desire flickering throughout my body. I ignore it, knowing Remlee is awake in the living room, watching some obnoxious kid's show. I purposely stay away from him, not wanting to give either of us the opportunity to start something we shouldn't.

"C'm'ere," he drawls, a sleepily seductive gleam in his eye. He pats the bed next to himself, inviting me into my own bed.

"Oh, no, big boy," I say, mock sternly. "No hanky-panky during daylight hours. You know the rules."

He pouts his lower lip out, and I laugh at him. He pushes his lip even further out, milking his shtick for all it was worth. I shake my head no, but I can't help but smile. He begins to slowly pull down the sheet that is covering him, giving me a tawdry burlesque show.

"Stop!" I squeal, my voice rising two octaves. My voice startles me. It sounds foreign, like the voice of a stranger. A happier, younger stranger.

"Okay, okay," he says, still laughing a little. "Rain check?"

"Deal," I say, and for a moment, everything is fine. I continue bustling about the room, getting ready to head out. I think I'll take Remlee to get some ice cream. She's been so good lately, not giving me or Jolene any problems. It's just so hot and sticky. I'm sure she'll be happy to get some kind of relief. As I'm rustling through my purse, looking for a few dollars to take, I hear him speak behind me.

"Where do you think you're going?" he asks, his voice suddenly as cold as a Minnesota winter.

"Just over to the Tastee-Freez," I say, looking back at him. I'm confused by the look on his face. He looks irate, but I can't figure out what he could possibly be angry about.

"Dressed like that? Oh, no, you're not," he says, pointing at my clothes.

"Dressed like what?" I ask in disbelief. "What's wrong with what I'm wearing?"

"Nothing, if you're a whore," he spits at me, with a dangerous gleam in his eye. "No woman of mine will—"

"What makes you think I'm your woman?" I ask derisively, cutting him off before he can finish his thought. "Just 'cause I let you in my pants don't make me your woman. I don't belong to nobody no more." I plant my feet, cross my arms, and glower at him, daring him to contradict me.

"That's where you're wrong, see?" he says, his voice suddenly deadly quiet. He stands up slowly and advances on me, like a stalking tiger. He grabs my arm and pulls me close. His face fills my entire field of vision as he leans in, a grotesque smile on his face.

"You're mine now," he says, almost conversationally, and I realize he's crazy, crazier than I thought, by a mile. "You're mine, and you're going to fucking obey."

He hauls back and slaps me full across my face. My head rocks back, and my vision is clouded by thousands of tiny white flowers. The skin of my cheek is on fire, but I'm more enraged than hurt. This ain't my first rodeo.

"You hit like a bitch," I say with a wild laugh and see the last remains of rationality drained from his expression, replaced by white-hot fury.

"Wha…what the fuck did you just say?" he asks, his jaw dropping and his whole body quivering.

"I said you hit like a bitch, bitch," I say, edging toward the door. I am only a few feet away, and I remember seeing Elton's baseball bat leaning against the wall in the hallway, and I want desperately to get to it. I've survived my brothers and my husband because I'm not afraid to hit an attacker with whatever is handy. Fairness don't come into it when you're a small woman fighting a big man.

"You sure are brave, I'll give you that," he says, balling up his fist. "Not too fucking bright, I see, but brave."

I make it to the hallway, and I scan for the bat, turning my back to the snarling beast stalking me. I hear him right behind me, but I refuse to run. I will not give him the satisfaction of knowing that I'm scared. Suddenly, he's on me, his hands gripping my arms like two vices. He turns me around to face him, and I spit in his eye.

"You filthy fucking cunt!" he howls, and he buries his fist in my belly. I feel all my breath forced out of me in a rush, and I crumple over, gasping for air. He stands over me, his form blocking out the light, and all I can see is his fist as he smashes my nose flat across my face. A warm, wet explosion cascades down the lower half of my face, and I feel a tooth bounce off my chin on its way to the floor.

I scramble to my feet and run as fast as I can into the kitchen. I hear his heavy steps behind me, chasing me down. I turn to look at him, and as I do, I catch a glimpse of Remlee in the living room. She's white as a ghost, her eyes bugging out of her head as she gapes at me. I raise my hand to warn her, and she gets it instantly. She pulls the afghan over her head, hiding. I feel a momentary sense of relief, and then that sense is shattered by Darryl's fist connecting with my collarbone. I feel it give with an excruciating snap, and once again, I find myself fighting for breath.

"Stop," I cry weakly, sliding down the cabinets into a feral crouch. I have my left hand up, blocking my face, but in my right hand is a steak knife I'm hiding behind my back. I can hardly hold my left hand up, my

whole left side is on fire where he broke my collarbone, but I need to keep him distracted.

"You're gonna learn now," he says, the humanity completely erased from his face. He hardly looks human, his futures so contorted by fury. A chill runs down my spine as I realize he intends to kill me. Not beat me up, punish me, knock me around a little. Kill me. Dead. I think of Remlee and Jolene, all alone, and I jam the knife into his chest as hard as I can. His eyes go wide with surprise, and he lets go of me, clutching at the handle as blood begins to pour out around his fingers.

"You… You… You fucking stabbed me!" he says, his voice bewildered. Knowing I ain't safe yet, I rear back my legs and kick him in the chest with everything I have. My right foot makes perfect contact with the handle of the knife, plunging it further in. Darryl sucks in a wheezing breath, fear finally making an appearance on his face. I can't help but take satisfaction in this, him losing his confidence. He's used to getting his way, especially with women, and I can see he can't figure out how this all went so wrong.

"Damn right I did!" I scream through my bloody lips. "And I'll do it again, too, if you don't get the FUCK OUT OF MY HOUSE RIGHT NOW!"

I leap to my feet and grab another knife off of the counter, holding it out in front of me like it is Excalibur. He is sitting on the floor now, holding his wounded chest, and glaring at me with the eyes of an injured predator. A chill runs through me, but I keep my eyes on him. He's too dangerous to turn your back on or even look away from for just a split second. He's hurt, true, but far from broken.

"Remlee, quick, run to the neighbors and have them call the law," I say, hoping she will be able to comply. She's only four and obviously terrified. She pokes her head out of the blanket, her eyes huge with fear.

"It's okay, honey," I say, trying to keep my voice calm. "You'll be okay. Just run over to Mrs. Tremonti's next door, and she'll take care of it. I promise." Remley runs out of the house at this, screaming at the top of her lungs. I keep the knife pointed at Darryl, doing my best to keep him at bay.

"You're gonna pay for this, bitch," he says through gasps. I see the blood bubbling around the knife handle, hear the sickening gurgling

hitches his chest makes as he draws in a breath. He stands up, ignoring my knife, and comes at me like a freight train. I swing the knife wildly at his face, but he catches my arm. His bulk overpowers me, and I find myself on my back, arms pinned under me as he thrashes on top of me. Blows are raining down on me from all angles, and I try to wriggle free. I hear sirens approach, and I feel a sense of relief. If I can just take it a little longer, I'll be saved.

"If I go back to jail over this shit," he yells as he pounds away at my head and shoulders, "I'm damn sure gonna make it worth it. I'm gonna hurt you bad, Betty Sue."

"Does that make you feel like a man?" I spit at him, every ounce of disdain I can muster dripping from every word. "To beat on a woman? 'Cuz you're such a limp dick, you gotta beat me?"

"I. Will. Have. Your. Respect," he says, punctuating each word with another blow. Things begin to go gray around the edges, and I struggle to stay awake. I push back against the counter with my legs as hard as I can, and I manage to scramble out from under him. I get to my feet, holding the knife out in front again. I can't see almost nothing; the blood has run down my forehead and into my eyes. I can feel my hair plastered to the side of my swollen face. Darryl keeps lunging at me, and I just keep stabbing at the dark red shadow in front of me.

"Just get the fuck out of here," I say, swinging the knife back and forth in front of me in an arc. "The cops are gonna be here any minute now, and once they get a look at me, well, you know what happens next."

"Then why shouldn't I just kill you now?" he asks with a wolfish grin.

"What makes you think you can?" I ask, swinging a knife down hard into his shoulder. He throws his head back and screams, and I twist the knife as I push it in deeper. He claws at my face, digging furrows into my cheeks. He lunges again blindly, and I'm able to sidestep him. He careens past me and crashes into the refrigerator with the grace of a three-legged dog.

"Stillwater Police, open up!" yells a voice from behind the front door. I make a break in that direction, leaping over Darryl's bleeding body, just missing his grasping hands. I run to the door and throw it open and am momentarily blinded by the blazing noontime sun.

"Ma'am, are you all right?" the voice asks, and I nod weakly. I feel my knees give out, and the room turns a funny angle as I collapse to the floor. I watch two black-clad feet come up to me and stop. Another set walks back toward the kitchen, where I can hear Darryl swearing and struggling to get up. The room begins to spin, slowly at first, but gradually gaining speed. The gray on the outside of my vision goes black and begins to close up, like the iris on a camera.

"Remlee, where is Remlee? Where is my daughter?" I ask frantically, but I never hear the answer. The warm, dark place has me again. Before I let go and drift completely, I shed a single tear.

Remlee

We spent our day lazily milling about the countryside. We drove aimlessly for hours, stopping at yard sales whenever one appeared. It was good to just be together, having fun and not worrying about anything. The weather was postcard perfect, and the day had an almost dreamlike cast to it. I kept waiting for something, anything, to swoop down upon us and deliver the reality that seemed to be on hold, but it never came. After lunch, I took him to the flea market a few towns over. I don't know why, but the flea markets up North are nothing compared to the ones you find down South. The one we went to was the size of a small town. Rows upon rows of pavilions marched out as far as the eye can see, all chock full of vendors plying their wares. Jack was awestruck at the variety of swag available. He bought a Jolly Roger flag, a set of nunchucks, a copy of the Bhagavad Gita, and a bag of Cajun-flavored boiled peanuts, all at the first table we came to.

"Is there anything you can't find here?" he asked incredulously.

"Hookers," I said teasingly, and he laughed heartily.

"I'm not sure about that," he said, his eyes glinting in the sun. "Did you see that woman standing next to the sunglasses display back there? I guarantee she'd blow me for a ten spot."

We explored the flea market for hours, people watching more than shopping. This was the melting pot you always hear about, this glorious mess of commerce. Black, white, red, and yellow, all together for one purpose: to find the best deals on useless crap. Here was the mini-UN assembled in a field in rural Florida. It was a coalition of bargain hunters gathered together in the pursuit of peaceful transactions. We heard English, Spanish, Hindi, Arabic, Cantonese, and Ghetto all being spoken at once, the multilingual haggling creating a symphony of human sound. It felt like we were just two cells bouncing around the body politic of humanity, two small parts of a giant whole.

By late afternoon, we took our leave of the flea market. Our tummies were rumbling, and there's only so much fried food a person can eat. We walked lazily to the Jeep, each swinging bags full of tchotchkes that neither of us needed. We headed back in the general direction of Stillwater in search of a place to eat. We found a barbecue joint on the edge of town, and it took little convincing to get Jack to go inside.

All throughout our meal, however, I began to feel uneasy. I was trying desperately not to think about it, but Jack's pending departure was weighing on my mind. I could feel the minutes slipping away through my fingers. I started to get angry with myself for allowing myself to focus on the time, but that only seemed to make it worse. I found myself checking my watch repeatedly, trying not to do the calculations that would tell me how much time we had left. I wasn't able to pay attention to him. I kept getting lost in my thoughts. This set off a guilt chain reaction in my psyche, and suddenly I began to cry.

"Whoa! Hey, what's the matter?" Jack asked, his face full of bewilderment.

"It's nothing," I said, trying to compose myself. "I'm just being stupid."

"What do you mean?" he asked, his confusion growing.

"I just don't want you to go as all," I said, my eyes downcast. I felt silly, like a little girl going to summer camp for the first time.

"I know," he said, reaching across the table to take my hands in his. "I don't want to go, either, but you know I have to. The bills don't pay themselves for some reason."

"We've been together so long now," I said. "I'm just used to you being around. It's comforting to have someone there, someone to come home to at night."

"You won't exactly be alone down here," he said with a sardonic smile.

"Yeah, but it's not the same, and you know it," I said, pouting.

"Well, you made this decision. Nobody made you. Just come back with me tonight. You don't owe these people anything. It's not like you signed a contract or anything," he said, exasperation hiding just under the surface.

"I know, I know," I replied grumpily. "I just can't leave all this to Jolene. You've seen her. There's no way she could do this shit by herself."

"Yeah, but—" he said, his frustration showing.

"And it's not like it's forever," I continued, hoping I sounded even remotely convincing. "I can leave anytime I like."

"Then leave tonight, with me," he said, folding his arms across his chest and looking smug.

"Aaarrrrggghhh!" I said, voicing my disgust at the situation. "I can't."

"Mmmmmm-hmmmmm," he said, his eyes dancing with unsounded laughter.

"Dammit, you know what I meant," I blustered. We sat without for a moment, neither of us really knowing what more to say. Finally, he broke the silence.

"You know, this won't be fun for me either," he said quietly, not looking up from his mug of beer.

I looked up at him with moistened eyes and saw he was fighting tears of his own. I wiped at my eyes, embarrassed, and took a sip of my drink, hoping to break off the awkward moment. I looked around the restaurant for anything to focus on, anything but Jack's face, because I knew if I saw him cry, I would lose it. For my part, I didn't relish the idea of providing a show for the other diners to ogle.

We finished our meal quietly and quickly paid our check. Jack bought a six-pack for the road, and I held my tongue. Things were tense enough without starting up a second front of our Cold War. When we left, I drove us around town, circling around and around. I didn't have a destination; I was simply avoiding going back to Jolene's. Once we got there, Jack would be leaving, and I still wanted to delay. I was hoping that if I could drag this day out long enough, he would agree to stay one more night and leave in the morning. That would have put him home a day later than he had told Trevor, but I knew that Trevor wasn't going to fire him over one extra day, busy season or not. I also knew Trevor wasn't the real reason Jack was in such a hurry to leave.

Although he never said anything, I could tell my family made him nervous. He wasn't exactly sheltered growing up, but he certainly didn't know anyone in a situation like my family's in any kind of intimate way. Poverty was something he read about in books and saw on TV but rarely actually saw in his childhood Cambridge home. As long as certain exits were avoided on the highway, he could easily forget that the poor were actual people and not just toys for his mother to play with to make herself feel less guilty for all she had. It wasn't until he went to college at Northeastern University that he had occasion to be around people whose family's entire household income was smaller than what his father paid in property taxes each year. To say that we came from different worlds would be the understatement of all time.

None of this, however, is meant to paint Jack as a snob. He's not. I know that he truly doesn't care about a person's circumstances, and he's willing to be friendly to anyone, but there is often is what I guess you would call a culture gap. There are certain things about class, even in our so-called classless society, that serve to alienate us from each other. Take sports, for example. Jack, like most red-blooded males from Massachusetts, lives for the Sox, the Pats, the Celtics, and the Bruins. I'm pretty sure he can tell you what size and brand of underwear Tom Brady wears. My family, however, couldn't give two shits about any of those sports. NASCAR is what was on the TV on Sundays at our houses. Another example is music. Jack is always up on whatever trendy indie rock band is hip at the moment, but the Shaws and Tuckers have no time for that art fag stuff. At our house, it was Hank, Dolly, Waylon, and Willie. And Skynyrd. Anything else was just, well, downright un-American.

He was just overwhelmed by us all, just like I was when I first met his family. I was terrified that first Thanksgiving when we pulled into the driveway of his parents' palatial home. I was sure, at any moment, someone was going to give me away, to notice that I didn't belong. I remember sitting at his parents' dining room table and realizing that it was longer than the living room of the apartment

I shared with two other girls. I barely spoke all evening, and when I did, my voice wasn't my own. My usual raucous and rowdy voice became small in their house, mousy and meek. Just knowing more was spent on this meal than I paid in rent each month made me feel small and insignificant. I kept expecting someone to finally call me out for the interloper I was, but no one did. Not with their words, anyways. Their eyes told a different story, though. So, too, did the subtle patronizing tinge their voices affected when talking to me, as did the attitude I was faced with, the one born of irritation and smug superiority. Jack told me I was being paranoid afterward when I told him this, but I know I wasn't. Men just aren't that observant sometimes.

Eventually, it became obvious that I was stalling, so I gave up my ruse and made the turn to head back to Jolene's, and by implication, Jack's departure. Jack tried valiantly to keep my spirits up with his obnoxious commentary on the town and its residents, but my laughs were only for his benefit. I knew I was being a baby about all this, that this entire venture was my decision. Knowing that didn't make it any easier, though. Cold rationality doesn't keep you warm at night, secure and safe in its arms. Reason makes a poor bedmate.

It was all I could do to keep it together when we pulled into the empty parking space in front of my sister's. I still wasn't ready for the inevitable, so I returned to the time-honored, time-wasting activity that has been used as an excuse to delay for hundreds, if not thousands, of years; I lit a cigarette. Taking my cue, Jack lit one of his own.

"I hate this," I said as I gazed out of the window.

"Me too," Jack replied, his voice low and all trace of joviality scrubbed clean.

We sat quietly until our smokes were butts, each not wanting to be the one to initiate the leaving process. My mind raced desperately, trying to find a loophole and escape from my predicament, but I could find none. Mama needed me more than Jack did right now. It was as simple as that. I couldn't—no, wouldn't—allow myself to abandon her. I wanted to prove to the world, and more importantly, to myself that I was better than her. I needed to be the one to look out for her, almost as some kind of twisted punishment. I wanted her to see me caring for her every day, even though she didn't do the same for me because I wanted her to see that she didn't ruin me. I might be damaged, but she wasn't able to completely remove my empathy or my humanity. I wanted to forgive her, not because it was the right thing to do but because it was the best method I could think of to repudiate my mother's life. By not allowing her to poison me against humanity, I was able to somehow claim some form of moral victory. That was the irony; I was being good in kind in the service of spite.

"Rem," he said, finally breaking the silence, "I gotta get going."

"I know," I said quietly. I briefly considered faking a panic attack (which, honestly, would only barely be faking), in an effort to forestall him a little longer, but immediately dismissed the idea as a childish stunt. I was a big girl, damn it; now it was time to act like it.

"Promise you'll stop somewhere tonight," I said pleadingly. "Don't try to push all the way through. And by somewhere, I mean an actual motel, not some parking lot on the side of the road."

He grinned sheepishly as he replied, "Aaawww, c'mon! That takes all the fun out of it!"

I shot him a look that suggested he dispense with the attempts at humor. He obviously got the message because he dropped his head, chastened, and mumbled, "Fine, fine. I'll stay in a proper motel."

The atmosphere changed at that moment, going from sad to awkward. I could tell he was as conflicted as I was, and he just wanted to get started. That's just how Jack was. Rip the Band-Aid off all at once, never count to three, just go. He would simply attack unpleasantness head-on, hoping to catch it unawares and claim an easy victory. I was more of a procrastinator, the idea being that if I just stay still long enough, maybe the unpleasantness will not notice me and move on. Usually, Jack would compensate for my hesitance, but not always. Every once in a while, he would just jump without looking, pulling me along into the unknown with him.

Summoning all my willpower, I turned to him and said, "Okay. I guess I'm ready. You're all packed up, right?"

"Yeah," he replied, chuckling. "I only brought a backpack, remember?"

I laughed along with him, and suddenly, I knew it would be all okay. The weight of twenty planets lifted from my chest, and I began to smile. I opened the door to climb out and begin the next phase of my adventure but paused to turn and kiss Jack one last time before he left. I closed my eyes as I melted into him and simply savored the moment. When the moment was over, we came apart, and I clambered out of the Jeep. He smiled goofily at me as I shut the door, and I blew him one last kiss. He caught it with dramatic flair, pretending to bobble it before triumphantly catching it and doing an elaborate celebration dance in the end zone that was the driver's seat. The Jeep began to creep forward as his foot slipped off the brake pedal due to his wild gyrations.

"Dude!" I shouted, laughing a warning, and he got the wayward vehicle under control.

"I love you forever," he said, a faint but detectable hitch in his voice.

"And I love you that plus one more," I replied, repeating our mantra. He gave a slow wave and began to pull away.

"Miss you!" I called after him.

"I know!" I barely heard him answer, and soon the Jeep turned right, onto the main road and out of sight. I stood rooted to the spot, waiting just in case he changed his mind. I heard the door of Jolene's trailer open and shut behind me, but I didn't turn around.

"You all right, Remlee?" Jolene asked quietly from the porch.

"Yeah, I'm fine," I lied and put on my best fake smile as I turned to her. I made my way up on the porch next to her. We just stood there quietly for a while, drinking in the teeming beauty all around. I supposed that there were worse places to be separated from your other half. I resolved to try to enjoy this time, to try to erase the past in my mind, at least all the bad parts, and reconnect with these people I ran so far from. There was closure here, somehow, and all I had to do was find it.

I was finally ready to begin looking.

Betty Sue

It's funny the things that you think about when you can't talk to anybody. After a while, you begin to look at the world differently. Things that used to fit together don't anymore, and things that previously held no similarities become inseparable. Everything is topsy-turvy, like on the deck of a schooner on a stormy sea. I'm learning, slowly as usual, the shape of this new world I find myself in. Now I just need a strategy on how to fit into it.

I can't rightly say I'm too optimistic on that front. Fitting into this society has never been something I've had much success at under the best of conditions, so to think I can do it now, when I can't even make myself understood, is more than wishful thinking; it's madness. I doubt I have enough of what it takes left in me now. Life has kicked me right in the teeth too many times. I'm not saying that I'm quitting, just trying to temper expectations. I'm tired of being let down.

It's been quiet on the ward today. Nurse Tinkerbell is off today, and her replacement is much quieter, less syrupy. I like her. She comes in, does what she needs to do, then fucks off. She's not rude, but she doesn't waste time trying to cheer me up with a bunch of small talk. I appreciate this, 'cause everyone else in this place is always on me to try to talk. It's goddamn exhausting is what it is, and I'm glad this nurse leaves me alone. I know I need to practice, but frankly, I suck at talking now, and failing over and over gets to you. I ain't got much in life to be all that proud of, and this loss of ability to talk for myself like an adult makes it one thing less.

I don't wanna sit around feeling sorry for myself, but there isn't much else to do around here. All day long, the same worries play over and over in my mind, and I can't do anything from here. I'm not really sure if I can do anything about anything anywhere at all anymore, and this scares me most of all. Yesterday (or was it the day before?), this social worker lady came in to see me. She said something about "assessing me" and then asked me a bunch of damn fool questions she knew I couldn't answer. She hardly looked at me as she read from her clipboard and just jotted down a bunch of stuff as I mangled the language in answer. She then started telling me about all these places I would have to go, all these steps that would have to be taken. It dawned on me that she was threatening to have me put in a home, and I began to panic. After a few minutes of soothing talk, she managed to calm me down and assure me that the home was only an option, but I'm still not sure I trust that. I've been lied to before.

I'm lost in thought, wondering what my fate will be, when Remlee walks in the room. I feel my face break forth in a smile, pleasantly surprised at her appearance. She told me she would come back the last time she was here, but until now, I wasn't sure if she actually meant it. She sits down on the chair next to my bed and looks at me with unreadable eyes.

"Hi, Mama," she says, a tentative smile touching the corners of her thin lips.

"Yu yu yu Remll," I say, beaming that I can say her name. Mostly.

"How are you doing?" she asks, and I wonder if she's forgotten about my condition. Then I realize she's just looking for something to say. Neither of us seem to know what to do, what the proper etiquette is for this situation. Is she just supposed to sit there silently? Am I supposed to bother answering her at all, given that she won't understand me anyway? We just sit there, warily regarding each other, and I decide to push my luck, and I respond to her query.

"F…F… Fne… Fne…" I stammer. "Chupp yu yu yu hed."

"What, Mamma?" she asks gently, and I point to my head and shake my head no.

"You have a headache?" Remlee asks, her tone perking up.

"Whyte…yu yu…whyte…yeah," I sputter, nodding vigorously. I'm all smiles now, despite my throbbing temples. We're getting somewhere!

"Do you need an aspirin or something? Do you want me to call the nurse?" she asks. Again, I shake my head no.

"Yu yu usa sublim. No. Yu yu yu did not good," I say. I already took two; they ain't no good.

"I don't understand you, Mama, I'm sorry," she says, and I try to dismiss it all with a contemptuous wave of my hand. I think she gets the point because she quits that line of conversation.

"Juh… Juh… Juhleenn?" I ask, wondering if Jolene is coming too.

"Not right now. Maybe later," she replies. My heart is soaring, despite this news. I'm having an actual conversation with the daughter I was sure I had lost! It might not be much of one, I admit, but it can't be denied. There is back-and-forth, a give-and-take, however rudimentary. I'll take what I can get.

"I'm going to stay down here for a while," she says, and my jaw drops to the floor. I can't believe what I'm hearing. I start to wonder if this is real or just another one of those fucking dreams I have. I'm having trouble telling dreamlife from waking life lately, so either option is possible. A small hot coal of dread sparks to life in the deepest parts of my guts, and I brace myself for that evil turn I'm sure is imminent, but it never comes. This is the real world, and something good is happening in it, no matter how unlikely that seems. I begin to relax, and I feel the tension drain from me.

"Yu yu yu ssttaaay?" I ask, making sure I'm hearing her correctly.

"Yes," she says soothingly, like she's talking a jumper off a ledge. "At least until we can figure out what to do with you."

My eyes tear up as I look upon Remlee's face with admiration. I can hardly believe I created this person in front of me. Sure, she looks like me, but she's so much better. She's stronger, somehow. Life kicked the shit out of both of us, but it don't seem to have affected her the same way as me. Life has made me bitter, petty, and mean as a snake. Remley's life wasn't no picnic either, but she's not like me. She didn't let it get to her somehow. Life fucked her and fucked her, but she don't let that make her treat people badly. I wonder where this character trait came from, we've already established that it ain't me, and her Daddy is even more twisted than I am. I don't think that man is even human.

"Jack went back home last night," she continues. "I'm gonna stay with Jolene for now until we can figure out how to get you squared away. I can't stay forever, but I'll be here for a little while longer."

I'm just happy she's here at all. I know I don't deserve her attention. Not everything that happened was my fault, but enough of it was that I can't expect to be exonerated. It's too early to say if I can repair what was broken, but I'm more grateful than I have ever been to have the chance. I just hope I don't fuck it up like everything else I touch.

There's so much I want to ask her, so much of her life that I don't know. We haven't spoken in years; I don't know the first thing about her. I have to remember that. She isn't the fourteen-year-old I remember. This woman is a virtual stranger, even though looking at her is like looking into a mirror. Okay, maybe an old photo of myself, if I'm being honest. I don't know where she works, who her friends are, what she does for fun. What kind of music does she like? Can she cook? Everything that makes a person who they are, the little details that combine to form an individual, all of it is a mystery to me where Remlee is concerned. Christ, does she have kids? Are there more grandbabies out there somewhere? My mind reels as I consider the possibilities.

"I talked to the social worker before I came into your room," Remlee says, and I perk up. This could be vital information. "She doesn't think you're going to be able to go back to your trailer, at least not at first. You're going to need looking after, at least until you get some of your words back."

This is not what I want to hear, but pretty much what I expected. The nosy little social worker told me as much when we talked earlier, if in a less direct manner. A little wind leaves my sails with this confirmation, and I try to remain hopeful.

"Jolene and I have been talking, and we're gonna figure it out. Will probably have to have you move in with her..." she says, but it's not at all what I want to hear.

"Yambu gunga pas!" I interrupt. No fucking way.

She peers at me with her stern face, the face of authority. My baby no longer, I gaze up at her in awe as she towers over me. Where did this woman come from?

"Look, I know you don't like it," she says, her face impassive. "None of us do. But there's nothing else to be done. Do you think Uncle Clarence is gonna look after you?"

I laugh out loud at that. Pigs would fly over frozen lakes of sulfur in Hell before I'd ever trust that snake to care for me. He wouldn't walk across the street to piss on me if I was on fire and holding a five-hundred-dollar bill.

"Exactly my point," she says, laughing with me. It feels good, better than I have ever felt since this whole ordeal started.

"Yu yu stup stup stup oh Lord," I stammer, trying to confirm that she is sticking around. I can't help but feel like this is too good to be true, that she's going to just up and take off again.

"It's okay, Mama," she says, sitting next to me and sliding her arm over my shoulder. I'm shocked at how big she is. I still can't seem to account for the passage of time. My mind gets it, I can do the math, but the feel is wrong. The physicality of Remlee today just don't match with what I'm used to, and somehow, this kind of scares me. The weight of all those years is beginning to become apparent. Those years I missed had real consequences, and those consequences were now cradling me like a baby.

"It's okay, Mama, it's okay," she repeats over and over, like it's some kind of sacred prayer. I clutch at her, desperate to hold on, terrified that if I let go, she'll just disappear like smoke. I close my eyes and concentrate on the realness of her. I listen to her heart beating, the breath rushing in and out of her lungs. She strokes my hair lovingly, and I began to relax, slowly, one little bit at a time. I feel myself becoming drowsy, and I fight to stay awake, convinced if I slumber, even for just a minute, she will be gone, never to return.

"Dunt gow, Remlee," I say, unsure if she understands me.

"I won't, Mama," she replies, and I think she means it. I let go, and I allow myself to drift. Time…passes…on…

Remlee

I woke up early the next morning with a start, thrashing around in the dark, searching in vain for Jack. He was my protector in the deep, dark night when I needed him most. Several frantic minutes passed before my mind caught up with my body, and I remembered my circumstances. I began to calm down, but a new feeling was creeping in and taking the place of terror. It hadn't even been twelve hours, and I already missed Jack to the point of distraction.

I glanced at my phone, and to my relief, there was a picture message in my inbox. I opened it to see Jack's grinning face all but obscuring the Motel 6 sign he was standing in front of. The accompanying text said, "I'm a good boy!" and I chuckled out loud when I read it. Jack, always the smart-ass. I sent him a brief reply after much deliberation. I didn't want to start a text avalanche. I needed to keep my mind here, on task, not thousands of miles away. Jack was grown, and he didn't need me to worry about him. He'd be fine.

The sun was just starting to rise, and I heard the alarm in Jolene's bedroom. Much commotion ensued as Gary loudly and violently struggled to shut the infernal racket off. I heard Jolene's voice raised in protest, but the walls were just thick enough in the trailer to hinder me from making out any specific words. Before long, an underwear-clad and sleep-puzzled Gary came stumbling out of the bedroom and into the kitchen. He paid me no mind, and I realized he had forgotten I was even there. I sat rooted to the couch, embarrassed into complete stillness. My mind quickly flashed the image of a rabbit, or some other small prey animal, frozen solid in alarm at the appearance of a stalking and hungry predator. It was irrational, I know. Gary knew I was there; I was a guest. That knowledge didn't stop the shiver from traveling up and down my spine as I watched him go about his morning rituals.

Once his coffee was brewed, he poured himself a cup and sat at the island in the kitchen, his back still turned to me. I began to get anxious, my bladder now awake and hectoring me to please, if I would be so kind, allow it to find relief. I began to squirm in my seat, hoping the motion would distract my body, trick it into forgetting it needed to pee. I figured I could just outlast him; he couldn't just sit there in his tightie-whities forever. Eventually, he'd have to get up and get dressed, and then I could slip into the john.

"Good morning, Remlee," he said, not turning around. "Coffee?"

I felt my cheeks turn red as I meekly answered, "Sure, thanks."

I stood up and made my way back to the bathroom, refusing to look back and see if he was watching. I let myself in and hurried out of my pants and onto the toilet. I breathed an audible sigh of relief as I rid myself of the previous night's accumulated liquid waste. I finished up and washed up, then went back out to join Gary at the island, where a steaming mug of liquid ambition awaited me.

"Sticking around awhile then?" Gary asked amiably.

"Until we get Mama squared away, anyways," I replied through greedy sips of coffee. I tried not to make notice that he was all but naked sitting next to me. If he wasn't uncomfortable, I figured there was no reason for me to be.

"Good luck with that," he said with a sarcastic grin.

"Yeah, thanks," I said with equal in sincerity. "I'm going to need it."

He stood up at that and disappeared back into the bedroom, presumably to get dressed for the day. I picked up the fishing magazine on the counter in front of me and began skimming through it as I drank my coffee. I was halfway through a fascinating article on the art of fly tying when Jolene sauntered into the room, bleary-eyed and coughing her smokers hack. She poured herself a cup and sat down heavily in the seat next to me.

"Wanna come with me today?" I asked.

"Maybe. When are you going?" she answered, her voice still thick with sleep.

"First thing, I guess. I mean, I'm gonna clean up and everything, but no later than nine o'clock or so," I said as I pulled out my first Camel of the day and luxuriated in its tasty poisonous smoke.

"I'll have to go with you next time, then," she said.

"Why?" I asked, curious as to what she could possibly have to do otherwise.

"That's when I gotta be at the clinic," she said, looking away from me in shame.

"Oh, okay," I said simply, not wanting to create an issue. I didn't need her there with me, and I figured that suboxone was better for my sister than heroin off the streets. At least it was clean, the dosage guaranteed. With suboxone treatment, Jolene might still be hooked on something, but that something at least had some oversight, or quality control, or whatever. You never know what you're getting when you cop on the street. At the clinic, you could be assured that, at the very least, you wouldn't overdose. Small victories are sometimes the most vital.

"If you wait, I can go with you," she said earnestly, and I could see she felt shame and guilt for needing her fix. I felt a lump forming in my throat, and I pushed it down, not wanting Jolene to see that I was upset.

"No, it's fine," I said reassuringly. "I'll be fine. She's going to be there for a few more days, anyways. We don't have to make any decisions about that right yet."

"About that," Jolene said, her tone quieter. She gulped her coffee down in a seeming attempt to fortify herself for what was to come and continued, "Gary ain't too hot of the idea of Mama staying here."

Before I could respond, Gary reappeared from the bedroom, almost as if summoned. He walked over to the counter and poured himself another cup of coffee, then turned and faced the two of us.

"I'm headed to work now," he said, mainly to Jolene. "Don't forget to pick up that part for the boat at Skip's today. He's been holding it for me for a couple of weeks now, and Ray-Ray paid me last night for that wheeler I fixed for him. We can finally get back out on Lake George fishing again."

"I will, babe," Jolene answered automatically as if she wasn't really listening.

"Seriously," Gary said, his voice cutting through the morning fog. "Don't forget. I know how you are, and—"

"Yeah, yeah, get the part from Skip. I got it," Jolene said, waving him away like a mosquito.

"I mean it," he said, his eyes flashing, and he turned to walk out the door. He stopped to put on his shoes and grab his keys, and without another word, he stepped out into the already sweltering morning.

"Prick," Jolene muttered, and she stood up and stretched out languorously, reminding me of our cat back home, Wesley Willis. I wondered for a moment if he was okay, if the little neighbor girl had to remember to take care of him. I decided he must be intact. I hadn't heard anything from Dana since I gave her the keys and instructions, and she seemed like a more or less responsible kid. Either way, Jack would be there soon enough, so I put it out of my mind and got back to the task at hand.

"So Gary's a no-go, huh?" I asked, unsurprised by this information. Gary hadn't struck me as the most generous of men.

"So far," Jolene replied. "I tried explaining how she is, how she can't live alone no more, but he didn't want to hear it. Just kept saying that it wasn't his problem, it was mine. Like I didn't fuckin' already know that."

I looked at her as she spoke, and the changes the years had wrought were plain to see. Her gaunt body quivered with suppressed tears of rage, and I was aghast at how emaciated she was. She was only wearing a long tank top, likely Gary's, and I was able to see more of her body than I had previously been privy to. The rough-and-tumble girl from my childhood, my protector, my idol, the toughest chick I knew, was now this wisp of a woman, her sallow skin hanging loosely on her frame, her eyes sunken deep into their sockets, her hair lank and dull, its youthful luster gone with the youth that produced it. What was left was just a husk, waiting for the winds of fate to scatter her once and for all. I thought of all the betrayals that led her here, and a spark of anger began smoldering away, somewhere deep inside of me, but I had no target to direct it at. There was no single guilty party, except maybe God, and if he does exist, which I seriously doubt, he's far beyond my reach.

"It's not like we don't have the room," she continued, her tears spilling, but her voice even. "He just can't be bothered. Now, if it was his Mama, well, you see what happens there. He bought the trailer next door for her, no questions asked. But fuck my family, I guess." Her normally brown eyes were black as she seethed, and I felt a chill pass over me as I looked at her. The expression on her face was that of a person who intends to commit murder, and I decided to try to pull her back down to a more reasonable plane.

"Aren't there any other options?" I asked hopefully. "What about this trailer park? Could we have her trailer moved here, where you can keep an eye on her easier?"

"I thought of that too, but no," she answered, and I noted with satisfaction that she was coming a bit. I was glad of it. I didn't need her hysterical on top of everything else.

"First of all, she don't own that piece of shit, she just rents it, so she couldn't move it if she wanted to," she continued. "Second, there ain't no empty lots in this park to move in to. Plus, it would cost three or four grand to move it here, if she did own her own trailer and there was a lot available, and she ain't got that kind of money. That idea is out. We gotta think of something else."

"What about the County Home?" I asked, knowing what the answer would be.

"She won't willingly go there," Jolene answered with a derisive laugh. "You should know better than that."

"I know," I said, frustrated edge entering my voice. "Can't we just, I don't know, fucking make her, somehow?"

"Your hubby's the one with lawyers in the family, ask him," Jolene said sharply.

"What the hell?" I said, my defenses immediately going up. "Why are you starting with me?"

"I'm not," she said, her voice softening a bit. "I'm just pissed off. This isn't fair, and I don't know what the fuck we're supposed to do."

"Have you talked to that social worker lady at the hospital?" I asked her, hoping maybe she had more luck with her than I had.

"I think so," Jolene answered, "but I don't know for sure. Everything is kind of a blur since this all started. There's just so many different doctors and nurses and therapists and what-the-fuck-ever's running around, all telling you a whole bunch of different shit, all while you're trying to deal with the fact that your mom's a goddamn vegetable in the bed in front of you. Point is, maybe so, but I don't remember anything she might have said."

"Well, I'll make sure to talk to her again today," I said, hoping that reassured her. The knowledge that she had an active partner in this fiasco would make her stronger, or so went my logic.

She wandered over to the sink and started tidying up the few dishes in the strainer, her shoulders hunched in the posture of the perpetually defeated. As she fiddled with the silverware, she gazed out of the window, not appearing to be really looking at anything specific, just looking at the tableau of waking nature framed by the panes of glass.

"Well, I'm going to get around and head over there," I said after the silence grew too uncomfortable.

"This early? Christ, it's barely 7:00 a.m.," Jolene said incredulously. "They won't even be open yet."

"That's okay," I said, moving to the living room and grabbing my duffel bag of clothes. "It'll take me at least a half hour to get dressed and cleaned up a bit. I'll just drive around a bit and sightsee for a few minutes to kill the rest of the time."

"What sights?" she asked with a contemptuous laugh. "This is Stillwater. You going to go see the meth heads passed out in the park? Or maybe you can tour the ruins of the old ice plant. Sightsee, she says. Ha! There is a good one."

I ignored her scorn, determined not to let her spoil my day. I was certain Mama would try her best to accomplish this feat, and there is no need to let Jolene beat her to the punch. I dug out what seemed to be the cleanest clothes in my duffel, silently thanking whatever benevolent force that was responsible for making this happen in the summertime. The last-minute dash to Florida from Massachusetts via update upstate New York was made easier by the lack of need for a different wardrobe. Had this happened six months earlier, I'd have been stuck in jeans and sweaters. Thank God, or Goddess, for small favors.

Jolene followed me into the bathroom, where I began to change. I knew she had more to say but wasn't in the mood for further discussion, so I let her stare awkwardly at me, refusing to speak first. I could feel her eyes on me, appraising and evaluating.

"Damn! You look good, little sis," she said with a cheesy wolf whistle.

"I guess," I replied, slightly embarrassed.

"No, seriously," she said, her face the picture of earnestness, "you're so smooth and firm. Everything is where it's supposed to be. Not like me, with my road map of stretch marks and saggy old tits. I bet you don't even need to wear a bra."

"Oh, come off it, of course I do," I said, flabbergasted. "Have you seen these things? There f'n ginormous!"

"Okay, fine," she admitted. "But otherwise, I stand by what I said. You're gorgeous."

"So are you, you know," I said, hoping she wouldn't see the lie in my eyes.

"No, I'm not," she replied with a sad laugh.

I started to protest further, but she held up her hand, saying, "I know better, Rem. I'm not blind. Those kids of mine ruined my body. That's what kids do. You'll find out, one day."

"No, I don't think I will," I said quietly. Jolene stopped cold at that and looked at me quizzically.

"What do you mean?" she asked, her eyes narrowed with suspicion.

"Just what I said," I answered, my voice still barely above a whisper. "I don't think I'll find out what kids do to your body."

"How do you figure?" she asked, genuinely perplexed. "Ain't you and your hunky gonna have kids?"

"No, that is definitely not in our plan," I said.

"You mean HIS plan?" Jolene retorted, her voice full of rancor.

"No, I mean OUR plan," I said, my voice steady. "Neither of us want kids."

"Why… What… What do you mean?" she asked, her eyes widening as if I had just told her I planned to move to Saturn.

"Just that," I said with exasperation. "We don't want kids."

Jolene shook her head, clearly taken aback. She sat down slowly on the toilet and spied a pack of Marlboros sitting on the stand next to her. She lit one up and slowly blew smoke rings out, just like she used to, back when we were kids, and she wanted to entertain me.

"Don't get me wrong," she said, her voice taking on a faraway cast, "sometimes I fantasize about what life my life would have been like if I had never had no kids, but I'd never give them up if it came right down to it. They're my heart. What other reason is there to life?"

"Who says there *is* a reason to life?" I asked and immediately regretted the harshness with which I spoke. Jolene's eyes grew so comically wide. I almost thought they might fall out of their sockets. She huffed and puffed as she considered her answer, seemingly offended by my question.

"Well, of course, there's a reason," she blundered, her face a mask of incredulity. "God has a reason for everything. He—"

"Which one?" I interrupted.

"Which one what?" she asked, and she gave me a look that is usually reserved for particularly slow children.

"Which God?" I asked, clarifying my initial query.

"Well… *God* God… I mean, you know, God," she said, still misunderstanding me.

"I mean do you mean Zeus? Poseidon? Indra? Jimmu Tenno? Ahura Mazda? Horus?" I asked, barely suppressing the vitriol that was threatening to boil over and out of my mouth.

"What the… No! I mean God! Like Father, Son, Holy Ghost," she answered. She looked at me like she had never seen me before or anything even remotely resembling me.

"Look," I said, lowering my intensity by several hundred watts, "I'm not trying to get into a theological debate with you. I'm just saying that neither Jack nor I feel the need to procreate just to appease some deity that may or may not exist."

"Okay, I guess," Jolene said slowly, obviously trying hard to wrap her head around my line of thinking. "But ain't you lonely, with just the two of you?"

"Sometimes, I suppose," I admitted. "That doesn't seem like a good enough reason to create a life to me, though. Face it, Jolene, life fucking sucks. Not all the time, sure, but a lot of it. Why would I subject someone else to that?"

"Yeah, but you could change that for them. You could turn it around, make it better for them than you had it," Jolene said, pleading her case passionately.

"Who are you trying to kid?" I asked with a mirthless laugh. "Who, exactly, do I have to look to for a role model there? Mom? Dad? No, I'd be a horrible mom, it's in my genes."

"You got me," she said quietly.

"HA-HA-HA!" I laughed bitterly. "Really? You're going to go there? Okay, fine, we can do this. Where are your kids right now, Jolene? Tell me, just how fucking great are their lives? Don't answer that, I already know. That's how I keep in contact with you. You call me every time one of your kids is fucked up somehow. They are knocked up, or strung out, or locked up. That's all I ever hear about you from you. Spare me the bullshit, okay? Please? I fucking know better."

Jolene seemed to shrink at this, curling in on herself in a defensive crouch on the toilet. Her eyes were wide with shock and crimson from the tears that were coursing down her cheeks. She covered her head with her arms as if to deflect a blow, and a single howl escaped her lips.

"Go fuck yourself," she hissed, somewhere between a sob and a roared threat, and she looked at me with red hot anger. I instantly regretted my words; I had no intention to hurt her.

"I'm sorry," I said quickly, hoping to plug the hole in the dike before the ocean of tears spilled over the levees completely, drowning us both in sorrow and regret.

"No, you're not," she said, sounding tired and defeated. "But that's okay. You are not wrong. I guess that's why it hurts so much."

I stood silently, unable to say anything to erase the past few minutes. Something in our relationship broke that night, irreparably. Sure, she would forgive my words, but she would never, ever forget them. The sting would always be there, like a jellyfish sting that just won't heal. Some intangible facet of our sisterly bond was destroyed, and nothing would ever be the same between us. Not coldness or indifference, just a hollow feeling where that nameless piece used to reside.

"I'm going to head over there now, to the hospital," I said blankly, overcome suddenly by the awkwardness that had crept into the room.

"Yup," Jolene replied flatly. She stood up abruptly and shuffled out of the room and into her bedroom, where she shut the door behind her. I could hear a few sobs escape from behind the closed door, and I hurried to get out of there.

"I'll be back in a few hours," I called over my shoulder as I walked out the door.

"Whatever," came her reply from inside her sanctuary. I shut the door behind me inside loudly as I leaned against the trailer. Great, now I have another fire to put out, I thought and began my walk to the hospital, where I hoped things would go better.

I needed something to put in the win column.

Betty Sue

I open my eyes, and Remlee is gone. The hospital is gone, this godforsaken stroke is gone, and the past few years are gone too. It takes me a minute for my eyes to adjust, but when they do, I realize I'm in Tiger's saloon. There's a rum and Coke in one of my hands in a smoldering Virginia Slim in the other. I take long pulls from one, then the other, and give a silent prayer of thanks for small comforts. The warm flush of the booze helps ward off the willies I get from these bizarre time travel/dream walks.

"Are you going to answer me?" asks a strident voice to my left. I turn to see who the familiar voice belongs to, and sitting next to me is Sandy. She's frustrated with me now because I seem to have beamed down here in the middle of a conversation, and I have no idea what it is we have been talking about. I feel like Scott Bakula, only I don't have a Ziggy to feed me information.

"Answer you what?" I asked, raising my voice to be heard over the pounding Bo Diddley beat currently being belted out by Mr. George Thoroughgood.

"What should I do?" she asks, her voice nearly cracking in her vexation.

"About what?" I ask stupidly, almost ducking to avoid the blows I'm certain are about to fall.

"Jesus Christ, Betty! Are you even listening to me at all?" she asks, a genuinely hurt look on her face.

"Yes, I'm listening. It's just so goddamn loud in here, that's all. Can we step outside?" I ask, hoping to explain my way out of her disapprobation.

"It's raining, Betty Sue," she simply replies, looking at me like she cannot believe how stupid I am being.

"I mean to the car," I say hastily, trying to cover my slip. She looks at me suspiciously, then walks toward the door. I follow her outside, won-

dering if I drove this particular evening or if she did. I follow her to the little red Toyota truck that I'm still driving to this day, or was until this fucking stroke, thank you very much, and one of the mysteries I'm contending with is solved. She clambers into the passenger side, slamming the door to keep out the weather. I slide into the driver's seat next to her and shut my door tight as well. The rain pelts the roof over our heads, and the sound of it is relaxing, hypnotic. I began to pat myself dry with a towel, then I hand it to Sandy.

"Now, what's going on?" I ask, turning to face her. I hold both of her hands in mine, and I gaze directly into her eyes. I want her to know she has my full attention.

"I've been asking you all night if you think I should leave Hollis," she says, exasperated beyond all measure.

"Why now?" I ask. "It's not like you've ever actually been happy with him."

"I think he'll end up killing me if I don't," she says, and I can see the truth of it in her eyes.

"What's different now, though?" I ask, pressing her further. "You've been nursing bruises for years now. Why the sudden change? Don't get me wrong, leaving that no-good son of a bitch would be the best thing you could do, I reckon, but I've been telling you that for years. What changed all of a sudden that you're talking about leaving?"

"It's nothing really," she says, her face full of confusion. "Nothing specific, anyways. I'm just sick of it, that's all. I done put up with his beatings, his whoring and gambling, everything, and I'm just tired. I don't want to do it no more. Now that Stevie's moved out and off driving truck, there's just no reason for me to put up with it no more. I've just been hanging on these past three or four years, waiting. Now, I'm ready to go, I think."

"You know you're welcome to stay with me," I say, and she smiles sadly at me.

"You don't think that will be the first place he looks?" she asks, and I don't say anything. She's right, of course. We've been nearly inseparable for years now. There is no way Hollis Chalmers wouldn't be banging on my door first if Sandy came up missing.

"Where will you go then?" I ask.

"Don't know yet," she answers with a steely glint in her eyes. "Not sure I even care. I'd sleep in a tent in the swamp at this point if it got me away from that cocksucker."

I can tell she means it. Her jaw is set, as is her path. I know that now, she's finally ready. Those other times, they were practice. They were just feints, ruses to test his borders, his security. She tells me that she's been thinking about this for weeks now, that is now or never. She tells me it has to be tonight. She's ready tonight. She might not be brave enough in the morning. I'm not really listening, though. I'm frantic that I am unable to warn her, unable to impart the information I have, gained through living through this very night once before. I try to open my mouth, to scream, "No, don't do it!" but some unseen force stops me. The past is obdurate, unyielding to change. What happened, happened, and nothing I can do will change it.

I hear myself encourage her defection, plot with her a means of escape. I feel like I'm watching a horror movie of my life, and I want to scream at the screen a warning, but I'm unable to break away from the script as it was written, just over five years ago. I am unable to prevent myself from driving her out to the farm, where I proceed to convince Clarence and Earls Three and Four to hide Sandy there, just for a day or two, until other arrangements can be made.

Dread establishes a base camp in the pit of my stomach, preparing itself for the ascent to the top of my consciousness. I know the events that follow. They've haunted me since the time I first experienced them. I lead her to the couch where I tuck her in and tell her lies about her safety. I kiss her forehead and bid her good night for what I now know will be the last time. I try to hold on longer, to extend the moment. I want to smell her, the realness of her, just a little longer, but the past is relentless, and it pulls me away, dragging me to my truck and back out into the night.

My truck seems to have a mind of its own. It takes me back to my trailer without my input. I make my way inside and pour myself a drink, hoping to steel myself for what I know is inevitable. I sit down hard on the couch, suddenly dizzy. The room begins to spin, the edges of things blurring with the perceived motion. I feel myself fall back onto the couch, but I just keep falling instead of stopping on the cushions. Everything is black, and I realize, with enormous relief, that I'm back in the warm, dark place. Time goes on vacation again, and I float in the sublime nothingness.

I barely have time to enjoy the oblivion when I'm pulled violently back into the dreamscape. I open my eyes, and I'm in the waiting room of St. Mark's, the same place my body is lying right now, reliving this nightmare all over again. My cheeks are wet, my eyes feel swollen, and I realize I've been crying. Earl Three is sitting next to me, looking dazed. There's a line of blood running down the side of his face from the hanky he's holding to his temple. The hanky used to be a faded blue, but now it's a deep purple, almost black, soaked as it is with his blood. Earl Three has never been the smartest character, and I worry that the vicious blow delivered to his skull by Hollis Chalmers won't help matters much. Earl had the dishonor of being the one who answered the door when Hollis came knocking, looking for his errant wife, and now he's paying dearly for his momentary lapse into chivalry, telling Hollis Chalmers to go take a flying fuck at a rolling donut.

I look at my brother like I've never seen him before. While certainly not the meanest of my siblings, that honor goes to Jedediah, that snake; Earl Three wouldn't ever be mistaken for Mother Teresa. Yet here he sits, bleeding from the head, all to protect a woman who he ain't even sleeping with. I wonder for a second if maybe he's changed over the years. Lord knows I stay far enough away that I probably wouldn't notice, at least under normal circumstances. I'm trying to reconcile the man who risked his own neck taking on a well-known and feared professional psycho like Hollis Chalmers to protect someone else with the boy who used to sit on my chest and torture me with all manner of creepy crawlies, and I'm coming up short. It just goes to show that people can surprise you sometimes.

I'm reeling with shock as I wait to hear from the doctor. Hollis had gotten wind somehow that Sandy was hiding out on the farm, and he came out to collect what he considers to be his. I wasn't there when he arrived. Only Earl Three and Sandy were there. Earl Three fought him valiantly, but even he was no match for that wolverine. After clubbing Earl over the head with a tire iron and leaving him for dead, he managed to hunt down Sandy, and he then enthusiastically administered the beating to end all beatings to her terrified and quivering body. When Earl Three came to, he called the ambulance, then me, before gingerly picking up Sandy's ravaged body, barely alive now, and walked out to the dooryard to wait for help. Hollis had disappeared, and only blood and suffering lay in his wake. It would be nearly a week later when authorities would finally catch him in a Las Vegas brothel, drunk and crying in the bewildered prostitute's arms.

I fight myself to stay calm, to let the doctors do what it is that they've trained for. It takes all my willpower to remain sitting here, to not blast through the ER doors and locate my friend. I want to hold her hand and tell her she's not alone and that everything is going to be just fine. I know it's a lie, but the thought of her dying alone and terrified is more than I can bear. I feel guilty as hell, being the one stupid enough to think that the farm would be a safe place for her, to actually believe my family could have the discipline, just once, to keep their stupid fucking mouths shut and help me protect the only person who has ever stood by me. I find myself praying, hoping that my absence from the pews will have gone unnoticed. I have heard it said that God doesn't bargain, but I try anyways, just in case I've gotten some bad intelligence. I offer him anything, anything at all, if he will just let Sandy pull through. I don't think I can make it in this rotten old world without her.

My guilt is eating me alive. I can't forget that it was me who helped usher her into his grip; it was I who damned her. I'd give anything right now to take her place. She never deserved this, and I put her here, just as much as Hollis's fists. It was my cowardice in not standing up to Elmer and Hollis that put her in that hospital bed. Hollis is just like a cannon. He destroys whatever he is pointed at, and I aimed him right at Sandy. Because I was lonely. I knew what I was condemning her to, but I put her on a dinner plate and served her right up to be devoured, just so I wouldn't be devoured alone. I was already in hell, and I dragged her down in with me, just so I wouldn't be alone. My selfishness is what is going to get her killed.

I stand up and begin to pace. The wait for the bad news seems to take forever. Every minute is dragged out, stretched to its breaking point until it snaps and the next minute begins. I feel anxious, but I shouldn't, because I already know the outcome. It's like my mind has doubled, and I am simultaneously experiencing this for the first time, but this is also a memory I've relived countless times. This doubling, or rather my rec-

ognition of this doubling, has me almost giddy. I just want the doctor to come out and say the horrible words, the words that finally break me, the words that convince me that there truly is no hope.

Yet at the same time, there is a small part of me that thinks that maybe, just maybe, things will be different. Maybe Sandy will pull through after all. There's no doubt that Hollis will go to jail for this. This is attempted homicide, or I'll eat my hat. Maybe she survives, and I get my friend back. I won't have to be alone in this world. I never deserved it, but Sandy never abandoned me, not like everyone else I ever cared about. We can move in together, two old birds against the world. I'll have her back, and she'll have mine. Most of all, I won't have to feel this crushing guilt. I'm pretty sure this guilt is going to be a big burden for me to carry. Oh, please, God, please, let her make it through. Just this once, let the past be changed.

It isn't to be, though. The doctor comes through the door separating the injured and the dying from the looky-loos and the mourning, and I feel my knees grow weak, almost pitching me onto the floor. No, no, no, no! This has to stop now. Oh, God, please let me go back to the warm, dark place, back to my uncommunicative body, anything but this. I can't hear the words again. I just can't.

"Ms. Shaw? Mr. Tucker?" the doctor calls, searching for the unfortunate hearers of the bad news that is his displeasure to have to impart. I consider running, simply bolting like a thoroughbred out of the gate. Maybe, if I can just outrun this, it will keep it from being real.

"Yes, sir, that's us," I hear Earl Three say, and I want to kill him. Why are you giving us away? Don't you know what he's going to say? Oh, dammit, Earl Three, why can't you just keep your fool mouth shut?

The doctor approaches us, and I can see the news in his eyes before he utters a single word. There is genuine sorrow there. He is truly heartbroken that he's lost her.

"I'm sorry to have to say this," he begins, his high voice full of gravitas and sincere sympathy, "but Mrs. Chalmers didn't make it. We did all we could, but she simply lost too much blood. The amount of trauma… Well, it was massive. Honestly, I'm surprised she even made it to the hospital. I'm so sorry."

"I don't want it," I say, barely above a whisper.

"How's that?" the doctor replies quizzically.

"I don't want your sorry," I say, the dam bursting and tears pouring down my face. "I want my friend!"

I collapse in a puddle on the floor, all strength leaving suddenly. I feel my heart breaking in half, and I haven't heard this bad since Jesco died, maybe ever. I had more time with Sandy than I had with Jesco. There's more history there. Either way, I'm destroyed, immobile, and bawling in the middle of the waiting room. Earl Three reaches down to try to comfort me, but I push his hand away. I don't blame him, not exactly, but he's also the last person I want comfort from right now. I have no way of proving it, but I'm positive it was his big dumb-ass mouth that led Hollis to the doorstep of Sandy's sanctuary. I know the dumb oaf didn't mean no harm. He's just kind of slow, don't think before he speaks. Hell, he don't hardly think at all, truth be told, and his stupidity cost my friend her life. That kind of stupidity ain't easy to forgive.

All eyes in the waiting room are on me now. I can feel the weight of their collective stare. Most people would rather you just keep your despair to yourself, thank you very much. Nothing seems to make people more uncomfortable than the public display of utter sadness. The human instinct to nurture goes AWOL when a stranger's world falls apart in front of us. It's just easier to watch from the sidelines than it is to actually help a human being in the depths of the most physically debilitating of emotions. We say, "There but for the grace of God go I," and then step right over the person as they wail, forgetting all about the unpleasant little incident by dinner. I ain't got no room to talk. Lord knows I never give money to the panhandlers downtown that pass through from time to time. There's plenty of old folks dying of terminal loneliness in these nursing homes, but I don't go befriend them, even though it would brighten both of our lives. That would take effort. What a terrible species we are. No wonder God tried to drown us all.

Presently, I manage to gather myself together. Earl Three is standing over me, looking confused. He is concerned and wants to help, but I can tell he's afraid I'll bite his damn hands off if he gets too close. It's not that he's afraid of me. He's kicked my ass too many times for that to be a possibility, but he's hurting enough already from getting walloped by a tire iron, and any more blows would be more than he is willing to tolerate today. I see his swollen, bloody knuckles, and a small sense of pride blooms in me for my brother. Hollis didn't get away unscathed, Earl Three took a big chunk out of his ass, and he's gonna have scars for the rest of his life to remember us by. I guess I'll have to take satisfaction where I can get it.

I manage to get to my feet, but I'm seeing double, my tears acting like prisms. I wipe my eyes to clear them, and when my vision clears, I'm no longer at St. Mark's. It's three days later, and I'm at the graveyard. There's a gaping maw in the earth that Sandy's casket hangs over, and I imagine hungry noises coming out of it. The stench of death is everywhere. I look around at everyone gathered, and I'm frozen with terror. These aren't people mourning a loved one. These are the damned, here to claim another soul.

"No!" I scream, my voice ragged and chill. "No! You can't have her! She ain't never hurt nobody!"

I hurl myself at the closest wraith, pounding its chest uselessly. It seems immune to my wrath; my blows have no effect whatsoever. Undaunted, I batter on, focusing all my hatred, all my righteous indignation on the unfeeling specter that is absorbing my onslaught.

"You...can't...have...everyone!" I shriek, punctuating each word with an impotent punch to the revenant's unfazed rib cage. I feel the bones snap under my fury, but the damned continues to stare right through me at the object it truly desires, Sandy's casket. It begins lurching toward it, and I try desperately to hold it back. I've got a hold of its leg, and I'm holding on like Daddy taught me to hold on when riding our old stallion, Midnight. It drags me along like I weigh nothing, and I feel the rough ground tearing at my clothes, scraping my knees. Its companions are converging now too, closing in on poor Sandy. I know that when they reach her, they'll drag her down to hell. If I let the creature pull me along, maybe I'll get sucked down along with her. So be it, if this is what's to come. Hell is no worse than I deserve. I might as well get on with it.

I can see the flames pouring out of the hole in the earth. I'm right at the edge now. The damned have reached Sandy's coffin, they're lovingly caressing it, and strange sounds are emanating from their motionless mouths. It sounds obscene, like a demonic parody of a baby cooing. I begin to feel nauseous, the fumes pouring out of the grave are poison. I cough and hack. I can't seem to quite catch my breath.

I'm beyond fear now. All rational thought is gone. I'm on the brink of madness. A deep voice comes out of the fire, speaking a language I've never heard, but I can feel the malice of the words like I can feel the rays of the sun. I don't know if it's talking to me or to the horde I'm surrounded by, but the words fill me with the nameless, singular dread. My despair is total. All is ruin. I see a dark shape sitting within the flames, seeming to be both inside them and somehow of them, like a spirit constructed of flame and sulfur. The shape gets closer and closer, filling my entire field of vision. Two giant green eyes open, eyes filled with hatred and revulsion. Horrified, I try to look away, but I can't. The eyes have locked me in. I'm hypnotized.

"I'm here for you, too, Betty Sue Magoo," the voice sings, suddenly childlike and teasing. I try to scream, but the inferno rushes into my mouth when I open it, burning me all the way through.

"Dear God, please help me!" I scream with all I have left and immediately begin choking on the rancid air.

"He can't hear you here," the voice mocks and I'm falling, down, down, down into the deepest, darkest pit. The pit is Gehenna, and it is forever.

Remlee

After visiting with Mama, I found myself alone in a familiar yet ultimately foreign place with nowhere to go and nothing to do. Despite Jack's provenance, we weren't idle rich. His family may have given us a decent start, but we worked for all we have. I wasn't used to having nothing to do on a weekday afternoon, and I was out of sorts, unsure of what to do with myself. Normally, at 10:30 a.m. on a Thursday, I'd be ordering my supplies for the weekend and leaving early to make the deposit. I had my staff taking care of that now, and I felt out of place. I had a position in life, a function, be it ever so humble, that I served. It may not have been at the forefront of my thoughts, but I drew pride from that. I pulled my weight by the sweat of my brow. I fed the masses their breakfasts and lunches, fueling the construction workers, firemen, insurance salesmen, and cops that made our city run. Maybe I was only a small part, seemingly insignificant, but I slept better at night knowing that what I did that day made some people's lives better, if only by giving them a satisfying meal. It was honest. Everyone walked away happy, their situation improved. My bills get paid, and their bellies leave them alone for a few hours. Win-win, all around.

I pulled out my phone and called Jack, just to hear his voice. That nasal Boston accent was a sound that had become part of the background, as much as a part of my home as the four walls that housed me. He answered on the second ring, ever the dutiful husband, and I dashed off a silent prayer of supreme gratitude to whoever was responsible for placing him in my path.

"Hey, babyface," he said brightly, his breath heaving. "How goes it?"

"It goes well enough, I guess. What are you doing, anyways? Why are you breathing so hard?" I replied with queries of my own.

"I just ran back to the truck to grab my phone. I'm at work right now," he explained.

"So you made it back, I see," I said imperiously, leaving unsaid the rebuke for not calling me immediately upon arrival.

"Yeah, late last night. I was bushed, so I passed out almost immediately. I never made it off of the couch," he said, and I accepted without note his unsaid apology for the non-offense he didn't commit.

"And you went to work today?" I asked, surprised he was able to drag himself out of bed. Most mornings, I had to practically pour a pitcher of water on him to get him to stir.

"I'm just dedicated, you know?" he said, laughing.

"No, you're just dick-whipped by your boyfriend, Trevor," I said, teasing.

"The fact that Trevor has a lovely penis is irrelevant," Jack deadpanned, and I lost it at that, breaking down into gales of unbridled laughter. After a few moments, I was able to pull myself back together.

"Seriously, though," I began when my laughter abated, "everything's okay up there? No fires to put out?"

"No, ma'am, the view's clear from here," he said. "Listen, Rem, I gotta go. We've got like, eight lawns to do. Trevor's been whinging all morning about how behind he is because I was gone."

"No, I understand," I said, suppressing the urge to urge him to tell Trevor to go fuck himself. Not that Jack would've obeyed me, but Trevor's always been good to us, put up with a lot of bullshit from Jack that would never be tolerated elsewhere. It would be rather gauche to disrespect him now, not to mention wildly self-destructive. It wasn't really Trevor I was upset with anyways, so biting the hand that fed would have led me to doubt my own sanity.

"Look," he said, his voice lower, almost conspiratorial, "I'll call you back later tonight, when I get off, okay?"

"Okay, love y…" I started to say, but the clicking in my ear made it clear that the recipient of my sentiment wasn't there anymore. I stared in shock at my phone, disbelieving that he had just hung up on me. While it wasn't done in anger, his motives were beside the point. For a second, a wave of despair so black it terrified me washed over me. I felt I would drown in it, lost forever in a sea of grief. I fought the feeling, and it was quickly replaced with self-recrimination, and I began my usual process of self-flagellation, disgusted as I was by the absurdity of my emotional excesses. The man and I had barely been separated for a day, and it already felt like an eternity. A queasy sensation gripped my core as I attempted to calculate the minutes until I could be with him again, but I suck at algebra, and I couldn't figure the unknown factors.

I started walking, not to any specific destination, just aimlessly strolling along the streets that still haunt my dreams. Things began to take on a surreal cast as every corner I turned brought out surprising memories, the minutiae of a life I had once run from. Looking back, I think it was the subtle changes that led to such a topsy-turvy feeling. Houses were painted in different colors. Businesses had moved and renamed themselves. Different faces were sitting on the porches that used to belong to someone else. I felt out of place, even though this was the town that spawned me. I walked past my elementary school and sitting there, where I first learned to read, where I made my first friends, the first place where my particular interests were encouraged rather than ridiculed was a Dollar General. They had come in, knocked down one of the only bright points in my otherwise dismal childhood, and replaced it with a box full of cheap household supplies and discount clothing. I turned and ran the other way, desperate to put distance between myself and that obscenity.

I headed back in the direction of Jolene's mainly because I was at a loss as to what else to do. It was far too early to go sit in a bar, the library was closed, and I didn't know anyone anymore. The rapidity with which loneliness was asserting itself in my psyche surprised me. I expected to miss Jack, terribly even, but it was almost embarrassing how quickly that happened. I had always prided myself on my independence. I wasn't going to be one of those pathetic housewives who can't shit without their husbands' input. The fact that I felt so lost, so quickly, was a giant blow to my ego. I was a modern woman, dammit; I didn't need no man to make me whole.

By the time I made it back to Jolene's, I was sweaty and hangry. The midday sun had warmed the air rapidly, and the humidity was compounding the problem exponentially. It felt like walking through a wet electric blanket without the risk of electric shock. My body felt twenty pounds heavier, like the gravity had ratcheted up in intensity. I trudged my way up the steps and into her house, collapsing in a heap in front of the air conditioner. As I lay there, cooling myself to a more reasonable body temperature, I began to marvel at how much the heat had affected me. As a child, I could run and play all day, rain or shine, all year round. The climate wasn't a factor, somehow. It's as though the exuberance of youth somehow acted as a shield, blocking me from the effects of the world, and as I aged, the protection wore off.

I got up and began to search for Jolene. Her car was gone from out front, so I figured I would be unsuccessful. When I was unable to locate her, I decided to raid the fridge and placate the growling nuisance in my belly. I found the remains of some kind of Mexican casserole and decided that it was likely my best option. I heated it up in the microwave, then took it to the couch, where I sat and put on some daytime trash television to keep me company with my meal. I flipped through the stations and finally settled on the Ellen show, content to watch her awkwardly dance with celebrities hawking their newest offering. Today, Jennifer Lawrence was gushing about her oh-so-spiritual vacay to Bora Bora, and I zoned out and ate, only half listening to her adventures. I was uneasy about Mama, and my thoughts kept wandering back to her and her dilemma.

I must have fallen asleep because the next thing I knew, Jolene was standing over me, calling my name and tickling my ears with a feather. This was always how she would wake me as a child, and for a moment, I almost thought I was back there, in the past.

"Wake up, sleepyhead," Jolene cooed, and I swatted at the feather, knocking it out of her hand.

"Wha… What's going on?" I asked thickly, the unexpected sleep still fogging my brain.

"Just got home," she replied, and she sat down next to me. "How was Mama?"

"Basically the same, I guess," I said. "She managed to say my name again. And the word 'stay.' Not much else."

"God, it's horrible," Jolene said, her voice full of pity. "Can you imagine what it must be like for her? Not being able to talk? It must be like being a baby all over again."

"Yeah, except baby doesn't know what's going on," I pointed out.

"But does Mama? Really? I mean, who knows what's going on in her head? She can't tell us. She might be completely gone in there. How would we know?" Jolene asked.

"Well, she can basically answer yes or no questions," I said.

"But can she?" Jolene pressed. "I mean yeah, sort of, but she gets that wrong too, sometimes. It's not like she's been doing well otherwise, before the stroke, I mean."

"What's that supposed to mean? Not doing well?" I asked, completely at a loss as to what she was talking about.

"She's been going downhill for the last few years," Jolene explained. "Just like Granny. She's losing it, Rem. The big D—Dementia."

"I didn't know," I said, horrified.

"Of course, you didn't. How could you have? You'd have to actually talk to us to know that," she said, the rancor in her voice readily apparent.

I ignored her jab and asked, "How bad was it?"

"Bad enough to be a problem, not bad enough to do anything about," she answered, and I could see the struggle had worn on her.

"You're gonna need to explain better than that," I said, a sharp edge creeping into my voice.

"Just that," she said, shrugging. "Like, she forgets what day it is, or forgets to pay the light bill..."

"How is that any different for her?" I asked, interrupting her.

"Haw-haw," Jolene replied sarcastically. "You know what I mean."

"No, I don't," I said, my tone rising. "That's why I'm fucking asking! This isn't a joke, sis. She's been a drunk for decades. She always was bad with responsibilities. What's different now?"

"I don't really know how to put it," Jolene said, her face the portrait of confusion. "She's just been different. Off. It's not like her usual forgetfulness." She fell silent at that, and it seemed like she was trying to remember something, digging deep into her own psyche to unearth a nugget of understanding to share with me.

"It's like just last month," Jolene began after a minute, her voice and expression far away. "She was giving me a ride to the store 'cause the car was in the shop. After we were done, she started heading to the old apartment by the ice plant. The one we lived in when you was little. I realized where she was heading, and I asked her, 'Where are you going?' and she told me, 'To our house, Remlee, remember?' I knew right then, and there something was off. Not only was she taking me to a place we haven't lived in for twenty-some years, but she thought I was you!"

As she relayed this to me, I could see that Jolene was scared. Our mother was falling apart before her eyes, and she had no one to help her with her. Guilt began tapping at the edges of my mind, howling their mad pleas to be granted access and allowed to run riot.

"It's just small stuff like that, really. Little slip-ups, here and there, nothing major. I mean, she was still going to work, paying her bills, mostly, you know, keeping up. I was worried a little but not freaking out yet. I guess I just hoped she would get over it, like a cold, you know?" she said, and I understood completely. I, too, have the tendency to try to ignore unpleasantness in hopes that it clears itself on its own.

"Jesus," I breathed, overwhelmed by this new information.

"Exactly," Joleen agreed.

I could see the toll all this had taken on Jolene. It was no wonder she was an addict. I don't think, had I never left, that I would have turned out any different. All that stress, all the time, from every corner, would have to wear you down eventually. Life had defeated Jolene, completely trounced her, and it was evident in her posture, her every gesture, even the quality of her voice. A dullness had crept into her eyes, a deadening. To survive her own family, my poor sister had to basically kill herself off slowly. It had been so long since she had seen anything even remotely resembling hope, that she probably wouldn't have recognized it if it blew in through the door.

The guilt monster began rapping even harder on the door of my mind as Jolene continued her description of mom's descent into madness, demanding entry. I held off as long as I could, but eventually, like always, it managed to work its insidious fingers through the cracks and ripped the door clean off its hinges. Once inside, it began trashing everything insight, once again set on its course of destruction. It wasn't fair that all of this had fallen on Jolene's shoulders. One night of careless teenage passion was all it took to plant the seed that would grow to be the tether that held her in Stillwater. I, however, got out before I could be trapped, and I felt like a soldier who left his buddy behind to face certain doom. I had the chance to live my life, free of this place and these people, free from the infamy that my name held.

In Massachusetts, I was just another working-class woman. The stories of the numerous crimes and other notorious acts that led to the negative notoriety my family held had never been heard there. I could apply for a job at the grocery store without having to explain that, no, I wasn't the Shaw that robbed the place last year, and no, I'm not the one who took out the Christmas display with my car after a weeklong meth binge. Jolene never had such luxuries. Everywhere she went, people knew who she was, what family she belonged to. Small towns are unforgiving like that.

"What the hell are we gonna do with her?" I asked after a moment.

"Don't know," Jolene answered, "but we better come up with something soon. The social worker called me while I was out and said that they're probably going to discharge her in the next day or so, as long as we got a place for her to go. I didn't tell her we didn't have that yet."

"Why not?" I asked, flabbergasted. "I mean, will they keep her longer if she don't have a place to go?"

"Sort of? Maybe? I don't know," Jolene said with a frustrated sigh. "I didn't say anything because I don't know what *to* say. She don't want to go to a home, and even if she did, she ain't got no money to pay for that. Those places are fuckin' expensive. And she can't go back to her trailer, we done already been over that."

"So what does that leave us?" I asked. "The farm?"

"Naw, that won't work. She won't go there either, even though there's plenty of room. Her and Clarence..." Jolene said, pausing for dramatic effect. "They just don't like each other. Period. One of them would end up offing the other before a week was out."

We were in a bind, and none of the possible solutions were likely to work. Mama was just too difficult, too stubborn. There was too much bad blood, too many petty wars between ever-shifting factions over the years, for my family to ever function as a healthy unit.

"What about next door, with Gary's mom?" I asked suddenly, brightening at the prospect. "She's got an extra room over there, and it's right next door."

Jolene shook her head slowly and replied, "Gary probably won't go for it."

"What?" I asked, shocked. "Why the fuck not?"

"It's not his mama," Jolene said, and I could see that even she wasn't buying her own bullshit.

"You haven't even asked, have you?" I ask, the situation resolving itself in my mind.

"Yes, I fucking did!" Jolene replied haughtily, and I knew she was lying. "It was the first thing I thought of."

"And he just said no. No explanation as to why, just straight-up no?" I asked derisively.

Jolene squirmed under my interrogation but held firm, saying, "Well, he had his reasons."

"Like?" I pressed.

"I don't know! He just don't want her here, that's all," she said, her voice full of nervous tension.

"Well, maybe I should talk to him," I offered, and Jolene's face went pale as milk.

"That wouldn't be a good idea," Jolene quickly said, her nervousness edging toward raw panic.

"Why not?" I asked, knowing full well what the truth was. Jolene didn't want the responsibility. I didn't blame her. I didn't either.

"He'll say it's none of your business," Jolene answered, her eyes darting about as she searched desperately for an escape from the conversation.

"Of course, it's my business, she's my fucking mom!" I countered.

"Yeah, but it's *his* trailer, he owns it. It's in *his* name, not *mine*, I got no say," Jolene said, a new to finality in her voice.

"That's fucking bullshit, Jolene, and you know it," I said through clenched teeth.

"Sure is," Jolene agreed, her face the portrait of resignation, "but that don't change nothing. It is what it is."

I sat quietly for a moment, trying to think of anything that might help our situation. I kept drawing blanks. I couldn't seem to make things fit. It was like trying to construct a new chemical using the most volatile elements on the periodical chart without blowing up half the world in the process. We were attempting to create cold fusion in the living room, and neither of us knew what the fuck we were doing.

"We're just going to have to ask him again," I said resolutely. "The two of us, together, like a tag team."

"That makes sense," said Jolene, "'cause it's going to be one hell of a fight."

"So you'll try?" I asked hopefully.

"I guess," Jolene answered unenthusiastically. "I don't see what other choice we got."

"We could let them put her in the County Home," I said, leaving her room to try to wriggle free, if she wanted to.

"No, we can't," she replied, her voice maudlin. "I can't have those poor workers' blood on my hands."

I broke out laughing at that, and before long, Jolene joined in. We spent the next few months in hysterics, each laughing at the other in a chain reaction of hilarity. Before long, my sides hurt, and I was gasping for breath, and I saw that Jolene was similarly afflicted.

"Seriously, though," Jolene said after we had managed to pull back from the brink of lunacy, "I would feel bad for anyone who had to look after her."

"Me too," I agreed. "So we'll ask Gary tonight? To save the lives of a few candy stripers?"

"I guess so," she answered apprehensively. "I just hope he agrees."

"He has to," I said. "What other choice do we have?"

Betty Sue

I open my eyes with a start, my breath coming in short, ragged gasps. The inhuman voice of the pit is still ringing in my ears, laughing in triumph. It knows it has me, that my soul belongs to it, and it is content to wait and bide its time. Nature will have her way with me, like she does with all things that live, so my escape is never is even considered. Sooner or later, I'm going to croak, and Old Scratch has all the time in the world to wait. I don't have the same luxury.

I start to run blindly, not really seeing anything. All I know is that I want to get as far away from the voice as I can. I've never heard anything like it in my life. It has a greedy sound; I can hear the furious need lurking just under the surface. This is the voice of pure hate, the total sum of all that is hurtful and vicious in the entire universe. It is blackness personified. Not darkness but blackness, un-light. Darkness is just the absence of light; this is beyond that. This is the voice of the combined evil of everything, the distilled essence of all that is wrong, twisted, and perverse. I flee from it in horror, unable to look behind me, heedless of where my terrified legs are taking me. As long as it is away from the foul beast I know is breathing down my neck, I don't care where I go.

I careen into the hallway and crash into the wall across from my door. I ignore the sharp pain that erupts in my shoulder and dash away as fast as my sixty-plus-year-old legs will carry me. Alarmed faces appear on all sides, but in my panic, I don't recognize them as the help that they are, and I flee from them as well. I know they are demons, sent by the Devil himself to collect his prize. I scream wordlessly at them, hoping I can intimidate them, maybe scare them off.

"Ms. Shaw! It's okay, Ms. Shaw! Calm down, everything is okay!" one of the faces says as it advances on me with arms extended.

"Just relax, Ms. Shaw," says another, from behind me.

I feel them closing in, and I realize I'm cornered. I scream again in impotent fury. I'm outnumbered by a lot. I count four, no five faces around me, soft words coming out of their lying lips. They try to tell me I'm safe and I'm okay. They just keep repeating it, like that will somehow make it true. Their faces begin to change, becoming somehow longer. The skin pulls tight; it shines bright in the light as it is pulled taut over rapidly growing skulls. They stop looking like humans; they remind me of lizards, especially that one from the car insurance commercials. Only these guys ain't cute. They're a nightmare come to life. My knees go weak, refusing to hold me up any longer, and I sink to the floor under their terrifying gaze.

"Everything is fine, Ms. Shaw," one of the voices says, and I feel a hand grab my upper arm. Its grip is soft, supple, but I can feel the iron underneath. This hand could snap my arm in two in the blink of an eye without even trying, but it's not hurting me now. It's just insistent, unyielding. Another hand grabs my other arm, equally firmly but not quite as gently. The second hand digs its fingers into the flesh, not enough to leave a mark, just enough to let me know it means business. I can't look at my captors. I'm too scared. I'm afraid I'll lose what's left of my mind if I were to lock eyes with one of these demons sent from hell, so I keep my eyes shut tight, and I allow them to lead me away.

Seconds later, I'm sitting back on my bed. The voices are still all around, but they no longer sound so menacing. I stoke up my courage and open my eyes again, ready to face whatever horror is in front of me. I shake my head rapidly, confused, because the demons are gone, replaced by the hospital staff. The monsters who were about to eat my soul for lunch are gone, and the much safer, although admittedly less interesting, nurses and orderlies had taken their place, and I immediately began to feel silly. It was just another nightmare, only this time carried over into what I'm calling the "real" world. Honestly, though, I'm not sure I believe in any such place anymore.

Once they realize I'm not going to bolt, the nurses leave me be, glad to go back to their Bookface and Lettergram or whatever it is they're always doing on those stupid little computers they call phones. I begin to relax. The fear has faded, leaving only the bitter aftertaste in my mouth, a taste like copper, like blood. I wonder if this is all from the stroke or if maybe I have even more problems than I realized. I remember my step-

mom, and I remember my Granny. They both got the dementia, and it wasn't pretty in either case. I hope to God that I'm not losing it. That's all I need right now.

I sit and mull this over for a while. Everything is so different now. The world I used to know is gone. No, that's not right. The world is still there. I'm what has changed. I'm broken, and they tell me that they can't fix me. Not completely. Oh, they can make me a little better, sure. Baby steps. But Betty Sue Shaw, terror of Alachua County? She's gone. Well, not gone but unavailable. Separate now. I'm on my own private island now, among people but no longer with people.

I think maybe it's this place. I've been here. I don't know how long, but it feels like forever. The world I knew outside these walls seems so far away now. I need to get out of here. I need air. Fresh air. Air that hasn't been circulated and recirculated, all life sanitized out of it until all that's left is stale and dead. I need to feel the sun on my skin, the wind in my hair. I need to see a fucking tree. I've been in this box too long. It's closing in. Every day the walls get closer, like a giant team of carpenters sneaks in during my sleep and rebuild the walls, an inch closer to my bed every night. If they keep it up, my feet will be in the hallway when I lie down before too long.

I've never been a nature girl, I'd much rather sit in a bar than go on a hike, but this complete lack of nature is getting to me. Everything I can see, hear, touch, or smell is artificial. Everything is glass, plastic, and steel, hard lines and ninety-degree angles. Everything is where it is by design. There is no creative anarchy here. I don't think people are meant to live this way; it feels false. I need to see something that exists only for itself, not as a thing of utility to be used for purposes it has no stake in. The flower may be beautiful, but that is a side effect, a matter of opinion, really. It just is what it is because it is. It exists because it does, not because it was created with a purpose. That chair over there? It's just the bones of trees in the skins of animals, twisted to our use. The trees and cows themselves? They weren't consulted. We just took them for our own. They have their own purposes, unknown and unavailable to us, and they have an energy that I can't find in this tomb, and it's an energy I'm realizing I depend on more than I ever guessed. Everything is dead here, and I don't want that infecting me.

As I think about this, Jolene and Remlee walk through the door. Their sudden appearance jolts me out of my thoughts, and I smile in spite of myself. The negativity washes away when I see their faces. I'm just so happy to see them, and I feel the stirrings of shame over my mood. I should be happy. Sure, I can't talk, but seeing my two daughters, together after all this time is far beyond what I ever expected, and I'm ashamed that I keep dwelling on the downside. I have another chance at having a family. I can't let myself get in the way of myself.

"Hi, Mama," Jolene says, and I try to respond in kind.

"Huy Juuleeen," is what comes out. Goddammit! I try again, bearing down with all the might my wrecked brain can muster.

"Ha... Ha lo Jak... Jon... Oh Lord!" I splutter, my frustration boiling over.

"It's okay, Mama," Remlee says, pity etched into her face.

"No! Not... Not... Not... 'Kay," I say, spitting out each syllable with contempt. This is not okay, not at all. Maybe it could be worse, but this is far from okay.

"I know," Remlee says, and she sits down on the bed next to me. A sense of unreality hits me. She's so big now. Not fat, just grown. I still remember her as the coltish little girl, sleek and lanky, the fullness of womanhood still years away. This woman beside me has lost that child-like figure. She's fuller, rounder. She's not my little girl anymore. She's a young woman now. Her presence next to me makes the passage of time real, tangible. Her new (to me) body is evidence that time has passed, that the past really happened, and the future will come. The only constant in life is change, and my daughter is living proof, sitting next to me.

Jolene's voice cut through the clouds in my mind, saying, "The hospital is probably going to discharge you in the next few days. Have they talked to you about that?"

Barely. They have mentioned it a few times, but they haven't given me any details, so I'm excited to hear what more she has to say. It's Remlee who speaks next, however.

"You know you can't go back to your trailer, right?" she asks, and my heart skips a beat.

"NO, NO, NO, NO, NO, NO!" I say, shaking my head back and forth so violently that my glasses fly off my face.

"You can say "No" all you want," Remlee continues, ignoring my protests. "It's not safe there for you. There isn't anyone to look after you there."

"Yu... Yu... Yu... Yu... Yes, yu..." I say, pointing at her.

"Mama, I can't move in with you," she says firmly.

"No, no," I say and begin jabbing my finger in Jolene's direction. "Juh..."

"You know Gary won't let you," Jolene says, refusing to look at me. She feels guilty, I can tell. Good, she should. While she lets that man rule over here like he does is beyond me.

"Don't worry, Mama," Remlee says in a voice that is more appropriately used with children. "We'll figure something out."

Don't worry, she says. What a laugh. That's easy for her to say. It's not her that was just informed of her impending homelessness. I just want to go home, that's all. I'm a grown-ass woman. I can take care of myself. I suppose I'll need a little help now, making phone calls for appointments, for example, but I ain't no invalid. I can wipe my own ass, shower myself. I haven't had the opportunity to try yet, but I'm pretty confident I can still operate a microwave. All I really need is someone to take me places every now and then help me make my phone calls. Far from the round-the-clock care these two seem to think I need.

"We've got an idea we're working on," Jolene says hesitantly.

"Gumble tow?" I ask. What idea?

"Well, you know how Gary's Mama lives in the trailer next to ours?" she asks nervously. I nod yes, but I make sure she sees the death glare I'm giving her. I know Gary's Mama, all right. That old bitch and I got a bit of a history, you might say. You might also say I once caught that floozy with her lips wrapped around my husband's crankshaft, and you would be more accurate. After she picked her teeth up off of the floor, she left my house in a real hurry, and she hasn't been too keen on spending much time with me ever since.

Before I can verbally object, using one of the two or three words I can be relied upon to actually be able to utter on command, Jolene says, in a rush, "I know all about you and her. You don't have to remind me. I know it would be awkward."

I laugh at this. I see Remlee's rolling her eyes too, and I take hope in that. Maybe she's on my side. I sure could use an ally.

"That was a real long time ago, Mama," Jolene continues, pleading her case. "You were both young. Things happen. But we got to face the facts. You simply cannot live alone, and we can't afford to put you in one of those fancy retirement places. You won't go back to the farm, and that's probably for the better. You and Clarence would probably end up killing each other anyways, so that's out. There aren't any other options. Ida lives there alone. She don't hardly have nothing. There's an empty bedroom there already, and I'd be right next door."

I hear what she has to say, and I can't argue with most of it. Hell, I can't argue with any of it because I can't argue at all. How am I going to live life like this? Other than yes or no, I can't really say much else. Any detail, any at all is lost. Am I at the mercy of somebody else now, be it one of my daughters or some bigwig at the County Home? I have no intention of giving up my freedom, but I have no idea how to fight for it.

"I know this isn't easy," Remlee says, and I can see this is upsetting her too. "Nothing's set in stone anyways. We haven't even talked to Gary about it yet. It's his trailer, so it's really up to him. It's just the best option we've got so far. Don't get all worked up yet. Things can easily change."

I nod at her solemnly, wanting to believe her. I should be happy that they ain't packing me off to the home, that they're trying to help me somehow, but I ain't. I can't let go my independence without some kind of fight. It was hard-earned. I had people telling me what to do and when to do it from the time I was born until the day the law dragged that old skunk Elmer off to prison and out of my life. My freedom was fought for. I got the scars to prove it. How can I just let it go, knowing how much of my own blood had to be spilled to get it?

"Listen," Jolene says, "we don't have to make any decisions right now. They want to keep you a few more days, give the therapist and doctors a few more looks at you. But you have to cooperate with them, Mama! They're just trying to help you."

"Yu…Yu yu yu… Oh Lord…deyno caar," I mumble, and even though my words are unclear, my meaning isn't. I know these people in here don't give a damn about me. I'm just a body in a bed, another check on their checklist. I ain't saying that they're mistreating me or anything.

I'm just not so naive as to think I'm surrounded by Mother Theresa's. These jobs pay well, the work is steady, and the buildings you work in are air-conditioned. No sweating in the sun or in the factory. No worries about jobs being eliminated due to a bad economy. Health care is always booming. Death and taxes, right? These people are smart, and I don't mean just book learning. They figured out how to live comfortably without having to get too uncomfortable.

"We're going to leave now," Jolene says. "Shane got back into town last night, and he wants to see Remlee, so we're going over to St. Augustine next."

"Gassk... S... Oh Lord... Yu yu... Shaaan?" I ask. I haven't seen my oldest son in five years or more. I want to ask Remlee to make him come see me, but I know he won't. Not if he don't want to. I want to think he at least cares if I'm okay or not, but I won't get my hopes up. Jolene's expression confirms my suspicion, but she doesn't answer me.

"We'll be back tomorrow, Mama," Remlee says, and she leans in and hugs me. I close my eyes and take her in, basking in her glow. I hold on as long as I can. I don't want to let her go. I'm embarrassed to admit it, even to myself, but I don't want to be alone here anymore. Sure, there are people all around me here, but I'm still alone. They ain't my blood. I'm just a job to them. It ain't their fault. I'd be the same way if I was in their position, but it's getting harder and harder every night. I can't do this much longer.

Reluctantly, I let go of Remlee. Jolene steps into her place, and once again, I'm lost in the embrace of my offspring. Jolene feels different, of course. There is more familiarity there. It feels less forced on her part. It hurts me that Remlee is so closed off to me, but I understand. It's funny, in a way. Jolene was stuck with me for much longer than Remlee was. She was exposed to my chaos more than her sister. Yet somehow, she loves me more than Remlee does. Of all my kids, it's Jolene who bore the brunt of my shittiness, but she's the one who loves me the most. I don't think I'll ever truly understand people.

Jolene pulls away, and we say our farewells. Okay, they say farewell, and I grunt in unintelligibly, but either way, they leave and once again I'm alone with my thoughts. Before all this, I would have told you there weren't that many thoughts available to keep me company, but now that my voice has been stolen, I realize how active my mind really is. Being forced to be quiet makes everything else that much louder, it seems. I used to be able to just kind of zone out, let my mind be blank, but now I find my mind is constantly racing. Of course, I ain't had a drink in God knows how long, and I don't doubt that maybe that's part of the problem.

This thought makes me thirsty, but I know that the cafeteria here don't serve what I'm hankering for. It's all I can think about now. I can picture the glass, the dew on the outside, the brown liquid joy on the inside. I crave it like a lover. I need to feel its warm, gentle fingers relax me from the inside out. This is probably the longest I've been sober for years, and I don't like it. This is all just too much without the support I usually get from Captain Morgan. He's been by my side, through thick and thin, and he's never let me down. He does his job, and he does it right, without complaint, every single time. That makes him more reliable than any flesh and blood man I've ever met. He's the perfect lover: he gives his all and asks nothing in return. Who could ask for anything more?

I lie back on my bed and force my eyes closed. Hopefully, I can sleep this craving away for now. There's too much new information to process, and I'm too exhausted to try without some brain lubrication. I try to push myself down, down, down, away from the light and sound of the world and into the warm, dark place. I need my brain to stop. I need these cravings to stop. I need it all to stop.

The dark opens up in front of me, glad to accept my sacrifice. For now, there is peace.

Remlee

The road to Saint Augustine is straight and flat, passing over farmland and dozens of lakes as it makes its way to the coast. Jolene and I were barreling east with the windows down, blasting old Cyndi Lauper songs and singing (horribly) at the top of our lungs. I felt like a kid again on one of the many days spent at the beach, just us girls. The sun was high in the cloudless sky, and the day had a dreamlike quality to it. Everything was almost too real, like the seedy underside was trying too hard to fit in. My spirit was lighter, though, lighter than it had been since this whole affair started, so I decided to ignore the Potemkin Village vibe I was getting and just enjoy the moment.

As we grew nearer to our destination, the conversation turned to Shane and what I could expect. I still hadn't completely wrapped my mind around his marital status and was unsure how to proceed. Jolene had years of practice by this point. The strangeness of his union with our (half) cousin had long since worn off. For her, it was just part of the landscape of her life that she had learned to live with. I, however, didn't yet have the benefit of years of exposure, so I was grilling Jolene for details.

"Isn't it weird, them being together like that?" I asked.

"At first, I guess," Jolene replied, shrugging. "But honestly, it really wasn't that surprising. You're a lot younger, you wouldn't really remember, but they was always together as kids. She'd always stay with us overnight, but she spent her time with Shane more than me. They just liked the same things, had the same bad ideas. I know it's wrong in most people's eyes. Hell, maybe it just *is* wrong. I don't know. What I do know is I ain't never met two people who just… completed each other like they do. It's like they're the same person,

almost. I don't know how else to describe it. It's weird, but somehow, it's just right, you know?"

"Yeah, sure," I said skeptically, "but don't they have kids? I mean, I'm not trying to be rude here, but are they...well, fucked up?"

Jolene flashed me a look of supreme disapproval and replied, "There ain't nothing wrong with them kids, you hear me? Them kids ain't no different from anyone else. Both of them are doing better than any of mine are, and you won't hear a word against them cross my lips. And Lord help anyone else I hear saying anything bad about them." Her face flushed, and I was taken aback at the ferocity of her defense.

"Whoa!" I said, my voice full of contrition. "I was just asking! Geez, I meant no disrespect. It's just you hear that kids born like that..."

"Like what?" Jolene interrupted, her tone brooking no challenge. She opened her mouth to continue her tirade but then thought better of it.

"I'm sorry," she said, and she sighed sadly before continuing, "it's not your fault. You got every right to be curious. Them kids take so much shit is all. That's why he and Lindie moved over here. It's only an hour from home, but that's far enough that everyone don't know them. They ain't heard all the stories. They came here to get away from all that shit back in Stillwater, where everybody knows them, knows all about them. They can just live their lives here, you know? Their names don't hold them back here, not like back home."

I kept quiet, but I understood. That was one of the prime motivations I had when I left. I knew the stares all too well, and I resolved to remove myself from the line of sight. Life is hard enough without having to carry the baggage that other people packed for you, without your request or consent. I knew how hard it was for Jolene, trapped as she was by motherhood and poverty. Her need for chemical comfort, while ultimately destructive, made perfect sense. I myself had been known to spend time in a self-medicated haze, albeit a more benign one, and knew better than to judge.

That's why drugs exist. They work. Sure, there are often horrific side effects, but the fact remains, if you feel bad, taking drugs usually makes you feel better. If they didn't make you feel good, nobody would take them. The real problem is that for some people, life just hurts too much, too often, and the only reliable relief comes in a pill, or a powder, a bottle, a needle, or a joint. We're told to just exercise, pray, or volunteer in a soup kitchen, but who are we kidding? All of those things take the two things most people, including me, are most loath to give: time and effort. Happiness, at least the so-called natural kind that holy men and other busybodies are always prattling on about, requires a diligence of the spirit that most people simply do not possess. It's so much easier to just consume something, wait a few minutes, and let big pharma (or some dread-headed trustafarian) do the heavy lifting. It's the way of the West, better living through science. We might be destroying our souls in the process, but I, for one, am not even convinced that such a thing exists, so I don't give such thoughts much consideration. People like us don't have the luxury of lofty pursuits; we just have to survive.

"Well, this is it," Jolene said as she pulled into a driveway, the entry to which was almost obscured by the thick growth of wisteria that lined the road. I was charmed by the bright blue wall of blooms that acted as a privacy barrier but also vaguely surprised. As we crept further onto the property, I took note of the neatly maintained grounds. I was pleasantly shocked when I didn't see the rusting corpses of various hoopties littering the lawn, but instead, I found simple but tasteful landscaping elements dotting the tiny estate like little oases is of organized beauty. I immediately felt guilty for expecting squalor and silently reprimanded myself for my small-mindedness and casual bigotry. What did it say about me that I expected to see filth and degradation instead of the lovely, well-designed delight of a garden that I was now witnessing? I was no better than the people who shunned us on reputation alone, and that realization stung. I always had thought I was better than that.

Jolene pulled to a stop behind a well-worn GMC Sierra, its bed overflowing with tools and various building supplies. I lit a cigarette to fortify myself, and then I exited the car. We walked leisurely over to the deck that was attached to the handsome ranch house and knocked on the door. I heard rustling inside and then the sound of heavy feet pounding the floor as they approached the other side of the door. I took a deep breath, suddenly nervous, and the door opened inward, revealing my brother to me for the first time in almost twenty years.

"Fucking Jesus Christ!" he bellowed through an enormous smile. "Remlee! Holy fuck, how long has it been?"

He roughly gathered me up in his arms, and a cascade of memories fought each other for primacy in my mind. He squeezed me for ages, then held me out at arms-length, inspecting me from top to bottom.

"You look…grown," he said, laughing. "You weren't more than, what, twelve, thirteen last time I saw you? You, you was just a skinny little girl. But now… Geez."

"Thanks," I said, chuckling along with him. "You look great."

He did too. As my oldest brother, he was pushing fifty, but the years had been kind to him. His looks favored Daddy, and his dark wavy hair still showed no signs of greying. His permanently tanned skin was taut, and it was obvious that hard physical work was no stranger to him. Truth be told, Jolene looked far older, even though Shane had five years on her. Hell, he had eleven on me, and we probably could have passed as the same age.

"It's good to see you, come in," he said, ushering us inside. We followed him into a sitting room where Lindie was sitting, watching some reality show on the television. She looked up, smiled wanly, and said hello. She seemed slightly out of it, and I could tell Shane was irritated with her. She continually fidgeted with her hair, and her jaw was swinging back and forth in a sawing motion, her teeth grating together. I knew immediately what was going on with her but decided to keep mum. I glanced at Jolene and caught her eye; she had seen it too. A silent conversation erupted between us, and we agreed, by means of the telepathy that exists between sisters, that we shouldn't bring up the obvious fact that Lindie was high as fuck on speed.

Instead, we talked of the usual things that people talk about when they've been apart for a long time. We traded abridged life stories over beer and bong, and the years seemed to melt away. I teased them for being old enough to be grandparents, and they picked on me for my Yankee accent, renaming me traitor and turncoat. It felt good, wholesome. This was what family was supposed to be, a group of flawed individuals who love and enjoy each other despite their imperfections. I saw what Jolene had meant. Shane and Lindie were perfect together. Sure, she had her problems, but you can see that she adored our brother, and he adored her. Nothing could split these two, not the sensibilities of polite society, not the scourge of meth. No matter what road Lindie went down, Shane would be right behind her, ready to carry her when she fell. He knew her demons, and he accepted them without question.

"Have you talked to Elton lately?" Jolene asked after a lull in the conversation.

"Couple of weeks ago," Shane replied. "Why?"

"Well, does he know about Mama?" she asked.

"Probably not," Lindie answered, taking over from Shane. "Shane's been down Daytona way, working for the past three weeks, and Elton don't call here in less he knows Shane's going to be here. He don't like me much."

"He don't like anybody much," Jolene said sardonically.

"Yeah, I think you're right about that," Shane agreed.

"Someone should tell him, though, right?" I asked. Awkward silence filled the room as we all understood what that meant. Someone would have to go visit him.

"We could write him a letter," Jolene said hopefully.

"Come on, man, that's fucked up!" Lindie said, her voice edged with the taste of contempt. "Y'all got to go see him. It ain't right to have to get that news in a letter. What the fuck is wrong with you guys?"

"I know, I know," Jolene said, chastised. "I just hate going there, you know? I'm always afraid I'll see ***HIM*** there."

"Him who?" I asked, oblivious to the obvious.

"Daddy," Jolene said, and immediately I felt like an idiot. Of course, that's who she meant.

I had forgotten all about the male contributor to my genetic makeup. I hesitate to use the word father, as I have no memory of the man at all. I was two when he got his double life sentence, and all I'd ever known of Elmer Ray Shaw is what had been told to me. I had no personal connection to the man other than sharing his surname. He was a phantom in my life, the boogeyman I would be threatened with to coerce compliance, the stain on my name that I could never erase. People would always think of him and his wretched deeds when my name was spoken. No amount of decency I exhibited would ever fully exonerate me in the eyes of Stillwater. That was my birthright.

I can only imagine what it was like for my older siblings, Jolene most of all. Jesco's death nearly destroyed her, and it left her weak and vulnerable. Shane and Elton had their own ways of dealing with the infamy, with Shane simply leaving town and Elton zealously keeping the family tradition of criminality alive and well, using the name to command the respect of the denizens of the underworld. Jolene just withered under the scrutiny, let the haters define her, and became everything they told her she was. I began to feel guilty about this, like I unjustly avoided the punishment due. Sure, I suffered through the same prejudice when I was a child, but I left and did so very young. Instead of standing by my family, I ran as far as I could the first chance I got, and I didn't look back. I left them all to drown in the shame, and I didn't like myself very much for it.

"Do you ever talk to him?" I asked Shane, curious as to how he felt about the old man.

"Not really," he answered. "He calls maybe twice a year, but if I ain't home, he's out of luck."

"Does he ask about me ever?" I asked, almost timidly. I wasn't sure I actually wanted the answer.

"No," he replied.

It was the answer I expected, but the brevity of it cut me deep. There was no hesitation, he didn't have to think about it. Just "no." My father didn't think about me at all, and while I wasn't surprised, another little bit of the world went dark for me. Hypothetical concern was better than no concern at all, which was what I was now left with. It seemed silly to mourn for a relationship that was never real, but it's what I felt, nonetheless.

Shane stood up and stretched, then motioned me to follow him. He let me out into the yard, where the smell of honeysuckle and wisteria filled the evening air. It was peaceful there, like he and Lindie had carved out a little bit of Eden for themselves, there in the middle of the Florida swamp. It felt good knowing that someone in the family had their shit together. Despite her love of meth, or maybe because of it, Lindie had created a wonder here, and for a moment, I was reminded of Jack. He would have loved the design. He likely would have talked Lindie's ear off about it, grilling her about this plant and that, storing the information for later use. I made a note to snap a picture and text it to him. I knew he'd appreciate it.

"So how is Jolene really doing with this?" Shane asked conspiratorially.

"About how you'd expect," I replied, and he nodded in agreement.

"So, terrible then," he said dourly.

"Yeah, that about sums it up," I said. He turned away, looking off into the horizon.

After a moment, he asked, "Is she using again?"

"She says no," I answered cautiously. "I mean, she's still going to the clinic every day. So yeah, as far as dope is concerned, I think so. But I know she eats Xanax like Skittles, Klonopins too. So no, not exactly. I don't know."

"It don't matter," he said, resignation causing him to wilt slightly. His shoulder sagged, and he seemed to shrink before my eyes. My Big Brother, my protector, the hero of my youth, was becoming human, superhuman no longer. Time and experience had whittled the mythical proportions he once held down to a more reasonable, realistic size.

"Your place looks fantastic," I said, trying to steer the conversation into more pleasant territory.

"Huh?" he asked, confused by my gambit. "Oh, yeah. Thanks. Most of it is Lindie's handiwork. I just paid for it." He gave a sarcastic little laugh as he surveyed his domain.

"Looks like there's money in roofing," I said, looking around for effect.

"Can be," he said, "but if you want to make that money, you end up working so much, you never have time to enjoy it."

"Seems like Lindie enjoys it enough for the both of you," I said, and his eyes shifted toward me, glinting with a fierce warning.

"Yeah, well, you let me worry about that," he said, the edge in his voice matching the steely gaze he regarded me with. "That's my business, not yours."

"I ain't trying to get in your business," I said.

"That's a good idea," he said, his voice cold. "Look... Lindie... she gets lonely out here, now that Ashley's growed up and moved out. Junior's getting close to eighteen, he ain't around much either. Between school, his job out at the truck stop, and hanging out chasing tail with his buddies, he might as well be gone."

"So...meth is the reasonable replacement?" I asked incredulously.

"Well, no," he said, his cheeks flushing. "But what am I gonna do? I can't be here all the time to babysit her. I got to work. She's a grown-ass woman, and she's a Tucker. You know what that means. Do you let your old man tell you what to do?"

He had me there. What was he supposed to do? Noncompliance is baked into our DNA in this family. I looked at him and shook my head.

"Exactly," he said with a smug smile. "All I can do is just keep going and just love her."

"Don't you worry that she'll OD or something?" I asked.

"Not really," he said. "That's kind of a hard thing to do. It ain't exactly unheard of, but it's not like dope, where you hear about people falling out all the time."

"What about cops?" I asked, and I could see he was losing patience with my interrogation.

"What about them? Are you worried about them?" he asked pointedly.

"Why would I be worried about the cops?" I asked, not following his line of reasoning.

"You think I can't smell that bag of skunk you got in your pocket there?" he asked, grinning like a Cheshire cat. "If the five-oh stopped you and Lindie right now, both of you'd be off to the hoosegow."

"Come on, that's not the same thing," I protested, but he held up his hand to silence me.

"I know that, and you know that, but the law don't know that, and they are the ones who make the decision," he said.

He walked over to a nearby lawn chair and sat down heavily in it. He looked up at me, and I could suddenly see the years in his face. It wasn't wrinkles or age spots that belied his age but his careworn expression. It was a look of long-suffering in service of love.

His voice cracked a little as he explained further, "It's been really hard for her, you know? Life, I mean. Well, I don't have to tell you, you know how things are. You were smart enough to get away before Alachua County could really get its hooks into you."

"You got away, too," I pointed out.

He laughed bitterly at that and said venomously, "Hardly. I'm an hour away. Sure, I guess I have to deal with less bullshit here than if I was back in Stillwater, but it's not like the bullshit has to travel all that far to land on me."

He picked up a rock and threw it into the bushes, scattering the sparrows that had gathered there to feast on the berries that sprouted. He looked at me for a minute, studying me.

"God, you look like her," he said, shaking his head. "It's just so weird. It's like looking at Mama when I was a teenager, only you got that goddamn Yankee accent that ruins it."

"I guess I do," I said thoughtfully. "I never really thought about it before, but I've lived in Boston way longer than I did here. Only makes sense that I'd sound the way I do. Does that mean you're gonna disown me now?"

Shane laughed hard back, his eyes tearing up with delight. "And let you off so easy? I don't think so," he said. "No, you'll never escape this family."

That's exactly what I was afraid of.

Betty Sue

The sound of an organ belting out a dirge startles me awake. The song that is playing is loud but somber musical tears for the assembled to mourn too. I look around and see I'm in church, my family crowded around me in the pew. I'm afraid of this place. The statues are so spooky. Their eyes stare at me, accusing me of every foul deed known to man and a few yet to be discovered. I bury my face in the hymnal, hoping it will shield me from their terrible gaze. I notice tears on the faces of all those gathered, the grief in the air is palpable. Daddy is holding my hand, his eyes bloodshot and staring. Mama Lettie's on my other side, silent and stoic. I wonder what's going on, why everyone is so sad, why we are even in church in the first place. We're a Christian family, don't get me wrong; we ain't no heathens, but we don't come to church but once or twice a year. Unless there is a wedding. Or funeral.

Oh God! That's what this is. I remember when I'm at now. This is Bobby Lee's funeral. I stand on my tippy toes, hoping for a better look, and there, at the front, sits Bobby Lee's coffin. It's draped with the flag, like that's supposed to make his death better somehow. Everybody tells us how proud they are of him, how great he was for laying down his life for his country. I couldn't give a fuck less about my country. I want my brother back. Let those people over there be commies if they want to. I don't care. What does their freedom mean to me? Or Bobby Lee? Nothing. I got to go through life without one of the few bright points I had now, just so some people on the other side of the planet can be free. If they want freedom so bad, let them fight for themselves, leave my brother out of it.

The music ends, and the preacher begins his eulogy. He quotes a bunch of Bible verses and talks about duty and honor and a whole bunch of other nonsense. What about his duty to me? Don't I count? Why are the problems of some foreigners something that is Bobby Lee Tucker's duty to fix? No Vietnamese people ever did nothing for us. I never even met one, so why is my brother in a box for them?

Eventually, the preacher wears himself out and thankfully shuts up. If I have to hear any more of his excuses as to why this all happened, I might scream. The people in the front row rise and begin to file past the coffin, each person stopping to mutter some words before moving on. I don't want to go; I want to stay here in my seat. I don't want to say good-bye. I won't do it. Saying goodbye is admitting he's dead, and I can't do that. Maybe they got it wrong, made a mistake somehow. Maybe Bobby Lee's dog tags got switched somehow, and he's still out there, trying to find his way back home. I refuse to give up, even if everybody else here has.

Daddy's hands are on my shoulders now, pinching the muscle, urging me to move. Reluctantly, I allow him to guide me along to my date with my dead brother. A sense of dread begins to take hold, a fear I can't quite put my finger on. I just know something awful is going to happen, but I don't know what.

I look around for clues, trying to find anything out of place, but this is not possible. Everything is out of place. Colors are too bright, sounds too sharp. The tears of the mourners seem fake, like a trap, something to get me to let my guard down so they can devour me when my back is turned. I have the uncanny feeling of being watched, but I can't find the spy. Everybody is looking at me, and no one is looking at me. We're nearing our turn at the casket now. There's only two people in front of me. I'm near panic, my heart races, and I feel like I might pass out, or vomit, or both.

When my turn comes, my traitorous eyes lock themselves on the body. It's not him, though. This person don't look right. He's too pale. The lips are unnaturally red, and he's wearing his dress uniform, complete with a tie. That's how I know it can't really be him, 'cuz Bobby Lee ain't worn a damn tie a day in his life. But if this ain't Bobby Lee, then where is he? Is he still alive? And who is this poor soul wearing my brother's uniform and stealing his name?

A white-hot spark ignites deep in the darkest corridor of my heart. It's the spark of anger and hatred that will eventually be fed and fed until it grows into a towering inferno that will eventually lead me to the hospital bed my body is lying in, back in the now. This is it, the very moment where it all goes wrong. Life wasn't perfect before, but there was still hope. This fire will consume that hope and much else in the process. The world took my big brother, my best brother, the only man I ever felt cared that much for me at all. He's the one thing I have, the person who remembers me, celebrates my birthday, doesn't beat me on general principle. I'm alone from this moment on.

I twist free of my Daddy's grasp as he kneels in front of the casket. I hear him give one loud sob, and it is the sound of despair personified. It feels like the walls shake from the power in Daddy's voice. There is no other sound in the world. I begin to run, madly dashing to the exit, to escape the oppressive weight of my father's grief.

Once outside, I sit down in the grass to catch my breath. My head is pounding, my heart racing. I focus on relaxing, willing myself calm. Bobby Lee's pale face in the casket keeps bouncing around the edges of my thought, occasionally poking through into the forefront, and it's all I can do to keep his ghost at bay. My back is to the church, and I can feel it looking at me with its giant stained-glass eyes. Everything feels sinister, every little detail suffused with threat. I'm just a small little girl in the shadow of this giant cathedral, shaking with an intensity I scarcely thought possible, drowning in a crushing tsunami of grief.

Soon, the other mourners begin to file out, their faces dour, their voices hushed. I watch them all go, marking those I know and those I don't. There's plenty of people here. Bobby Lee is (was) loved. I see uncles and aunts, cousins, and nieces and nephews. I recognize most people, but not all. I start to wonder about them, these people from the outside. Who are they? How do they know my brother? I realize there's a whole side to him, likely the biggest part, that I never knew. And now I never will. I'm just his kid sister. I only know a small part of him. I've never met the soldier, the friend, the coworker version. I only know him as the older brother who is sometimes nice to me. These people know him in ways I never will, and it's just not fair. Not to anybody involved.

I see Daddy and Mama Lettie come outside, and they're obviously looking for me. His face is red and puffy, and his head is moving back and forth, scanning the crowd for me. Mama Lettie seems less concerned and more irritated. I stand up, waving my arms wildly, hoping to attract their attention. They don't see me. They are surrounded by hangers-on, all tripping over each other to offer their condolences. I start to head over to where they are, and a large hand grips my shoulder.

"I thought I'd find you out here," a reedy voice says from behind me. I turn to see the preacher standing behind me, a kindly smile upon his lips.

"I... I was just... Just getting some air," I stammer. The preacher has always given me the heebie-jeebies, and his sudden appearance does nothing to comfort me.

"Oh, it's okay," he says with a laugh that doesn't reach his eyes. "I don't much like funerals myself. Least favorite part of the job."

Something about him makes me disbelieve this. I bet he just loves funerals. He feeds off of them somehow, almost like a vampire. I don't recognize it yet, but I will come to learn that men like this savor other people's suffering like you, or I would enjoy an ice cream cone. Why is it that the sick bastards are always the ones in charge? I look up at him with what I hope passes for trust and respect, even though every instinct I have is screaming at me to run, run far and fast. A fresh wave of unreality washes over me as snippets of a song that hasn't been recorded yet play through my head: "Psycho killer, qu'est-que c'est... Fah fah fah fah fah fah fah fah fah far better... Run, run, run, run, run away..."

"I know how you must feel," he continues, "losing a brother like that. You wonder, "Why? What did he do to deserve this?' It doesn't seem fair, right?"

I nod at him, playing along. I wonder if he realizes how fake he sounds, if he knows he ain't fooling anyone. Probably not, recognizing reality ain't exactly what psychopaths are known for.

"Well," he says expansively, like he's letting me in on a wonderful secret, "that's not the right question to ask. God is God. What he does is fair, by definition. It may hurt, and we may not understand, but God has a plan. Everything that happens, whether or not we see it as good, is good, because it's part of God's plan, and God is good. He is the potter. We are but the clay. It is not for us to ask why, but to rejoice and give thanks, for it is His glorious plan that is unfolding."

I look at him with astonishment, realizing what it is that he is trying to say. For a moment, I'm speechless. I cannot believe what I'm hearing. Is this for real? Did I just hear him say that Bobby Lee dying is a good thing? Because God planned it? The spark of anger that first came to be in the church is whipped into a frenzy, and I see red. My vision narrows down to where all I can see is the preacher. Everything else is gone. My muscles are taut, every sinew at attention, ready to spring, ready to attack this horrible man and the horrible things he is saying.

"Plan?" I seethe, dangerously quiet. "My brother had to die for God's plan? Are you fucking kidding me?"

"Young lady!" the preacher gasps, taken aback, but I ignore him, determined to have my say. A small crowd gathers, eager to witness the next train wreck. Fuckers.

"This is the worst excuse I've heard yet!" I shout, oblivious to the stares. "You're telling me God's great plan needs my brother to die young? My brother has to miss out on everything because God needs him to? There ain't no better way? Are you saying that all-powerful God can't think of a better way of doing whatever it is He's doing without killing my brother? Well, I'll tell you what I think. I think that is a lousy plan. A lousy fucking plan, and I ain't afraid to say so!"

The chattering of the crowd suddenly stops, and shocked silence gathers. People look at me as if they've never seen something like me before, like I'm some undiscovered species. The preacher goes red in the face. He's not used to being questioned like this, especially not by some ragamuffin child like me.

"Excuse me?" he says, his voice rising two octaves. "Are you questioning the will of God?"

"No, sir," I counter, my eyes boring deep into his. "I'm questioning whether or not you have any fucking idea at all what God's will even is."

He recoils as if slapped, and there are a smattering of oohs and ahhs at my foolhardy response. His face is so red, I almost think it's going to pop, spraying blood and brains everywhere. I should be scared. I just publicly disrespected my preacher, in front of my whole family, and half the town, no less. We may be poor, and we might not exactly conduct all of our business aboveboard, but we ain't no heathens. I frantically scan the crowd, hoping maybe my parents are already at the station wagon and missed out on this little show. A cold voice to my right stops that hope train right in his tracks.

"Betty Sue Tucker, you apologize to the reverend right now, or so help me, I will tan your hide, right here in front of God and everybody," Mama Lettie says furiously.

I turn to face her, ready for war, and the world turns on a dime. The blue spring sky solidifies into four walls and a ceiling. The bystanders disappear, the trees disappear, and everything disappears. The world of my brother's funeral in 1970 is gone, replaced by the hospital room from forty some odd years later. The switch, if that's what you can call it, leaves me dizzy. The transition from standing to lying down without actually moving causes my mind to reel from the ensuing paradoxes. If I can't quit this time travel dream walking, I'm pretty sure I'll go crazy. If I'm not already there, that is.

That's the thing: crazy is a place. It's not a state of mind, not really. It's a physical place you go to without ever leaving. If you don't understand that last sentence, then you're not crazy, because you shouldn't understand it. The fact that I can think such thoughts is just proof that I'm in Crazy Town right now, staying at Madness Manor on Lunacy Lane. Up is down, left his right, black is white. Nothing else explains this. I must be mad.

I look around my hospital room, the cell I've been imprisoned in for longer than I can remember. I think it's real, I think I'm awake, but I can't be sure, not any longer. Sleeping and waking are almost the same now. I don't think I'm ever fully either. My sleep is broken and fitful, my waking hours fuzzy and lethargic. I'm always bone-tired, and everything hurts. I need to get out of this place, out into the sun and air before I lose my mind, if I haven't already, that is.

Restlessness takes hold of me, and I get up out of bed, but it's too fast. Everything goes gray for a minute as I struggle to remain upright. Eventually, my senses come back down from their smoke break, and I'm able to walk. I need to move around. I feel all compacted, like somebody stuck me in the car crusher out at Rennie's Salvage Yard. I'm about to make my way out into the hallway and resume my pacing when the social worker lady appears, seemingly out of nowhere. She startles me, and I gasp loudly.

"Oh, sorry, Ms. Shaw," she says, "I didn't mean to frighten you."

"Yungwud ogat neemo," I reply dryly. You couldn't frighten a child.

"Why don't you come back in here and sit down," she says, gently pulling me back into my cell/room. "I've got some good news for you!"

I look at her for clues as to what she may mean. I've come to realize that these people's idea of "good" and mine ain't exactly the same. Not by a country mile. My guess is that she really has something awful to say, but she thinks if she sugarcoats it, that will somehow make it better as if I'm some ignorant child.

"The doctor is going to discharge you tomorrow," she says, her voice bubbly. "Your daughters are coming in for a meeting with your care team to go over some details tomorrow morning, and then, as long as everything still looks good, you can go home in the afternoon sometime. Isn't that exciting?"

You'd think so, but I'm anything but excited. Just a minute ago, leaving this place was all I could think about, but now I'm scared. Jolene says I can't go back to my trailer, at least not right now. She's gonna try to make me stay with her old man's Mama, and I really don't want to. Problem is, I don't know how to fight her. I hate to admit it, but she's probably right. I can't do all that much for myself right now. That's the worst part of all of this, really. I've been doing for myself for so long. I ain't comfortable living any other way. That and the fact that I don't exactly trust Jolene that much. She's on them pills, I know it, and I ain't sure she's really all that better off than me.

"Let's get you back in your bed so you can get some rest," she says, and I go willingly. I'm almost out of here, no reason to upset the applecart. I'm still nervous about what it's gonna be like out there, or more to the point, what I'm gonna be like, but that's not as scary as spending the rest of my life here or in a home. This is a case where the devil you don't know is actually better than the devil you do.

"Get some rest, honey," she says as she tucks me in. I give into the comfort and allow her calm words to soothe me. I can relax now; the light has finally appeared at the end of the tunnel. I think the worst is about to be over, and maybe things can start to get better now. Maybe I can finally quench that fire that has been driving me for so long. Maybe I can repair some of the damage I've caused my kids. I can't talk and fuck it all up now, can't say the wrong thing. I can't try to defend the indefensible anymore. All pretense is gone now. I have to accept what they say. I can't

twist it anymore to my advantage. A strange new spark lights up in my heart, next to the dying embers of the hatred that drove me for so long. I don't recognize it at first. I haven't seen it's like in so long, I'm surprised I'm able to discern what it is that seems now to be my fuel. A year ago, I would have told you such a thing didn't really exist. It was just some shit they made up to sell greeting cards and sappy movies. Now, though, I'm staring right at it, its brilliance dazzling me, overwhelming me with its stark power. I have a new fire now, brighter and stronger than the old. I know its name, and I hold it dear now, clutching it like a drowning woman.

Its name is hope.

Remlee

The visit with my brother ended well. Shane built a fire, and we sat around it, casually drinking and talking about times past. There was so much that happened before I was born, stories I had never heard. Shane and Jolene were closer in age than I was to either of them. They were more like an aunt and uncle than siblings to me. I'm pretty sure they felt the same way. Jolene practically raised me as one of her own. I'm only four years older than her eldest, Colton. Shane had moved out on his own before my third birthday, so I had no memory of ever actually living with him. They grew up together, learned about the world together. They actually remember a time when our parents were not only together, but actually mostly glad to be so. They knew Elmer Ray Shaw before he went sour, when he still held down a steady, legitimate job at the ice plant and "mostly" kept his hands to himself, sexually and otherwise. I felt a stab of jealousy as they talked, knowing they had a closeness with each other that I'll never have with either of the two. I was an outsider in my own family of notorious outsiders.

It's not that anyone ever said anything to me. My otherness wasn't something that was talked about, something consciously noted and filed away for future use. There were no overt actions or specific utterances that I could point at as examples of my unofficial semishunning. It was just a certain wariness, a furtive gleam in the eye, that alerted me to my othered status. I didn't think it was some kind of grand conspiracy to ostracize me; they simply didn't really know me. The intervening years had erased the Remlee they remembered, and the new Remlee wasn't much like themselves. Not better, not worse, just different. The world had always been indifferent to downright hostile to my family, so faces that haven't been around were seen as a possible threat, familiar surname be damned. I couldn't really blame them.

By eleven, the fire had burned to embers, and the beer had been exhausted. A comfortable silence had descended upon us, and we were content to bask in the magical summer night air, its warm dampness comforting. The peepers and cicadas were in full swing, blasting their music into the living night. I felt sleepy and content, nestled in the bosom of my family. For the first time since Jack left to go home, I wasn't worried about him or really even thinking about him at all. I felt a little twinge of guilt when I realized this but immediately dismissed it for the codependent nonsense that it was. The guilt fairy wasn't finished with me, however. Instead of departing respectfully as requested, she just pivoted her aim. I began to regret all the years of virtual radio silence I had imposed upon my family. I suppose at first it made sense to keep my distance. I didn't want to be dragged back, kicking and screaming. But once I reached the age of majority, when there was nothing anyone could have done to force me back? Why not then? Sure, I kept in touch with Jolene, but only on an extremely limited basis, in which I controlled all the variables. The fact was, ugly as it might have been, that I was ashamed of my own blood. That led to a vicious cycle of shame and recrimination, as recognizing my own distaste for my kin created even more shame. I realized that shame had been piggybacking on to my life for so long now, I didn't even notice it. It was just a part of my life, the backdrop upon which my life played out.

Shane had a hammock stretched out between two cypress trees at the back of their property, and I laid claim to it. I was drunk and tired, certainly in no condition to drive the fifty- or sixty-odd miles back to Stillwater. I stretched out in the hammock and let the slow rocking soothe me off gently into the land of nod. My last waking moments were spent listening to the sounds of my siblings talking together, murmuring low to each other so as not to disturb me. I drifted off to sleep, imagining the adventures they were cooking up, just like they had years ago, in the golden days of youth, before all the ugly invaded and destroyed paradise forever.

My sleep was plagued with surreal nightmares all night. I dreamed of calamity on top of calamity, horror upon horror. I watched family members grow old and die in the span of seconds, one minute hale and hearty, the next withered corpses teeming with maggots. My cries went unheard as I watched faceless beings stalk and torture everyone I had ever loved. I ran through the empty streets of Stillwater, chased by phantoms bearing the faces of dead relatives. Their haunted cries pursued me like hell hounds, implacable foes intent on dragging me back to face judgment for my sins. I fled past swirling images depicting every impure moment throughout my life. I watched myself shoplifting from Walmart, lying to my teachers about who was smoking in the girls' room, ganging up on the weakest child on the playground, just to feel a sense of power for a change. Every wrong I had ever done, or even considered doing, was playing on an endless loop in my mind. I begged for mercy, my voice ragged, though I knew not who or what, it was that I addressed my pleas. The only response I received was mocking laughter, as my tormentors drew their sustenance from the misery of those unlucky enough to find themselves under the terrible gaze of those unseen justices. All was despair; all was ruin.

Then it wasn't. I woke up suddenly, the morning sun just peeking over the horizon as it began its daily trek across the sky. My heart was racing, the echoes of the damned ringing in my ears. It took several minutes of deep breathing to calm myself down. I was feeling off-kilter; it had been years since a dream had affected me that much. I was frankly embarrassed at my reaction. Grown women shouldn't be shaking like a leaf in the light of day due to a dream. That was for children, not fully sovereign adults. Terror like that should be reserved for earthquakes, child molesters, and bureaucrats, not the ephemeral phantoms conjured by one's own overactive imagination gone wild. I was supposed to be past this stage in life, my id should have been more under my control.

After a few more minutes of obligatory self-flagellation, I stood up and began my morning stretching routine. It's not exactly yoga. There's no set poses I follow, no particular emphasis on a specific discipline. I just let my body tell me what it needs, then proceed to comply. It's always been more about breathing deeply and being one with myself than any kind of dogmatic physical ritual. No new age whale song music, no hippy-dippy chimes and shit, just me, myself, and I. After my body felt loose and lithe, the night's suboptimal sleep posture's ill effects ameliorated, I felt refreshed and new, ready to face the potential calamities that the day may have in store.

I made my way into the house, careful to remain quiet. The clock on the kitchen stove read 7:03, and I didn't want to wake anyone who may still have been sleeping. I crept to the bathroom, intent on carrying out the usual morning necessities, but found it already occupied by my sister. Pleasantly surprised, I ambled back to the kitchen to make coffee while I waited my turn. Once I had the go-go juice on the brew, Jolene emerged from the bathroom, and we switched places. I got my preliminaries sorted, then joined my sister in the kitchen.

"Shane still sleeping?" I asked.

"Oh, no, he left for work an hour ago," Jolene replied, wiping the sleep out of her eyes with the cuff of her sleeve.

"Wait… He left already?" I asked, taken aback.

"Well… Yeah, he had to go to work," she answered, her eyebrows furrowed with confusion.

"But he knew he had to leave for that meeting with the hospital staff this morning," I said, my annoyance growing. I lit a cigarette and brooded over it while Jolene looked at me curiously.

"So?" she asked, clearly not understanding my distress.

"He didn't say goodbye, Jolene," I said, explaining the obvious.

"And I repeat: so?" she countered, obstinance ever her watchword.

"What do you mean 'so?' I fumed, my patience wearing thin. "I haven't seen my brother for twenty years, and he leaves without saying goodbye, and your response is 'so?'"

"What did you expect?" she asked coldly, her eyes suddenly frozen amethysts in their sockets. "Did you say goodbye to anyone when you left?"

Stunned, I answered incredulously, "Are you kidding me? Still? You're still going to beat that dead fucking horse?"

The sheer malice in her voice when she answered took my breath away. She sounded like she truly hated me at that moment, and I withered a little under the intensity of her glare.

"Did you ever once think about us?" she hissed, sonic venom pouring from her sneering lips. "How we'd worry? You left without a trace, Rem. Just gone, without a word. It was really fucking selfish of you—"

"Selfish?" I exploded, my voice booming throughout the house. "Are you really trying to say that? Granny had lost it, Jolene. I was the one who was carrying her, not you, not anyone else. And I was just a fucking kid. That's too much to ask of anyone. Where were you, Saint Jo? Huh? Where the fuck were you when your kid sister was drowning under the weight of caring for a crazy old lady? Oh, I remember, out getting knocked up again for the umpteenth time. Don't give me the fucking martyr act Jolene. I know better. I was there too, you know."

Jolene took all this in silently, but I could see the shadows of rage at work just under the surface. She began to tremble, and tears threatened to spill over the banks and flood her cheeks.

"You don't know what you're talking about," she said, her voice small and trembly. She was close to her breaking point, I could see it, but I didn't care. I had had enough of the pity party, the self-victimization.

"Yes, I do, and you know it," I said, heedless of any damage I might inflict. "All your life, all I've ever heard is poor me, poor put-upon Jolene, her twin died. Poor Jolene, she has to look out for her siblings because her mom's a drunk. Poor Jolene, that boy who knocked her up took off. Poor Jolene, she just can't stay off smack, she's just addicted, the poor thing. Well, I'm tired of hearing it, you hear me? Most of the bad shit in your life is due to your own stupid fucking decisions—"

Her eyes grew to the size of soccer balls, and she almost choked on her own words as she spat, "Are you seriously telling me that Jesco getting killed was my decision?"

"No," I said quietly, hanging my head. "Not that."

"Then what are you trying to say?" she asked so coldly. I swore I could see icicles shooting from her mouth.

"I don't know, I guess," I admitted sheepishly. "I'm just tired of the victim game. I know your life was shit. I know what cards you were dealt. I had to play with the same hand. But I played. Maybe I come out on the losing side more often than not, but I still play. You never have. You fold every hand you're dealt. You don't even try to bluff your way through. You just keep chipping in your ante, but you always fold. You can't win that way, don't you see?"

"Life is not a game, Remlee," she replied with a contemptuous sigh.

"But it is," I countered. "It is a game, but you can't win if you don't play."

Jolene chuckled sardonically at that but didn't challenge me on my assertion. She lit a cigarette of her own and desultorily exhaled the pale blue poisonous vapor that we were both so hopelessly addicted to. She regarded me through the haze she so recently unleashed, her eyes guarded, watchful. She studied me the way a small critter might observe an apex predator, something to be keenly wary of.

"I don't want to have this conversation," she said abruptly, breaking the awkward silence that had filled the room. "We've got to get to the hospital for that meeting in two hours, and that's stressful enough."

I nodded in silent agreement, inwardly grateful for the opportunity to escape the previous line of inquiry. It felt horrible, calling her out like that. I hadn't intended for our morning to start out so contentiously. It's just that I tend to get carried away with my own sense of self-righteousness from time to time.

We gathered our belongings in sullen silence and made our exit without further incident. We left a note for Lindie, bidding her farewell and offering thanks for her hospitality. I initially pushed for an in-person farewell, but Jolene insisted it was safer to let sleeping dogs lie, so to speak. I grudgingly accepted her assessment, and quietly, we let ourselves out into the golden morning light.

The ride back to Stillwater was uncomfortably quiet. Both of our feelings were raw, each of us wounded by the other. The silence was only broken by the inane shenanigans of the local morning radio show morons, tittering their way through dozens of tired dick and fart jokes accompanied by cheesy stock sound effects patched together by their unpaid, overworked interns. I tried to lose myself in their banter to stave off introspection, but the utter banal humorlessness of the troglodytes issuing from the stereo made the roar in my head all the louder.

About halfway back, my phone rang, and I scrambled to answer it, knowing it was likely to be Jack. I sighed audibly with relief when the caller ID display confirmed my hunch. His voice cut through the din, brightening my day as he greeted me.

"Jesus fucking Christ, it's good to hear your voice," he said breathlessly, in lieu of the traditional "hello."

"That's what I was going to say!" I replied with a joyful laugh.

We exchanged recent histories with each other, him detailing the travails of his return to landscaping duty, me explaining the most recent developments in the case of the addled mother. It felt so good to talk to him again, even though it had only been a day. I explained our gambit for stashing Mom and next door to Jolene, with Gary's mother, and he agreed that there didn't seem to be a better option. He wished me luck with the meeting, and I wish him luck with dinner, ribbing him over his abysmal cooking skills. He laughed and promised not to burn any water and then was gone. I had lost the signal before I could say goodbye. That was starting to become an annoying trend.

When we finally made it to St. Mark's, we parked and lit one last smoke to fortify ourselves for the impending unpleasantness. Neither one of us wanted to be the first to go. We both searched desperately in vain to find reasons to procrastinate. Things were about to progress; the safety net of the hospital was about to be dissolved. The full-time care of our mother was about to become our sole responsibility. The luxury of paid workers to babysit was set to expire in a few short hours. Looking at the doors mere feet away from where we sat filled me with superstitious dread, and I knew that when I returned through them, it would be with Mama, obstinate and unyielding as ever. The idea made me nauseous, but I resolved to be a big girl, so I pushed the bile back down and put myself into motion.

Jolene fell in step beside me, clutching my arm for support. I looked over at her and saw the fear and sorrow bubbling just below the surface. I smiled gently at her, silently lending her my strength.

"You ready for this?" I asked.

"No," she replied, barely above a whisper.

"Me neither," I said, and holding her hand tightly, we stepped through the doors to face whatever came next. Together.

Betty Sue

I'm up before the sun. I just can't sleep anymore; it seems like that's all I've done for the past month. Sleep and jump through hoops to please the staff. All that ends today, though. Today, I'm free again. Sort of. I still have to go live with that nasty old bitch, but I can tell her to go fuck herself. Okay, I can't really, but you know what I mean. Ida Greene ain't got no power over me, not like they do here at the hospital. I gotta play along if I want them to spring me, so that's what I've been doing. I'm all smiles an "yes, sir" and "no, ma'am." I'm so close to freedom I can smell it, and I ain't gonna mess that up for nothing. I'll play the sweet old lady for Nurse Tinkerbell or the Robot Therapy Guy if that's what I got to do to get out of here. Because I need to get out of here.

I'm restless beyond measure. I can't sit still. I wouldn't be surprised to find out that I've worn a groove in the floor from pacing back and forth so much. Everything's quiet on the ward, only I'm awake, save the nurse sitting at the station. I don't know much about this one, she only works nights, so I rarely see her. The cheap slippers I'm wearing go pat, pat, pat, as I pad along my path, and I peek out the door to see if the night nurse notices my noises. She's wearing headphones, and her face is buried in one of those cell phone doohickeys. Good. She won't be a problem.

I don't know what it is I'm so paranoid about. They can't keep me here against my will. This ain't jail. I'm not under arrest. I ain't been in front of no judge to say I'm too crazy for my own good. I could just walk right out the door right now, and there ain't nothing in the world anyone could do to stop me. So why don't I? Why am I waiting for their permission? I don't need it. I might not really be able to talk, but I know what's going on, dammit. I'm not crazy, not yet anyways, so why am I letting these doctors tell me what to do? That just ain't like me. I don't let nobody tell me what to do, not a man, not a boss, not Johnny fuckin' Law. Did the stroke take my guts when it took my words?

No, I'm still one high-riding bitch. I'm just being smart, that's all. Mama Lettie always said you catch more flies with honey than with vinegar, and in this case, at least, I agree. Maybe I'm just getting older, or smarter, or both, but I finally understand that being a bull in the China shop don't usually get you anywhere. If I were to show my ass and make a ruckus to get myself out of here, it would just be a red flag, something they could use against me later. If I'm sweet as pie and just be a little patient, they'll let me out, and there won't be no record of me being troublesome. I gotta fly under the radar. That's the only thing for it.

I go stand in front of the window and watch the drawn break pink across the sky. Everything is golden. Everything is new. The day is still full of possibility, even more so than usual, somehow. The dew on the grass outside reflects the sun, making the ground look like it's covered in millions of sparkling diamonds. I feel giddy, younger, more vital. I struggle to maintain my composure. I want to skip and run and sing, but besides making me look like a damn fool, I'd probably fall and break my hip, so I content myself with a gigantic goofy grin. I can't seem to stop smiling, in fact. My cheeks actually kind of burn from my perma-grin.

I wonder how long it will be before they cut me loose. Tinkerbell told me that they have to have a meeting with my daughters and the staff so they can get all the paperwork bullshit dealt with and get me set up with outpatient therapy and whatever other red tape needs attending to. After that, I can be on my way. I just have to make it through, and by this afternoon, I should be out of here, out of these awful pajamas, and back to rebuilding my life.

The first thing I'm gonna do is have me a smoke. This is the longest I've gone without tobacco since I was nine or ten, and I fucking miss it. I know I should be smart and stay quit. I should use this time out as my stepping-stone to emancipation from that filthy habit, but I don't think I can. Sometimes, I want a cigarette so bad, I can actually feel my lungs itching, begging to be coated once more with smoke and tar. Not smoking here in the hospital is easy, you ain't allowed. In the world, it ain't like that. If I have to the urge to smoke in my living room, there ain't nobody to stop me. It's much easier to kick a habit if you don't have access to it.

The doctor tells me that not only do I got to quit smoking, but she wants me to eat better too. No more fried chicken, no more truck stop pizza, no more flavor. Rice and veggies, veggies and rice. Just picture the blandest, most unappetizing food you can think of and then put that on the menu while taking anything with any flavor whatsoever off of it. I guess I can try, but I can't promise nothing. If I could just give up one or the other, I might be okay, but no gravy with dinner and no cigarette after? That's a tall order. I don't know if it's really worth it. I mean, what good is life if you can't do anything you enjoy?

Stop it, Betty Sue. I gotta quit feeling sorry for myself. It don't fix the situation any; it just takes energy away from doing the things I can do. I gotta keep positive, for Remlee. I got a chance to make it up to her, at least a little bit, and I don't intend to fuck it up. I don't have much time; she's going back to Boston once I'm settled. I don't blame her. She's got a life for herself up there. There ain't nothing for her here. There's no jobs worth having in Stillwater, except for the prison. Sure, it pays decent, but who wants to be locked up every day? Those guards don't seem to get that; they're doing time too. They just get to go home at night. But you make a career out of it, and you'll spend more time behind bars than some criminal in for bank robbery. You might get a gold watch and a pension at the end, but you still lost all those years being locked in a cage with a bunch of animals.

I just have to make the best of what time I do have with her. I don't expect a miracle. I just want to be allowed to be a part of her life. That's all. I don't want her to disappear again. She don't have to babysit me; I just want to hear her voice from time to time. I'm hoping that ain't too much to ask.

An orderly comes by with breakfast, but I'm too keyed up to eat. I try anyway, if only to kill time. Mostly, I just push the yellow goo they tell me is eggs from one side of my tray to the other. I turn on the TV, hoping it might distract me, and for a while, it almost does. I almost lose myself in the insignificant prattle that comes pouring out of that infernal box on the wall. I find myself actually caring what my choice in curtains says about my personality. Finding the ultimate stain fighter to battle my pernicious grass stains takes on near-mythical significance. I shed a sincere tear when I hear that after years of trying, Adele is finally preg-

nant. I'm so happy for her and her lovely husband. My sense of righteous indignation is triggered when I watch Dr. Phil tear into that ungrateful, disobedient brat with the cute yellow dress. I celebrate with Marlon when Maury informs him that he is not the father. I'm devastated when I hear about the fire at the orphanage; those poor children have a hell of a time. I can live my life vicariously through strangers and never have to leave my bed. The life I watch is so much more glamorous, so much more interesting than the drab reality I actually inhabit.

That drab reality comes roaring back into my room, accompanied by Nurse Tinkerbell, the nosey Social Worker Bee, Mr. Robot, and my daughters. The way they stalk into the room makes me nervous, and I instinctively crouch in the corner. The cheeriness in their faces drains and is replaced by looks of confusion and concern. Tink and The Robot rush over, spouting what I can only assume they think are comforting phrases at me, but in my foggy state, I'm unable to understand. They gently guide me to the bed, explaining their benevolent intentions the whole way. I sit down and close my eyes, hoping I can somehow banish this sudden irrational fear. I know these people. Nobody is trying to hurt me. Everything is peachy keen.

"Mama! Woah! It's okay, it's just us," Jolene says, her voice high and thin. She is as white as a ghost, and I wonder if the fear monster that I just banished attached itself to her. It had to go somewhere, didn't it?

I try to tell them that I'm fine, that they just startled me, but the new reality is stubborn, like me, and it seems that my voice is still MIA. A stream of gibberish is all I can manage. Everyone crowds around me, and the weight of their combined presence pushes on me heavily.

"B…BBB… Bbbaaaaccckkkk," I say, waving them away like a swarm of mosquitoes. They all look at each other with surprise, but they do what I tell them. I try to smile at them, hoping that they understand I'm being a good girl. I'm so close to being free of this place, I can't mess this up. The squadron in front of me eyes me warily, looking to see if I'm gearing up to pounce. I can't blame them, I have gone after a few of my minders since coming here, but dammit, I was provoked.

"SSS…SSSS… S'oookkaaaa," I say, summoning my all my will. I smile at them so hard that my cheeks begin to burn.

"Is everything okay, Ms. Shaw?" Worker Bee says, and I can see the cold calculation behind the superficial benevolence. This one is watching me close.

I nod yes, keeping the smile painted on my face. It isn't that hard of a task, I am genuinely excited to be leaving, even if my destination isn't ideal. I don't think they can keep me here or make me go somewhere I don't want to. I ain't seen no judge, but the idea is pernicious. It has burrowed down deep in my head and sunk hardy roots. No matter how many times I rip the poison fruit of paranoia out of the garden, it just grows back. I don't think I'll truly feel good about all this until I see St. Mark's in the rearview mirror. I just have to make it until then. I can do it. I will do it.

"Well, Ms. Shaw, today is the big day! Are you excited?" Nurse Tinkerbell asks, chipper as ever.

"Yu… Yu… Nau bo… Tank and albaugh," I say, and for once, I'm glad my language is garbled. Telling her that I am excited to get the fuck away from her is safer for my precarious situation when she can't understand me. Maybe this is a good thing, now that I think about it. My mouth, up to this point, has gotten me nothing but trouble. Maybe this is God's way of saving me from myself. I ain't no spring chicken no more. I can't scrap like I used to. It's hard to pick a fight when you can't insult no one.

The staffers yammer on and on, giving me instructions about this pill and that, but I can't follow them. Jolene and Remlee are here. I'm sure they'll pick it all up. I'm too restless to focus on their words. I just want them to finish. They stick a stack of papers in front of me and tell me to make my mark. I try to sign, but the end result looks like Japanese kanji drawn by an orangutan. Apparently, this is satisfactory because as I finish the last of the seemingly endless signatures, Miss Nosey Social Worker Bee snatches them from me and grasps my hand in a firm, businesslike handshake.

"Good luck to you, Ms. Shaw," she says, turns on her heel, and primly walks out, followed by Mr. Robot and Tink. As she exits the door, Nurse Tinkerbell looks back at me and smiles warmly.

"We'll miss you," she says, all saccharine. I flip her off.

"Mama!" Jolene squeaks, looking at me with mingled annoyance and amusement. Remlee looks at the ground, and I can see she is fighting laughter.

"Sumble?" I ask. (What?)

I give my daughters my best attempt at an innocent look. Jolene and Remlee look at me, then each other, and burst out laughing. I join in, thrilled to be able to take part. I've felt outside of humanity ever since the stroke, but this moment, laughing with my daughters, brings me back into the fold, for the time being, anyways. We laugh until our sides hurt, and tears are streaming down our faces. We must sound like lunatics to anyone walking by, but I don't care. This is the best medicine anyone could prescribe.

We finally settle down and begin gathering what few belongings I have. Remlee produces a fresh outfit that she picked up at Target for me to wear. It's not really my style, I'm not usually into sweat suits, but I'm just so happy to wear normal clothes that don't show my ass to the world that I happily scramble into it. Once I'm changed, I all but run to the door, like a kid who can't wait for recess.

"Geez, Dale Earnhardt!" Jolene exclaims as I rush past her, nearly knocking her over in the process. I make a mental note to get on to her about her eating. She's too damn skinny. If I ever can talk again, that is.

I make a beeline for the elevator, leaving my daughters in the dust. I mash the call buttons and grumble under my breath, my impatience growing by the minute. The car shows up just as my girls catch up, and we all get in together. Time starts fucking with me, slowing down to a crawl, and I swear it takes sixteen years for the elevator to descend the three floors to the lobby. When the doors finally opened, it's like the scene in The Wizard of Oz *where Dorothy first steps into Oz, and it goes from fuzzy black-and-white to dynamic full Technicolor. The sun bursting through the floor-to-ceiling windows in front of me blinds me and takes my breath away. I feel like I'm marching to the pearly gates instead of a boring old exit. This isn't just a change of scenery for me; it's a religious experience. I am baptized anew, reborn, as I walk through the giant revolving door and back into the world.*

Now, all I have to do is fix everything I've broken.

Remlee

Our meeting with the staff of St. Mark's was blessedly brief. I got the feeling that they were as excited to see Mama go as Mama was to leave. They gave us a rundown of her new medications (warfarin, aspirin, Flexeril for her back) and set up home visitation for a nurse and an occupational therapist. They gave us a folder, jam-packed full of information that neither Jolene nor I would ever have the time to read. They were pleasant enough to us, but it was obvious that Mama wasn't exactly their favorite patient, and most topics were glossed over, rushed through. They wanted her to no longer be their burden, and understandably so. I can only imagine how difficult it must be to work in a field where there is so much suffering when the patients are cooperative and friendly. Dealing with a mean old twat on top of everything else must be murder. I know I couldn't do it. I'm just not that good of a person.

After the staff was certain that they had dotted all their i's and crossed all their t's, they let us in an odd procession to my mother's room. She seemed disoriented at first, like we interrupted her trip to La-La Land. She backed into the corner like a rabid animal, looking wild, ferocious, and ready to attack. The nurse and occupational therapist managed to rein her in quickly, and Mama came to her senses, if you will. I knew she was back for sure when she flipped off the nurse as she left. Pointedly obnoxious behavior is far more my mother's style than the frothing wolverine we encountered upon first entering her room. I'm not sure what it says when antisocial behavior is a sign of things returning to normal.

Once we got Mama squared away, she all but ran out of the hospital. I was slightly amazed that I really had to try to keep up with her. Her excitement to be free once again overrode her decrepitude, and at that moment, I bet she would have beaten Jackie Joyner-Kersee in the hundred-meter dash. She burst through the front doors of the hospital like an allied soldier entering a German pillbox, wild and ravenous. Once outside, she stood stock still, her arms outstretched, her eyes closed, and face tilted up toward the sun. She looked like the world's biggest sunflower in her new yellow tracksuit, growing tall out of the cracks in the pavement. Her shoulders heaved as she drank the fresh air in like a drowning woman. A single tear escaped her eye, but she didn't make a move to wipe it away. It was like she was photosynthesizing, drawing nourishment from the sun and uncirculated, unconditioned air. Jolene and I watched her, giggling at each other.

"I don't remember the last time I seen her so happy," Jolene said, beaming.

After a few moments of celebrating her newly regained (semi) freedom, we corralled Mama and let her to the car. She seemed indignant at having to sit in the back, but not enough to put up a fuss. She spent the ride to her new digs staring out of the window, wide-eyed and oddly curious. She had lived in Stillwater and the surrounding area for her entire six and a half decades, but it seemed that she no longer recognized it. Her face was a trippy mix of excitement, concern, confusion, and suspicion. I think she was worried that we were tricking her, and any moment, we would turn into the parking lot of the County Home to abandon her to the mercy of underpaid, overworked strangers. Her expression wavered between wide-eyed, dopey grinning, and squinty, naked hostility. I wondered what half-crazy thoughts were bouncing around the inside of her skull; how much of what was happening was being processed accurately.

We stopped at the drug store, then the grocery store, before finally making our way to Mama's new home. Mama insisted on carrying out her own transactions, leading to much commotion in both stores. The poor pharmacist at Walgreens was nearly apoplectic by the time Jolene swooped in to rescue her from the babbling and wildly gesticulating customer that was our mother. Mama tried to pay with cash but kept getting her bills mixed up. Jolene and I just followed behind her, pleading and cajoling her to let us handle her light work. She basically ignored us and just jabbered her nonsense into the perfectly perplexed faces of the poor, unprepared employees. It took ten times longer than it should have in both stores, so by the time we pulled up in front of Gary's two trailer complex, the sun had already passed its midpoint, and the afternoon was upon us.

Mama looked at the two trailers like she had never seen any such thing before in her life. She looked questioningly at Jolene and me and made some interrogative noises, but we weren't able to suss out her meaning. She just sat stock still, asking her wordless question over and over, always displeased with the replies we were supplying.

"Dissen yu yu… Dissen yu yu? Oh Lord, yu yu dissen yu?" she asked over and over, genuinely distressed by both the original stressor and by our inability to understand her queries. It felt like we were playing Twenty Questions as we tried to figure out exactly what it was that she was trying to ask. Eventually, we were able to ascertain that she had forgotten that she wasn't going back to her trailer or else thought we were going to ignore the doctor and take her there anyways. It wasn't entirely clear which of the two scenarios was the correct one, but it didn't matter. Mama didn't want to stay here. She wanted to go to her own place, medical orders be damned, and no amount of reasoning would change her mind. Jolene and I sat in that car, pleading with our mother, for a solid forty-five minutes before I finally lost my temper. Arguing with a semilucid, misanthropic mute with something neither of us had ever prepared for, and we were greatly outmatched. No matter what we offered, threatened, or promised, Mama refused to budge. Eventually, she quit talking, choosing instead to simply point down the road and shake her head no.

"That's fucking it!" I shouted, my voice booming in the confines of Jolene's Cavalier. "I've had enough! You are going in that god damned trailer, and that's that. You are an invalid, Mama. I'm sorry to say. Truly, I get no joy from telling you that. Do you think I wanted any of this, either? I have a life, Mama. It's on hold now so that I can take care of you. And that's fine. You're my mother, and I love you. Despite all the shit you put me through, that you put all of us through, I still care what happens to you. Some people say I shouldn't, and maybe they're right, but I do. So let me, Mama. Let us. Let us take care of you."

"No… Yu yu… Oh Lord… Yu yu yu… No… Icantu…" she said, her petulant face red and shiny with sweat.

"This isn't a fucking debate, Mama," I said, my voice cold and stern. I got out of the car in a huff, violently opening and slamming the door. Mom's eyes grew wide as I tore her door open. She cringed away from me in the corner, eyes rolling in blind terror. Seeing my once fierce mother reduced to a cowering, quivering puddle of broken humanity shocked me into softening my approach. An almost matronly feeling came over me, and my anger was gone, replaced by sadness, pity, and concern. I sat down on the back seat beside her, doing my best to present as unthreatening of body language as possible. Jolene sat in the driver seat still, traumatized into inaction. I made eye contact with her, silently asking her to help me calm our mother down, but she either ignored me or was too upset herself to be of much use. I turned back to the pitiful creature that was my mother and tried a new tack.

"I understand, Mama," I said soothingly, my voice low and breathy. "This is all a big change. It's all new. Nobody is trying to hurt you or take anything from you. Let's just go inside, Mama. It's hot as balls out here. I'm sweating like a pig, ain't you?"

She nodded yes, but slowly, like she didn't really want to admit it. Damn, she's a stubborn old bitch!

"C'mon, Mama," I trilled, almost singing at her. "Wouldn't a nice, cold beer sounds just about perfect right now?"

Bingo. Her eyes lit up at that, and I knew, with grim satisfaction, that the fight was over. Oh, she still might make a show of resisting, if only to placate her own ego, but she would go. She hadn't had a drink in nearly two weeks, and the monkey on her back needed scratching.

Jolene caught on to my ploy immediately and said, "Yeah, Mama. I know for a fact that Ida has a case a Bud Light in there. Gary just picked it up, night before last. Ida only drinks every once in a while, I guarantee there's plenty left in there. C'mon, let's go in and cool off and have a beer together. Lord knows I could use one too."

Mama gave us both a suspicious look, but her need for a drink overrode her uncharacteristic caution. She made her way out of the car and allowed me to lead her to the door of the tidy little trailer that would now be her home for the time being. Jolene followed behind, carrying the small duffel bag of mom's clothes and our recent supply purchases. I knocked on the door rapidly and pushed it open, not content to wait for an answer.

"Who dat?" a small, confused voice called from within, and Ida Greene appeared, small and withered, from the hallway to the left. She was roughly mom's age but shorter and squatter. She was scowling at us, and her attitude told me that she was about as happy with the arrangement as Mama. At least they had that in common; neither wanted to live with the other.

"Oh, it's you," she said dismissively and turned and slunk away. We stood there, taken aback for a moment before I stepped inside, tugging my reluctant mother behind me. Jolene came in last, shutting the door a little too quickly, resulting in an echoing boom that brought prison doors to mind.

"See, isn't it nice in here?" Jolene asked as she gestured around the room like Vanna White revealing prizes. Mama rolled her eyes and made a beeline for the kitchen and the refrigerator she knew would lie within. She walked right past Ida, who was sitting in her easy chair in the sitting room, glaring at us and all the ruckus we were bringing into her life. Momma flung open the fridge and rummaged through it violently, paying no heed to the packages, bottles, and other bric-a-brac stored inside. She finally found her quarry, opened the bottle of brew with her teeth, and started gulping it greedily, the yellow nectar spilling all down the front of her chin and neck.

"A "please" would have been nice," Ida grumbled from her chair.

"Summbla doubey," Mama said in return, and nobody present thought "please" was what she meant. She grabbed a second beer from the fridge and shuffled over to the love seat and sat down heavily.

"Well, I know you guys know each other already, so I guess I won't bother with introductions," Jolene said, a nervous tremor in her voice.

I could see that taking charge of a situation was something she was not well suited for, and I understood how it was that her kids were able to walk all over her. She was a mouse in human clothing, and like the hyenas that children are, her kids took full advantage.

Mama eyed Ida warily, and Ida returned fire. Their mutual distaste for another was palpable. It filled the air with a heavy gloom that was felt instead of seen. I wondered if maybe this wasn't a mistake; it couldn't possibly be good for either of them to be stuck with each other. How could Mama focus on getting better if she was miserable about her circumstances all the time?

Just as the tension was getting to be too much, Jolene broke the silence, saying, "Why don't we show you your new room, huh? That'll be nice, won't it?"

Mama looked at her witheringly but stood up and followed Jolene down the hallway toward the rooms in the back. I followed behind her, preparing myself for the sudden move toward escape I almost expected her to take. No such evasion occurred, however, and she went to her new digs as docile as a lamb to slaughter. She entered her room with little interest and flopped down onto the bed. She laid her arms across her eyes, blocking out the light, and proceeded to ignore us aggressively.

"Mama..." Jolene began, her voice raw with exhaustion and exasperation, but gave up before she finished her thought. Her shoulders slumped in defeat, and she turned to look at me, hoping I knew what to do next. I didn't, so we both sat down on the bed next to mom's prone form and waited for her to reappear out of her ineffective hiding place. When it became clear that she wasn't going to relent, that her pouting would continue for the foreseeable future, Jolene gave her what was left of her tour presentation.

"The bathroom is right across the hall, Mama, and the clicker for the TV is on the stand next to you. We're going to leave now. I'm tired. I'm sure Remlee is too. I need a shower, something terrible, and I need my bed," Jolene said. Mama didn't say anything or even acknowledge she heard in any way.

"Mama? Did you hear Jolene?" I asked and irritated edge to my voice. My daily allotment of patience was almost exhausted, and it took considerable effort to remain calm and pleasant.

"Dimmu gaffay low," she muttered, not lifting her arms from her face.

"Let's go, Jolene. She'll be fine," I said, pulling on her shirt to get her moving.

"We'll be right next door," Jolene called over her shoulder as I half dragged her from the room. We walked past a scowling Ida, hastily said our goodbyes, and walked out into the steamy late afternoon.

"Do you think she'll be all right?" Jolene asked fretfully, tugging absentmindedly at her lower lip.

"She'll be fine," I said dismissively. "She's got AC, she's got TV, she's got beer. What else could she ask for?"

"The company of people who care about her," she retorted, looking at me like I was incredibly stupid, or insensitive, or both.

"Yeah? And who exactly is that?" I said, twisting the knife sadistically.

"Jesus Christ, you're cold," Jolene said breathlessly, taken aback by the vitriol that issued forth from my mouth.

"This is Florida, Sis. Ain't nobody cold," I said dryly.

Jolene stopped in her tracks and stared at me for a moment, suddenly bereft of words for likely the first time in her life. An enormous grin began to break slowly across her face, lighting it up from the inside. She exploded into gales of hysterical laughter, doubling over and clutching her sides. I quickly joined her, smugly satisfied with my cutting wit. We sat down on the curb between her trailer in the street, arms around each other, shaking uncontrollably with psychotic laughter. The seriousness of the situation had grown to be too much, and my gallows humor had saved us from drowning in the sea of despair we were both dangling precariously over.

"It's gonna be all right, ain't it?" Jolene finally asked me after the hysteria had abated.

"Probably not," I said truthfully. "But we'll get through it anyways. We always do."

"Speak for yourself," Jolene said darkly. "There ain't been a 'we' since you run off."

"Fine, I will," I said, ignoring her jab. I stood up, stretching, and turned toward Jolene's trailer to go inside.

"Let's go inside and cool off. It's like soup out here today," I said, reaching my hand out to help her up. She took it and hauled herself to her feet.

"Okay, good idea," she said wearily. "I really just want this day to be over. It ain't even suppertime, but all this drama got me wore out."

She laced her arm through mine, and we made our way inside, into the electrically created winter, where we would lick our wounds and prepare to fight another day.

Betty Sue

I don't think this new living situation is going to work out. I just got here an hour ago, and already I want to leave. If you had told me I would be shaking up with that world-famous hussy, Ida Greene, I would have called you a damn liar. Like living as a mute ain't bad enough, now I got to do it with one of my husband's whores. Every time I look at that nasty old bitch, I see Elmer's cock in her mouth, and I want to tear her tits off with my bare hands. I shouldn't care. That was ages ago, and I didn't like him anyways. It's a territorial thing, I guess. Elmer Ray Shaw ain't worth a kernel of corn in a pile of pig shit, but he was mine, and I don't share my things.

When Jolene and Remlee ditched me here, I tried to sit with Ida. Much as I hate her, I don't want to have to hide in one room like an inmate, so I thought I'd try to be civil. She's just a lonely old broad like me. People like us should stick together. I sat down on the chair opposite her and tried to make my face as pleasant as I could. She made a show of ignoring me, sighing theatrically as she turned each page of the newspaper she wasn't actually reading but using as a prop to aid her in ignoring me. Out of sight, out of mind.

"Teebloo reemo?" I asked. Where is the TV remote?

Nothing. Silence from behind the news-print wall.

"Teebloo reemo?" I repeated more forcefully. Ida lowered the paper and glared at me like I was the antichrist.

"I don't like you," she said, her voice flat and emotionless. "I don't want you here, but it's my son's trailer, and I got to do what he says, but I don't have to like it. We ain't gonna be friends."

"Fukyu, sumble neebo," I retorted. Fuck you, I hate you too, cunt. I stormed back to my new room (cell) and slammed the door. I turned on

the TV for company, and now here I sit, alone again with the electronic ghosts in the box.

In some ways, this is better than the hospital, I guess. I can close the fucking door and get some privacy here, for one. There ain't an army of faceless worker bees zipping in and out, pestering me at all hours of the night, and that is a major improvement, I tell you. I don't have to listen to Nurse Tinkerbell's revoltingly adorable voice spouting vacuous platitudes about "remaining positive" and "looking on the bright side." If I would have had to listen to her try to explain how good the world is one more fucking time, when she ain't hardly seen any of it, I probably would have crammed that stethoscope down her precious little throat. As long as Ida leaves me alone, and she seems to want nothing more than to do just that, maybe this will be okay. I'd rather be at my own trailer, but I guess this will have to do.

Speaking of my trailer, I wonder what's going to happen to it. Ralph Mercer, my landlord, may want to bone me, but money is money. He ain't gonna hold that place for me for long. If I ever get better enough to be on my own again (fingers crossed), I'll have to start over again somewhere else. That's okay. I ain't love with the place or anything, but I'm used to it. I know where not to a step to avoid squeaks. I know the trick to get the closet door to stay shut. I'm too old to have to learn the mysteries of a new (to me) house. You can't teach an old dog new tricks.

I'm watching some murder mystery on Dateline, the story of a fairy tale romance gone wrong. These stories get me every time. I don't understand how these broads never see it coming. They marry these monsters, knowing how they are, knowing how all men are, and then act all surprised when he acts monstrous. If you lie down with scorpions, you can't be surprised when you get stung.

I begin to feel drowsy from the events of the day. Yawns break forth from my mouth with regularity, and my eyelids suddenly weigh a ton. I close them gladly, not that I could keep them open if I wanted to. I feel a sinking sensation, and the ambient sounds begin to fade out, like at the end of a pop song. Soon, all sound is gone, all light is gone, all senses are gone. I'm back in my little comfy pocket of nowhere, and I let myself drift through the nothingness.

Something brings me back to myself. One minute, I'm nothing, the next, something. My thoughts restart or reboot as the current terminology goes, and I'm a person once again. A tiny pinprick of brilliant white light pops into existence, somewhere far ahead (behind, beside, below—hell, if I can tell) of me. It's so small, I normally wouldn't notice it, but in the void, it's impossible to miss. It is the only thing that exists, other than my thoughts. It starts pulsating, growing slightly larger with each pulse. I notice a sound now, and it seems to be tied somehow to the light. It gets louder and clearer in rhythm with the pulses, quiet and garbled on the dim cycle, loud and clear on the bright. It grows steadily in intensity and size until it fills my entire field of vision, and it solidifies, somehow, into a giant, radiant door. It stands, shining forth its blazing white light, nearly six stories tall. I can barely see the top.

The light the door emits is swallowed up by the infinite blackness on either side of it and all around it. Other than the door, only I am visible now. I look down at myself, and I'm shocked to see the state I'm in. My youth is back, my skin once again taught, my hair golden and lush. My skin seems to be glowing, like some of the light from the door resides in me as well. I hear triumphant, glorious music coming from within, the voice of thousands of heavenly voices combining with a musical virtuosity I hardly believe possible. Dozens of melodies cascade through the air, coming together to dance with each other, then coming apart in the most intricate of ways. I don't understand the lyrics of this magnum opus. They're in a language no human being has ever spoken.

"Come, Betty Sue," a separate voice says, but I don't hear it with my ear. It's coming from inside me somehow. I'm mildly surprised that this doesn't scare me until I realize that I don't even understand the concept of fear any longer. It's like some invisible surgeon excised that emotion from my palate completely. I no longer even have a word for it.

"Come inside, Betty Sue, I've been waiting for you," the voice says, and I recognize it from somewhere. I can't quite put my finger on it, it's almost like it's a voice I've only ever heard in dreams, yet somehow, it's as familiar as my own.

"Come inside, come inside," the voice chants, and hundreds of other voices join in, creating a din so loud I can actually feel the sound waves pushing against me. Only they are pushing from behind somehow, defy-

ing physics, and guiding me slowly but inexorably toward the door, which is now opening in front of me. As I pass over its threshold, I turn around and look behind me. Instead of the inky blackness I expect, I see myself, asleep in my new room. I look down at my hands, and yes, they are there. Somehow, I am both here, standing in the doorway and, also there, sleeping peacefully in bed.

I'm suddenly lightheaded as I look at myself from a distance for the first time. I look old, tired, and defeated, a pale imitation of what I once was. If I saw myself in that state walking down the street, I'd likely called 911 to send an ambulance, just out of Christian duty. It horrifies me to see how much I've let myself go, how weak and feeble I become. I'm revolted by myself, and I turn away and step through into the light beyond.

The light is so bright, so intense. It takes several moments for me to adjust to it. I rub my eyes and blink rapidly, and suddenly, everything pops into focus. I'm standing on top of a great hill, overlooking a sea of lush greenness, stretching to the horizon and beyond. Immediately I immediately recognize it for what it is: sugarcane. It ripples in the gentle breeze, sighing a quiet tune of peace and contentment. Dotted here and there in the verdant tapestry before me are small clearings in which quaint little cabins stand, wispy tendrils of smoke curling from their charmingly crooked chimneys. I can see people milling about these little estates, made small by distance. It's like looking at an ant-farm of sorts, everything laid out in front of me to study.

"Betty Sue," says the voice that drew me here, "I'm so glad you came."

I turn to look at whoever is addressing me, and my breath stops in my throat. Standing before me is the most radiant woman I have ever seen. Her face is hauntingly familiar. I know this face from somewhere. I've seen this face in my dreams, all throughout my life. This woman is always there, I realize, in every dream I've ever had, but in the background of the dream; she's never been in focus until now.

"I've been waiting so long to meet you," she says, smiling at me with such benevolence. It takes my breath away.

"You have?" I ask, genuinely perplexed. "But why?"

"You know why," she says, a mischievous twinkle in her amethyst eyes.

She says this with such confidence that I'm forced to believe her. I search the file cabinets of my memory, trying to match this face with a name, but I come up empty. I simply have no idea who she is, or I don't know that I know. That doesn't feel right, though. I do know who she is. There's just some kind of shield around her identity that I can't get past.

"I'm so sorry for how bad it has been for you," she says with such compassion that the words seem to have substance, acting as a balm for all my scars, physical and mental. I stare at her, fascinated by every detail my eyes greedily devour. The glowing, golden hair; the high, noble cheekbones; the full, sensuous mouth. Waves of love and goodwill pour from her every pore, visible like heat on the highway. I feel such indescribable joy that I don't know what to do. Every molecule is charged with this positive energy, and I feel like I might burst into a spectacular fireworks display, lighting up the already sunny sky with thousands of colors.

"Is this…heaven?" I ask her, finally finding my voice.

"I don't like that word…" she says absentmindedly.

"Well, is it?" I ask again, impatient.

She laughs her huge laugh and replies, "If you insist on giving this a name, I suppose that one will suffice. I sometimes forget how it is, down there."

"Down where?" I press, growing frustrated with her riddles.

"Earth. The world. Arda. Du monde. Third rock from the sun. The place where you live. Lived," she says offhandedly as if the answer was of no importance.

"Lived? Wait… Am I dead? I am dead then, huh? This is heaven. It has to be," I say, the confusion slowly draining away.

"Hold on, not so fast," the glowing lady says with a gentle laugh. "Not exactly. You're not exactly dead, and you're not exactly alive. I guess you could call this a preview or maybe a trial offer. You've got a choice in this, believe it or not. You can stay here, or you can go back. It's up to you."

Stunned, my mouth falls open, and I ask, "It's up to me?"

"Completely," she replies.

I'll look away from her and back to the giant door. It's just a few feet behind me, standing wide open. Through it, I see my sleeping body still breathing, albeit shallowly. I turn back to the woman and regard her warily.

"Who are you, really?" I ask.

It's her turn to look away, and she walks slowly down the hill, beckoning me to follow her. I hesitate, worried I might lose the door and get trapped here, but her voice rings out, clear and strong.

"It will still be there. The Great Door only closes when your decision is made. We're big on free will around here," she says and winks playfully at me.

She leads me to what I can only assume is her homestead. It's a simple little abode, stucco with a thatched roof. A cow and two sheep mill about the yard, lazily chewing the grass to a manageable length. There is a well in the center of the property, and I see a man bent over in front of it, seemingly applying mortar to the sides as a repair. He hears us coming, and he stands and turns to face us. My heart stops in my chest when I see my father's smiling face regarding me for the first time in decades.

"Daddy?" I gasp, my voice suddenly weak.

"Hello, little muffin," he says, beaming. I rush to him and lose myself in his arms, burying my face in the beard that hangs to his chest. He's just as I remember him when I was a kid: tall, tan, and tougher than a razorback. He even smells the same: sweat, sawdust, motor oil, and Old Spice aftershave. I lean back to look at his face, and a tear sneaks out of the corner of my eye.

"What are you doing here?" I ask breathlessly, still in shock from his completely unexpected appearance.

"I'm dead, silly. Where else would I be?" he replies, giggling at his own joke.

I turn to look at my guide, the beautiful, glowing woman, and suddenly the final veil falls from my eyes. She is right. I do know who she is.

"Mama," I breathe, the word almost a prayer. She smiles at me with a brilliance that almost hurts to look at.

"Betty Sue," she says in her melodious voice. "I've been waiting so long to be able to say that to you. I was only ever able to say it in your presence one other time: the day you were born and the day I died."

"I am so sorry I killed you," I say, at a loss to describe the guilt I feel at being the cause of her demise, however unwittingly.

"Oh, no, darling! Don't say that!" she says, her voice thick with motherly concern. "It was just my time, is all. You didn't have nothing to do with it. My body was worn out. I was too old to be trying to have more kids. I got greedy and put everything I had into you, my one and only daughter. My life might have ended, but in doing so, I was able to give you yours. It was my gift to you, no strings attached."

"Well, I'm sorry to have to tell you, but you probably wasted it on me then. I'm just a fuck-up," I say, and my mother's eyes grow red with sadness.

"How can you say such a thing?" she asks, and I look at her with confusion.

"Ain't you been watching?" I say, my voice full of self-loathing. "I ain't done one right thing in my whole life. My kids are all messed up, except maybe Remlee, and that's only 'cause Daddy kept her away from me as much as he could. Well, and Jesco. Jesco's dead because I was such a lousy mother."

"He's here, you know," Mama interrupts, and my mind stops on a dime.

"He stays over yonder a piece," she says, nodding eastward, toward the still climbing sun. "You can visit him anytime you want. He don't blame you, you know."

For some reason, this angers me, and I snap, "Well, I still do. It was my job to protect him, and I didn't."

"You're just one person, Betty Sue," Mama says, touching my shoulder. Heat radiates from her fingertips and into my arm.

"It can't be that easy," I say. "I stole his life from him."

"No, the truck took it," she says patiently.

"Because I wasn't paying attention," I retort.

"Nor was the truck driver, the twelve other motorists who passed by and saw your Jesco fooling around but kept going, or the half-dozen neighborhood kids who were also standing right there," Mama says, the hint of a smile playing at the corner of her lips.

"But he wasn't their responsibility, he was mine," I say, holding my ground.

"Wasn't he? Are we not to look out for each other?" she asked.

"Well, maybe," I reply, confused by this whole line of conversation. This is like anti-court; I have to convince the judge that I am guilty. I giggle to myself at the ridiculousness of my plight.

"Fine," I say, not yet giving into this unexpected grace, "even if I say that he wasn't my sole responsibility, he was mainly mine. I brought him into the world."

"Not alone, you had help. There was only ever one virgin birth, and it wasn't from your womb," Mama says, determined to win her case.

"Yeah, if you can count what Elmer did as help," I say.

"Look, Betty Sue," she says, looking deep into my eyes. "It's true that what happened to your son was a tragedy. He missed out on most of life, and you missed out on sharing it with him. You both lost something. If anything, it was worse for you. Jesco has been here ever since that horrible day, safe and happy. You had to live with it every day. You punish yourself in ways you don't even realize, more than enough to pay for your transgressions. Everybody seems to think that the Big Guy is all about punishment. Everybody couldn't be more wrong. We punish ourselves; our "hell" is our own minds refusing to let go. Let go, Betty Sue."

The truth of what she says hits home like a freight train. All these years I've hated myself for my failures. All these years I held myself back because I felt unworthy, simply for being human. I have weaknesses. I fuck up from time to time. But I don't hate blindly. I don't have vicious intentions. Any harm I've caused is due to my own human frailties, not malice.

"They say it backward on earth, you know," she says, smiling at me with perfect love. "It shouldn't be 'The road to hell is paved with good intentions.' Good intentions are the only way to avoid hell, the only things that actually matter to the Big Guy. We're imperfect creatures, created so. We aren't expected to be perfect; we're just expected to try our best. We fall so we can learn to get back up."

My mind reels as all this sinks in. I began to feel embarrassed, like I've been wasting all this time worrying about the wrong things. I'm halfway through my sixth decade, more or less, and I just now understand the game I've been playing all this time. My old friend shame creeps into the room in my head and makes himself at home. I've wasted most of my life on bitterness and self-flagellation. I look up at the angel that is my Mama with quivering lips.

"I really messed up, huh?" I ask her, my eyes pleading for pardon.

"Hardly," she replies. "The fact that you care that you might have is proof that you haven't."

"So, Betty Sue," she says after a few quiet moments, "how do you feel about staying?"

"It's awful nice here," I say, overwhelmed by the enormity of the decision I'm being asked to make. "I can stay if I want?"

"Like I said, it's up to you," she says.

"If I go back to the world, can I come back here?" I ask, hedging my bets.

"All journeys end here," she says enigmatically, her face suddenly in an impassive mask.

I think about my life and try to weigh the options. The past several years have been gray and lonely. My spark was almost gone. I was practically the walking dead *anyway. I just went through the motions. I was just surviving, not living. Then the stroke comes out of nowhere and knocks the words right out of my mouth, knocking me out of the world almost completely. If I go back, my life will never be the same as it was. I'll be dependent on someone, either family or some disinterested mercenary, and I don't relish that thought.*

But then there's Remlee. She's back in my life now. I thought I had lost her, but she's here, and she's here for me. She's giving me a chance. Maybe I can salvage the time I have left, if I choose to have more time, that is. That's scary, though. The world isn't a cooperative place. Thousands of factors conspire daily to wreak havoc on the enterprises of men. There will be suffering; there will be pain. I can avoid all that nastiness if I just stay here.

I don't want to be a quitter anymore. I've got all this fight in me. Maybe it's time I used it to fight for myself. I spent enough time holding myself back, punishing myself for sins, real and imagined. Doesn't it say to judge not? Maybe that rule isn't about judging each other. Maybe it's about forgiving yourself.

I look at Mama with firm resolve and say, "I want to live."

As the words leave my mouth, I feel myself being gently pulled away. My eyes lose focus. Everything becomes a vibrant swirl of moving rainbows.

"That's my girl," I hear Mama say, but she's far away now. The Great Door is looming in front of me, and I'm drawn to it, like I'm standing on one of those moving sidewalks, like they have at the airport in Jacksonville. I hear the angelic music for a second as I'm on the threshold, a loud burst that hurts my ears, and then all the silent and dark once again. I turn to look behind me to catch one last glimpse of Paradise, but it's gone. The Great Door is closed, and its light is fading rapidly. Soon, I'm back in the void, like nothing happened.

Time passes, I don't know how much. I start to worry that something went wrong, that maybe I got lost. I strain my senses for any sign of the world, and I can hear birds singing to each other, quietly, almost imperceptibly. The song grows louder and is joined by other noises. I hear a dog barking in the distance. A truck starts up someplace closer. I open my eyes, and it's morning. I'm back in the world, alive and kicking.

It's time to get things right. I have a life to live.

Remlee

Getting Mama settled in proved to be even more difficult than I had imagined. None of the involved parties seemed inclined to cooperate with me or each other, for that matter. Mama and Ida couldn't get past their mutual disdain for one another, and every day, I had to step in and settle some ridiculous quarrel. You wouldn't think that two old, decrepit women would have the energy to spend on such pettiness, but those two were only held back from each other's throats by the most fragile of treaties. Ida was nearly deaf, and Mama couldn't really talk, but that didn't stop them from bickering nearly every minute they were in the same room.

Minor oversights and sincere accidents took on near-mythical proportions. Something as innocuous as the method for peeling potatoes (over the sink or over the garbage) became a flashpoint in their cold war, threatening to bring on mutually assured destruction. Neither wanted to give an inch. Compromise wasn't possible. They had embarked on a war of attrition, and both planned to see it to the bitter end. I was running next door to referee the twelve-round no-holds-barred deathmatches four or five times a day. Every time, I would chastise them after pulling them apart (metaphorically, mostly), and they would both hang their heads like children in the principal's office. I would send them to their neutral corners and leave them with instructions to behave, knowing full well they wouldn't. It was a vicious cycle that I grew to resent quite rapidly.

I kept in touch with Jack, talking with him several times a day. He seemed to be faring well in my absence, and I felt a bit guilty at my annoyance regarding that. Part of me wanted him to be lost without me, unable to make it throughout his day without my assistance. It was ludicrous because I knew if he had taken it poorly, reacted with outrageous jealousy, say, or partied irresponsibly, I would have been more than just annoyed, yet somehow, his competence made me more uncomfortable than I cared to admit. I missed him profoundly, and phone calls and text messages didn't really satisfy.

I had gotten so used to leaning on Jack over the years that now that he wasn't around, I felt strangely incomplete, like I was missing some vital organ. I felt almost like a junkie whose connections have dried up, my need just growing to ever-increasing levels of discomfort. Jack was more than just my husband and my friend; he was also my counselor, shaman, and my favorite fix. Without him, I felt unsteady, unmoored, like the world could shift at any given moment. I longed to return to him, and my resentment at my present circumstances grew as time wore on.

Mama began isolating herself in her room so as to avoid having to spend any time with Ida. After the first few chaotic days, she began to tire of the endless strife and chose to avoid Ida altogether. Soon, she only left the room to use the bathroom. She wouldn't even emerge for meals. She would just wait patiently in her easy chair, watching trash TV, and eventually someone would bring her some food, usually me. I started to wonder if she wouldn't just starve to death in that room if her meals stopped being brought to her and she were forced to leave her self-imposed exile.

I figured that Mama's isolation was better than the bickering. Normally, I'd say the opposite, that secluding yourself away from the world is a surefire way to drive yourself mad, but I don't think that applies to the already batty. It certainly was a superior mode of living from my perspective. Anything was better than having to mediate daily ceasefires to end the hostilities.

By the end of the second week, my frustration was coming mainly from a new source: Jolene. As time went on, she became more and more absent, leaving the bulk of Mama's oversight to me. Every day, there was a new catastrophe, a new unavoidable, unforeseen development that cropped up and kept Jolene from carrying her share of the weight. One of her grandbabies would come down with a fever, or one of her kids would need a babysitter at the last minute. She actually went as far as purposely flattening her tire by running over some nails, just so she could procrastinate on the side of the road while she waited for a tow truck. This team effort wasn't doing anything to make it easier on me because my team was mostly AWOL.

At first, I took it in stride, bottling up all the snark that was the byproduct of my unspoken grievances. I ignored the inconsistencies in Jolene's alibis and pretended I didn't notice how her pupils were almost nonexistent or how she kept nodding out in the middle of the day. I gathered up all the slack and just kept my nose to the grindstone. I spent most mornings on my phone, doing my best to manage my business from afar. Luckily, McCurdy's grill was a well-oiled machine and mostly ran itself. There was one minor hiccup when a waitress quit suddenly, but Kelly was able to replace her relatively quickly, and no real harm was done. The rest of my day was spent waiting on Mama, practicing her words, scheduling and attending her therapy sessions, driving her to the doctors. I got the distinct feeling that Mama was taking advantage, that she was capable of more than she let on. I started to suspect that she enjoyed being pampered and wasn't averse to fudging her symptoms to facilitate such treatment. It would have been amusing if it weren't so damned infuriating.

I continued to muddle through, though the chip on my shoulder was growing steadily by the hour. I felt trapped by my own desire to be decent. Mama needed help, and Jolene wasn't willing or able (I'm not sure which) to provide what was necessary. I knew that Jolene's main problems were chemical, that it was her addictions that made her so useless as a caregiver. I'd heard all my life how it was the disease, that the addict couldn't help themselves, how I should take pity instead of showing scorn, but that idea always rang hollow to me. Generally speaking, I'm uncomfortable with the idea that people aren't responsible for their own actions. I'm not disputing the fact that some chemicals can cause physical dependency. I just hate putting junkies in the same category as childhood leukemia patients. While both are tragic, the junkie played an outsized role in his own fate, where the cancer kid just lost life's lottery. I just can't put the two on the same moral footing. Call me an asshole. Nobody is ever forced to start fucking around with opiates, underage hookers from Mexico notwithstanding. Even those poor souls who get hooked after some kind of injury have a choice. I've had teeth pulled and been given Percocet, but I managed to control myself. If I can, anyone can, if they only try.

I probably sound like a hypocrite, what with my love for cannabis in my husband's affinity for alcohol. All I can say in my defense is that those drugs simply aren't the same as narcotics. In theory, I suppose they all should be treated the same, but theory rarely holds up to the scrutiny of reality. The reality is opiates aren't just any drug. I've never really believed in the soul, but if I did, I would say opiates are the quickest, surest route to losing whatever you have that qualifies as one. I'm pretty laid-back, I don't care much what other people do, but opiates are the goddamned devil in chemical form.

Everything came to a head in the middle of the third week. I was thoroughly disgusted with the whole situation by then. I was one irritation away from washing my hands of the whole mess. Jolene was useless, Ida was purposely obstructionist, and Mama was Mama, stubborn and irrational. The cherry on top of this shit sundae was my longing for Jack. I felt the need for him in my bones. These texts and phone calls were no longer enough. I needed to experience him with all my senses, not just my hearing. My initial embarrassment at my borderline codependency was forgotten, along with my pride.

In an effort to truly set my affairs in order in preparation for my return to Boston, I decided to visit Elton in prison. I had no plans of returning to Florida any time soon, and I wanted no stone left unturned. I didn't want there to be any loose ends. I'd come to make peace with the past, and I meant to do it. When we were kids, I always looked up to Elton, thought he was the coolest guy on the planet. His juvenile delinquency didn't make me wary of him, quite the opposite. He was like a real-life supervillain living across the hall from me, and for a time, I nearly worshipped him. He would steal things for me all the time, for the thrill of the hunt and the thrill of making me happy. I cried for a week the first time the police took him away to juvie.

I set it up with Jolene to have her babysit Mama. I didn't want to leave her alone that long, and Jolene refused to set foot in the prison anyway. She still remembered Daddy and would do anything necessary to never run into him again. Luckily, his incarceration made that task rather simple. As much as she missed our brother and wanted to see him, her fear of our reviled father kept her away. She simply wouldn't risk the possibility of ever seeing Elmer Ray Shaw for even a split second in passing. I guess maybe not remembering my father is a mercy, because he can't haunt me like he does Jolene.

"It will be fine, quit worrying," Jolene called to me from the porch as I pulled away in her car.

"Fat chance," I muttered under my breath in reply. I smiled at her as I drove past the porch and headed out to the main road. I paused at the stop sign for longer than strictly necessary as I fought an internal battle. Something, call it intuition, call it my guardian angel, didn't want me to leave Mama with Jolene, not that day, anyways. Somehow, I just knew catastrophe was hiding just out of sight, waiting to pounce the second I turned my back. I knew I was being silly. There was no rational reason to think that Mama wouldn't be just fine where she was for two measly hours while I visited Elton. I pushed the feelings of impending doom down deep into my psyche and entered traffic, bound for my reunion with my favorite brother.

The drive to the prison was short and uneventful. The prison itself sat on the outskirts of town, a bustling little city in its own right, surrounded by razor wire. The low, squat building seemed to suck all the positivity out of the surrounding atmosphere. The sun shone less brightly there, somehow, as if it couldn't stand to witness what went on went there. I could feel the weight of the air seemingly grow, the prison's malevolence thickening its substance in some occult manner. I wondered if J. K. Rowling had been here and used the place as inspiration for Azkaban. I decided probably not; the wizards' prison at least had a less punishing climate.

I parked my car as close to the entrance as I could; I wanted to be able to make a quick getaway if necessary. I wasn't sure what would necessitate such extreme measures, but I wanted to be prepared for any eventuality. I was about to willingly walk into a building that housed the worst specimens humanity had to offer. This was the home of killers and rapists, thieves, and molesters. This was the home of my father.

I walked inside and was corralled into a reception area, where I was asked to show identification, had my purse searched, and was brusquely told to have a seat while I waited. The guards looked bored and nervous, all at the same time. Their expressions did little to make me feel better about my surroundings. Their faces told me that danger was omnipresent here; it was baked into the very concrete the place was constructed of. I sat down in one of the hard plastic chairs and waited uncomfortably for my name to be called. As I waited, I looked around at my surroundings. The walls were painted a putrescent institutional green, and said paint was peeling profusely. I wondered if the paint was lead-based, if Ralph Nader's crusade to rid the world of all that is unhealthy but financially advantageous had extended its influence behind these walls, but I immediately thought better of it. The Department of Corrections probably used lead-based paint on purpose to shorten the lives of the inmates, thereby cutting costs.

The waiting room was relatively quiet that day. There were only a handful of other people there to visit their walking tragedies. One woman had a child with her, and he was sitting listlessly on her lap, a large runner of snot slowly descending from his nostril. He kept staring at me vacantly while his mom ignored him in favor of the little plastic box in her hand that told her all she needed to know about the world. I wondered how many years it would be before she was visiting the slug on her lap here as well as whoever she was visiting now. One-stop shopping. Family reunion in the rec yard.

After forever and a day had passed, someone finally called my name. I stood up abruptly, the summons startling me out of semislumber. The summoner was a large black woman, dressed in the Gestapo-like uniform that all the guards in this wonderful establishment wore. She looked thoroughly uninterested in life in general as I walked over to her. Her eyes never met mine. She simply looked through me as if I was just a shadow on the wall. She turned and produced an enormous key ring, expertly choosing the correct key instantly from the hundreds collected upon it. She unlocked the giant steel door and ushered me into a long, narrow corridor lit by flickering fluorescents that were floundering from a lack of maintenance. At the end, we turned right and went through another giant steel door into the visiting room.

There was a row of odd cubicles against the wall with windows looking into a room on the other side. Each cubicle was equipped with a telephone handset, like used to be on the payphones that have now gone extinct. The guard led me to the furthest seat from the door and indicated that I should have a seat. I complied, and she turned and walked to her post in the corner, where she preceded to continue aggressively ignoring me.

A door opened in the room on the other side of the window, and the final piece of my familial puzzle walked through it and sat down across from me, on the other side of the glass.

"Hello, Remlee," Elton said with a thin smile. I thought I had prepared myself for what I might see when I was reunited with my brother, but I hadn't. Of all of my family members that I had recently been reacquainted with, Elton had changed the most since I had last seen him, on my last birthday in Stillwater before I ran away. The lanky teenager with the mullet and wispy wannabe mustache was gone, replaced by the heavily tattooed and heavily muscled convict that sat before me. There was a vicious scar running the length of his left cheek, most likely the result of a particularly nasty dust-up with another inmate. His head was shaved to the skin, but a ZZ Top-worthy beard spilled down from his cheeks and over the front of his orange jumpsuit. I wasn't entirely sure they gave me the right criminal until he grinned, and I saw that old mischievous spark in his eye.

"Hello, Elton," I said, smiling tentatively. "How have you been?"

He cackled and spread his arms out, gesturing at our surroundings, and replied, "Why don't you take a guess?"

I laughed nervously at his quip, surreptitiously trying to gauge his level of crazy. Even though there was an inch and a half of bulletproof glass separating us, I wasn't taking any chances.

"Seriously, though," he said, his laughter petering out, "it's good to see you, sis, it really is. I'm just curious, is all. Why are you here? Why now?"

He looked at me with a smile on his lips, but the smile didn't extend to his eyes. His eyes were the eyes of a shark, unfeeling and calculating.

"It's Mama," I said solemnly. "She had a stroke. It's real bad, Elton."

"Yeah?" he replied, his granite face impassive. "And?"

"And she's all fucked up," I said, disoriented by his nonreaction.

"That sucks," he said with unconcealed disinterest. "What do you want me to do about it?"

"Nothing," I replied, my feelings beginning to feel the sting. "Maybe just, I don't know, give a fuck."

"Why? She never did," he said almost petulantly, echoing my own initial reaction, the childish tone he affected so hilariously out of line with his imposing appearance that I had to struggle to stifle a laugh.

"Look," I said, mustering all of my courage, "I'm just relaying information. What you do with it is your affair. I just thought you might like to know, that's all."

He looked at me through lizard's eyes and replied, "And you've done it. Thanks a bunch, sis. I don't know how I would have gotten through my day without that vital information."

I stood up, incensed. Obviously, I had made a mistake. The Elton I knew was gone, replaced by this inhuman doppelganger in front of me. He looked at me with surprise, and I heard him speak through the handset I was still holding by my hip.

"Chill! Geez!" he said, sounding like the protestations of a spoiled kid who regretted chasing his playmates off with his bullying. "Sit down, sit down. Don't get your panties in a wad. I got ten more minutes on this visit, might as well use them. How have you been? What you been doing?"

I sat back down slowly, giving him my patented death stare, and said, "Fine. I'll stay. But you gotta be nice to me. I'm taking enough shit right now, and I don't need yours. I wanted to see you before I went back home. Don't ruin it."

He looked at me, the slightest trace of humanity gleaming in his eye, and said, "Fair enough. I'll be 'nice.' That's just not a skill that pays off well in here, you know? I'm out of practice, you could say." He chuckled to himself, and I joined him.

We spent the rest of our allotted time giving each other the CliffsNotes versions of our respective lives. I told him about Jack and the restaurant. He told me of the dizzying highs and dreadful lows of his criminal career. I had to admit that I was impressed with the sheer scope of his illicit enterprises; the man dreamed big. The tragedy was how his talents were wasted. If he could only have pivoted that razor-sharp mind to legitimate purposes, he could have been a master of the universe, the head of some Fortune 500 company. Instead, he was raised by a series of juvenile detention centers, where keeping control took precedence over the actual reform of delinquent children. If you ever want to see the prime example of the unintended consequences of poorly thought-out public policy, look no further than the juvenile (in)justice system. People like my brother aren't born; they are made.

Too soon, the guard brusquely notified us that our time was up. We both stood, regarding each other with mingled feelings of nostalgia and sorrow.

"Hey," he said, his face brightening, "I get out in eight months, barring any unforeseen events. Maybe I come up Boston way, check it out. I hear they have a great restaurant there."

"Won't you be on parole?" I asked with a chuckle.

"I don't know if you've noticed," he said with a grin, "but I don't tend to follow the rules all that well." With that, he allowed the guard to lead him back into the tombs, laughing heartily as he went to his state of state-enforced suspended animation.

The behemoth in the guard's uniform behind me indicated that I should follow her, unless I wanted to make myself a guess for a more extended stay. I followed her back out through the claustrophobic corridors and back into the waiting room from whence I came. I signed out at the "reception desk," if that's what euphemism you'd prefer, and made haste to the parking lot. Once outside, I felt relief from a pressure I hadn't realized I'd felt until it had been released. Somehow, the combined negativity of the hundreds of miserable souls created a vortex of discord that could be keenly felt. The very air inside was poisonous, and I was grateful beyond measure to no longer be breathing it.

I drove back to Jolene's by a circuitous route. I needed a few minutes to gather myself after such an intense rendezvous. I let Jolene's Cavalier meander wherever it would. I was only there to keep it from colliding with something. My mind kept coming back to the smile that Elton flashed, that soulless, unfeeling smile meant to lull prey into a false sense of security. I felt bad for Elton, but I was glad he was locked up. Society had broken him and turned him sour, and he was mayhem walking. I felt safer knowing he was behind several feet of steel-reinforced concrete and razor wire, and I felt guilty because dangerous misanthrope or not, he was my blood.

When I turned into Jolene's trailer court, the sight that appeared before me drove all thoughts of societal decay from my train of thought. Instead of the bucolic scene of small-town tranquility I expected, I was presented with chaos. Three police cars and an ambulance were parked haphazardly in the street in front of Ida's trailer. First-responder types were milling about, and I saw Jolene, hysterical, in some kind of heated discussion with a cop. My mind immediately began calculating the odds on which nightmare scenario was the most likely to have occurred. Did Mama have another stroke? The doctor warned us that it was an inherent possibility, especially if she didn't take her medicine as prescribed. I tried to remember if I had been keeping up, but my panicked brain couldn't locate the information.

The other possibility, just as likely, was that Mama had snapped and attacked Ida. It certainly wouldn't have been out of character. Ida had been wearing dentures for twenty-five years because of Mama's fists. If Ida just said the wrong thing, or even if Mama thought she did, a violent reaction was the very likely outcome. I began to imagine the phone call with Jack where I had to ask him for bail money to spring my mother. I didn't relish the possibility that I might have to have that conversation, and I wasn't sure how I would even ask.

I pulled to a screeching halt just feet from where Jolene was having a very public nervous breakdown. I threw the transmission into park and leaped out of the car, not bothering to turn it off. I ran to Jolene, my heart and mind racing, and grabbed her just as she was about to collapse in front of the bewildered police officer. She looked at me through teary, frightened eyes and let us let out a soul-rending howl.

"It's Mama," she said, through sobs of extreme despair and terror. "She's gone."

Betty Sue

Things are getting better by the day. I'm still stuck living with that old hag Ida, but otherwise, things are on an upward swing. The invisible weight of self-hatred and depression is gone now. I feel twenty pounds lighter. When I wake up in the morning, I don't just want to go back to sleep. I actually have energy now, more than I've had in years. I'm not going to run a marathon or anything, but I don't feel exhausted from just walking to the bathroom and back anymore.

At first, Ida and I fought constantly. You wouldn't think that would be possible, what with my lack of communication skills, but we found a way. She don't want me here, and she'll be damned before she lets me be comfortable, not if she has any say. At first, I let her bait me, and I'd get pissed and start showing my ass. Joline and Remlee would have to come over and play referee a couple of times a day. Finally, I realized that letting that old floozy upset me is just giving her what she wants, so now I just ignore her. She's just a part of the furniture to me now, and I feel better ever since.

Remlee has been spending a lot of time with me ever since they let me out. Even though we can't really have an actual conversation, I'm still just content to listen to her talk. She tries to get me to practice talking, and sometimes I do, but it gets too frustrating. I struggle and struggle, but I'm still lucky if I can get two intelligible words strung together before it all falls apart, and I'm back to babbling. Remlee tries to be patient, but I can see it takes all the effort she can muster to not just give up and walk away. I wonder sometimes if maybe I'm sandbagging my own efforts, just so she will stay longer. I know her life is up in Boston, but I'm just so happy to be around her that I don't want her to go. I'm not purposely trying to stay broken, but I'd be lying if I said I was in a hurry to recover too much. I may have lost most of my independence, but I got my daughter back, and I'm thinking that's a pretty decent trade.

I'm really starting to worry about Jolene, though. She thinks I don't know, but she's all strung out on them pills. She thinks she can hide it from me, like I didn't push her out of my womb, like I don't know every little thought she has, even before she has it. I can see how skinny she is. I can see her nodding out in the chair across from me during the middle of the day. She ain't got no job. Her kids are all grown, what other reason than drugs does she have for being so tired? I don't know who she thinks she's fooling. I ain't saying I'm no angel. I done my share of partying, but whatever it is that Jolene is doing right now don't look like no party to me. It looks miserable, like a waking death. I worry so much about her, but I don't know how to help her. Even if I could talk, she won't listen.

That boyfriend of hers ain't no help. He's over here, holding onto his mommy's fucking apron strings way more than he is at his own place. Jolene's probably lonely, that's all. Okay, maybe not ***ALL****, but a good bit of the problem. I see that man child and his mama every night, sitting together watching TV, and I wonder why he isn't at his own home with his woman who he is supposed to love. What kind of man wants to spend all of his free time with his momma instead of a beautiful young woman? Norman fucking Bates, that's who.*

I hold them kids of hers partially responsible, too, but only a little. They ran her ragged, walked all over her. She couldn't never hold on to a man, so none of her young'uns really have a daddy. She was on her own with all of them. Ain't a one of those deadbeats who knocked her up ever stuck around to help clean up the mess they made together; they just left her to her own devices. By the time her youngest, Gavin, came along, she had pretty much given up trying to civilize her brood. As long as they didn't starve, she was satisfied. That was about all she could offer. Life had just beat her ass too many times.

She don't come around that much, truth be told. Remlee's always making excuses for her, but I know she's avoiding me. I can't really blame her. I'm sure I ain't much fun to be around. She ain't got time for me now, and seeing how I wasn't the best mother to her, I shouldn't be surprised. I had good intentions, but intentions don't cook dinner and help with homework. I tried my best, and it wasn't enough. I don't exactly blame myself anymore, but I get why Jolene does. She's not wrong, from her perspective. All she knows is that I failed her. The why don't really matter. Maybe it should, but I can't tell her how to feel.

I'm really just happy to be here. Heaven, or whatever that place was, was wonderful, but I ain't ready for that. The whole time I was there, something was pulling me back here. I still ain't sure what it is that makes me want to be here. There just seems to be something I'm supposed to do, but what that something is ain't exactly clear. It's just nagging at the edges of my thoughts that I can't quite make out. The demand is hidden from me somehow. I don't know what it looks like. I can only barely sense its presence. It's a good feeling, actually, like the anticipation of some favorite holiday. I know that once I do whatever is being asked (demanded) of me, things will improve. It's like going to the dentist, I know that there will be some momentary discomfort, but once that is passed, a much more pleasant future lies in store. I just don't know what that will look like, but I no longer fear the future.

Remley's gone today, out visiting Elton. It does my heart good to know that she's reconnecting with her kin. Her being gone without no contact all those years was just plumb wrong, but I forgive her. I forgive everybody lately. All that hate, all those years, only hurt me. None of that negative energy did a damn thing to hurt the people I wanted it to. It only destroyed me, and it took my kids down the same awful path to varying degrees. If I want to be forgiven, I have to forgive. It only makes sense. I can't expect to receive what I refuse to offer. The past is over anyway. Holding grudges is just a waste of time, and I've done wasted enough. I can sit in this misery stew and let myself rot, or I can get up and get on.

It's in the spirit that I march into the living room, the territory of my sworn foe, Ida Greene. She seems like a wonderful candidate to test my theory on. I've hated that bitch with an unholy passion for as long as I can remember. Even before I caught her suck-starting my husband's engine, we were never friends. I don't even really remember why or where all the enmity started, we've always just been arch enemies. I figure if I can forgive her, bury the hatchet without burying any actual hatchets, so to speak, I can forgive anyone, even myself.

I walk through the doorway from the hall with what I hope is a warm, inviting smile on my face. I can't be sure if it is because my face has been fucked up ever since the stroke. It don't do what I tell it to anymore, not exactly. I start to open my mouth to say something, anything to break our mutually agreed upon silence, and I see her face up close as I approach her. Her eyes are bugged out, full of panic, and her face is nearly purple.

"Help!" she croaks. "My chest… Call the ambulance… I think… I'm having a heart attack!"

She clutches her chest and moans some more, but I can't make out what she is saying. Pain has taken her away from the human language.

"Jumon! Kepee in tipoh!" I shout. What do I do?

I try to decide on a course of action, but I don't know what to do. I could call 911, but I can't talk to them to tell them what the problem is. I look at Ida in desperation, but she can't help. She's on the floor now, having toppled out of her chair, and she's crawling slowly toward the phone. I rush over and hand it to her, and for a second, Ida smiles at me weakly. She starts to press some buttons. Her eyes screw up furiously under her sweaty brow, all of her attention on the phone in her hand. I stand beside her, dumbfounded, and watch. She manages to push two numbers before her eyes roll up into the back of her head, and she drops her head to the floor. The rest of her body follows suit, and I scream as she goes stock still.

I run to the door, desperate to find some kind of help. I fling it open and step out of the trailer and onto the street outside. I look around to gather my bearings and horrified when I realize I don't recognize a thing. I have absolutely no idea where I am. All the trailers look the same. Which one is Jolene's? I've been to it dozens of times over the past five years, ever since she's been with Gary. There ain't no reason why I can't find it now, it should be right here, but it don't look right. I thought her trailer was blue, but this one is yellow. I knock on the door anyway, hoping whoever answers can call the ambulance, Jolene or some other neighbor. I don't care.

No one answers, though, so I try the next house. And the next. After the fifth trailer, I give up. Nobody is home today, it seems. I need to find help, but there don't seem to be no help around here to find.

I wander out to the main road, looking for any human at all, anyone I can flag down. I wave wildly at the few cars that pass, but they ignore me and continue past, leaving me more and more frantic as the minutes pass. I can't let Ida die, not now, not before I can tell her I've forgiven her.

The further I wander, the more confused I become. I realize I don't recognize anything. I don't know where I am at all. I turn around and head in the direction I came from, but nothing looks familiar that way either. I may have just passed that gas station, but it looks like every gas station, and I can't remember anymore. Now, not only do I have to help find help for Ida, but I have to figure out where I am. I decide to try the gas station. At least there are people there.

I walk inside and go up to the counter. The clerk is some bored stoner, and he looks blearily at me as I smack the bell in front of him.

"Yu yu… Oh Lord…simblah gins… No… Oh Lord," I sputter.

"Huh?" he says slowly, his eyes as red as the stupid vest he is wearing. "Can I help you?"

"Caw… Caw… Blamps… Caw blamps," I say, hoping he's not too high to understand that I'm begging him to call an ambulance.

"I don't know what you're saying, lady," he drawls, his sense of alarm not reaching the appropriate level.

I reach across the counter and grab him by the lapels of his stupid fucking red vest and pull his face close to mine. His eyes grow too the size of pumpkins as he realizes for the first time since I wandered in that there's something wrong, that attention must be paid to the here and now.

"CAW BLAMPS!" I roar into his stupefied face, and it seems that the fire has finally been lit under his ass. Unfortunately for me, it isn't the fire I'm looking for.

"Listen, lady," he says, suddenly alert and indignant, "you're gonna have to settle down. Let go of my shirt, okay? What's your deal, anyways?"

I growl unintelligibly in frustrated reply. I don't know how to convey the message I need to convey, and even if I had an idea, this cannabis added addled moron in front of me ain't likely to get it. There's not much going on behind his bloodshot eyes on his best days, I bet, and he smells like he just walked out of a Black Sabbath concert.

"Look, if you're not gonna buy something," he says, nodding toward the door. I pick up the first thing I can put my hands on, which happens to be a BIC lighter, and chuck it at his dumb face. He howls in protest, clutching at his nose and almost crying. Pussy.

"Yu yu fackin zolo," I spit at him, and I all but run back out into the street.

"Calling the cops," I hear him call after me, and I hope he does. The cops ain't the ambulance, but it's a step in the right direction. I know he won't, though. He won't want the law poking around, smelling the smells I smelt. Not over some crazy old lady who didn't hurt nothing but maybe his pride.

I wander off, frantic and discombobulated. I don't know what to do, I'm out of ideas. I walk for blocks and blocks, looking for anything familiar at all. The concern I feel for Ida's safety is starting to fade as my concern for my own well-being starts to grow. The longer I walk, the more scared I get. I keep expecting to turn a corner and see something familiar, a landmark, a business, anything at all that seems like I remember it, but that recognition never comes. I grew up here in Stillwater, spent damn near my entire life here, but I don't recognize this place. I would swear in a court of law on a whole stack of bibles that I ain't never been here before. This could be Indiana, Illinois, or fucking Idaho, for all I know.

Eventually, I come to a park. I don't recognize it either, but I'm tired now, and I need to sit down for a minute. I find a bench and try to make myself comfortable. My mind races as I try to consider my predicament. I'm hopelessly lost, and Ida is lying on her floor somewhere, possibly dying. The world begins to spin around me, making me dizzy. I lie down on the bench to fight off the vertigo, and I close my eyes. The spinning stops, my mind stops, everything stops. I let go, exhausted beyond measure, unable to go any further. The void opens, and I allow it to consume me once more and turn the problems of the world into my own sweet oblivion. Today has just been a little too much. I need a break. Just…a…little…break…

Remlee

"What do you mean 'gone'?" I asked Jolene as my blood froze in my veins.

Jolene was on her knees in front of Ida's trailer, looking up at me through bleary eyes, red and puffy with tears. Two cops were talking to her as I approached, and they looked almost as bewildered as I felt. Jolene's voice cracked as she explained the chaos that surrounded us.

"She's gone," she said through sobs. "Like, missing. Not here."

"Not dead 'gone,' though, right?" I asked, my worst fear not yet ruled out.

"Well, I don't think so," Jolene replied. "She's missing. No one can find her."

"What did Ida say?" I asked.

"That's the other thing," she answered, hysteria threatening to take control. "They think she had a heart attack. That's why the ambulance is here. The medics are inside right now, working on her."

"Oh shit!" I said, stunned. "What happened?"

"That's what we're trying to figure out," she said witheringly.

The police walked away, apparently satisfied that Jolene had provided as much information as she was able to. They began to herd the small crowd that had gathered away from the ambulance, and I pulled Jolene to the side as the EMTs wheeled Ida out on a gurney. She was pale and waxy-looking, and I couldn't even tell if she was breathing. There was an oxygen mask over her face, and I shuddered at the unbidden image of Mama's face on her body that flashed through my mind.

"Jesus Christ!" I yelled at Jolene, my fury at the situation directed with laser precision squarely between her eyes. "I leave for three and a half hours and look what happens! Where the fuck were you, Jolene?"

"I was next door, at home," she replied, a glint of fear in her eyes.

"Fucking nodded out, I presume," I said with as much contempt as I could muster.

"Fuck you," she said in a whisper, her eyes glued to a spot about six inches from my foot.

"Fuck me? Oh, no, sis, fuck you," I said through clenched teeth, my voice low and dangerous. "You're such a fucking junkie that I can't leave our basically immobile mother alone with you for the afternoon without you misplacing her."

"In my defense," Jolene began with an awkward laugh, "our assessment of her mobility seems to be faulty."

I opened my mouth to say something hurtful and counterproductive, but the words died in my mouth, killed by gigantic belly laughs that erupted out of nowhere. Jolene looked at me warily for a few seconds, then tentatively joined in. Before long, we were both on the ground, arms around each other as we simultaneously laughed our asses off and cried her eyes out. I noticed one of the cops noticed us and rolled his eyes, but I ignored his scorn. I had bigger problems than the fact that I was just another Tucker/Shaw notch in his professional belt, another anecdote to laugh about at the precinct softball games this season.

"Look, you walk down toward Cypress, and I'll drive toward her old trailer. Maybe she'll go there. It's in the trailer court out past the old Army base, right?" I asked, refreshing my memory.

"Yeah," she said and immediately walked off in the direction I had indicated.

"Call me if you find her," I called after her as I reclaimed my seat in the Cavalier, the seat cushion still warm from the last time I had occupied it. I revved the engine, threw it into gear, and peeled out, spraying gravel all over the assembled cars, trailers, and people. I turned right at the exit to the park without even stopping to look, cutting off a harried soccer mom in her Caravan in the process. I sped off in search of Mama, ignoring surprisingly filthy tirade issuing from the incredibly loud mouth of the aggrieved driver behind me.

I didn't have any idea how long Mama had been loose, so I had no idea how to estimate search parameters. I began a slow zig-zag across town, my eyes constantly searching for any sign of my errant parent. I imagine I must have presented quite a shady sight, a harried, wild-eyed woman lurking along the street, appraising every pedestrian with a queer intensity. I became more and more frantic the longer I fruitlessly searched. By the time I reached the playground by our old apartment across from the ice plant, I was nearly beside myself with dread.

I knew I couldn't really blame Jolene. Jolene had problems with life. She wasn't very good at it. I should have never expected that she could manage our mother's life, even for just a couple of hours, not when it was a daily struggle for her just to manage her own. The plain fact was that Jolene was an addict. How she got the addiction could be debated upon, but the addiction wasn't an opinion. It was real, and I should have recognized that. It wasn't even fair to be mad at her about it at this point; whether or not the cause of the addiction was her fault was irrelevant. She was an addict, and I should have known better.

As I came to a stop sign, I noticed what appeared to be a homeless person sleeping on one of the benches in the park. Just another throwaway person, the refuse of the disposable culture we live in. When something breaks, even just a little, we throw it away instead of fixing it. Everything is so cheap in this plastic world, even people, so instead of doing a little work, we just buy a new one. Television on the fritz? Chuck it, they sell sixty-four-inch models for two hundred bucks. Granny's brain is a little bit clunky now. Maybe it runs a little slower than it used to. Throw her in the memory hole we call a nursing home. Don't worry; the state will pick up the tab, and that will leave you with so much more time to like memes that strangers post on Facebook. Electronic friends and family are so much tidier than the flesh and blood versions. You can ignore their suffering with the click of a mouse. Somehow, digital hand jobs have displaced actual embraces, and we call it progress.

A horn erupted from behind me, interrupting my reverie. Embarrassed, I waved the offended motorist around me as I pulled slowly to the curb. I needed to collect myself for a moment. My nerves were frayed to their breaking point. I lit a cigarette and breathed its noxious fumes deeply, savoring the comforting destruction they wrought upon my poor, abused lungs. I turned the car off and got out, remembering to grab my phone on the off-chance Jolene accidentally succeeded in finding Mama. I needed to walk for a minute. The confines of the compact car I had cribbed from Jolene had me cranky and cramped. I wandered in the general direction of the lost soul on the bench, almost drawn to the person by some primal need to look despair in the face. As I approached the gently snoring form, I felt my heart began to rise when I recognized the yellow tracksuit it wore. There, sleeping like Goldilocks in Baby Bear's bed, lie my mother, safe and sound.

"Oh my God!" I shouted once I regained my breath, and I rushed to her side. I shook her gently and called her name, and presently, she came around.

"Wha… Yu yu… Rembly?" she asked, looking small and scared.

"Yes, Mama, it's me," I said soothingly, gathering her into my arms like a terrified toddler. "It's okay, everything is okay now. I got you, you're safe."

"Yu yu…art akk… Yu… Art akk," she said, her eyes filled with concern.

"It's okay," I repeated, unaware of the message she was trying to impart.

"Art akk… Art akk!" she shouted, near hysterical. Whatever it was that she was upset about, my generic reassurances weren't placating her. She grew even more agitated, standing up and hopping up and down while clutching her breasts and shrieking her wordless pleas into my perplexed face. Nothing I said would calm her, whatever it was that she needed me to know wasn't getting across the communication barrier, and she erupted into tears of frustration.

"Come with me, Mama," I said, gently taking her hand. "Let's go home and get a nice bath. That will make you feel better."

After a few more minutes of the most inexpert game of charades ever played, she gave up and meekly followed me to the car. She seemed to have accepted the fact that whatever signal she was sending out wasn't being picked up, and she silently shuffled along beside me, docile as a lamb. I let her into the car and buckled her in with her looking through me at some vision only she could see. I got in the driver seat and started the car, dialing Jolene's cell simultaneously.

She answered on the second ring, breathlessly asking, "Did you find her?"

"Yes," I replied, and my eardrums exploded from the sudden eruption of squealing that issued from the earpiece as Jolene hooted in relief in triumph.

"Where was she?" Jolene asked when her celebrations died down.

"Asleep on a park bench in the playground by our old apartment," I said. "We'll be back in five minutes or so."

I hung up before she could say anything else and pulled away from the curb and headed back to the Jolene/Ida trailer complex. Mama just stared out of the window the whole time, seemingly fascinated by the scenery, like she hadn't seen that Taco Bell, or any Taco Bell, for that matter, a million times previously. I realized that she truly was lost. She really had no idea where she was. She was seeing Stillwater for the first time again, even though she had lived her entire life here. Her face had a bemused expression on it, like she didn't know what she was looking at but found it mildly pleasing, nonetheless.

I spent the drive trying to calm down. While I ultimately didn't blame Jolene for the day's little trip into the land of desperation, I was still irked at her. I just couldn't completely absolve her of any responsibility, addiction or no. There were steps that would need to be taken, and I needed a clear head to determine what those steps were and how to best accomplish them. I wouldn't have that if my mind was focused on my personal favorite of the seven deadly sins: wrath. My desire to punish would outweigh my desire to effectively manage this situation if I gave into the raging voice I heard urging me to war. I had to leave my emotions out of it and just do what needed doing. I could feel all I wanted to after the bomb was defused.

When we pulled to a stop in front of Jolene's trailer, she was sitting on the steps, head hanging down, a cigarette in one hand, half-empty bottle of Bud Light in the other. She was swaying a little, like a breeze that only affected her was blowing in random gusts. Her skin was milky pale, and as she looked up at us, I saw that the pupils in her green eyes were all but gone. She scratched herself indolently about the forearms, hardly aware of what her arms were doing without her direct input.

"I'm so sorry," she slurred, but she managed to gain her feet and shuffle over to us. She grabbed the both of us in a fierce hug, and I could feel her sinewy muscles shaking as she held us as close as she was able.

"It doesn't matter now," I said, dismissing her contrition. "Let's just get Mama inside and settled for the night. I'm pretty sure it's been rough for her too."

Jolene nodded in silent agreement and helped me lead our semi-addled mother to her room. Once inside, Mama collapsed onto the bed, and turning her back to us as she pulled the blanket over herself, she promptly fell asleep.

Jolene and I walked out into the living room and sat down on opposing sides of the room. I stared intently at her, daring her to try to justify herself. I was curious what tack she would take; her pretzel logic was often unintentionally hilarious in its sheer boneheadedness. Finally, she spoke, and what she said knocked all the arrogant self-righteousness right out of my head.

"I can't do this," she said quietly, her face roiling from the internal war being waged behind her eyes. "I thought I could, but I can't. I'm a hot fucking mess. I know I am. It's obvious to anyone with eyes. I lost my mama today because I nodded out, got too fucking high to maintain my responsibilities. And as soon as I knew you had saved the day, I ran home to fix again. I couldn't even wait until you got Mama home, and I saw with my own eyes that my fucking negligence didn't end up killing her. I couldn't face you, not without help. So here I sit, high as hell. I ain't no good for nothing, Remlee. I can't take care of her."

"I know," I simply replied. There was no need for me to say anything else. We both knew the truth of our situation. I was effectively on my own with Mama. Jolene would only be able to provide token support at best.

"I'm—" she started to say.

"Sorry," I finished for her. "I know. You keep saying that."

With that, I stood up and walked out of the trailer into the darkening evening. Jolene stayed where she was, prudently providing me with the proper space to put together the particulars of what I was preparing to do. I knew what was required of me now. I just had to do what needed to be done. I had to call the person who had been my lifeline for years and ask him to once again sacrifice for the benefit of someone, who by all accounts he had received, deserved it not. I felt bad for the gigantic favor I was about to ask of my spouse, but I could see no other viable options. I was going to have to ask Jack to move Mama to Boston with us.

I wandered through the trailer park aimlessly for a while, working myself up for the conversation I was so dreading. I wasn't at all worried that he'd say no, quite the opposite. My generous husband would agree almost at once, and I'd forever feel in his debt. There was no comparable scenario I could think of that I could do to reciprocate the support Jack always gave immediately to me upon demand, with no thought of reward. It would always be my side of the family that would need help getting along this world. The Shephards could provide themselves with whatever they could possibly ever need. Our marriage seemed lopsided. I had so much more to gain from our union. I resented that imbalance and Jack by implication. I held him responsible for the unforgivable crime of access to resources and a willingness to part with them selflessly for the benefit of people he cared about. He was just too damned good sometimes, and I silently thanked Dionysus for the gift of alcohol, as Jack weakness for it was the only thing keeping him from sainthood, and therefore, his association with the likes of me and my kin could somehow be accounted for, if only a little bit.

Finally, after half a pack of cigarettes and two joints, I had mustered up enough courage to call and make my desperate request. My fingers shook visibly as I pushed the numbers, and I fought hard to suppress the urge to void the entire contents of my stomach all over the sidewalk in front of me. He answered on the third ring, his melodious voice honey to my ear.

"Hey, babe, I was just going to call you," he said.

I immediately launched in my narrative, detailing the day's events. I started by explaining my growing disillusionment with Jolene, describing her gradual but total abdication of responsibility concerning Mama. I tried to remain calm and distant as I relayed the facts, but before I said more than six sentences, all pretense at cold objectivity melted under the sudden downpour of frustrated tears that fell from my overwhelmed eyes. I finished my tale of woe through choking sobs and fell silent as I waited for a response.

"Jesus," he breathed, clearly unprepared for the torrent of tribulation I had just poured into his unsuspecting ears. "So what do you want to do?"

"Well," I began, taking a deep breath, but he continued on, taking my words away before I could say them.

"I mean, should I clear out the spare bedroom or the attic above the garage?" he asked, and I exhaled the breath wordlessly, stunned by the implication in his question.

"I love you so much," I said, my voice cracking as I sobbed once again.

"I know," he replied smugly.

"Are you sure this is what you want?" I asked, ignoring the time-honored advice to not look gift horses in the mouth.

"Of course, I don't ***want*** this," he said, laughing. "I just don't see how I have much of a choice—"

"Of course, you do!" I interjected.

"Not really," he replied, his tone suddenly uncharacteristically serious. "I want you back. You won't leave your mom alone unattended. It seems I really only have two choices: move us to Florida or move your ma to Boston. I just did the math. Our whole life, my job, your business, our friends, everything is here. What's holding your ma there? A job she can't work anymore? Family who don't care about her? Nothing, that's what. I know you, Remlee. You're stubborn as a mule and as loyal as a golden retriever. I know you ain't gonna abandon your ma to her fate, no matter how much she may deserve it. So it's either restart everything down there or just modify what we already have going here. You know how lazy I am. It's just easier this way."

"It won't be easy," I warned. While I was relieved that Jack was fine with the plan, I was still uneasy. It was easy enough to be okay with the idea when it was still abstract. Would he still be so magnanimous a few months down the line when the novelty is worn off and the banal routine sets in? I wondered.

"I know," he said, trying to reassure me. "It's gonna fucking suck giant, hairy mastodon balls. But you're my wife. Your problems are my problems."

"I'm not sure she'll be too keen on the idea either," I said after a moment's reflection. "She's never really lived anywhere else, except the back of a semi from time to time, when she'd run off for a week or two with some trucker that she picked up at the Flying J. She might try to fight us."

"Let her," Jack said, and I could hear the grin in his voice. "I can take her. She's just a feeble old lady."

"It's that kind of thinking that's led to dozens of black eyes and missing teeth for arrogant men who tried to make Mama do something she doesn't want to do. Just saying," I said, only slightly joking.

"I can be pretty persuasive, you know," he said impishly.

"You're gonna have to be," I said.

"What she gonna do, call the cops and tell them we kidnapped here? Not likely. She can't even dial the number. That's what led to all this mess today. Trust me, she'll come."

"You're probably right," I said. "I'll just make it out like it's going to be a big adventure for the two of us."

"Won't it be?" he asked.

He had a point.

Betty Sue

Apparently, I'm moving. The morning after the hullabaloo with Ida, Remlee, and Jolene informed me of this. They didn't ask me; they told me. Jolene seemed uncomfortable with the idea, but she didn't say nothing. She just went along with Remlee. So tomorrow morning, I'm climbing in this basically empty U-Haul with Remlee and leaving everything in everyone I've ever known behind. When this trip is over, I'll be damn near two thousand miles away in some big nasty Northern city. Daddy's probably rolling over in his grave knowing his daughter is not only gonna be a Yankee, but a big-city Yankee to boot. I'd be lying if I said I wasn't scared, at least a little bit.

I'd also be lying if I said I wasn't a little bit excited. This is the first new thing to happen in my life in years, other than this godforsaken stroke, that is. I ain't never been that far north before. I thought, at my age, that my days of adventure were long behind me, but I guess I was wrong. Funny how life catches you off guard all the time. If you'd told me six months ago that I'd be moving in with Remlee in Boston, I would have laughed in your face. I never thought I'd even see her again, much less live with her, yet here I am. I guess Yogi Berra was right: it ain't over till it's over.

What scares me most is the city part. I don't like cities, never have. I dread anytime I have to go into Gainesville for anything. It's too hectic for me, and here I am moving to fucking Boston, of all places. Remley tells me her place ain't directly in the city. It's in one of the suburbs, someplace called Malden. Jolene showed it to me on a satellite map on her phone thingy, and I gotta say, it sure looks like a city to me. The name on the top of the street signs may be different, but it still looks like thousands of people, all stacked on top of each other, like sardines. It don't look like there's nowhere you can breathe up there. Everything is all jammed together in an ugly little knot. I feel mildly claustrophobic already, just thinking about it. I think all those people are what's going to take the most getting used to.

I will get used to it, though. I know that now. My little visit to the afterlife, or whatever that was, has left me hopeful. It's funny, really, when you think about it. I'm more confident now when I'm less capable than I have ever been since I was a toddler, then I was when I could run all aspects of my own life. I'm pretty sure that's what the eggheads call irony. I wasn't no good at school, though, so I may have that wrong.

Remlee and Jolene spent the last two days combing through my stuff at my trailer. I sat in the kitchen chain-smoking as I watched my daughters sift through my life and decide what should make the trip and what should be jettisoned. At first, I tried to help, filling a box with a few sentimental odds and ends that I didn't want to part with, but in the commotion, it somehow got tossed in one of the several trash bags that now dotted the lawn. I felt out of place in my own home, almost like a ghost. I began to imagine that this was the aftermath of my funeral, and I was just watching my offspring toss the accumulated pieces of my life into the trash as if it meant nothing. It was as though they couldn't even see me. I was just a phantom spying on my own disposal. I had to get away after a while, the impersonal way they disposed of my things, the things I worked for, however cheap and useless they may have seemed, was causing me to get too worked up.

Tonight, Jolene and Remlee are taking me to the farm for one last Tucker blowout. We may not always get along on a day-to-day basis, but I'm glad for the opportunity to say my goodbyes. Well, grunt them anyways. I've been practicing talking again, but I still ain't made much progress. It will be just good to be with them all, having a good time. It's been a while since I showed up to one of these shindigs, there will be folks there I ain't seen since they was kids. I'm looking forward to seeing Lola Mae's kids, for example. The last time I saw them, the oldest had just lost his first tooth, and the youngest wasn't even born yet. I only ever seen Daisy in pictures, and precious few of them, to boot.

I put on my nicest jeans and my prettiest blouse. I put on makeup for the first time since Sandy's funeral. I'm a new person now, and I want everyone to meet the new me looking my best. Maybe it's because I can't talk to no one anymore, but I suddenly care what I look like. I guess I need some point of pride, something that proves that this stroke ain't beat me, not totally. I'm still in here, even if I can't tell you so. I'm still a person, a whole entire person, not just a collection of body parts that sort of functions. I'm still Betty Sue Tucker Shaw. I'm bigger than this stroke. I'm bigger than life itself. I'm not broken. I look in the mirror at the final product and see a younger me smiling crookedly back. It ain't perfect, but it will do.

I'm nervous as hell on the drive out to the farm. I don't know what to expect, I don't know what's expected of me. I almost jump out of the car at a red light. I just want to go back to my room and watch TV. The only thing that keeps me in the car is the fact that I'll get lost trying to get there. There ain't no use in denying it. I'm lost all the time now. It's like the map in my head is all mixed up, and things ain't where there supposed to be. Nothing looks familiar, yet everything looks the same. I made this particular drive, from Stillwater to the farm, thousands of times in my life, but right now, I couldn't tell you the next turn to save my life. It's too late to turn back now, as the song goes, so I better just get used to the idea.

Jolene pulls the car into an overgrown driveway and sitting before me is the house. It is the first thing I recognize since this trip started, but even it looks different. It's shabbier now, just this side of rundown. Daddy would be ashamed if he saw how Clarence and Earl Three have let this place go. I feel my temper begin to pound on the bars of her cage, but I keep that door locked. What is, is. I can't do nothing about how my brothers keep the place. I should just be happy they ain't burned the place down or lost it to unpaid taxes or some such shit. That's the positive outlook here. That's what I got to focus on. I gotta find the good and forget the bad. The good is there in any situation. You just got to be clever enough to recognize it.

We all exit the hooptie and stretch ourselves out. I can't help but notice that we all reach for a cigarette at the same time. It seems just perfect that we would all be so much the same. I can see my influence on them as we all take part in our ritual. I can see it in a thousand little ways, not just the obvious ones. It's the way they both hold their cigarettes like me, in their left hands, not their right. It's the way they both twist their hair around their fingers when they're thinking, just like me. Even Remlee, with their foreign Yankee accent, still uses downhome phrases I ain't heard spoken north of Atlanta. I can see that even though I wasn't around enough. I still managed to make a giant mess. Poor things. I always figured that since I was such a lousy excuse for a person, I'd be doing them a favor by staying out of their way. Turns out that they turned out like me anyways, so I missed all that time for nothing. It's not only sad; it's fucking embarrassing. I wasted all that time to make sure they don't end up like me, yet here I stand, looking at two women who could never be staking for anything but my offspring. I feel so stupid.

I can hear all kinds of commotion coming from the barn. It's dark now, and the light from inside spills out through the cracks between the boards that make up the walls. The door swings open, revealing an incredibly drunk Earl Four, crawling on his hands and knees. He retches, vomits, and falls face-first into the muck.

"Looks like things are already in full swing," Remlee says, stepping over poor Earl as he lay moaning in a puddle of his own puke.

I follow my daughters inside, and immediately I am surrounded by family, all smiling and asking me things all at once. It's overwhelming. I can't make anything out that anyone is saying. It all just sort of melts together, making one loud question that makes no sense.

"How when car you trailer his doctor job had?" they ask.

I smile weakly and mumble my nonsense in reply. I'm not even trying to actually say anything. I didn't understand the question. I'm just replying to be polite. I know nobody expects me to be able to actually communicate, so it's really easy to get away with my ruse.

I make my way to a picnic table set up in the corner and try to fade into the background, like them lizards they have at the zoo in Gainesville. After a while, the novelty of me wears off, and I'm more or less left alone as everyone works hard at making all the alcohol in North Central Florida disappear. Loud music plays, and the younger ones dance the night away. I don't much care for most of the newer music they play, but my toes get to tapping when I hear our local boy, Tom Petty, singing about his American girl. I always used to dream that he was singing about me. Before I realize it, my feet get happy, and I'm out in the middle of the floor, dancing my heart out. Everybody is pointing and laughing, but I don't care, because I'm laughing too. It feels so good to let go and let loose. I'm lost in the driving rhythm and the glorious melody caught up in the intoxication of the dancing youth I'm surrounded by. All the rivalries and petty feuds of the past melt away, made in insignificant by the truth of rock 'n' roll in sacrament with the celebration of kin. This is what matters, family laughing and playing together, enjoying each other in the world we share.

The song ends, replaced by some modern trash that leaves me uninspired at best. That's fine. All that dancing wore me out. I must really be out of shape, geez! I sit back down and wait for my heart to slow down to a more reasonable pace, and I look around at the generations of kin that are gathered. I feel sad that I'm leaving all of this. Remlee tells me I can come back someday if I get better enough, but I know that possibility is a long shot. In all likelihood, I'll never see this place again. This hurts a lot, but it also feels right. This era is over for me. I just feel it in my bones. This feeling I have right now, where everything is nice and sweet and cozy between everybody is an illusion. Tomorrow, we will all wake up and remember that so-and-so owes us money, or other so-and-so took Uncle George's gun cabinet when he died, even though he promised it to us. All the petty, backstabbing bullshit will return, and I should be glad I'll be gone to where it can't find me.

The revelry picks up in intensity as the night wears on. I start to notice people disappearing in groups of twos and threes, only to return a few minutes later, suddenly full of energy. I know what's going on. I ain't naive. Someone, or someones, has broken out the new family product, and all the real party is just starting. I look around for Remlee and am relieved when I see her relaxing peacefully in the hammock up in the hayloft. Good, at least she isn't fucking around with that poison. I done my share of partying, but I was smart enough to never fuck around with nothing you put up your nose. That shit just ain't natural. It changes people in ways alcohol and pot just don't. I can see it at work right now. The atmosphere in here has changed since somebody started in with that shit. The relaxed, peaceful vibe is gone, replaced by this weird anxious energy. I don't like this feeling, it makes me dizzy, so I quietly make my way out of the barn and the ugliness growing inside and head to the house. I'm just bone tired now, and all I want to do is sleep.

I walk into the house, and everything is how I remember it, only now it's all covered in a layer of dust. Obviously, Clarence ain't heard about cleanliness being next to godliness. There's a couple of young'uns sitting on the couch, passing a joint back and forth, but I don't know who they are or who they belong to, so I ignore them and head up the stairs, looking for a quiet place with a soft bed to collapse into. When I reached the top, my breath stops in my throat as I look at the open door of my old bedroom. Dozens of traumatic memories assault me when my eyes land on the violets in a row wallpaper that still covers the walls of the room where my innocence was stolen from me. I'm frozen in place. I can't even turn my eyes away from the repulsive little flowers. I can feel my uncle's every slimy caress, smell his acrid sweat. I relive every illicit touch all over again, feel all that fear as keenly as the first time my Uncle Leo taught me the special game I learned to dread so much. Adrenaline kicks in, and I'm able to break free of that haunted room's unholy grasp, and I rush into the next room and slam the door behind me. I lean up against it, blocking access for any monsters who might be chasing me, and begin the process of calming myself down. It takes quite a while this time.

When I feel like I'm more in control again, I pad over to the bed in the corner and flop down into it with the grace of a three-legged elephant. I realize I don't know whose room I'm in, but it is obviously lived in. I decide I'm too tired to care, and I'm not moving from this spot until morning. Anyone who has a problem with that is out of luck. I'm where I'm at for the night. I ain't moving. I suppose the owner of this bed is welcome to lay in it with me, if they're willing to share, but if they want me to move, they're gonna have to move me their own damn selves.

I feel sleep taking me, and I greet it like an old friend. I got a big day tomorrow; I need my rest. Tomorrow I start my new life.

Remlee

Getting Mama all squared away and ready to move went about as expected. It wasn't the hardest thing I'd ever done in my life, but it definitely made the top five. Everyone involved seemed to have made it their personal mission to obstruct me at every turn. If Mama wasn't throwing temper tantrums of almost comical proportions, Jolene was throwing one of her own passive-aggressive variants. I never realized how complicated a modern life is until I had to completely uproot and transplant my mother's. There are so many little details that need attending to: shutting off utilities, closing out bank accounts, returning library books (we're not philistines), rerouting the mail, and the most dreaded task of all, packing.

I rented a little U-Haul truck, the smallest available, and a tow behind dolly for her truck. I tried to get her to sell it, explaining that she had no business driving anyway, but she wouldn't budge. Jack and I only had one vehicle, so I decided having a second vehicle at our disposal would be quite advantageous. The day before we were set to leave, Jolene, Mama, and I descended upon her trailer for the last time. The plan was to pack only what was vital, chuck the rest into the dumpster, and leave the keys for her landlord. Mama wasn't a hoarder, per se, but she was definitely hoarder-adjacent. I expected her to put up a fight over the unceremonious checking out of the remnants of her life, but she surprised me by remaining mostly subdued. When all was said and done, we managed to fit her whole life into the back of that U-Haul with plenty of room to spare.

That evening, we were invited to the farm for a giant sendoff bash. Earl Four promised me that it would be the party to end all parties, and I believed him. He had gotten a mild reputation for his elaborate soirees. He was like a redneck Jay Gatsby. His voice twinkled with delight as he described the night he had planned: the drink menu, the musical entertainment, and the (illegal) fireworks display. He promised that he was sparing no expense, cutting no corners, and that we could be assured of a night we'd most certainly forget but never forget that we forgot.

I was vaguely excited to go, as was Jolene, but Mama took some convincing. I wasn't able to discern what her exact objection was, but I assumed that it had something to do with some petty feud or another. That had been her excuse for her avoiding her family in the past. It only made sense that she would carry those grudges with her. I tried to lecture her about water under bridges, and she grew agitated.

"No!" she said vehemently, wagging her finger at me. "Not yu… No… Barst…"

"That's all in the past," I said, still not recognizing what she was trying to get across to me.

"No! Not pass… Barst me…" she said, reporting at her lips as she spoke.

"Are you saying you're embarrassed?" Jolene asked, her voice softening as a look of dawning realization washed over her face.

Mama nodded furiously, tears welling up in her clear blue eyes. I immediately felt like a dunce. Of course, it would be embarrassing, losing the ability to communicate like that. It's the ultimate loss of sovereignty, the lack of ability to make one's feelings and needs known. All other freedoms that we associate with adulthood hinge on the ability to be able to exchange information with other people. Without that ability, one is dependent on others in the most profound of ways.

"Oh God, Mama," I breathed and gathered her into a hug. She cried a little into my chest before letting go and smiling at me expectantly.

"Yu yu yu… Dress?" she asked coyly, pointing at the shabby tracksuit she was wearing.

"I got you, Mama," Jolene said with a grin and whisked her away to play living Barbie doll.

Watching Mama get herself together gave me some hope for her prognosis. It was good to see her trying again. The Mama I remembered before the stroke wasn't necessarily what you'd call a classic beauty, her features too blunt, her frame too solid for that. She had a different sort of attractiveness, a rough handsomeness combined with a palpable energy that somehow elevated her beyond the sum of her parts. Any generic description would mention her thick blond hair, fair complexion, and fit form. It's the intangible that is so hard to describe. Life burned brighter in her, somehow, transforming what were rather generic characteristics into something remarkable, unforgettable. That light was gone for a while, hidden away by the ravages caused by a blood clot no bigger than a sesame seed. Whatever those barriers were constructed of, I delighted in watching them stripped away as that fire began to consume them. My mother was the phoenix rising in flames out of the ashes of ruin.

When she was done, a chill ran down my spine as I looked at the final product. Standing before me was the woman I remembered, not the pathetic wraith I met in the hospital. She was standing tall and confident, twenty years of age miraculously melted away. She practically glowed as she beamed at me, and I felt myself grinning goofily back. This was the happiest I had seen her since I had been back, maybe even ever. I quickly rummaged through the old memory files, searching for any other joyful moments, and came up blank. I hoped we could maintain that emotional high for the duration of the evening. My biggest fear was that some form of familial chaos would break out at the party that evening, causing turmoil and making our departure in the morning all the more difficult. As long as Mama was happy, she was compliant, and I needed all the compliance she could offer.

Mama was cagey on the ride out to the farm. Her head was on a swivel, looking here, there, and everywhere. At one point, I was certain she was going to leap out of the car and make a break for it. I got myself ready to pounce on her if she tried, but she seemed to think better of it and remained where she was. I could tell she was completely lost, and my heart went out to her. I couldn't imagine what it must be like, feeling lost in the only town you've ever lived in. She must have felt like the ultimate refugee, cut off from all humanity in such a basic way.

When we pulled into the driveway at the farm, I saw the first flickerings of recognition in her eyes. We all got out and lit cigarettes, and I watched her look around, remembering. I could tell she wasn't really with us. She was scattered throughout time, reliving the small moments that were awakened by seeing the stage upon which they had been played out. She had a bemused smile on her face, like she was eminently pleased with herself, and I felt myself relax a little. Whatever reservations Mama had on the way over were gone, and I was confident that she would behave.

We entered the barn where the festivities were centralized, careful not to step on a hopelessly hammered Earl Four. We were almost immediately mobbed by well-wishing family members. For a second, I understood the panic those mop-headed Brits must have felt when they stepped off the plane in 1963 to make their debut on *The Ed Sullivan Show*. Everyone was talking at once, their voices blending together into an unintelligible word soup. Mama looked dazed, like a deer in headlights, what Hazel-Rah would have called *tharn*. I worried that all the attention might freak her out, but Mama managed the quasi-paparazzi like a seasoned pro. She smiled and waved at everyone, never allowing anyone to impede her progress as she made her way to a picnic table in the back. The hangers-on gradually peeled off to join the rest of the party, their respect paid to one of the senior members of our sprawling family.

Once I was sure Mama was settled in and comfortable, I began to make my rounds. I said my farewells to the gathered masses, one small cluster of revelers at a time. I promised to keep in touch more than I had in the past, and I actually meant it. I realized how much I had missed out on over the years of separation. There was a whole life for me that I ignored out of self-imposed shame, and I understood that I had only cheated myself. Here was an entire army of people I was connected to in ways that could never be severed, and I had thought myself too good to even associate in the most superficial ways with them. I had allowed strangers to dictate my opinions about my own blood, and it made me feel microscopically small. I was determined to no longer be that person. I would be better.

At one point, Uncle Clarence pulled me aside and said, "This is a good thing you're doing, looking out for your mom like that. I know she wasn't no good as a mama, ain't no use in lying. You'd be well within your rights to let her drown in her own shit. I probably would if I was you. You ain't doing that, though, why?"

Shrugging, I looked at him in the eye and answered as truthfully as I was able, saying, "I don't really know. I guess I'm doing it for me, not her. She's the only Mama I got, and she's still here. I didn't even know I missed her until she almost fucking died, but I did all the same. She may not be able to do anything for me anymore. That's fine. I learned how to do for myself. That's not what I'm looking for. I just want… I want a mother. She don't have to do much, just be there."

Clarence looked away, seemingly studying the antics of the people dancing around the stereo. "It wasn't never personal," he said quietly.

"Huh?" I asked, puzzled by his statement.

"I mean, she loved y'all. When that baby died, she just gave up. Part of her died on that pavement right along with Jesco. She wasn't right after that. She cared about y'all. She was just hurting too much," Clarence said, almost tenderly. I looked at him in askance. This kind of sentimentality didn't jibe well with the image I had always held of my most powerful uncle.

"Did you just say something nice about your sister?" I asked, genuinely surprised at his momentary lapse into empathy.

"Don't tell anyone," he said with an impish grin.

"Far be it for me to reveal to the world that you are a human being after all," I replied, rolling my eyes.

I stayed up late into the night, enjoying the comfort of communion with my kin. I knew I would pay for it the next day, when I began the cross-country migration in the unfamiliar vehicle I had rented, but I didn't care. I wasn't likely going to see these people again anytime soon. I doubled the number of contacts on my phone, and I swear I repeated my phone number hundreds of times. I knew I probably would only actively talk to a handful of these people on a regular basis going forward, but I felt better knowing that the channels were open now, if the need or urge to communicate ever arose. I built connections that night that might help sustain me through hard times in the future, if only by providing myself with more shoulders to cry on.

I finally crawled into the house just before the sun started his daily journey across the sky. I was almost asleep as soon as my head hit the cushion on the living room couch. My dreams were hazy and unfocused, mostly just feelings and amorphous shapes lumbering around a desolate landscape. I felt like I was searching for something, something very specific, but I had forgotten what that was, only that it was lost, and it was my duty to retrieve it. I woke up a few hours later, achy and still tired, but rested enough to get on with our departure. I moseyed my way out into the kitchen in search of the first of what would likely be many cups of hot brown liquid energy. Mama and Jolene were already in there, drinking and smoking their own breakfasts. I poured myself a cup and joined them at the table, where we sat in awkward silence. Zero hour was upon us, and apparently, none of us had prepared ourselves for the coming fare-thee-wells. I could see that Jolene's eyes were red and puffy, and I suspected it was more from tears than from her apparent recent exit from dreamland. No one wanted to be the first to speak, to be the one who set everything into motion. We just sat there, basking in each other's presence, the three Shaw women, together and undefeatable.

Mama reached out, grasped our hands, and beamed, saying, "Yu yu yu… Oh Lord… Yu luv… Gambuh… No… Luv grrls."

"I love you too, Mama," I said, squeezing her hand and fighting back the tears.

"Oh, Mama!" Jolene sputtered, bursting into tears of her own. I couldn't hold out any longer, and I joined in the waterworks. Mama gathered us both into her arms, holding us close as we sobbed, out of both joy and sorrow. I was so happy that my family was healing, becoming whole again, but the sweetness was cut with the bitterness of our impending separation. My whole body was heavy with emotion, and I struggled to let go. I wanted to stay in that group embrace forever, and the future could go fuck itself. Eventually, Mama relaxed her iron grip, and I felt myself pulling away and standing up. The moment was over, and the road home was beckoning.

Jolene and I made one last leap sweep of the property, making sure all of our belongings were stowed in accounted for. I said my final farewells to the few family members who were up and about and to the property itself. I took one last look of this at the sea of cane rippling in the breeze and at the swing hanging from the old willow that I tried to use as my launching pad into the great beyond. I made a silent promise to myself that I'd see this place again, that this wouldn't be the last time I breathed this sweet air or the last time I would hear the sounds of the farm. I would return, and often. I had regained my birthright after so callously throwing it away, and I would be damned before I made that mistake again.

Once I was satisfied the mental images were burned into my mind's eye, we gathered Mama up and got into Jolene's car. As we were pulling out of the driveway, Mama suddenly jumped out of the car and ran over to the mailbox. She planted a kiss on the palm of her hand, then lovingly placed it on the mailbox in a touching kind of benediction. She stood there with her eyes closed for a few minutes, then got back into the car.

"Yu yu go now," she said, and Jolene complied, bring us to the U-Haul quickly, as the early morning traffic in rural Florida is all but non-existent.

"Be careful out there," Jolene said once we had Mama transferred to the moving truck. Her eyes were downcast at a bashful angle, and I grabbed her into a fierce hug. We cried on each other's shoulders for a long time until there were no tears left, all available moisture wrung out of us.

"You be careful right here," I whispered into her neck. "I don't think I can handle the both of you if you stroke out too."

She giggled and released me, giving me an appraising look. "I'm really proud of you, you know," she said, her eyes clear and sober. "You are the best of us. I was always pissed at you for leaving, but now I'm glad you did. The rest of us weren't able to hold you back with you living a thousand miles away."

"Don't say that," I said. "You guys never held me back—"

"Yes, we did," Jolene interrupted. "Or we would have. There's too much drama in this family. If you are too close, you can't help but get sucked in."

"Well, I'm back in the fold now, for better or for worse," I said, sighing.

"My condolences," Jolene replied with a snort.

Jolene went over to say her goodbyes to Mama in the truck, and I took the moment to take one last pee break before starting the journey. I went inside and took care of business, and on my way back out, I ran into Gary, who was just coming out of the bedroom. Once again, he was clad only in his undies, and once again, he didn't seem the least bit concerned by this. I kept my gaze strictly on his face as I asked him about his mother.

"Doc says she's going to be okay," he said in response to my query. "They're springing her tomorrow or the next day."

"That's good," I said. "By the way, I want to thank you for letting Mama stay in your other trailer. I know it didn't work out, but I appreciate it all the same."

"Well, you just do what you have to, I guess," he said, shrugging.

"Yeah, but you didn't have to, and you did anyways. That's no little thing. Seriously, thank you," I said.

"You about to head out?" he asked as he set about making coffee.

"In a few minutes. Just got to say goodbye to Jolene," I replied.

"Well, it was good to finally meet you. Don't be a stranger," he said, and with that, he sat at the island and buried his nose in the newspaper.

"Bye," I said back, and I walked back outside to say my peace to my sister.

She was leaning on the hood of the U-Haul, smoking a cigarette and gazing off into the distance. She looked so small and vulnerable, like the slightest wind could blow her away. She looked at me with bleary eyes and did her best to smile.

"It's time, ain't it?" she said, a hollow finality in her voice.

"It is," I agreed.

She rushed over and crushed me tight to her in a hug so intense it bordered on assault. The strength of her grasp surprised me; I would have never guessed such raw power existed in such a shriveled specimen. I hugged her back, focusing all my love and goodwill into her. I wanted to convey all I felt for her in that hug, to show through physicality what words were inadequate to describe.

"I have to go, Jolene," I said gently after a few moments had passed.

"I know," she said petulantly. "I just don't have to like it, is all."

She released me reluctantly, and I scurried into the cab of the truck, less she changed her mind and try to attach herself to me again. I started the truck up and smiled at Jolene one last time.

"I'll miss you, sis. I love you," I said, and I pulled away from the curb.

"I'll be up to visit y'all real soon," she called after us, and I watched her follow us in the rearview mirror.

"You better," I shouted back at her, and I waved goodbye one last time as I turned onto the main road, and Jolene shrunk from sight.

I turned to Mama as I urged the truck up to speed and said, "Here we go."

"Heer go," she agreed, flashing a satisfied smile.

I drove slowly into the center of town and took a right onto the highway, northbound. I took one last look at the town of my youth and made a vow to return someday soon. The place had changed, some for the better, but mostly for the worse. Like small towns all across the country, Stillwater had been dying a slow death for decades; it only still existed due to inertia. It would never be a dynamic place to live; it would just sit there in its own slow decay, unable to come up with a way to save itself. I mourned Stillwater, the Stillwater that once was, but time marches on, regardless of our feelings. The town wasn't able to keep up with the furious pace of modernity, and another piece of America's soul died without having the decency to tell the people who still live there. The town would lumber on, but only a shell of what it could be, if people just gave a shit again.

We reached the city limits, and I reached over and held my mom's hand. She squeezed it tight, urging me on out of Stillwater and into our future. Together.

Betty Sue

If anyone ever asks me, I'll be sure to report that U-Haul trucks ain't designed with comfort in mind. I've been bouncing down the road in this overgrown closet on wheels for the better part of the day now, and my ass is as sore as can be. I keep shifting my weight from one side to the other, just to give each hemisphere a break. It's like there ain't any shocks in this thing at all. Every pebble feels like a boulder. It reminds me of an automated version of that fairy tale about the princess and the pea, only I ain't never been considered delicate. The prissy little princess in the story would have given up five hundred miles ago.

Other than the uncomfortable ride, the day is postcard perfect. The sun is bright in the almost cloudless sky. You couldn't ask for better traveling weather. We've gone as far north as North Carolina, and we're in the mountains. The sky is so close here. I swear I can reach out the window and touch it. Everything looks so peaceful from up here. All the little towns spread out in front of me like a giant toy train set. All those lives seem so small from this far away, just tiny little people doing tiny little things under a giant blue sky. All those little houses hold stories, though. Stories, if told correctly, that are as big as the mountain itself. I think about my story and what the storyteller would say about me. Would they get it right?

The further north we get, the more I feel the past slipping away. Somehow, the miles are creating the separation I need to put the past in the past where it belongs. I've never been able to do that before. The past is all around. Every building in town holds some kind of memory. Every person has an opinion of me. I still have to go to the grocery store that fired me for no good reason. Christ, I have to live with the wench who screwed my husband. There ain't no escaping the past in Stillwater, because Stillwater ain't never left the past.

Remlee tries to make small talk, but I don't really participate. Talking takes too much concentration anymore, and I'm just too keyed up to concentrate. The idea of moving my entire life across the country both terrifies and exhilarates me. Boston couldn't be any more different from Stillwater, and I don't really know what to expect. The TV would have me believe that all American cities are war zones, but I've been to Jacksonville before, and nobody ever shot at me. I'll probably be too chickenshit to leave the house anyway, who am I kidding. It seems a good portion of my often-ill-considered bravery has gone with my speech.

I'm most nervous about meeting Remlee's husband's family. Remlee hasn't told me much about them, mainly just that they're rich and snobby. I don't know how I'm supposed to act around people like that. I guess my lack of speech might actually help in this case, 'cause I can't say anything to embarrass anybody. Normally, I couldn't possibly care any less who I offend, but this is different. These folks are important to Remlee, so I got to mind my p's and q's. She's got a good thing going on. I don't want to mess that up.

Family is a weird thing, really. The people who can make you feel the best can also make you feel the worst. They can make you feel bad without even trying. I'd bet a million bucks Jesco would rather have not died, but he did, and it hurt me more than anything. For the longest time, I hid myself away to avoid that pain. Because it's inevitable. People you care about will hurt you, sometimes on purpose, sometimes not. After enough wounds, I just kept people away. That worked, in a way, but I see now that that ain't no way to live. That's just existing. Sure, it don't hurt, living that way, but nothing feels good either. If you suppress one feeling, maybe you suppress them all. I don't know, I ain't no headshrinker, but it only makes sense. I don't think emotions are like the a la carte line in the cafeteria; you can't pick and choose.

The feeling I have most nowadays is gratitude. It probably don't seem like I got much to be grateful for, I admit. Two months ago, before the stroke, I certainly wouldn't have called myself thankful. All I saw was the bad in every situation. I took so much for granted. It never occurred to me that one day I might not be able to speak for myself, that I would be dependent on the help of others just to conduct my day-to-day tasks. Sure, I worried about cancer and the clap and got my flu shot every year, but this kind of medical catastrophe never even crossed my mind.

That's over now. I see so much more clearly now, and there are blessings everywhere. All it takes is a shift in perspective to see them. Apparently, massive brain trauma is good for causing such a shift because my perspective is almost completely different now. Instead of dwelling on the handful of things that I can't do, I just remind myself how much I still can. I can still walk in the sun and see the beautiful flowers. My ears can still hear Patsy Cline's angelic voice. I can still savor the flavor of a well-cooked meal, and I'm still able to cook it (long as I ain't got to read no recipe). All of this is great, but it pales in comparison to the best thing of all: I have Remlee back.

She's really the key to all of this. I think I had given up on life, long before the stroke, really. Losing Jesco hurt bad, so did losing Bobby Lee and Sandy. But none of them chose to leave. Death stole them from me. Remlee didn't die, though. CPS didn't take her neither. She wanted to leave, so she did. And she wanted to because I was a lousy mother. I may not have wanted to be bad, hell, I tried real hard not to be, but I was all the same. I never really thought I'd ever have a chance to make it up to her. I wasn't even sure if I'd ever hear from her again at all. Had this stroke not happened, I think I probably wouldn't have. Yet here she sits, not two feet from me, driving me and all of my belongings to her house, where I'm now going to live. I've got a chance to fix a part of the mess I made. I ain't got time for anything but gratitude.

That's really what it's all about: time. Anything else can be replaced. You can get more money. You can buy a new car. You can build a new house. Hell, you can marry a different person and make new kids. But you can't buy more time. I wasted a lot of mine so far, but I don't have to waste anymore. I treasure every minute now because once they're gone, they're gone. There ain't no time store where you can buy an extra hour. The amount I have left in my account can't be that much. I'm sixty-two years old and ain't a one of them years been easy. I ain't wasting what's left on hate, not hatred of those who done me wrong, not hatred of myself. What's done is done, and dwelling on it only keeps the hate alive. I ain't saying I forget the bad; remembering is how you learn. But you can remember without letting the past control the present. You can't improve your future if your present is controlled by the past.

I used to be scared of the future. I expected to die alone and forgotten in the County Home, surrounded only by machines and the disinterested humans who operated them. I didn't see that as an injustice, quite the opposite. A part of me craved it even, the part that wants to be punished. I think that maybe I thought I could get the punishment out of the way somehow, maybe cheat hell of one more soul. I'm starting to think I had it all wrong now. No torturer could ever be more precise, more efficient at doing the most profound of psychic damage than I was. I knew all my own weaknesses, where to push the knife to slip past my armor.

On this day, however, the future no longer holds the dread for me that once did, as recently as a month ago. There's a light ahead now, illuminating all the possibilities that my self-imposed exile had cast into darkness. I know things won't be all roses and wine, but that's okay. Life isn't always pleasant. Life is always wonderful, however. I mean that as literally as it can be taken. Life is full of wonder. Every day is a new opportunity to fix the mistakes you've made, a new chance to do things better. I can let the past define me, or I can make the decision to decide myself. I choose the latter. I choose life.

The sun is starting to slip below the western horizon, tucking itself in for another night's slumber. I can see that Remlee's getting tired. How could she not be? She's been driving all day. I want to tell her to pull over for the night, even in a parking lot, if she has to, but I don't know how.

"Yu yu yu gimbal eiht... Summa toua?" I ask uselessly, pointing at the clock in hopes that is enough of a clue for her to guess what I'm getting at.

"Huh?" she asks, startled by the sudden intrusion into her cultivated silence. She looks at the clock I'm pointing at and says, "Oh, yeah. It is getting late. We'll get off at the next exit and find us a room for the night."

I smile with relief, glad that my message has been received. A nice, hot shower and a soft, clean bed sound wonderful. Remlee is true to her word, and within the next forty minutes, we're parked outside room 116 at the Motel 6 just outside of Harrisonburg, Virginia. Them damn do-gooders have gotten smoking banned in hotel rooms, even in fucking Virginia, home of Marlboro, for Chrissakes, so we're getting in another puff before we go inside. I catch Remlee looking at me, and I make a questioning noise.

"Nothing," Remlee says, answering my unasked question. "It's just...good to see you, you know? The real you, not that washed-out,

hopeless patient I met in the hospital. You look so much better now, that's all. You look…younger? No, not exactly. More…alive, somehow. When I first saw you in the hospital, you looked like a wax figure or something. You didn't look real, not like the Mama I remembered. You do now."

I smile at her because it's all I can do. There are so many things I want to tell her, and it's more than a little frustrating that I can't. I'm getting better, but I can't do anything more than get my most basic needs met. I can't really just talk for talking sake, the kind of talk where real communication happens. I mean the kind of conversation that bonds people together through ideas, not the strictly utilitarian kind. I miss the conversations where the minds can really connect and share the world together. Even now, as great as this is, Remlee and I are still separated by a barrier. I'm chipping away at that barrier bit by bit as the days go on, but despite all my recent character improvements, I still haven't mastered the art of patience. I know that someday, I'll be able to have a real conversation with my daughter. I just have to allow myself the time to be ready for that.

We finish our smokes and go inside our room for the night. We take turns showering, me first, then her. After we've washed away the dust of the road, Remlee orders a pizza from the little Italian joint across the street. For some inexplicable reason, she has them put ham and pineapple on it. It must be a Yankee thing. When it arrives, I try a piece, just to be polite. Much to my surprise, the strange concoction is actually delicious. Who would have thought it? I eat three whole pieces in celebration of my newfound culinary courageousness. Maybe that's the secret to life. Just keep trying combinations. Sometimes the strangest mixes make for the most delicious discoveries.

After I've eaten my fill, I settle myself in for bed. Remlee tucks me in and kisses me tenderly on the forehead.

"I love you, Mama," she says.

"Yu yu luv yu," I say back.

I close my eyes and begin to drift. I need the rest; tomorrow is the first day of the rest of my life. This time around, I plan to make the most of it.

November 4, 2020–April 2, 2021

About the Author

Before embarking on the endeavor that you now hold in your hands, R. C. Wagner took part in many adventures, most of which shouldn't be recounted in polite society. He currently resides at Wag-End in the Shire, where he and his family are valiantly trying to recreate Eden.

CPSIA information can be obtained
at www.ICGtesting.com
Printed in the USA
LVHW052231021121
702257LV00006B/105